PINO

"NOW, TOUCH ME ..."

White Wolf said, his eyes filled with a loving need.

Without thinking, Dawnmarie moved closer to him, letting him shower heated kisses down the full length of her body as she moaned with pleasure.

"My love for you is greater than my need to breathe," he whispered huskily, as sweet currents of warmth swept through her.

When White Wolf's mouth seized hers in another more demanding kiss, Dawnmarie was shaken by a river of sensations she had never experienced before. She was lost in a wild, abandoned bliss that she never wanted to end. . . .

"Cassie Edwards is a sensitive storyteller who always touches readers' hearts."
—*Romantic Times*

ANNOUNCING THE
TOPAZ FREQUENT READERS CLUB
COMMEMORATING TOPAZ'S
1 YEAR ANNIVERSARY!

THE MORE YOU BUY, THE MORE YOU GET

Redeem coupons found here and in the back of all new Topaz titles for FREE Topaz gifts:

Send in:

 2 coupons for a free TOPAZ novel (choose from the list below);
- ☐ THE KISSING BANDIT, Margaret Brownley
- ☐ BY LOVE UNVEILED, Deborah Martin
- ☐ TOUCH THE DAWN, Chelley Kitzmiller
- ☐ WILD EMBRACE, Cassie Edwards

 4 coupons for an "I Love the Topaz Man" on-board sign

 6 coupons for a TOPAZ compact mirror

 8 coupons for a Topaz Man T-shirt

Just fill out this certificate and send with original sales receipts to:

TOPAZ FREQUENT READERS CLUB-1ST ANNIVERSARY
Penguin USA • Mass Market Promotion; Dept. H.U.G.
375 Hudson St., NY, NY 10014

Name_____

Address_____

City_____State_____Zip_____
Offer expires 5/31/1995
This certificate must accompany your request. No duplicates accepted. Void where prohibited, taxed or restricted. Allow 4-6 weeks for receipt of merchandise. Offer good only in U.S., its territories, and Canada.

Wild Bliss

by
Cassie Edwards

A TOPAZ BOOK

TOPAZ
Published by the Penguin Group
Penguin Books USA Inc., 375 Hudson Street,
New York, New York 10014, U.S.A.
Penguin Books Ltd, 27 Wrights Lane,
London W8 5TZ, England
Penguin Books Australia Ltd, Ringwood,
Victoria, Australia
Penguin Books Canada Ltd, 10 Alcorn Avenue,
Toronto, Ontario, Canada M4V 3B2
Penguin Books (N.Z.) Ltd, 182–190 Wairau Road,
Auckland 10, New Zealand

Penguin Books Ltd, Registered Offices:
Harmondsworth, Middlesex, England

First published by Topaz, an imprint of Dutton Signet,
a division of Penguin Books USA Inc.

First Printing, June, 1995
10 9 8 7 6 5 4 3 2

 Topaz is a trademark of Dutton Signet,
a division of Penguin Books USA Inc.

Printed in Canada

Wild Bliss is dedicated to Rhonda Fochs,
a sweet friend, and her mother, Jacque Weber,
who are both proud Native Americans from the
Lac du Flambeau Lake Superior band of Chippewa,

and to Alice Robertson, a dear friend
from the beautiful state of Washington.

A Warrior, A Man, A Friend

Who is this man who I don't know?
I love him, care for him, I can't let go.
His tawny dark skin and jet-black hair,
The feel of his touch I know he cares.

He's wise for his age, yet looks so young.
The words that he speaks are never undone.
He cares very deeply for those he loves.
His faith is hidden but not from Above.

He's a true man, a full breed, he's one of a kind.
Forever he will be in my heart and my mind.
There's a distant saddening in his eyes,
A forever gaze that won't subside.

There's a loss in his heart that's deep inside,
An emotion only he can hide.
He's a very strong, prominent man,
And is very proud of his homeland.

There's nothing in this world he fears,
Although I feel he hides his tears.
A mighty, mighty man is he.
A Warrior he will always be.

He's suffered all the scars of life,
The pain, the agony, sharp like a knife.
I love this man and who he is,
Deep in my Heart I know I'm his.

Two different worlds of which we're from,
Loving each other as if we were one.
Within our hearts our love did grow,
A love so strong we'll never let go.

This war of worlds that we are in,
Keeps challenging our strengths within.
Why does this war, the scars, the tears,
Always seem to reappear?

How much more must a Warrior take?
He's not one to run, to hide, or shake.
The time is near, my Warrior, my Friend,
The wounds will heal and the hurt will mend.

Far away above the sky so blue,
Lies a happy memory of me and you.
I love you more than words can say,
I should have learned to love your way.

I hope along life's path you'll see,
The love we shared was meant to be.

—Jacqueline Lee Holst

Chapter One

A land of trees, which reaching round about,
In shady blessing stretched their old arms out.
—Leigh Hunt

Miini-giizis, the Blueberry Moon time of year, 1823

The warm weather of August had spread a green blush over land that was part forest and part water. Hawkweed and buttercups dotted the ground with a riot of colors. Bordered with birch and aspen, the many lakes and rivers beckoned with unbroken shorelines.

"We only watch the trading post again today, not enter?" Yellow Tail asked as he sidled closer to his chief. "Slow Running, have we not waited long enough for the firewater?" A cold bitterness entered his voice. "The white trader lies when he says that he has none."

Chief Slow Running stood stiffly on a cliff that overlooked the vast Wisconsin River and the small trading post situated a short distance from its banks. The sun sheened his bare copper chest and his raven-black hair that hung long and free of braids down his back. In the stiff breeze his breechclout fluttered against his muscled legs.

Slow Running's piercing black eyes narrowed as he watched the cabin below. Only moments ago he had seen the woman step outside to gather firewood. He had used the excuse of watching for the arrival of firewater more than once in order to see the woman who lived in the trader's cabin.

It was not yet known by Slow Running's warriors that he had chosen this woman to be his wife. He did not want to look weak in their eyes by voicing aloud the desire for a woman who did not return looks of admiration when he entered her father's cabin to trade furs for firearms and firewater.

He had decided that if she would not love him by choice, it would be done by force.

In time he would claim her as his.

In time she would bear him many sons.

"Slow Running, what is your decision?" Yellow Tail prodded. "My patience is thin for the firewater. Is not yours the same?"

"We have watched, Yellow Tail, have we not, for the arrival of the white man's river craft that brings fresh supplies? There have been no new shipments for weeks," Chief Slow Running said tightly. "One more day. We shall give them one more day. Then we will return to the trader's cabin and make him prove to us the emptiness of his store of firewater."

"*Hecitu-yelo,* that is true. We have not seen the white man's large river vessel. But I say we go *now* and force the trader's hand," Yellow Tail said, his hand instinctively going to the knife sheathed at his right side.

Slow Running turned to Yellow Tail and clasped the fingers of one hand around his throat. He glared at him with cold, intense eyes. "Never forget who is chief of our band of Sioux," he growled. "*I* make the decisions, not a mere warrior such as you."

Yellow Tail's eyes were wild. His tongue protruded from between his lips as he gasped for breath. He managed a slow nod, which was enough for Slow Running to drop his hand away from him.

"I will not forget again who is chief," Yellow Tail

said, anxiously rubbing the raw skin of his throat. "It is only that I cannot believe that the white man has no firewater in his cabin. How can he be without it? Too often I have seen that drink has stolen his senses away."

"Then one more day of waiting is in our favor, is it not?" Slow Running said, laughing shrewdly. "He will prove by the stench on his breath that he lies to the Sioux!"

Yellow Tail silently nodded.

Slow Running started to return to his canoe that he had left beached far from the trading post so that it would not be detected, then stopped. He did not yet want to turn away from the sight that spread out for miles below him. Behind the trader's cabin everything was heavily forested and bathed in exquisite stillness. Only the scream of a lynx now broke the silence.

He thought of the tracks of wolves that could be found anytime of day or night along the rock-strewn streams that ran pure and clean. It was a land worth fighting the Chippewa over.

One Chippewa chief in particular, White Wolf, had become Slow Running's ardent enemy. Not only because of the land they both claimed as theirs, but also because of the woman who lived below in the trader's cabin. Both Indian and white by birth, a *breed,* she was someone Slow Running could not do without for much longer.

And he would certainly never allow her to enter White Wolf's wigwam as *his* wife.

His jaw tight, his chin held high, Slow Running wheeled around and ran swiftly down the incline toward the sparkling river, Yellow Tail dutifully following.

A red-winged hawk, called a sunhawk, suddenly circled overhead. Seeing its shadow against the land, and hearing its *peent-peenting,* Slow Running stopped and stared up at the large, soaring bird. The sunhawk was one of the "winged peoples" and a powerful guardian spirit, giving the abilities of far vision and balance in all things.

It was a spirit messenger, a reminder to man of his connectedness with the Great Spirit.

Slow Running circled his hands into tight fists at his sides as the bird continued to cry loud and clear into the wind, as though warning those in the cabin below that their worst enemy was near.

Chapter Two

Turn I my looks unto the skies,
Love with his arrows wounds mine eyes;
If so I gaze upon the ground,
Love then in every flower is found.
—Thomas Lodge

Dawnmarie Garrett gazed with pity at her father, a small, balding man of fifty, as he staggered across the dim-shadowed outer room of the cabin they used as a trading post.

Since he had begun drinking heavily, his narrow shoulders slumped as though under a heavy weight and his buckskin clothes hung loose and disheveled on his small frame. He was no longer the same man who had been one of the first traders to winter among the Indians.

He used to be respected by everyone; now he

seemed only just tolerated by those who came to trade with him.

Dawnmarie flinched when her father tripped on a barrel covered by a stack of pelts.

She grimaced and placed a hand on her throat when he tipped a mug of ale to his lips. She watched in disgust as the amber liquid escaped from the corners of his mouth and bubbled down his chin.

With a loud hiccough, Cleaves placed the mug back down on the counter. Leaning heavily against the log wall, he wiped his mouth clean with the back of his hand. His eyes were blank and bloodshot as he gazed from his daughter, to his wife, and back again to Dawnmarie.

Without a word he reached for the mug of ale again.

Dawnmarie rushed to his side and tried to take the mug away from him. "Father, you have had too much today," she said, struggling with him as he refused to give up the mug to her. "Please, Father. Seeing you this way is frightening. And what if the Sioux should arrive while you are in such a state? Who can say what they might do if they realize they have the advantage over you?"

"We'll see about tha'," Cleaves drawled drunkenly in his strong cockney accent. " 'Twill be the end of th' 'ooligans if they come here wit' their threats again."

"Father, if you don't sober up, there will be nothing you can do to prevent anything they decide to do," Dawnmarie said, her voice shallow with fear. "While I was gathering wood only moments ago, I saw Chief Slow Running again. I have often noticed him and his warrior, Yellow Tail, on the cliff observing the activities here at the trading post. If the new shipment of alcohol doesn't arrive soon, the Sioux might be provoked enough to come and take our scalps.''

Cleave relinquished the mug of ale to Dawnmarie, then reached a hand to her copper face. Just the thought of something happening to his daughter made him quickly sober. Her beauty was such that no man would remove her scalp when he could take all of her instead.

Cleaves knew that if he didn't stop dulling his brain with alcohol, that bloody cur Sioux chief could take his daughter from him without so much as a struggle.

His gaze swept over Dawnmarie. He was proud to the core over what he and his Kickapoo Indian wife had brought into this world. Dawnmarie was what most folks derisively called a breed, but she was unquestionably the loveliest woman in the Wisconsin Territory. She had the golden skin and raven hair of her Kickapoo mother, the violet eyes of her white father.

She was a mixture of the best of both her parents. She could speak her mother's Kickapoo language flawlessly. Yet she could also speak the perfect English that her mother, Doe Eyes, had learned from the Jesuit priests before Cleaves stole her from a Kickapoo camp nineteen years ago.

Now eighteen, Dawnmarie was beautiful not only in appearance, but also in her heart and soul. Her dark hair hung in a single braid down the perfect straight line of her back, held by a strip of cloth decorated with quillwork and beads. From her braid, long streamers of ribbon flowed nearly to the floor.

She wore a deerskin dress resplendent with beaded designs and belted at the waist. She also wore leggings, moccasins, and fine nettle-fiber undergarments.

Cleaves's gaze shifted to his wife, Doe Eyes. Still as vivacious as the day he had stolen her away, she made his heart skip a beat even now to be near her.

Although he understood why his wife no longer looked at him with love, it hurt him deeply to see the pity in her eyes. Of late, his unquenched desire for alcohol had placed a barrier between them.

Given a choice between taking his wife to bed or a flask of brandy, these days he would choose brandy without hesitating.

Shamed by these thoughts, Cleaves ran trembling fingers through his hair as he gave his wife and daughter a look of apology. " 'Ere's what I'll do for both my luvs," he said thickly. " 'Twill give you ease of my presence while I go and sleep off the drink. Then, 'twill be my solemn promise to you to never touch the stuff again."

Relief flooding through her, Dawnmarie rushed into her father's arms. "Thank you," she murmured. "From the bottom of my heart, Father, I thank you."

He hugged her close for a moment, then eased away from her and went to his wife. He took her hands, gazed into her dark eyes, then drew her into his embrace. Then he pulled himself free and climbed the ladder to his bedroom in the loft overhead.

Doe Eyes took Dawnmarie's hand and led her to a blanket that was spread out before the fire in the large stone fireplace. Although it was summer, the wind off the river and the shady depths of the forest kept the cabin chilly all year round.

Doe Eyes placed a small log among the slowly burning embers, then gave Dawnmarie a pensive look.

"Mum, what *is* it?" Dawnmarie asked, seeing how

her mother sat so stiffly, her eyes sad. "Mum, you should be happy. Father has promised not to drink ever again."

"But he has made such promises before, has he not?" Doe Eyes said softly. "How long has he kept them? Never for more than a week. Tomorrow? He will forget his promises again and become someone you and I no longer know."

"Please, Mum," Dawnmarie whispered, casting a quick look up at the loft. "Father will hear you. We don't want him knowing that we doubt his word."

"And so you doubt it also?" Doe Eyes asked, placing a gentle hand to Dawnmarie's cheek.

"Very much," Dawnmarie said, swallowing hard. "Yes, Mum. So very much."

"Sweetheart, when your father stole me from my true people, the Kickapoo, I hated him with a vengeance," Doe Eyes said, her eyes taking on a distant look. She locked her fingers together on her lap. "But I grew to love him over time. He was handsome, virile . . . and he was a masterful hunter! And when you were born, oh, how it made your father's eyes dance. I loved him so." She hung her head. "I still do."

"Oh, Mum, I'm so sorry that Father has turned to drink," Dawnmarie murmured. "But it is always here at the trading post, tempting the men. I cannot understand its lure. To me the stink alone is vile. It resembles the spray of a frightened skunk. The only solution, as I see it, is to encourage Father to give up this trading post and go into another line of business that has nothing to do with alcohol."

"And where would we go for him to do that?" Doe Eyes asked. "A white man whose wife is an Indian, and whose daughter is labeled a breed? No.

He would not be welcomed in any white man's community."

"Then what is the answer?" Dawnmarie asked, secretly knowing what she wanted *her* future to be. To be married to the Chippewa chief White Wolf! But for now the dilemma of her family had to come first in her heart.

"I don't know, but I fear the Sioux so much," Doe Eyes said softly. "Not *all* Sioux, mind you. Mainly Chief Slow Running. He is shifty. He hands out too many threats to your father during their dealings. I'm afraid that ... that something will happen to us before I can teach you about my true people, the Kickapoo, who are also your people."

"What is it, Mum?" Dawnmarie asked, scooting closer. "What have you not told me?"

Doe Eyes took both Dawnmarie's hands in hers. Tears silvered the corners of her eyes as she began to speak.

Chapter Three

Wend I to walk in sacred grove,
Even there I meet with sacred Love.
                              —*Thomas Lodge*

White Wolf carefully aimed his rifle at the browsing deer, letting forth a gunshot into the afternoon air. He smiled to himself as the deer's body lurched from the bullet.

He then cast a quick look at Sharp Nose as his friend fired the mortal shot that finally downed the deer.

"Once again, my friend, we are successful," White Wolf said, clasping Sharp Nose's muscled shoulder.

"We are many times practiced," Sharp Nose said, chuckling.

"You placed the deadly bullet in the side of the deer. You can carry it to the riverbank where we will clean it," White Wolf said, his eyes dancing. "I shall carry the rifles."

"So now I know why you chose to shoot first," Sharp Nose said laughingly. Each time they hunted, they took turns as to who shot first and who carried the deer.

After thrusting his rifle into White Wolf's hand, Sharp Nose hoisted the deer over his shoulder. He proudly carried it to the riverbank where White Wolf's canoe waited.

Together, wordlessly, the two men stripped the animal of its hide.

Once it was removed, they continued to carve the deer's carcass, which they placed in White Wolf's canoe.

Finally, White Wolf stuck part of the deer's liver in the fork of a tree as an offering of thanks to the deer's spirit. Sharp Nose then tied the deer's tail to a tree limb. The two men contemplated their work.

"Another satisfying hunt," White Wolf said, sitting down on the riverbank to clean his rifle. "A kill shared by best friends makes for the best of times."

Sharp Nose sat down beside White Wolf and watched him shine the barrel of his gun. "*Ay-uh,* yes, it is the best of times for friends," he said, nodding. "Our rifles are worth the ten finely dressed robes we paid for them."

"They are adequate," White Wolf said, glancing over at Sharp Nose. "They kill quickly and cleanly.

The deer we shot will provide enough meat to last many sunrises."

White Wolf continued to move the soft piece of buckskin over the barrel of his rifle. "Yes, it was an easy kill today," he repeated. "As easy as the snares we place in the forest which yield many pelts which we trade to the white man. Oddly enough, the common beaver is the pelt most sought after."

"It is said that the white people use these pelts for felt hats," Sharp Nose said, tossing a pebble into the clear water. He watched it sink quickly to the sandy bottom. "They say these hats provide the white man elegant ways to keep their heads dry. Hats keep their *heads* warm; brandy keeps their stomachs warm."

White Wolf frowned. "My *nee-gee,* the firewater not only warms the bellies of the white man, but also those of foolish Indians," he said, his voice stern. "When brandy became a part of the trade with the white men it was a disaster for the Indian society."

"Brandy has become a passion of one Sioux in particular," Sharp Nose said. "Chief Slow Running becomes violent when he drinks. He is becoming more of a threat to we Chippewa who seek peace whenever possible."

"*Ay-uh,* that is so," White Wolf said sullenly. "It all began with the British intruders on our land all those years ago. With them came an almost unlimited supply of rum."

"*Ay-uh,*" Sharp Nose said. "The rum came from the West Indies as a part of the sugar trade that kept many white merchants in business. It became a mainstay of the British fur trade."

White Wolf nodded. He was bothered thinking of Slow Running hanging around the trading post. It did not take much thought to figure out why he was

there. It was certainly not to watch the delivery of
the firewater to the trading post. White Wolf knew
that Slow Running watched Dawnmarie hungrily.

A sense of foreboding swam through White Wolf
to think that Slow Running might somehow manage
to sway Dawnmarie into his arms before White Wolf
had the chance to let her know *his* feelings for her.

His hand moved to the small pouch that he wore
tied to his breechcloth at his waist. He clutched it,
as though he were clutching Dawnmarie's hand. He
knew now not to wait much longer to offer a bride
price to her father. He must be the first with such
an offering or lose that chance, forever.

Sharp Nose noticed White Wolf fingering the small
bundle he had been wearing for several days. He
knew the meaning of such a bundle, yet he did not
want to pry just yet in White Wolf's personal affairs.
It was no secret who White Wolf's eyes watched
while trading at the post: the beautiful young daughter of the trader whose blood was mixed, her violet
eyes the only betrayal of her Kickapoo heritage.

Sharp Nose saw his friend's attraction as dangerous. Although the trader had married an Indian, and
his daughter was more Indian than white, it was quite
obvious to Sharp Nose, by the trader's behavior toward Indians, that Dawnmarie's father wanted
"more" for his daughter than to marry a "forest
savage."

This thought caused bitter resentment within
Sharp Nose, for he had no love for the white trader
whose tongue was forked with lies and cheating, and
whose thoughts were muddied by the very firewater
he sold to the Sioux.

"The bundle," Sharp Nose quickly blurted, unable

to hold his questions back any longer. "You now wear a bundle at your waist."

White Wolf smiled over at Sharp Nose. "*Ay-uh,* my friend," he said. "It contains my love medicine. Within it is a love charm. I carry it so that Dawnmarie's dreams will make her think of Chief White Wolf."

"Is this *nee-bwah-kah,* wise?" Sharp Nose asked, hardly ever questioning his chief's decisions.

"It is the way of my *gee-day,* heart, that you doubt?" White Wolf asked, forking an eyebrow. "This is rare, my friend, that you doubt my judgment."

"I do not mean to even *now,*" Sharp Nose said, his voice drawn.

"Then I will forget that you *did,*" White Wolf said, inhaling a quavering breath.

"What charm does your bundle carry?" Sharp Nose asked, trying hard not to speak again against his friend, his *chief.* "How did you manage to get this charm from Dawnmarie?"

"Recently, while at the trading post," White Wolf said, chuckling low, "she removed her shawl and laid it aside. While she was making entries in a journal and her father was busy counting pelts, I managed to cut off the piece of her shawl. I placed it along with a small piece of wood which I carved and shaped like a person inside my 'love medicine bag.' I am almost certain the charm is working. I have seen her look at me with much interest."

"You are blinded by her beauty?" Sharp Nose said without thinking.

White Wolf felt that he must justify his attraction to Dawnmarie to Sharp Nose.

"Have you not noticed Dawnmarie's virtues?"

White Wolf asked patiently and calmly. "She is a good worker. Is not a 'good worker' the virtue most sought by the Chippewa men while considering taking a wife? Not only does she have good virtues, she *is* also quite pleasant to look at."

"When will you tell her of your feelings for her?" Sharp Nose asked blandly.

"*Wi-yee-bah,* soon," White Wolf said, his insides growing warm at the very thought of being near her again at the trading post. "She *will* be my *gee-wee-oo,* wife."

"Her father will not let her go easily," Sharp Nose said, rising from the ground as White Wolf got up. "It will take an enormous bride price to lay claim to this woman."

"No price is too large," White Wolf said, placing his rifle into the canoe. He then shoved the canoe into the water. "I will pay whatever price is needed to have her."

"When will you talk to her?" Sharp Nose asked, climbing into the canoe.

"*Very* soon," White Wolf said, sitting down beside Sharp Nose. He lifted a paddle as Sharp Nose lifted his, soon leaving the shore behind.

"*Ay-uh,* I must act soon or lose her to someone else," White Wolf grumbled. "I cannot allow Slow Running to offer his price first. At night when the future winters are cold and blustery, I must have more than my bundle to hold midst my blankets beside my fire pit. I must have more than that to *caress.*"

He smiled knowingly over at Sharp Nose. "*And,* my friend, I *shall.*"

Chapter Four

Felt on your face an air, watery and sweet,
And a new sense in your self-lighting feet.
—Leigh Hunt

"Dawnmarie, you are everything in life to me," Doe Eyes said as she began to spill out her heartfelt feelings to her daughter. "Yes, I love my husband. But *your* future is what I am most concerned over. Out of five pregnancies you are the only child the Great Spirit has blessed me with. I want the best for you. Now that your father has become a stranger to me, I fear so much for your future."

"Mum, I am no longer a child. I can fend for myself," Dawnmarie said, reaching over to pat her mother's hand.

"To me you are still a child, a child to whom I gave a Kickapoo name, Ne-shu-esk-a-go-kew, meaning 'lady of two worlds,' " Doe Eyes continued softly. "Your father had difficulty with the Kickapoo name and gave you a white child's name. But should anything happen to part us, remember my teachings of today and go back to your true people, the Kickapoo."

"It is true that I am part Kickapoo, but I am also white by birth," Dawnmarie said, torn between her two worlds.

Doe Eyes took Dawnmarie's hands. "My daughter, just listen patiently to what I have to say," she said, pleading with her dark eyes. "If fate should separate us, there is something you must know. Dawnmarie,

Kitzihait, the Kickapoo's Great Spirit, made all people of the world and provided each with a certain place to live and a place for their spirits to dwell in the hereafter. Upon dying, the children of Kickapoo mothers and white fathers are sent to the place where the spirits of the Kickapoo are dispatched."

Doe Eyes paused and gazed up at the loft where she could hear the rumbling noise of her husband's snores, then she stared into the slow-burning embers of the fire. "I fear that my child might not be accepted by the ruler in the spirit world of the Kickapoo because of the evil that her father has done while on this earth," she said, her voice breaking. "I am not blind to your father's scheming and cheating ways with the various tribes who trade at this post. Since his mind has become warped from the firewater, his actions against the Indians have worsened."

Doe Eyes looked quickly over at Dawnmarie, her eyes wide. "I fear that your spirit, when it arrives at the doors of the spirit world, might be questioned. I fear that your spirit will be turned away and forced to travel without end."

"I hear what you are saying, yet I do not understand," Dawnmarie said, puzzled by her mother's desperate attitude. "What has happened to cause this sudden fear? Did you see a sign in a dream? Have you received a warning that you are not revealing to me?"

"Dawnmarie, nothing but the constant threat of Slow Running causes my unrest," Doe Eyes said, patting her daughter's hand for reassurance. "But should anything happen to me or your father, you must find a way back to your true people before you die. You must be sure to make it clear to your Kickapoo people that you *are* Kickapoo, heart and soul."

"But I *am* also part white," Dawnmarie said, her voice breaking. "My eyes. They reveal my white heritage!"

"You are Kickapoo, *Kickapoo!*" her mother commanded, her voice shrill. "Listen well to my teachings, daughter. It is said that if a Kickapoo woman cohabits with a man of another nation, she can lose her Kickapoo identity to the nation of her husband. Remember well that *you* are of the Thunder Clan of the Kickapoo. Always remember that. For your afterlife in the spirit world it is important for you to always lay claim to your heritage."

"I will remember," Dawnmarie said, reaching over to draw her mother into her arms. "I *am* Kickapoo. I *will* find my true people one day."

Yet somehow when she hugged Doe Eyes tightly, all she could think of was a handsome Chippewa warrior. He had stolen her heart the very first time she had seen him. If she ever had the chance to become White Wolf's special woman, could she truly remain Kickapoo at heart should he demand that she become one with him and his Chippewa world?

It was something that she would have to sort out. For now she had to concentrate on making her mother feel more at peace with *her* world. Never had she seen her mother in such a state.

But never before had Chief Slow Running posed such a threat. Dawnmarie feared him and his Sioux warriors even more than her mother did. When he looked at Dawnmarie with his cold and piercingly dark eyes, it turned her heart to stone.

"Mum, while Father is sleeping perhaps we should do some beading," Dawnmarie said as she eased from her mother's tight embrace. "It will be best for both of our states of mind. Don't you agree?"

Dawnmarie lived for her beading. Her father had made her a special cedar bead loom on which she had beaded many beautiful garments. Her love of beading had begun when, as a child, she had learned her colors by stringing beads.

"I have only a few more beads to attach to the friendship bag that I am making," Dawnmarie said softly. "One day I wish to find that perfect friend to whom I can give the bag."

"Swallow Song, of the Potawatomis tribe, seems as anxious to have a friend," Doe Eyes said, momentarily forgetting her fears and dreads of the future. She reached over and got her bag of beads. "Perhaps we might travel to their camp soon so that you can build on the friendship you have already started. After all, her father trades at our post."

"Yes, perhaps," Dawnmarie said, slipping beads onto a string. In her mind's eye she recalled how beautiful Swallow Song was and how she stared so openly at White Wolf when they had happened to be at the trading post at the same time.

Swallow Song seemed to be more a threat than a friend in Dawnmarie's eyes and heart. If White Wolf chose Swallow Song over her, Dawnmarie felt she would die!

"Yes, we shall manage to get you two together," Doe Eyes said, her fingers busy sewing beads on a moccasin.

But Dawnmarie stared down at her beads and offered no response.

Chapter Five

Why sweet plants so grateful odours shower?
It is because thy breath so like they be?
                                    —Giles Fletcher

The next day, while her mother prepared the morning meal and her father looked over his ledgers before Indians from various tribes arrived to trade goods with him, Dawnmarie stepped from the cabin to gather an armload of wood for the fire.

After burdening herself with as much as she could carry, she paused and gazed toward the river. Through the gray, hazy fog that was just lifting from the water she saw a movement.

Her heart leapt as White Wolf emerged from the fog, his muscled arms pulling the canoe paddle through the water.

Even though she knew that her mother was waiting for the firewood, Dawnmarie stood, dazed, as she continued to watch White Wolf beach his canoe on the sandy shore.

The sun was melting its way through the fog now and gave Dawnmarie a better look at the man of her midnight dreams. A layer of handsome pelts was draped across one of his arms, and he carried a buckskin bag as he made his way up the riverbank toward the trading post. She was glad that he had not noticed her standing there yet, which gave her more opportunity to marvel over him in private.

White Wolf was dressed not only in a breechcloth, but also in tight leggings that reached from his ankles to his crotch, held up by a thong tied to a belt. The leggings were decorated beautifully with outer fringe and beadwork.

Made from one piece of buckskin with a plain seam up the back and a puckered seam up the front, his moccasins were Chippewa in style.

But it was his powerful, bare chest that made Dawnmarie suck in an appreciative gasp of air. He was like no man she had ever seen. His sleekly muscled body rippled as he walked, his power echoing within his long stride. Gleaming in the sunlight, his long black hair lifted with each step, a fancy headband holding it back at his brow, a feather tied in a loop in the back.

As he came closer and she saw his face more clearly, she noticed an inner strength that shone in his deep brown-black eyes ... eyes that were as bright as the moon. And she noticed that his sculpted, bronze face glowed with pride and peace.

When he caught her standing there, their eyes immediately locked, and Dawnmarie felt too stunned to move. She felt her face warm with a blush as his gaze raked slowly over her. She felt so foolish to have been caught staring at him and even more foolish for having seemed to have forgotten how to walk.

She silently ordered her feet to scurry away, but they would not heed her command. It was as though she was frozen to the ground.

White Wolf's heart soared when he gazed at Dawnmarie. She was beautiful and radiant, her violet eyes sparkling with wisdom. Her face, which surely felt as smooth as corn silk to the touch, glowed with joy. Her slim, sinuous body was well defined beneath her clinging buckskin dress, revealing her narrow and supple waist, invitingly rounded hips, and overripe breasts for someone of her age of eighteen winters.

The soft glimmer of her dark brown hair spilled over her shoulders and tumbled down her back.

Again he stared at her face. As always before, he found it flawless. And how her violet eyes intrigued him, despite the fact that they were proof of that part of her that was white. But he loved her no less for having been born into the world with a white father.

And he would have her soon. Her father was too greedy not to accept his generous bride price.

Dawnmarie's mother called her from inside the cabin, waking her from her reverie. She smiled shyly up at White Wolf as he stepped up to her, his height towering above her, then she rushed back inside the cabin with her heart pounding.

Doe Eyes turned and frowned at Dawnmarie, but did not have the chance to ask what had taken her so long to get the firewood. The answer became apparent when White Wolf followed Dawnmarie into the cabin.

Flustered by his entrance, Dawnmarie spilled the wood onto the floor before she got to the fireplace. Her face flooded with color while her father gave her a silent, agitated stare. To save herself further embarrassment, Dawnmarie carried the wood, piece by piece, to the hearth.

A quiet, knowing smile lifted the corners of White Wolf's mouth as he watched Dawnmarie. He then sauntered to the counter and laid his pelts carefully across it.

Cleaves, inhabitually sober, and more carefully dressed than usual, stepped up to the counter in his clean, white summer breeches and bloodred, velvet shirt, his hair pulled back neatly into a perfect silvering queue.

Wiping his quill clean on a rag, he silently assessed the pelts. His attention was drawn back to his daughter, when White Wolf went to her and offered her his buckskin bag. Dawnmarie turned and gazed with surprise up at White Wolf.

"Take. *Geen-gee-di-eem,* yours," White Wolf said, shoving the bag into Dawnmarie's hands. "See what is inside. I hope it pleases you."

"You have brought me a gift?" Dawnmarie asked, staring down at the bag. Her gaze moved slowly upward again. Her heart was pounding so hard she felt as though she might faint at the Chippewa chief's feet.

"*Ay-uh,* a gift of colors," White Wolf said, his pulse racing. When he was near this woman, his senses threatened to leave him. He dreamed of touching her, of holding her, of kissing her. It took willpower not to reach out and tell her his deepest feelings for her.

But this was not the time. When he arrived at the trading post again, it would be with *many* valuable pelts, so many that it would take her father many days to count their worth!

"A gift of colors?" Dawnmarie said softly, again gazing down at the bag. She was most certainly ignoring the glare from her father. She knew that he was not quite ready for her to leave him and marry anyone. He still saw her as a child, a child he scarcely let out of his sight.

"Often I have seen you beading and sewing while I am trading with your father," White Wolf said, ignoring the angry glare from behind him. He knew how possessive the white trader was of his daughter.

But that was going to change, White Wolf thought

smugly to himself. Very soon this daughter would be a *wife*.

"I have brought you berries of many colors to dye buckskin cloths and seed beads so that the garments which you sew will be much more beautiful," he said.

"Why, how thoughtful," Dawnmarie said, opening the bag. Her heart frolicked with joy when she saw the different assortment of colorful berries, and the amount that he had brought for her.

"Thank you so much," she said, touched deeply by the gift. She gazed up at him and smiled, mesmerized anew by this man who seemed to be able to read her mind. How else could he have known that she had been searching for the right berries to use in a dye for a belt that she was going to weave?

Rarely speechless, White Wolf could not think of the right thing to say at such a time as this. He smiled instead, then turned and walked back to the counter to transact his business with the white trader. But as he turned, the thin buckskin thong that held his "love medicine bundle" to the belt of his breechclout came loose.

He was not aware of it falling to the floor.

Her eyes wide, Dawnmarie stared at the bundle. She knew of such bundles and their meanings. White Wolf was charming some woman. She could not help but want to see what the bag held, and from whom it might have been taken.

Her heart throbbing nervously, Dawnmarie laid her bag of berries aside on a table, then bent slowly to the floor and swept the small bundle into her hand.

Ignoring her mother who shook her head to discourage Dawnmarie from snooping and looking inside, since it was none of her business who this handsome man wanted to charm, Dawnmarie's fingers trembled as she loosened the drawstring at the top of the bag and took a quick peek inside.

When she recognized a tiny piece of her shawl as well as a woman's figure carved from a tiny fragment of wood, she gasped softly and the pit of her stomach became strangely warm and weak. She stared disbelievingly down at the contents of the bag. Her mother had never allowed her to forget her people and their customs. The way to make love charms was the same in both the Kickapoo and Chippewa tribes.

She understood the meaning of this love charm and was in awe of White Wolf's feelings for her. They matched those she felt for him.

Dawnmarie looked quickly up at White Wolf as he stood conferring with her father over the worth of his pelts. This man, this handsome, wonderful man who was a powerful Chippewa chief, *was* charming her. No wonder she had not been able to get him off her mind.

She thought of him the instant she awakened each morning, and she thought of him the moment she placed her head on her pillow each night.

She thought of hardly anything *but* him these past weeks.

Her dreams were filled with him!

Smiling slowly, a thrill coursed through her veins when she realized that he loved her.

Feeling as though floating on air, Dawnmarie crept to her mother's side and proudly showed her the contents of the bag. Dawnmarie's mother smiled and nodded her approval of this man.

Dawnmarie leaned close. "Mum, he *loves* me," she whispered, the excitement pure and wonderful in her heart.

"Yes, seems he does," Doe Eyes whispered back, taking a slow look over her shoulder at White Wolf.

"I love *him*, Mum," Dawnmarie whispered again.

"I have known since you first set eyes on him how you felt about him," Doe Eyes replied.

"Father won't approve. What am I to do?"

"Wait and let nature work its magic," Doe Eyes said, smiling over at Dawnmarie.

"What should I do with the bundle?" Dawnmarie asked, drawing the strings tight at the top.

"There is no way to disguise your finding it," her mother whispered back. "Take it and place it on the counter beside his hand."

"My knees are so weak," Dawnmarie whispered. "I fear he will see my reaction. And what will Father think of me reacting so to the love charm?"

"Your father does not know what the bag contains," her mother said softly. "He does not even know what an Indian love charm *is*. He will think that you are just being kind by delivering a lost object to the Chippewa chief."

"Yes, you are right," Dawnmarie said, holding the small bundle in the palm of her hand as gently as she might a delicate baby bird. "Father has never joined our conversations about our heritage. It is as though he hopes that if he ignores it, it might go away."

Her mother nodded.

Dawnmarie turned on a soft moccasined heel and walked gingerly toward the counter where her father and White Wolf were still in serious, deep transactions.

One beaver skin paid for eight pounds of gunpowder and forty pounds of lead for bullets. Two beaver skins paid for a red or white blanket, as well as a one-pound ax.

White Wolf was going to go away today with quite a load of supplies, for he had brought in an impressive number of beaver pelts as well as other furs that were of less value.

When Dawnmarie placed the bag on the counter she accidentally brushed her hand against White Wolf's bare arm. She gasped softly. His flesh against hers was akin to a fire being ignited inside her. She flinched and drew instantly away, but not quickly enough.

White Wolf turned and saw her standing there, holding his "love medicine bundle." His heart skipped a beat.

But it began to sing when he saw by the warm glow of her cheeks and the wonder in her eyes that she had seen what was inside the bag and did not seem alarmed or angered by it. He was confident now that winning her over would be much simpler.

"*Mee-gway-chee-wahn-dum,* thank you," he murmured, gathering up the bundle into his hand. "I shall have to keep better watch on my bundle. I would not want just anyone seeing what I carry inside it."

"I shouldn't have looked..." Dawnmarie said, knowing that the words fell clumsily from between her lips and hating herself for it.

"*You* I do not mind seeing the charms," White Wolf said, securing the medicine bundle to his belt. "And you know the reason why."

Despite her father's glare, Dawnmarie gave White Wolf another winning smile.

She then returned to her chore of tending the fire so that breakfast could be warmed.

Scarcely a word was exchanged between White
Wolf and Cleaves as they completed their business
transaction. Once it was done, it took several trips
for White Wolf to carry out all of his supplies.

And then finally he was gone.

Dawnmarie wanted to run to the door and watch
him glide away in the canoe. She wished to see his
rippling muscles just one more time today. She
wished to see the fluttering of his beautiful hair.

But the smell of food and the footsteps of her
father going to the table lured Dawnmarie back. She
sat down and ate a hearty breakfast of eggs and
black coffee. Yet she tasted nothing. Instead, her
senses were centered on one thing: the magic of
being in the arms of her beloved—White Wolf.

A commotion outside made her jump.

Had White Wolf returned?

Had he forgotten some of his supplies?

She turned toward the sound of footsteps behind
her and blanched when she found Chief Slow Running standing there with his warrior friend Yellow
Tail. The looks in their eyes and the way they stood
there with their arms locked across their bare chests
made her stiffen inside. Fear raced across her flesh
like a cold winter breeze.

Cleaves rose guardedly from his chair as Slow
Running and Yellow Tail went to the counter and
began rifling through White Wolf's pelts. They
grunted as they shoved first one, then another pelt
aside.

Dawnmarie rose from her chair and went to her
mother. She flinched when Slow Running threw the
pelts on the floor and stomped on them. He raged
in his Sioux tongue, saying words that Dawnmarie
had not yet learned of the Sioux language.

But the rage she saw in his behavior and the way he shouted as he talked was enough to know that he was not there for a friendly trade with her father.

In fact, he had brought nothing inside the cabin *to* trade.

She feared his true reason for being there.

It was either for firewater or, she shuddered at the thought, *her*.

She could see the anger flaring in her father's eyes and hoped that he would hold his tongue. If not, this time he might lose in the game of switch and bait with the Sioux.

It was a shame that Slow Running was so different from the rest of the Sioux, Dawnmarie thought wistfully to herself. For the most part, the Sioux that remained in this area wanted peace as badly as those other Indians who no longer wished to settle disagreements by warring.

She wished that it was the same with Slow Running. But everyone knew that he was born to hate and born to war.

"Wotcha think you're up to, eh?" Cleaves said in his cockney accent.

"You paid in firewater for these pelts?" Slow Running asked in clear enough English. He gestured with a hand toward the pelts strewn across the floor.

"And if I did?" Cleaves said, leaning over the counter into Slow Running's face. "Wotcha goin' to do abaht it?"

Dawnmarie paled. This was one time she wished her father was drunk. He would not be this brave or this reckless in his behavior with the Sioux.

Yet she understood how he felt. Slow Running had worn out his welcome long ago. He was never as polite as White Wolf. In fact, his very presence spelled trouble.

"Chief Slow Running has watched day and night for the white man's river craft to deliver more firewater to your trading post," Slow Running complained heatedly. "It has not arrived. Does this mean that you lied before? That you give firewater to one Indian and not another?"

"If you watch my cabin so earnestly then you would know that White Wolf brought these pelts and he never trades for firewater," Cleaves blurted out. "The supply is gone. Now, outta here, 'ooligans, or I'll take me pistol from the rack and make a couple of 'oles in your stomachs."

Slow Running reached over the counter, grabbed Cleaves by the throat, and half lifted him from the floor. He drew Cleaves close enough to smell his breath and, satisfied that he did not smell any alcohol on his breath, dropped him back to the floor.

Dawnmarie paled as the Sioux chief turned her way and glared at her. "Give me firewater after the sun rises once more in the sky or I will take your daughter," he threatened Cleaves, even though he planned to take her anyway.

First he wanted to secure his canoe with firewater. He would be patient until it arrived. Then he would take everything and kill this worthless white man who played games more often than not.

Blinded by rage at the Sioux's threat, Cleaves reached for the rifle that he always kept beneath the counter for times like this. He brought it out into the open and aimed it at Slow Running.

"Threaten to take me daughter, will ye?" Cleaves said throatily. "We'll see abaht tha', cock! If ye ever so much as touch me child you won't live long enough ta regret it."

Cleaves aimed steadily at Slow Running, keeping a critical watch on Yellow Tail out of the corner of his eyes.

"It seems the white man's tongue is a bit loose today," Slow Running grunted out angrily. "Tomorrow it might be cut from his mouth."

"I don't take your threat seriously," Cleaves said, smiling smugly. "Tomorrow the shipment of ale should arrive. That's all that's important, isn't it? Now outta here, 'ooligans. Come again tomorrow. I'll give ye your firewater, ahright?"

Snarling beneath his breath, Slow Running backed away from Cleaves.

Then he and Yellow Tail rushed from the cabin, their threats and shouts loud and ugly as they ran to their canoe.

Dawnmarie was almost too petrified to speak or to move. Then when she saw what her father was doing, she moved quickly into action.

"Father, no, don't," she begged as Cleaves brought out several jugs of brandy that he had kept hidden beneath bear pelts and began mixing the brandy with a herbal plant. She knew his intent. This particular plant, mashed and added to alcoholic beverages, could cause severe cramping in those who drank it. It was an ailment that came quickly and passed away slowly. He had used it before when he had been cheated by Indians. This was his way of paying them back.

"Luv, mind your business now," Cleaves said, then took a long swig of ale from a jug that had not yet been tainted. " 'Tis best I teach th' 'ooligans a lesson now. Later may be too late!"

"Father, you are only asking for more trouble," Dawnmarie pleaded, her voice drawn.

"Hush, luv," Cleaves said, frowning at her. "The Sioux wants brandy? Ah'll give 'em brandy, ahright . . . the sort that'll burn the gut clean outta them!"

Knowing that nothing she said would convince her father of the wrong in what he did, or the dangers, Dawnmarie shied away from him and went to her mother. Clinging to one another, they watched him drink himself into a stupor, his drunken laughter touching their very souls with remorse and added fear.

Dawnmarie wished that White Wolf would return, but even if he did, he would also be powerless to talk sense into her father. He might even become her father's first victim.

Just when Dawnmarie had found hope and joy in the form of White Wolf's "love medicine bundle," her world seemed suddenly turned upside down.

Chapter Six

Love turned and looked on you,
Love looked and he smiled, too.
—John Bowyer Buchanan Nichols

It was already noon and still the shipment of supplies from the warehouses upriver had not arrived. Nor had Chief Slow Running come to claim his firewater.

All morning Dawnmarie watched the cliff where Slow Running often stood, but thankfully she saw hide nor hair of him.

She surmised from his absence that he figured out that a delivery date could not be exact.

It had happened in the past that deliveries were late, and it was bound to happen again.

Tired of thinking about the Sioux chief, and having recently seen turtles nesting in the sand along the shoreline, Dawnmarie went to the river to begin a search for turtle eggs. They were a delicacy worth the dangers of leaving the cabin. Not only were they delicious, they were filled with energizing protein.

Each turtle nested about four times during the April to October season. She had witnessed their arrival this one time. It had seemed mystical that day after a warm, refreshing shower. As the dozens of turtles had searched for nesting places in the sand a rainbow had arched overhead in its myriad of lovely colors. It had seemed to be a sign in the sky.

Dawnmarie had hoped that it meant good fortune for herself and her family. Surely nothing that beautiful could be a forecast of something evil.

Golden sunlight played on the water and warmed Dawnmarie's face as she carried a wicker basket that she used to gather the turtle eggs. The warm sand felt wonderful against the soles of her bare feet, and she scarcely felt the clamshells and small stones as she walked over them.

Her eyes searched for signs of the turtles. Usually the turtle nests were easy to find. All one had to do was follow the turtle's tail tracks.

But now that the rain had erased all markings, she had yet to find the trail of even one turtle.

Her attention was drawn suddenly to the water, to a movement in the shallow waves. Minnows. Tiny, gray minnows that looked like small missiles darting to and fro through the water.

Mesmerized by the sight of the tiny fish, she knelt at the edge of the river. Reaching a hand, palm side down, into the water, she laughed softly as the minnows made small ripples on the surface as they fled quickly away from her.

"Your inborn instincts are working well this morning," she whispered.

Frowning, she gazed over her shoulder to make sure she was still alone. She hoped that her reactions would be as crisp and as quick as the minnows should she *ever* find herself face-to-face with Slow Running or his warrior sidekick, Yellow Tail. She just knew that one day soon Slow Running would confront her. He was a man who would follow through on his threats.

Dawnmarie stood up and resumed her search for the turtle nests.

Suddenly her eyes widened when she saw the first signs of the turtle tracks. Breathlessly she followed the small indentions in the sand, searching for raised places that would indicate the nests. And where there were nests, there were hopefully eggs.

She carefully poked one of the small bumps. She smiled when she found it soft beneath the raised surface of the sand. She was certain she had located the turtles' nesting ground.

Falling to her knees, Dawnmarie dug in the sand and carefully uncovered a full nest of eggs. One by one, she gingerly picked them up. They were soft, round, and very delicate. She carefully placed them in her basket.

Her basket overflowing, she rushed back to the

cabin, stopping only long enough to take another glance up at the cliff.

Finding no one there she sighed with relief and went inside.

"Mum, Father, see what I have brought home for you," Dawnmarie said, her voice filled with excitement. "Eggs. Many turtle eggs."

Doe Eyes took the basket and gazed down at the eggs, then smiled up at Dawnmarie. "I shall prepare them," she said, then grew solemn as she gazed over at her husband whose head hung in a drunken stupor. "Your father's promise to us lasted as long as I expected. See how the firewater has robbed him of his senses again?"

Dawnmarie gazed wistfully at her father, then went and poured water into a pan from the teakettle. "Mum, come," she said, giving her mother a weak, forced smile. "We shall boil the eggs and offer one to Father. Perhaps this will bring him back to his senses for at least a moment. He has never turned down the offering of turtle eggs."

"Yes, that is true," Doe Eyes said, placing the eggs, one by one, into the pan. "My husband at least responds to the needs of his stomach when he cannot hear words from his wife or daughter."

Doe Eyes boiled the eggs for only a few minutes, then placed them on the table to cool.

Dawnmarie took one of them over to her father. She punctured the shell with one of her fingers and handed the egg to Cleaves.

"Father, I've prepared a turtle egg for you," she murmured. "It was boiled only long enough to give it substance. All you need to do is suck its contents. The egg will comfort your insides if you will only allow it to."

Cleaves's head bobbed. He ran his long, lean fingers through his thinning gray hair that hung long, loose, and unkempt over his shoulders today.

Slouched over the counter, leaning heavily against it, he took Dawnmarie's offering of egg and placed it to his mouth, sucking until the egg was nothing but an empty shell.

Pleased that she had been able to reach her father in at least this small way, Dawnmarie prepared another egg for him and offered it to him.

She sucked the contents from one of the delicious morsels herself, but she flinched and dropped the eggshell to the floor when she heard a noise outside the cabin.

"The Sioux?" Doe Eyes asked, nervously wiping her hands on the front of her buckskin dress.

"Perhaps," Dawnmarie said. "Or perhaps the shipment of supplies has arrived."

Wary with fear, Dawnmarie crept to the door and slowly opened it.

When she saw nothing but a raccoon staring up at her, she realized that the noise they had heard was this little creature begging for food as if it knew that Dawnmarie could be quite generous with offerings.

"Sweetie, it's only you," Dawnmarie said, laughing loosely with relief.

She bent to a knee and stroked the head of the raccoon, glad that it allowed such attention. She giggled when it even leaned into her hand for a more lengthy petting.

Doe Eyes came to the door and bent down beside Dawnmarie. Laughing, she offered the animal an egg.

In a blink of an eye the raccoon sucked away the

insides of the egg, holding it the same way a human
would. It tossed the shell aside, and eagerly
awaited more.

"She wants another one," Dawnmarie said, looking over her shoulder at her mother.

"Come on inside, sweetie," Dawnmarie said, giving the raccoon a gentle shove. "I gathered enough
eggs for us all to get our fill."

"Get tha' pesky varmint outta 'ere," Cleaves said,
stumbling toward the raccoon. "If not, it'll become
one of the pelts on me shelf."

"Father, you wouldn't," Dawnmarie gasped,
sweeping the small creature into her arms. "You
must not blame the raccoon. If anyone is guilty, it is
I, for having allowed the raccoon to depend on our
occasional food offerings."

Cleaves laughed throatily. "Ah'll leave 'er be," he
said, lifting a jug of ale to his lips. "Ah've enjoyed
'er presence from time to time, meself."

Dawnmarie gave her father a frustrated look, then
placed the raccoon back on the floor. She sat down
on a blanket in front of the fireplace and forgot her
troubles as she played with the animal.

For a while, even, she forgot the threat of the
Sioux.

Chapter Seven

Her presence fills with perfumes all the field.
—Nicholas Hookes

Silently and smoothly several canoes slid onto the sandy shore just out of eye range of the trading post cabin.

War paint smeared across their faces, wearing fancy feathers and other ornaments, and dressed in brief breechcloths, several Sioux warriors secured their vessels.

They ran stealthily across the warm sand. Some carried bows and arrows. Others carried rifles. Their moccasins scarcely made a sound as they ran through the emptied turtle nests, scattering sand into the wind.

Chief Slow Running's face was smeared with black and red paint. His scowl was dark and deep. When he got his first view of the cabin up the slight incline from the beach, his black, piercing eyes shone with anger. His jaw tightened.

He had watched for the arrival of the white man's water vessel until midmorning, growing more angry by the minute when it did not arrive.

Feeling duped, and tired of bantering with the white trader, he and his warriors had gone into council.

They quickly united in their decision to rid the land of the cheating, lying white trader forever. After all, they could always use the trading post down the river.

In fact, they would have done this sooner if it wasn't for Slow Running becoming infatuated with a woman who due to her heritage, bridged two worlds.

Despite the way that Dawnmarie gazed at him, with hatred and dread, Slow Running figured he could make her obey and respect him after she became his wife.

He could have any woman that he wanted from his tribe, so he reasoned that he could have Dawnmarie as well.

Despite the many women who had sexually pleasured him, their favors meant little to him. His thoughts always went, stopped, and stayed with Dawnmarie. And today he would claim her as his.

That was another reason why he must be sure that her father died during the attack today. Her father was an interference that needed to be stilled, forever. After a moment of ponderance, he quickly decided that Dawnmarie's mother was an interference too.

She must also die.

Now close to the cabin, Slow Running shouted an order to his men with a mimicked cry of a turtle dove. He then gave a war whoop and charged the cabin.

Clouds of arrows and a spattering of gunfire crashed into the log siding and open window and door.

"Huka-hey!" Slow Running cried over and over again, the war whoop stilling all sounds in the nearby forest.

Chapter Eight

How her feet tempt!
How soft and light she treads!
—Nicholas Hookes

Suddenly immobilized by the sound of war cries, gunfire, and arrows flying through the front window like deadly missiles, Dawnmarie clung to the raccoon. Then she dropped the animal to the floor and ran to her mother.

She could see Chief Slow Running approaching the cabin in a mad run. "The bastard! He's finally come to murder us!" she cried.

Cleaves was too drunk to realize what was happening. He stared blankly at the arrows that whizzed past him and lodged into the wall behind him.

Dawnmarie grabbed her mother by the arm and started to grab her father, but a scream froze in her throat as an arrow lodged into her father's chest, followed by another and another. He stood in place, eyes wide, then fell lifelessly to the floor.

Doe Eyes let out a loud wail of despair and tried to yank herself free from Dawnmarie to go to her husband. But Dawnmarie kept a firm grip on her mother and led her toward the door that led into the storage room in the hopes of finding safety.

From there they could make their escape from the back door and into the forest. However, just as they reached the door Dawnmarie heard her mother cry out in pain. Her body flinched and quickly stiffened in Dawnmarie's grip.

"I am hit," Doe Eyes cried, dizzy with pain. "Daughter, leave me! Go on alone! Save yourself! If the Sioux find you they will take you captive. You will be raped! You will be held in bondage as a slave to Slow Running for the duration of your life! You are young. You are pretty. You have so much life ahead of you. It should be spent with White Wolf."

Dawnmarie turned to face her mother who was clutching at her upper left arm, blood trickling through her fingers. "No, Mum! No matter what you say, I shan't leave you. Please find the strength and courage to go onward. I cannot leave you to die at the hands of the Sioux. Is it not enough that I have lost my father to that damnable heathen Slow Running, and that you have lost your husband?"

Tears rushing down her cheeks, Doe Eyes implored Dawnmarie with a quiet stare, then reached a shaky hand out for her daughter. "Leave, Dawnmarie," she cried. "Now! Do you not see? My life is all but over. Leave me here. Let it be done and over with now."

"You know that I cannot leave you," Dawnmarie said, tears streaming from her eyes. "And the longer I must argue with you about this, the less chance either of us have of surviving."

Doe Eyes sighed heavily. "Yes, I see that now," she murmured. "Take me with you. If we survive, we will find a way to return later to see to your father's burial."

Dawnmarie swept an arm around her mother's waist and half dragged her through the dark storage room, and then out the back door.

Her mother groaned in pain, blood pouring in a steady stream from the wound on her arm. Yet Dawnmarie continued to run into the forest.

Then Doe Eyes stopped, heaving hard in an effort to catch her breath. "I cannot go any farther," she said, her face drained of color. "I am dizzy. I am weak. I am losing blood. Go on ahead. Go for help. The Lac du Flambeau village of Chippewa is not that far from here. Go to White Wolf. Seek his help."

Doe Eyes sank to the ground, her head hung as she clasped her wounded arm. "I am tired," she said, stretching out on the ground beneath a tree. "I must sleep."

Dawnmarie stood in stunned silence as she stared down at her mother. She was alarmed at the amount of blood that was spilling from the wound on her mother's arm. She knelt down beside her and ripped a portion of the hem of her dress away and with trembling fingers tied it around her mother's arm as a tourniquet in an effort to stop the bleeding.

When the blood flow ceased, tears of relief flooded Dawnmarie's eyes.

But then she stared behind her. Her heart skipped a beat when she heard the continued shouts and war cries that came from the cabin where her father lay dead.

Closing her eyes tightly, she tried to keep the thought of seeing her father scalped from surfacing in her mind's eye. She prayed to Kitzihiat, her Kickapoo Great Spirit, that at least he might be spared that humiliation at the hands of the Sioux.

"Dawnmarie, you must go for help," Doe Eyes managed to whisper as she reached a shaky hand to her daughter's arm and clutched it. "Flee while you have the chance. Do you not realize that Slow Running will come searching for you when he sees that you have escaped his wrath? Please, daughter. Leave. *Now.*"

Seeing that she had no choice but to leave her mother for the time required to go for help, Dawnmarie leaned protectively over her for a moment and hugged her, then leapt to her feet and searched with eager eyes for a better shelter for her.

Her gaze fell upon a thick stand of brush where there was an outcropping of rock at least on two sides. She fell to her knees once again beside her mother.

"Mum, you must get better hidden before I leave," she said, placing an arm around her mother's waist. "Please find the strength to come with me just a little ways, where I believe you will be safe."

Limp, her eyes closed, Doe Eyes moved slowly to her feet and leaned against Dawnmarie until she was behind the bushes and resting her back against the rock.

"I will return soon, Mum," Dawnmarie said, embracing her mother one last time. "I promise that I will bring help for you."

Her mother nodded, then hung her head and softly dozed off as Dawnmarie broke into a mad run through the forest.

Dawnmarie's hand went to the pistol she always carried in her pocket. Thank God her father had taught her how to use it.

Chapter Nine

Since she would not have them seen,
The wood about her draws a screen.
—Andrew Marvell

Slow Running moved stealthily around the quiet confines of the cabin. He chuckled amusedly as he stepped over Cleaves Garrett, the white trader's body a pincushion of arrows. Then his eyes narrowed angrily as he searched in vain for Dawnmarie and her mother.

When he saw that the back door was open, which led outside into the forest, he realized that the woman with the violet eyes and her mother had fled to safety.

Stamping back into the outer room of the trading post where his warriors had just discovered the jugs of brandy hidden beneath several layers of blankets, he grabbed one of the jugs and yanked the cork from the top.

"He lied," Slow Running shouted. He kicked Cleaves in the side. "This firewater is proof of his lies."

After tossing the cork across the room, he tilted the brandy to his lips and took several deep swallows. When he lowered the jug from his mouth he looked at it questionably.

He arched an eyebrow. He ran his tongue across his lips. There was something different, something peculiar, about this firewater. Yes, he tasted a strange sort of bitterness.

He shrugged, blaming the difference on the age of the brandy, then tossed out orders to his warriors.

"Steal everything you wish," he said, taking another deep swallow of brandy. "Take all the firewater."

He singled out two warriors and took them aside. "Go and search for the women," he flatly ordered. "Kill the older one. Bring the young one to me at our camp."

The warriors nodded, then left in a run from the cabin.

Slow Running kicked Cleaves's body again, took more drinks from the jug in big, fast gulps, then rummaged through everything, laughing drunkenly.

Dawnmarie's collection of colorful beads fell to the floor and rolled in all directions.

Chapter Ten

If so I mourn, he weeps with me,
And where I am, there he will be.
—Thomas Lodge

So intent was she on reaching White Wolf's village and then returning for her mother, Dawnmarie ignored the ache in her side caused from running endlessly through the pathless wilderness. Sweat poured from her brow as she ran through the tunnel of pines that perfumed the air.

She ran onward through thick, young aspens and brambles, then up a slope toward a rocky outcrop. Halfway up the slope, blocks of basalt five feet thick protruded from the earth like great, gray buckteeth, slowing her climb.

But once she reached the top of the summit and it leveled off to something safe enough to stand upon, she went to the edge.

Shielding her eyes from the sun, she peered downward, scanning the occasional break in the trees below for any signs of the Sioux warriors.

She gasped and swallowed hard when she discovered two warriors running through the forest. The way they searched with their eyes she knew that she was the object of their search.

Breathless with fear, Dawnmarie ran down the slope and tried to lose herself in the thick forest again. She ran past fiddlehead ferns and *chante relles*, crushing the lovely golden mushrooms beneath her feet. She tripped over tree limbs that lay twisted and rotted in her path. Then she grew cold with panic when she heard the sound of padded moccasins crunching the dried leaves behind her. They were catching up with her.

As bone-weary as she was, she knew that she had no chance in hell of eluding her pursuers for much longer. She had no choice but to stop dead in her tracks and try to trick them. There were only two warriors. If she could shoot quickly and accurately enough, she could rid herself of both of them.

Her heart thudding like a hammer within her chest, she stopped and stretched out on the ground on her stomach, pretending to be unconscious.

Her hand slipped into the pocket of her dress. She circled her fingers around the handle of the derringer. She positioned her finger on the trigger, then slowly drew the small firearm from her pocket and kept it hidden beneath her.

When she heard the heavy breathing of the Sioux as they drew closer, Dawnmarie grew weak with fear.

They were so close now she could even smell the strong aroma of their tobacco. They smoked a different sort than the Chippewa or her father. The strong stench clung to them.

When Dawnmarie surmised the Sioux were close enough, she rolled over on her back and shot one of them in the chest. Wide-eyed and scarcely breathing, she watched the warrior clutch at his chest as he tumbled to the ground.

She looked quickly over at the other warrior but was not quick enough to shoot him. He lunged at her and pinned her to the ground. His one hand held her in place while his other grabbed her firearm and tossed it away.

His eyes hazed over with pain, the wounded warrior moved slowly to his feet. He turned and stumbled away, back in the direction of the trading post.

Dawnmarie kicked and squirmed as the other warrior yanked her up from the ground. Half dragging her, he followed the wounded Sioux.

When they reached the canoes that had been beached along the sandy shore out of viewing range of the trading post, he tossed her into one of them as though she weighed no more than a small bag of potatoes. She scrambled to her feet again to try to jump from the canoe, but she was stopped and shoved back in place by the warrior.

Pretty soon she could do nothing but lay in the bottom of the canoe. The warrior then bound her wrists and ankles with small strips of leather.

Totally helpless now, she watched the warriors fill their canoes with the stolen goods from her father's trading post. Then her eyes brightened when she recognized the jugs of brandy that her father had doctored up the previous evening. Soon these warriors would be back at their camp, drinking the vile, tainted brandy, and would become violently ill.

Only then might she find a way to escape.

Tears streamed from her eyes as she thought of the fate of her mother and father. Her father had died. But what of her precious mother?

Then she realized with a measure of hope that there were no signs of her mother in any of the canoes. That meant that the Sioux warriors had not found her. There was a chance that she might survive, and Dawnmarie *had* to find a way to escape, to go back to her mother with help.

Only one hope remained: White Wolf. If only she could reach White Wolf in time.

Chief Slow Running headed down the slope toward the canoes, his gait clumsy, faltering. In one hand he held a jug of brandy. In his other, he carried Dawnmarie's father's favorite rifle.

The bastard Sioux had surely taken everything of value from the trading post. Dawnmarie told herself that she would make the Sioux pay for what they had done. She vowed to see that Slow Running would regret the day he was born.

Slow Running stepped into his canoe and settled himself on the seat close to Dawnmarie. "I see my warriors found you," he said drunkenly. "That is good. Now you will be my companion as we return to my village with all our spoils of war."

He laughed throatily. "*You* are the most lovely of these newly claimed possessions," he bragged.

"I would not celebrate too much," Dawnmarie said, staring icily at him.

"And why not?" he asked, weaving in his drunken stupor.

"I may have been caught, but I was not taken

without a fight," Dawnmarie said menacingly. She pointed toward the canoe at her right side. "Look in that canoe. What do you see? Do you not see a wounded warrior? Well, it is _my_ bullet that is lodged in his chest."

Slow Running's eyes widened. He stretched his neck and looked over at his warrior who lay comatose, his death soon approaching.

Slow Running gazed at Dawnmarie. She wondered whether he was going to hit her or remain impassive.

"It seems I have found a woman who is not only beautiful, but who is also a good shot," Slow Running said, chuckling.

Dawnmarie gasped. "You don't even care about your warrior, do you?" she said, shocked to learn that he could be so heartless. It only reconfirmed her earlier suspicions—that he cared only for himself.

"My warrior is not worthy of my worries," Slow Running grumbled. "He allowed a woman to get the best of him. He is disgraced. He is better off dead."

He lay the rifle aside and set the jug on the floor behind him, then reached his fingers to Dawnmarie's lustrously long hair.

"Take your hands away from my hair," Dawnmarie hissed, wrestling with her bonds, trying to get free. A chill soared over her flesh at the thought of him contemplating scalping her. In his war paint he looked fierce enough today to do anything and everything hideous.

When he lowered his hand and ran it softly across the contours of her face, another fear entered Dawnmarie's heart. He was touching her like a man who wanted a woman sexually. She could see the hunger in his eyes.

When his hand cupped a breast, his thumb finding

the hard nub of her nipple through her soft buckskin, she tried desperately to pull away. But he held her immobile with one hand as he took more liberties with his other.

He circled the nipple with his thumb, his lips quavering into a slow smile as she groaned with disgust. Slow Running simply took the groan as a sound of pleasure.

But when she managed to lift her bound feet and kicked him in the groin, his smile quickly faded, and he clutched himself, moaning with pain.

After his pain subsided he raised a hand and slapped her across the face. "You are too spirited," he said, leaning down into her face. He grabbed her hair and drew her lips close to his. "Slow Running will use that spirit soon in between his blankets. We will see then who wins this battle between man and woman."

Her face stinging from the blow, Dawnmarie glared at Slow Running. When he reached for his jug of brandy and took several swallows of it, she smiled smugly. Thanks to her father, Slow Running's threats would be short-lived. She doubted he would have the strength to take her into his blankets with him. The pain in his stomach would be even worse than that which she had inflicted in his groin only moments ago.

Slow Running caught Dawnmarie smiling. He set the jug aside and grabbed her by the shoulders and lifted her closer to him. "You smile?" he said, mistaking the smile as something akin to flirting. He yanked her close against his strong body and kissed her long and hard.

When he released her and let her fall clumsily to

the floor of the canoe, Dawnmarie coughed and choked, the need to retch dizzying her.

Slow Running ignored her reaction to the kiss. He knew he must escape before the Chippewa came and discovered the murdered trader, and the thievery that had taken place at the trading post. He took one more drink of the firewater, then shoved his canoe into the water. His warriors followed his lead.

Dawnmarie watched the shoreline as it moved swiftly past her. She hoped that White Wolf or some other friendly Indian might see the Sioux and realize that they were up to no good.

When she gazed up at Slow Running, watching the muscles ripple down his copper back as he paddled methodically through the water, all she could think of was another strong, muscled back: White Wolf's. But would she ever see him again?

She then thought of the "love charm bundle" that White Wolf wore. If he loved her, surely he would search until he found her!

She smiled thinking of him.

As quickly as she had gained a fraction of hope within her heart, she thought once again of her mother. Could she survive much longer alone in the wilderness?

Or would she die alone, left with the dream of finding her true people.

Dawnmarie bowed her head so that the Sioux warriors could not see her tears.

Chapter Eleven

The wind, enamóred, streaming round thee,
Painted the visions I had seen.
                              —John Clare

White Wolf placed one last pelt into his canoe. He then smiled. His canoe was too full to add another pelt. That was proof that he was taking enough to Dawnmarie's father for a bride price. He was a greedy man. No man filled with such greed could turn his back on such a wealthy offering.

"You still believe the white man will trade the pelts for his daughter?" Sharp Nose asked.

"Believe me, I know how Dawnmarie's father operates. When I return to my village you will see the white woman sitting behind me in the canoe, instead of the pelts. I am that confident that she will be mine to take into my blankets with me tonight."

"Even if the trader agrees to the bride price, are you certain the white woman will come with you that willingly?" Sharp Nose questioned.

"Do you not remember her reaction to my love charms?" White Wolf said, frowning over at Sharp Nose.

"She did not act offended," Sharp nose said, then shrugged. "But that does not mean that she wishes to be your woman."

"My warrior doubts his chief again?" White Wolf said, swinging an arm around Sharp Nose's shoulders. "My friend, could jealousy be the cause of this doubt?"

"No. My eyes have sought and found another woman," Sharp Nose said. He was thinking of Swallow Song of the Potawatomis tribe.

However, he feared that she too was already in love with White Wolf. It seemed Sharp Nose never got even half the attention that White Wolf got from women, and for this reason he was starting to resent his best friend, his *chief*.

But he had to learn to fight off the resentment, for better to have White Wolf as a friend, than an enemy. White Wolf held much power in this community. And being a friend to such a powerful man gave Sharp Nose a good measure of power himself.

"Are you speaking of Swallow Song?" White Wolf asked. He shoved his canoe out into the water. "Why do you not tell her about your feelings?"

"In time, my brother, in time," Sharp Nose said.

He planned to make a love charm for the beautiful maiden. This way he could charm her, then have her.

When White Wolf took leave of his friend, Sharp Nose called out, "Be safe, my friend!"

And White Wolf replied, "I am safe. Wenebojo, the Great Spirit, rides my canoe with me today. I am confident that all that happens today will be good, not ugly!"

Chapter Twelve

I must not tell, how dear you are to me.
It is unknown, as secret from myself.
Who should know best, I would not if I could
Expose the meaning of such mystery.
                              —*Vita Sackville-West*

Anxious to get to the trading post, hoping to soon be on his way back to his village with his new wife, White Wolf drew his paddle earnestly through the water.

He cocked an eyebrow thinking about the bride price that he would offer the white trader. "One hundred expensive pelts," he whispered.

"It *will* be adequate enough," he said, his voice no longer a whisper. "It is more than most warriors pay for their women."

But Dawnmarie was not just any woman. He closed his eyes and pictured her pretty smile, her intriguing eyes the color of violets in spring, and a body that had blossomed into womanhood at such a tender age.

Ay-uh, yes, she was far from ordinary. She was special in all ways that mattered to a man's heart.

He glided the canoe smoothly through the pristine water and followed a turn in the river. Once the turn was completed, he got his first sight of the trading post through a break in the trees only a short distance away. Having never offered a bride price before, White Wolf's heart raced nervously as he headed the canoe toward the shore.

White Wolf lay his paddle down inside the canoe and stepped out into the water. After dragging his vessel farther up onto the sand, so that it would not float away while he was tending to his personal business, he turned and stared toward the cabin.

. His gaze shifted upward. He was surprised that he did not see any smoke spiraling from the fireplace chimney. Usually Doe Eyes was always at the fire preparing a meal or hot coffee to offer those who were trading.

Then he noticed something else that caused his insides to stiffen. There were objects all strewn along the ground: a jug, a bolt of cloth that was half unrolled, its one loose end fluttering in the breeze, cooking utensils, such as spoons, pans, and plates.

Fear grabbed at White Wolf's heart when he looked up at the cabin again. He shadowed his eyes with a hand and peered more closely at the log structure.

Then he saw the arrows that were stuck into the sides of the cabin and the door that stood partially agape. He swallowed back a gasp of horror.

"*Gah-ween,* no!" he rasped as fear grabbed him at the pit of his stomach. He broke into a mad run up the hill.

All that he could think about was Dawnmarie! It was obvious now that she and her family had suffered an attack. Had she survived? Was she wounded? Had she been taken captive?

Anger flooded his senses when he suddenly realized the only person who could have wreaked such damage. Slow Running! The snakelike Sioux had posed a threat to the white people from the day they arrived at these shores.

The only thing that had kept Slow Running at bay

was his love of firewater. As long as the trader kept
him supplied with brandy and rum, the Sioux leader
would only voice his threats, never act on them.

But now it seemed his patience had run out. And
not only had his patience run out for firewater, but
perhaps also for Dawnmarie!

"Aieee!" White Wolf cried to the heavens. "I
waited one day too long to bring the bride price for
my woman!"

As he reached the cabin absolute silence met him
like a splash of cold water in the face.

He listened, but he heard nothing.

His hand reached instinctively for the knife he usually wore sheathed at his waist, but he realized it
was gone. In his haste to bring his bride price for
Dawnmarie he had forgotten his knife.

He felt awkward, even *naked,* without a weapon
for protection, but Dawnmarie, not weapons, was the
only thing he had been thinking of when he left.

She was the first thing on his mind when he woke
up. She had been his *reason* for waking up; for
breathing.

All he could think about was her loveliness and
how it was going to feel to be able to finally hold
her in his arms and whisper to her how much he
loved her.

He thought he might lose all reason, perhaps even
his sanity, if he could not claim her as his.

Stepping cautiously toward the open door, White
Wolf walked in. Sun was spiraling its beams through
the window, leaving everything else in shadows and
making it almost impossible for White Wolf to make
anything out.

But as soon as his eyes adjusted to the darkness
of the shadows he could see the disarray and the

mayhem of the cabin. He had to grab for something in order to steady himself, so great was the shock.

The white trader lay just inside the door, his body riddled by arrows, his dead eyes staring straight ahead. Everything inside had been overturned and ransacked, making it hard to move around.

"Dawnmarie?" he whispered. "Where are you?"

He moved stealthily toward the back room where he knew the supplies were kept. His pulse raced as he slowly pushed that door all the way open.

White Wolf took one step inside, his eyes quickly shifting to the floor where he saw a great puddle of blood that soaked the wood.

He knelt and scraped his finger across the dried blood.

His gaze quickly turned to the open back door and he realized it was possible that Dawnmarie and her mother had escaped. Then he spotted the bloodstains just outside the door.

"Someone *did* escape," he whispered.

So far he had no reason to believe that Dawnmarie was dead. Perhaps she *had* escaped. Yet it was also possible that she *was* a *gee-tay-bee-bee-nah,* captive.

If so, he reasoned, he would release her from captivity.

His shoulders stiff, his head bent, he broke into a run and began following the trail of blood into the forest. But suddenly the trail ended.

Realizing it was futile to go any farther, he cried, "I must go and gather a search party!"

When he returned to the cabin, he heard a noise coming from the outer room.

When he sniffed the air, his trained nose immediately identified the smell of Sioux tobacco, so different from that of the *kinnikinic* smoked by the

Chippewa. He wondered whether the smell was fresh or whether it was left behind from the attack.

Placing his back against the wall, White Wolf inched his way toward the door that led to the outer room. His eyes were alert as he watched for any sudden movement. He knew that his hands were his only weapons. He stopped in midstep, his eyes narrowing. He heard that same noise again. Obviously someone was rifling through what remained in the outer room. It wasn't enough that they had already destroyed the family's home; they had returned for whatever small piece of their lives remained intact.

Not enjoying this cat and mouse game, and needing to get some answers, White Wolf burst into the outer room.

His eyes widened at what he found. It was a raccoon innocently going through the pots, pans, and upturned cans.

White Wolf went to the raccoon, which seemed friendly enough. He reached a hand out to it, palm side up. "My furry friend, were you here?" he asked thickly. "Were you witness to what happened here? Oh, if only you could talk."

He glanced over at Cleaves again, then got a blanket and covered his body, the blanket unable to hide the arrows that White Wolf did not take the time to remove. Time was of the essence now. He had to go and search for Dawnmarie, and every minute counted. He had already taken too much time contemplating things.

Now it was time for *action*.

He turned to leave, wincing when something poked through his moccasins. When he lifted his foot, he discovered several colorful beads.

"Dawnmarie's," he whispered, bending to gather

several of them in his hand. "Is this all that remains of my Dawnmarie?"

He let them roll out of his hand, then broke into a run out of the cabin. He must return to his village. Not only would he organize a rescue party, but a warring party as well.

Stopping to gaze sadly at the pelts in his canoe, the bride price that he had been so proud to offer, White Wolf prayed softly to Wenebojo, the Great Spirit, that he would find Dawnmarie.

He prayed that if she was at the Sioux camp, he could arrive there before they harmed her. He only hoped that the Sioux's main interest lay in his fire-water, not Dawnmarie.

White Wolf shoved his canoe out into the water. With several quick strokes he soon had his vessel headed back toward his village.

He glanced up at the sun. It was slipping much too quickly downward on the far side of the sky.

Time was his enemy now, and without Dawnmarie, he could know no tomorrow.

Chapter Thirteen

Love laughed again, and said,
smiling, "Be not afraid."
—*John Bowyer Buchanan Nichols*

Dawnmarie sat stiffly beside the fire in Chief Slow Running's tepee. Her legs and wrists were no longer bound. In fact, she didn't even feel like a captive. However, she knew that if she tried to escape, she would be stopped before she took one step outside the Sioux chief's lodge.

Dawnmarie played along with the other women in the tepee. For now, she had no other choice. But when the time was right, she *would* find a way to escape. She had to. Not only for her own welfare, but also her mother's. She had to get back to her. She had to care for her.

When she arrived at the Sioux camp, Dawnmarie was offered a heaping tray of food, but she felt too heartsick to eat. She ate only enough to keep up her strength.

Dawnmarie was being pampered by the Sioux women. When Slow Running's young sister, Star Flower, brushed her hair with a porcupine quill hairbrush, she informed Dawnmarie that she was going to become her brother's *wife*. Dawnmarie's heart sank.

"*Hinu, hinu,* I know not why my brother chooses you over the beautiful Sioux women," Star Flower said spitefully even as she smoothed bloodroot color onto Dawnmarie's cheeks with her fingertips, reddening first one cheek and then the other. Smiling wickedly down at Dawnmarie and casting her a hateful glance, she rubbed Dawnmarie's cheek much too hard.

"Woman with the violet eyes, you think your life will be easy just because you marry a powerful Sioux chief," Star Flower tormented.

"I ask nothing of you, and I do not plan to be here long," Dawnmarie said, her voice edged with anger.

"And where do you think you are going?" Star Flower taunted.

"Anywhere but here," Dawnmarie spat back. "Given the chance, just see how quickly I leave."

"You will marry my brother soon and then you will be a wife who obeys orders from a *husband*,"

Star Flower said, laughing under her breath. "Then try to leave the Sioux camp. Your husband will beat you for your insolence."

"Your brother will not touch me *ever*," Dawnmarie hissed out between clenched teeth.

"And how do you intend to stop him?" Star Flower asked. The other women giggled and looked mockingly at Dawnmarie.

"I see many weapons in your brother's lodge," Dawnmarie said, her eyes moving slowly over the store of weapons that lay at the back of the tepee. "If your brother preoccupies himself with things like forcing himself on me sexually, then I will grab a knife and plunge it into the depths of his evil heart."

Star Flower slapped Dawnmarie across the face. Dawnmarie's neck snapped with the blow, yet she kept her composure, knowing that she had to look brave. After all, the worst was yet to come—when she would have to face *Slow Running.*

That was when her true courage would be needed.

Dawnmarie grew quiet. She wanted to ready herself for the arrival of Slow Running. She was not sure what preceded a Sioux wedding ceremony, but it was not the ceremony she dreaded, it was the events that might follow. She *must* find a way to escape before he defiled her body. She was saving herself for another man, for White Wolf.

"Look at what a mess you are," Star Flower fussed, wiping smeared bloodroot from Dawnmarie's face. "My brother would not be pleased to see you looking so. Sit still. Let Star Flower finish preparing you for the marriage ceremony."

Dawnmarie glared up at Star Flower, yet held her tongue. She could hear the warriors outside the tepee. Slow Running's voice and drunken laughter rose above everyone else's. It was boisterous and loud as he bragged about his day's exploits.

She could tell just from his voice that Slow Running and the rest of the Sioux warriors were terribly intoxicated. Yet her fear ebbed away when she remembered what her father had done to the brandy. These Sioux would be ill very soon. The tainted brandy would attack their insides like maggots feasting on dead flesh.

With this in mind, Dawnmarie was put at ease. She even played along with the women as they continued pampering her, and she did not object when Star Flower added bloodroot to the part of her hair.

Nor did she object when she was ordered to put on her wedding dress, a white doeskin dress with beautiful designs of beads and porcupine quills.

"The dress is so lovely," she said. "I would love to wear it. *Thank* you for your kindness."

Dawnmarie almost laughed out loud when she looked up and saw the surprise that leapt into Star Flower's eyes at Dawnmarie's comments, and at her sudden decision to cooperate.

Ignoring Star Flower, glad that she had found a way to unnerve her, Dawnmarie removed her own dress and slipped the new one over her head. She ran her hands down the full length of the buckskin fabric. It felt like soft velvet to her flesh.

And she could not help but admire the beadwork. Someone quite skilled had beaded this dress for the ceremony. The designs were intricate, and the colors blended together so beautifully.

"Who of your women is so skilled in beadwork?" Dawnmarie blurted out, her curiosity aroused.

"This sister took many pains with this dress for my

brother," Star Flower said sullenly. "Had I known it was going to be worn by *you*, a half-breed who bridges the world of white and red people, I would have made it *ugly*."

"You are quite skilled at beading," Dawnmarie said, unable to stop herself from complimenting someone whose work came so close to perfection. "You should be proud of what you have done, not resentful."

Star Flower's eyes widened. She stared silently at Dawnmarie, obviously stunned by her kindness. Dawnmarie smiled to herself, glad to have finally shut the mouth of this spiteful witch, even if her words had been heartfelt.

She stiffened at the sound of groans and retching outside the tepee. Then she smiled when she realized that the poisoned brandy had taken effect. She knew the men must be mindless with pain and discomfort. That meant *she* would be the last thing on their minds for many hours to come.

The time had come to take advantage of their discomfort and escape.

"What is wrong with our husbands and brothers?" one of the women cried, rushing to the entrance flap.

When she lifted it and looked out, she emitted a cry of despair. "*A-i-i.* They are all so violently ill. My husband. He has turned green."

She covered her mouth with a hand and looked away. "Just watching them retch makes me want to myself," she choked out, visibly shaken.

"Are they all ill?" Star Flower asked, rushing to the entrance flap. "Is my brother?"

Star Flower shoved the other women aside and gazed outside. Forgetting her duties to Dawnmarie, she gasped and left the lodge. She went to Slow Running and held his head between her hands as he vomited over and over again.

"What is wrong, my brother?" Star Flower cried. Horrified, she watched Slow Running become more ill by the minute. "What has caused this?"

"My stomach," Slow Running managed to stay between violent eruptions. "It is on fire. I feel I may die! Help me, Star Flower. Help me."

"What can I do?" Star Flower cried.

Slow Running vomited again. He hung his head and coughed and choked as his insides emptied out all over the ground.

Star Flower looked around and saw that all of the warriors were equally sick. Their women were with them, holding their heads and hands.

Dawnmarie crept to the entranceway and slowly edged the flap aside, just enough to see what was transpiring outside. She gasped and covered her mouth with a hand. She knew the men were going to be ill, but not *this* violently! She had never seen anything like it.

But they deserved it, she thought angrily to herself. And *worse*! Even death was not good enough for them. What they had done to her family merited a slow and painful death. Perhaps some of them *would* die. They seemed that ill!

She closed the flap and looked slowly around her, then smiled triumphantly. The women had left her alone to go and tend to their husbands and brothers. They had forgotten about her.

She lifted her eyes upward. "Father, wherever you are in the spirit world, thank you," she murmured. "Although I asked you not to do this to the brandy, oh, how glad I am that you did. Father, you may have just given me a second chance at life."

Not sure when Star Flower would suddenly remember that she had left her prisoner alone in the tepee with all of her brother's weapons, Dawnmarie knew that she had no time to lose. She must escape now. Otherwise it might be too late!

Her pulse racing, her throat dry, Dawnmarie rushed to the back of the tepee and sorted through the weapons until she found a knife. She whisked it from its sheath and scrambled over the piles of blankets and supplies.

On her knees, she placed the tip of the knife to the buckskin covering of the tepee. Slowly, pale with fear, she made a large cut in the buckskin, large enough for her to crawl through.

She then scurried outside to the back of the tepee and looked around her on all sides. She saw no one, only heard them. Their moans and groans continued to fill the afternoon air.

Breathing hard, her eyes wide, Dawnmarie stared toward the river. She saw canoes lined up on the beach. There were so many and no one was guarding them. Surely no one would notice if she stole a canoe. With it she could get to White Wolf's village very quickly.

Her feet adorned in beautifully beaded moccasins, Dawnmarie ran steadily toward a covering of trees. Dizzy with the fear of being caught, she quickly chose a canoe and shoved it out into the water. Without looking back, she climbed into the vessel and grabbed the paddle. Straining every muscle, she soon managed to gather momentum.

The wind ruffled her hair as she drew the paddle

through the water. She did not allow herself to stop even when her arms began to ache. She had to get to White Wolf's village. "I must get to White Wolf's village," she kept repeating to herself in a whisper.

Chapter Fourteen

She hath smiles to earth unknown.
—Wordsworth

A sudden revelation caused White Wolf to turn back. He could not waste time by forming a search party. By then Dawnmarie might already be defiled by the Sioux chief!

It was up to White Wolf, alone, to save her.

There were dangers in arriving alone, but he had to chance that. He could not take the time necessary to return to his village. He had wasted too much time as it was.

His heart throbbed impatiently as he recalled the woman for whom he was willing to risk his life. He pictured her violet eyes, her wondrous. sweet smile, and her long and flowing hair.

He thought of her body. How often had he dreamed of smoothing his hands over her flesh. of claiming her every secret place with his lips.

"Wenebojo," he cried to the heavens. "Save her for me. Please save her for me. She is my very soul! My reason for living! She is the reason you placed me on this earth and gave me breath. From the moment she and I were but seeds in our mothers' wombs our destinies were charted. Her destiny is *neen-nee-dah-ee-een*, mine."

A soft breeze caressed his cheeks as if in reply, and the cry of an eagle flying overhead made White Wolf's heart soar. He knew by these signs that the Great Spirit had responded to his plea.

When Dawnmarie came into his arms he would never let her go!

Chapter Fifteen

The perfect moment briefly caught,
As in your arms, but still a child, I lay.
—Vita Sackville-West

The summer heat blanketed the woodlands and river. Dawnmarie moved her canoe relentlessly through the water. She gazed at the patterns of lichens and moss mats on the rocks along the shoreline. A rock locust whirred by and a deerfly persistently circled her head. Through the curling waters, the long, dark stones on the river's bed looked like otters at play.

She looked heavenward and, in her loneliness and despair, offered a soft prayer. "O, great expanse of the blue sky, O, Great Spirit, see me lonely and fearful here," she cried. "I trust in you. Protect me. Follow me safely to White Wolf's village."

She gazed around her at the hills, trees, and water. And she looked overhead at the blue canopy stretching over everything like a dome without pillars.

But within the blink of an eye, it seemed the sky's mood darkened quickly and gale winds rushed in as though from out of nowhere. Clouds scudded across the sky in a wild and aimless flight.

Was this how her prayers were to be answered? she despaired. With black thunderheads mushrooming swiftly in the western sky?

She cringed when she heard dark-clouded rumblings and saw lightning zigzagging the sky. It was so bright and intense that it appeared not so much in the distance, as in her face.

She flinched and gasped when she heard an earth-shaking crash, a clap of thunder so loud that it shook the very water in which her canoe was cradled.

Knowing that her life depended on it, Dawnmarie struggled with all her might to turn her canoe toward shore.

But the winds were too strong, and the waves were too high. The currents seemed to suck at her canoe, while the thrashing waves seemed ready to swallow her whole! The rain continued to fall in blinding torrents.

Dawnmarie struggled a moment longer with the paddle, her muscles feeling as though they might collapse with the effort.

And then the inevitable happened. A large wave swept over both her and the canoe.

She screamed as the canoe overturned.

The waves unmercifully beat at her, pushing her into the depths of the river. She swallowed great gulps of water.

Finally, after what seemed like a lifetime, the river became calm, and the storm passed over.

Weak-limbed and water-soaked, Dawnmarie treaded water while trying to get her bearings. Smoothing her hair back from her eyes she squinted into the oncoming darkness. All that was left in the sky were salmon-colored clouds hanging low against the horizon.

Tears of relief flooded Dawnmarie's eyes as she spotted land in the not-so-far distance. With scarcely enough strength to get her to shore, she struggled to lift her arms, and swam for safety.

When she reached the shore, she crawled upon the sand and lay there breathing hard. Her lungs ached with each indrawn breath. She was limp with exhaustion. Although she knew the Sioux might find her, she also knew she had no choice but to rest.

She also knew she must hide herself well and eventually find a safe shelter. She only hoped that her mother had survived the devastating storm as well.

The thought of her mother was enough to get Dawnmarie shakily to her feet. She could not stop tonight. She had to move onward, back to her mother.

She stumbled through the darkness, unable to see where she was stepping, then screamed as she fell into a pit of some sort. Before she had time to catch her breath, she felt something even colder than her wet dress coiling around her ankles. The moon appeared from behind its cover of clouds and gave her enough light to see what she had stepped into: a pit of snakes!

Eyes wide, too stunned to move, she stared down at the snakes that crawled and writhed around her.

She was surrounded by every snake imaginable: heavy, thick snakes, thin, multicolored snakes, and small, plain snakes.

When one of them began to slither up her leg, she screamed and brushed it away. Motivated by repulsion, she somehow found the strength to climb from the pit and run away.

When she finally stopped to examine herself, she thanked the spirits that none of the snakes had been poisonous, and that she was unbitten. Even so, she realized, she was too weak to go farther. She must rest.

Her legs would no longer hold her up. She had no choice but obey the commands of her weakened body. Tomorrow she would continue.

Tomorrow she would get White Wolf's help. Together they would find her mother.

Dawnmarie collapsed under a juniper tree. She curled up on her side, but her wet clothes and hunger kept her from falling asleep.

She shivered and hugged herself, but nothing could ease the ache in her stomach. She had not eaten that much at Slow Running's lodge. Now she wished that she had not been so stubborn. She was not certain when she would eat again.

Dawnmarie moved shakily to her feet and began to search around her. By the light of the moon, she saw something that made her heart leap with joy: sugarplums! There were so many they hung heavy on the limbs.

Dawnmarie scooped the sugarplums into her mouth with both hands like a hungry animal. When she was pleasantly full, she returned to her hiding place.

Hugging herself, she curled up beneath a tall maple tree. Yet fearing what might come upon her in the night should she fall into the defenseless clutches of sleep, she tried to fight it off.

But the night sounds soon lulled her to sleep . . . the tremolos and yodels of loons sounding their eerie chorus across the water, the croaks of frogs, the howls of coyotes.

Soon Dawnmarie was lost to everything but her dream world.

She dreamed that she heard a patter of paws, and when she looked up, a long, furry white nose sniffed at her face. Sharp, white teeth shone out from under thick, white-furred jowls, and silver-blue eyes looked up into the night.

A bloodcurdling howl cut through the night like a knife and awakened Dawnmarie. She almost fainted with fright when she looked and saw a white wolf loping away into the darkness.

And then, as if part of her dream, White Wolf was there. He knelt down beside her where, illuminated by the moon, he resembled a spirit.

She felt disoriented, wondering if what she had just experienced was a dream? A white wolf had been there, and now the Chippewa chief White Wolf stood in its place!

Reaching a hand out for White Wolf, Dawnmarie softly touched his face. "Are you real?" she murmured. "Is it you, White Wolf?"

"*Ay-uh,* it is I," White Wolf said, helping her to her feet. He held her at arm's length, his eyes devouring her. "You are wet and cold, but otherwise all right?"

The wind blew against Dawnmarie's soft, young face. Her large, piercing violet eyes stared up at White Wolf in wonder. Relieved that he was there, she fell into his arms.

Taking strength from White Wolf's powerful body, she clung to him. Her legs wobbled as she leaned against him.

"I *will* be all right," she finally said, once again looking up at him. She felt blessed that he was there. The Great Spirit had heard her prayer. He had answered her in a way much better than she would have ever thought possible.

But that was the way with Kitzihiat, the Kicka-poo's Great Spirit. His wisdom was way greater than all creatures on the earth put together.

"I am all right. But my mother. I fear for my mother," Dawnmarie blurted out, her voice breaking with remorse. "And my father. He ... is ... dead."

"How did this happen?" White Wolf asked. "Who did this to you and your family?"

But he knew the foolishness of such a question. Who else but Slow Running could be responsible? Slow Running's mind was twisted, as though poisoned at birth by some unseen force.

"Slow Running," Dawnmarie sobbed out, taking refuge against White Wolf's hard body once again. It seemed only natural that she should be there, hugging him, relishing the very feel of his flesh against hers. She felt that she had never known life without him.

His chest became wet with her tears. She trembled with ecstasy when he stroked her hair in an effort to give her comfort.

"I found your father," White Wolf said thickly. "*Ay-uh,* yes, he is dead. And I found a trail of blood from the back of the cabin. I followed it until I saw it no longer."

"That was my mother's," Dawnmarie said as she crept from White Wolf's arms. "She was shot in the arm. Before I left her to come to you for help, I tied off the blood flow. She may have lost some more blood, but it should not be enough to kill her."

"You were on your way to seek my help?" White Wolf asked, placing gentle hands on her shoulders. His gaze moved over her. The dress she wore was wet and clinging, outlining her beautiful curves. Her hair hung wet and long across her shoulders.

"Mother and I got just so far and then she could not run any farther," Dawnmarie quickly explained. She shivered when another brush of cool river air swept across her face and bare arms. "When she could go no farther I promised to get your help. But ... but ... I did not get that far before Slow Running's warriors caught up with me. I shot one, but the other one was too quick and grabbed me. He took me to Slow Running's village where I was to be readied for marriage to Slow Running. Instead, I escaped."

White Wolf's lips lifted into a slow smile. "You are a clever, courageous woman," he said, running his fingers through her hair, lifting it from her shoulders. "You outwitted Slow Running. That is good."

"But my *mother*," Dawnmarie cried, shivering again as the wind persisted at tormenting her cold, wet flesh. "Please, you must come with me to find my mother."

Again White Wolf noticed Dawnmarie's uncomfortable, wet clothes. He grabbed her suddenly into his arms and carried her toward the river where his canoe was beached. "You must get out of that wet dress," he said, his voice full of command. "The top pelts in my canoe got wet from the storm, but those beneath them are dry. You should wrap yourself in a bear pelt. After you are dry, we will go find your mother. But first, you must get some nourishment into your body."

Hearing White Wolf's gentle words, Dawnmarie felt protected and loved. It had to do with the way White Wolf held her and spoke so gently to her. Gentleness shone in his eyes as he gazed down at her.

When White Wolf reached the beach and placed Dawnmarie on her feet close to the canoe, she was amazed to find it piled so high with pelts. She turned questioningly toward him.

White Wolf tossed the wet ones from the canoe, not stopping to think of their worth. He had to find dry ones with which to cover the woman who was worth everything in the world to him. "These pelts were to belong to your father. They were the bride price I was going to pay for you. I had planned to be with you tonight. But in a different situation from this one. I had hoped you would be in my lodge warming my blankets at my side. I had hoped to celebrate our marriage soon with a feast of feasts."

"Truly?" Dawnmarie asked, blushing. "You would part with so many rich pelts to have me as a wife?"

"You are worth triple these pelts," he said matter-of-factly. "Had I had room for more, I would have placed them there. I would never want you to believe that I think less of you."

"White Wolf, I am so honored," Dawnmarie murmured, touched deeply by just how much he loved her. How could he have known that she loved him as much?

White Wolf placed his hands to her waist and drew her into his arms. His lips trembled as he lowered them blissfully to hers.

He kissed her softly, everything within him becoming weak with passion and need of her. He had wanted her for so long. Time and again, he had dreamed of a moment such as this.

And now that it was happening, it was more than he could have ever envisioned. It was sheer paradise to kiss her.

He swept his arms around her and yanked her close. Her body next to his, her breasts pressed against his bare chest, was something never known to him before. He wanted to never let her go. Her kiss, her tiny, sweet hands on his cheeks, gently framing his face, dizzied him.

Then he managed to return to his senses. Remembering how he had found her, and why, he relinquished this moment of rapture with her. He leaned down and grabbed a thick bear pelt.

"I shall turn my back while you remove your wet clothes," he said, his voice drawn with passion. "Then you can wrap yourself in the warm pelt. You shall sit among the others and eat my offering of food."

Dawnmarie had never thought that anything could make her any weaker than those moments after swimming to shore, exhausted. But now she knew differently.

White Wolf's kiss and the wonders of his arms had weakened her so much she was not sure if she could move without collapsing. Being with him, being kissed by him, was sheer bliss.

Never in her midnight dreams, when she had dreamed of him, had it been as wonderful; as perfect. It was now that she knew for certain that their destinies were meant to be intertwined. Her rapture was so complete, she could hardly breathe!

But when he laid the pelt across her arms and turned his back to her, she realized the reality of the situation and the haste in which she must act. He had offered to help her find her mother. Not only was he the answer to all of her dreams, but he might also solve her problems.

Surely the Great Spirit must be looking down on her, smiling and giving his blessing. White Wolf was the best of everything on this earth. It seemed too good to be true.

He wanted her.

He loved her.

They would be together as man and wife.

Smiling, she tossed her dress away, then her underclothes.

The pelt felt warm and delicious as she snuggled it around her shoulders.

"It is all right," she murmured. "You can look now. The pelt is covering me."

White Wolf turned around. He smiled down at Dawnmarie, then lifted her into his arms once again and carried her to the canoe where he placed her midst the warm, dry furs. He sat down beside her and offered her food wrapped in leather and a small sealed basket of water.

She opened the bundle and found two pieces of jerky and two loaves of flat cornbread that she ate ravenously. She then swallowed the delicious water in fast gulps.

After she was done, she turned to White Wolf. "How did you find me?" she asked softly. She recalled the white wolf and the eeriness of waking to White Wolf standing in his exact spot.

"I was on my way to Slow Running's camp to see if you were there," White Wolf said, smoothing her hair back from her brow. "From the river I heard the cry of a wolf. This drew my eyes to the shore. I caught sight of the wolf in the moonlight. It was sniffing at something, so I decided to stop and see what had drawn the wolf there. That is the only reason I found you. My namesake, the white *myeengun,* led me to you."

"Then it *was* real," Dawnmarie said, trembling at the idea of the wolf being drawn to her. "I didn't dream it."

"The wolf was as real as White Wolf who sits with you now," he said, taking the empty piece of leather and basket as she handed them to him. He placed them at the bottom of the canoe. "Now we will go and search for your mother."

He left the canoe long enough to shove it out into the water, then sat down on the seat, his back to Dawnmarie. Lifting the paddle, he turned to her. "Which direction should I go?" he asked thickly.

She pointed the way.

He nodded.

Lifting his paddle, he guided the canoe around and began the journey back down the river.

Dawnmarie's heart pounded like thunder at the thought of seeing her mother. But could she remember the exact place where she had left her? She did recall seeing the shine of the river close by and the boulders of rocks that she had led her mother to. In the moonlight, surely she would find them.

But even if she did find her mother, would she be alive or dead?

She shuddered at the possibility of the latter.

Chapter Sixteen

Say over again, and yet once over again
That thou dost love me.
—*Elizabeth Barrett Browning*

The canoe moved quietly and smoothly down the avenue of the river. Owls hooted in the woods, and somewhere in the far distance a wolf bayed at the moon. Dawnmarie wondered if it was the same wolf that had led White Wolf to her hiding place. If so, it was the same wolf that had saved her life.

Dawnmarie kept a sharp lookout on the land to her left side, trying to calculate when she might see and recognize the outcropping of rocks where she had left her mother.

She realized that she was not that far from her home now, and that if she did not see the rocks soon, that meant they had already passed it.

Growing more tense by the moment, Dawnmarie gripped the bear pelt around her shoulders. She should have seen the outcropping of rocks by now.

"Oh, where are they?" she fussed to herself.

Her heart did a strange sort of flip-flop when they suddenly appeared, so clear and high, so silver and bright in the moon's glow.

"Stop! Here they are!" she cried, grabbing White Wolf's arm. "Over there, White Wolf. I finally see them."

White Wolf swung the canoe around and guided it toward shore.

The very instant Dawnmarie's feet touched the ground she broke into a mad run, the pelt clutched around her shoulders.

Then she stopped. Tears stung the corners of her eyes when she discovered that her mother was no longer there.

She stifled a sob behind a hand and fell into a hopeless heap on the ground and began to cry.

White Wolf stood over her, helplessly watching. His heart went out to her. He knelt down beside her and placed his hands gently on her shoulders and turned her around.

Dawnmarie welcomed White Wolf's strong arms as he held her close to comfort her. "It is as I feared," she cried, trying to close her thoughts to what may have happened to her mother. "I was gone way too long. What should I do? I do not know where to search for my beloved mother. I don't think she was taken a captive at Slow Running's village; I would have heard something about it. And I don't know of any other Indians in this area who take captives. Besides, everyone who traded at my father's trading post admired and liked my mother. I can't imagine anyone wanting to cause her harm."

"When we return to my village, we will send out a search party," White Wolf said, trying to soothe her pain. He stroked her hair that now lay dry and in long waves over her shoulders.

"You are so kind," Dawnmarie murmured, leaning away from him enough to gaze up at him. "You are so caring."

"For so long I have wanted to be there for you," White Wolf said thickly. "I should not have waited so long."

He placed a finger to her chin and tilted her lips to his as he kissed her.

Loving him so much, and so thankful that he cared as deeply, tears of joy streamed from Dawnmarie's eyes. She returned the kiss.

Then feeling guilty for this moment of bliss with him, when she knew not of her mother's fate, she drew quickly away. She rose to her feet to return to the canoe, then stopped and gasped as she stared down at the dark stains of blood on the ground. She covered her mouth with a hand, almost choked with the feeling that this was all that was left of her mother—her life's blood that had poured from her body!

She turned and began to run toward the canoe.

White Wolf followed her and caught up with her. He stopped her and swung her up into his arms, the bear pelt slipping from her shoulders enough to reveal to him the satiny curve of one of her breasts.

Seeing how exquisite it was, he sucked in a wild breath and looked quickly away. This was not the time to allow heat to rise in his loins. He was there to protect, not seduce her, even though he knew now that when they came together as men and women do when they loved, she would be a willing participant in the lovemaking.

Imagining this happier future gave White Wolf a feeling of quiet peace within his soul. He smiled down at Dawnmarie just as she turned her gaze slowly up to him, as though reading his most intimate thoughts about her.

When she smiled, every nerve within White Wolf seemed to melt. He was glad when they reached the canoe and he could busy his mind and hands with the paddle, *some*thing to keep him occupied and erase his desperate need for her, a need that was not easily extinquished.

A fire was lit inside of him, so hot that he feared it might burn out of control.

"Please take me to my home," Dawnmarie murmured. "I must see that my father gets a proper burial."

White Wolf hesitated. "You do not want to see your father," he said, his eyes wavering. "I will take you home. But I will handle the burial. After he is buried, then you can pray for him. Not before."

"I must see him one last time," Dawnmarie said, her voice breaking.

"I must insist that you do not," White Wolf said, recalling the many arrows that pierced her father's body. "You will stay in the canoe as I bury him. Then I will come for you."

"Does he look so horrible that I cannot say a final good-bye to him?" Dawnmarie asked, tremors cascading down her flesh. She knew that White Wolf was right. She should remember her father alive, not dead. She would recall being a child, sitting on his lap and listening to his wonderful stories.

She would remember the times, before her father started drinking, when all was peaceful within her family.

"Yes, please do bury him," Dawnmarie said, looking quickly up at White Wolf. "But how can I ever repay you for your kindness? It seems endless. How can you give yourself so generously to others?"

"I give myself wholly to you because I love you," White Wolf said, placing a soft kiss on her lips. "Now let us go to your home. Let us put *that* behind you. Then I will take you to my lodge so that you can rest. Tomorrow I might have better news about your mother. My warriors will turn over every stone in the forest until they find her."

They walked to the canoe, and he made sure she was properly covered in pelts before he pushed the canoe into the water.

He followed the quavering white path drawn by the moon until he recognized the land where he had beached his canoe so often in hopes of glimpsing Dawnmarie from afar.

Now this same path would lead him to death and destruction. The forest was quiet as though it too sensed the cloud of doom that lay over the trader's cabin.

After beaching the canoe, White Wolf knelt beside it and took Dawnmarie's hands. "Stay until I come for you?" he said thickly.

Dawnmarie gulped hard, then nodded. "Yes, I'll wait here for you," she murmured.

He brushed a soft kiss across her lips, then hurried to the cabin and to the chore at hand. When he entered the cabin the moon spilled its white sheen over the blanketed trader. Everything was peaceful. Eerily so. Remembrances of his many times at the trading post swept through White Wolf's mind. He could almost smell bread baking, coffee brewing, and stew cooking.

He remembered well the many times of bartering with Cleaves. Sometimes there was laughter while trading. Other times suspicions.

But what he remembered most was Dawnmarie's pleasant smile and pink cheeks whenever his eyes would lock with hers. For so long now there had been those secret, shared smiles between them.

Now they could be worn out in the open, for all to see.

That hurried him along to his task. Bending to one knee beside Cleaves, he gazed at the arrows that pierced the body. He decided that it was best not to disturb them. They were too well lodged in his body. The blood that had dried around them had acted as glue, securing them fast into his flesh.

White Wolf lifted Cleaves's body into his arms and carried him outside. He stopped to take a look at Dawnmarie, then carried her father up a small incline and lay him beneath the wide-spreading arms of an oak tree.

After returning to the cabin for a shovel, he then dug a huge hole in the ground.

Dawnmarie could see White Wolf tossing dirt over his shoulder as he continued digging the grave. Shivers raced up and down her spine at the thought of *whose* grave. She hung her head and cried again, hoping that one day she could get this grieving all behind her so that she could live a normal life again. White Wolf offered her so much more than she had ever expected. He truly loved her and wanted her to be his wife.

She allowed herself to dream of how it would be each night as everyone in the village retired to their lodges. She would be in White Wolf's arms when she fell asleep at night. He would be there when she awakened.

A thrill coursed through her just to imagine how it would feel to know that he would always be there for her, and how it might be to make love with him.

A strange melting sensation swam through her at the thought of lying unclothed with him, his masterful hands touching her, caressing her . . .

"It is done," White Wolf said, suddenly there beside the canoe, gently touching her cheek.

She looked quickly up at him, their eyes locking. She quickly forgot her fantasies.

"Is he buried?" she asked, her voice drawn and shallow. "My father. Is he in the cold, dark ground?"

"I folded many blankets around him before lowering him into the grave," White Wolf said, feeling her grief. "Come now. Say your prayers over the grave. Then we will leave this place forever."

Dawnmarie nodded. She allowed White Wolf to slip her into his arms so that she would not have to wade knee-high to the shore.

When White Wolf reached dry land and placed Dawnmarie on her feet, her knees grew weak with dread of having to stand over the grave in which her father now lay. It would be her last good-bye. For all that was holy in this world she would never return to this place of pain and death. This place was now forever sullied by the work of Slow Running.

She wanted to forget the Sioux chief.

But she could never forget what she and her family had suffered because of him!

When she reached the grave she clung to the bear pelt as she knelt to her knees beside the raised hump of dirt. Tears streamed from her eyes. Hoping that somehow even her father would gain some comfort from the words that came from her heart, she whispered a soft prayer.

"Great Spirit, please lead my father along the comforting road of the hereafter," she whispered. She felt White Wolf's hand on her shoulder and cherished its touch.

She continued her prayer until she no longer had words left to speak. She leaned over and kissed the cold earth, patted it softly, then rose slowly to her feet.

"It is done," she said, looking up into White Wolf's eyes. "He is now a part of the spirit world. He now walks the spirit path to the heavens."

White Wolf drew her into his arms and hugged her close. He burrowed his nose into the soft fragrance of her hair, then when she eased away and took his hand, he walked with her from the grave site.

As they approached the cabin, Dawnmarie could not help looking. As they walked past, she stopped and looked pleadingly up at White Wolf. "I must take one last look inside," she murmured.

Anticipating this request, White Wolf had carefully covered the blood on the floor of the cabin with a rug. He nodded to her. "Go, but do not be long," he said softly. He looked over his shoulder, into the depths of the woods. "The Sioux have surely discovered that you are gone. They will be looking for you."

"Neither Slow Running nor his warriors will be in any condition to worry about me for quite some time," Dawnmarie said.

Yet she knew that as soon as Slow Running's senses returned and the pain left he would begin a search for her. He seemed obsessed by the very thought of her.

And she wondered if she had done something to cause this? Had she somehow enticed him? Flirted with him?

No, she decided. It was not possible.

She had hated the very sight of him ever since his first visit to the trading post. He had never been a reasonable or pleasant man. She trusted him even less than her father had.

No. She had done nothing to incur his desire for her. She had just been at the wrong place at the wrong time for a man who suddenly felt the need for a *wife*.

"Why do you doubt that Slow Running won't look for you?" White Wolf asked, forking an eyebrow.

"My father was enraged by the Sioux chief's threats and warnings," she said, looking wistfully up at the grave on the hillside. "He prepared brandy that would make them all quite uncomfortable."

She turned smiling eyes up at White Wolf. "And, White Wolf," she murmured. "I have never heard such retching outside Slow Running's lodge as I heard after he and his warriors drank themselves senseless from my father's tainted brandy."

White Wolf chuckled. "This Chippewa chief is glad he never crossed your *gee-bah-bah*, father," he said, looking up at the grave, recalling the many moods of Dawnmarie's father. He was a soft and mellow man when he was not drinking, someone with whom White Wolf had enjoyed trading.

But when her father had lifted too many jugs of ale to his lips, he was not a man with whom anyone could reason.

That is why White Wolf had waited so long to go and offer a bride price for Dawnmarie. More oft than not these past months her father had been one with whom no one could bargain, especially for a daughter's hand in marriage.

"Father always admired you," Dawnmarie said, turning to move slowly to the open door of the cabin. She gave White Wolf a quick glance as he walked beside her. "But I doubt even those pelts you had planned to offer him would have swayed him into allowing you to take me to your blankets with you."

White Wolf's eyebrows arched, then lowered. "Then I would have continued bringing more and more pelts until he could not refuse my offer," he said determinedly. He swept a possessive arm around Dawnmarie's waist. "Now who do I exchange pelts with to get you to my blankets?"

"You need pay no one," Dawnmarie murmured, blushing as she returned his steady gaze. "I am yours, White Wolf. Totally yours. Use your pelts now for a different purpose. Take them to the trading post just up the river."

"There is no beautiful woman there," White Wolf teased.

"Of course I know that. Otherwise I would not send you there," Dawnmarie teased back, glad to find something lighthearted to say, to lift the heavy burden of the moment.

The tension returned and her face drained of smiles and color when she stepped into the cabin. The moon cast spiraling, white ribbons through the open door and windows, revealing the total destruction, the actual desecration of what had once belonged to her and her family.

Horrified, she held her hand against her mouth as her eyes surveyed everything.

When she took another step farther into the cabin and her bare feet came into contact with something that hurt her flesh, she winced and lifted her foot. She stared down at what remained of her beloved beads. They were scattered and smashed all over the floor.

"My loom," she moaned, her eyes wide as she went around the cabin, rummaging through the destroyed contents. "The loom that my father made me. Oh, how I would love to have it now to remember him by."

She stopped and stared down at the tattered remains of the loom as she slowly uncovered the pieces from beneath a strewn, blood-streaked blanket. Tears flowed from her eyes as she picked up the pieces one by one and laid them in her outstretched hand.

"It is gone from me forever," she whispered, then let the pieces slide back to their final resting place on the floor.

She rose to her feet and looked through the cabin for a moment longer, then stopped and shouted with glee when she found something of her mother's that had not been destroyed.

A friendship bag.

Its beautiful beads shone in the moonlight as she lifted it up from the floor. "My mother received this friendship bag from a close friend while she still lived among her Kickapoo people," she murmured, showing it to White Wolf. "The meaning behind this bag is so special. I hope one day to have as close a friend as my mother's."

She lay the bag aside momentarily. Clutching the pelt at her throat, she tried to find her own bag, the one that was almost completed. When she found it, as well as all of her clothes that lay strewn with it across the floor, she could hardly believe her eyes. They were shredded to pieces. Everything.

She was too numb to shed more tears.

But her clothes. She had nothing left to wear. The pelt that she now wore would have to do, at least until she reached White Wolf's village. Surely someone there would be merciful and offer her a dress to wear.

She picked up her mother's friendship bag and looked quickly over at White Wolf. "You have never told me much about your family," she blurted out. "Do you have sisters? Brothers? Parents?"

"I have none," White Wolf said stiffly. "I was the only child born to my chieftain father and his wife. They were killed during a Sioux raid when I was ten winters of age. I was raised then by an aunt and an uncle who became chief after my father. When he died, I became chief. Now my beloved aunt is all that I have left in the world."

He placed a hand to her chin and steadied her eyes into his. "And you," he said huskily. "Now I also have *you*."

He paused, questioning her silently with his eyes. "I *do* have you now, don't I?" he said softly. "Will you not be my wife and fill the emptiness of my lodge with your laughter?"

"I *am* yours," Dawnmarie murmured, her rapid heartbeat almost swallowing her whole. "And once my grieving is all behind me you will hear much laughter in your lodge. I will be so happy to be your wife I shall never stop smiling and laughing."

White Wolf leaned a soft kiss to her lips, then glanced over his shoulder at the door when he heard a scratching noise. He stiffened.

Dawnmarie laughed softly. "I recognize the sound of my raccoon friend," she murmured. "Take a look, White Wolf. It will be outside ready to beg for my handouts."

"I saw the raccoon when I was here before," he said, taking Dawnmarie outside. She was right. The raccoon was there, its eyes wide as it gazed up at them through the moonlit darkness. "It found a turtle egg and sucked the egg from the shell."

Dawnmarie's heart lurched at the memory of the fun she had while gathering the eggs. She turned her eyes away from White Wolf. He had already seen too many of her tears. She fought back those that threatened to spill from her eyes now.

"We should go now," he said, seeing how the mention of the eggs had disturbed her, yet not asking why. "I must get you to safety."

"Just being with you makes me feel safe," Dawnmarie murmured. She wiped the tears from her eyes and watched the raccoon run into the woods. She could not stop from yawning, her weariness was so complete.

"You have had a traumatic, tiring day," White Wolf said, whisking her into his arms again. He trotted down the hill, toward the river. "You shall rest in the canoe as I take you to my village."

Dawnmarie nodded, closed her eyes, and rested

her cheek once more against his bare chest. It seemed to her that she had known the thrill of being held by him, and of being able to take comfort against his powerful chest, forever. And it would be forever now that she would.

That caused a smile to ripple across her lips. At least she could hold on to that at a time when she had lost everything else that she had known during her lifetime. Her future now lay before her, a future that sent a wild bliss through her to even think about it. She had the man of her dreams.

But she would never be at peace until she found her mother ... until she knew that her mother was alive and well.

Before White Wolf reached the river Dawnmarie was asleep in his arms. He waded out into the water and gently placed her on the cushion of pelts in his canoe. He gazed down at the friendship bag that she still clutched in her hand. Perhaps she saw it as a sort of lifeline to the world that had been taken from her today. He did not dislodge it from between her fingers. He drew a pelt over her and covered her to her chin.

White Wolf took a moment longer to soak up the beauty of Dawnmarie's face, of her vulnerable innocence. He was shaken from head to toe by just how severely he *did* love her. His body throbbed from his swift heartbeats. His mouth was dry.

Shaking himself from his reverie, he shoved the canoe out into deeper water, climbed aboard, and drew the paddle deeply and swiftly through the gentle waves. He paddled rhythmically without pausing to rest until he reached the beach that lay only a stone's throw from his village.

As the sun rose with all its splendor in the new

light of day, White Wolf carried Dawnmarie to his wigwam made of poles that were bent and covered with tree bark. He lay her on weaved cattail mats, then covered her with a plush white rabbit robe and removed the one that had been snugly wrapped around her.

Woman Dancing, his elderly aunt who lived in a separate lodge, was faithfully attentive to him. A fire burned in the middle of his lodge, and a pot of food hung over the flames, kept warm for his return.

White Wolf sat down opposite the fire and watched Dawnmarie. He loved her now as never before. He wanted her so badly his body ached with the need. He flinched when she emitted a low sob in her sleep, a desultory tear slipping from the corner of one of her eyes.

He felt her sadness and her pain for he too would never recover completely from having lost his parents at the hand of a band of Sioux during the times of border wars with them.

White Wolf's jaw tightened, vowing to himself that he would find this woman's mother for her. He wanted to end Dawnmarie's pain and fill her heart with a warm peace.

He left the wigwam and went from one lodge to another until he had gathered together several of his warriors. He explained to them what had happened to Dawnmarie's parents and instructed them to search for her mother.

When the warriors left, each going in different directions down the river in their canoes, White Wolf returned to his lodge. He stood over Dawnmarie and watched her for a while longer, then turned from her and busied his fingers. He knew that sleep would not come for him even if he tried, not with Dawnmarie so close.

He prepared smoking tobacco by greasing tobacco leaves and drying them over the fire.

But nothing would keep his eyes from straying to Dawnmarie, her very presence a magnet to his soaring heart.

Chapter Seventeen

"Speak once more . . . thou lovest!"
Who can fear too many stars?
        —*Elizabeth Barrett Browning*

Dawnmarie awakened and slowly raised herself up on an elbow. For a moment her thoughts were muddled. She clasped the rabbit robe close to her bosom and pains of anguish grabbed at the pit of her stomach when she suddenly recalled the events of the prior day.

Her parents.

One was dead.

The other?

She did not know.

And would she ever? she silently despaired.

Her gaze went quickly to White Wolf, and her heart skipped a beat. She quickly remembered whose bark wigwam she was in.

His.

He was on his knees beside the fire, his back to her. She realized he was praying.

She listened, loving not only him, but even the very sound of his voice. It thrilled her heart and weakened her knees with passion.

She could tell he was a very religious man who believed in his Great Spirit just as she believed in hers.

"And so this morning, Wenebojo, I offer my tobacco to clear my mind of irrelevant thoughts," White Wolf said as he sprinkled tobacco into the flames of the fire. "But also to give a simple thanks for existence and the little things in life, like food, shelter, and other caring human beings."

Dawnmarie listened, yet took this opportunity to gaze slowly around her, to see how the man she loved lived. The dome-shaped wigwam was larger than she had imagined. A person could walk around inside without stooping their shoulders.

Dyed bulrush mats twined over basswood bast to make the wigwam more pleasantly colorful were spread over pine branches on the floor. A pleasant pine scent lifted from the pine branches, perfuming the air with its woodsy smell.

She turned over and looked farther into the shadows of the wigwam. Braids of corn, about four feet in length, hung at the back wall over White Wolf's store of weapons, rolled blankets, and various other personal belongings.

Many beautiful pelts hung from the wall as decoration.

Dawnmarie gazed up at the smoke hole that opened directly above the fire pit where smoke spiraled upward even now into the gray sky.

Seeing the threat of rain in the sky, she snuggled the rabbit robe closely around her shoulders, then stared down at the robe. She couldn't recall having seen it before. She certainly didn't recall drawing it over herself before she fell into a deep sleep the prior evening.

Her gaze shifted quickly to White Wolf as her face
grew hot with a blush at the thought of him having
replaced the other pelt that he had given her earlier
when she had discarded her wet dress, with this robe
that was softer and more beautiful.

While doing so, he must have seen her total
naked body.

Had he glanced or gazed at length at it?

Somehow the prospect did not shock or abhor her.
Instead, a shiver of pleasure ran through her, wishing
even now that he would come to her, throw aside
the robe, and take her into his arms.

How wonderful it would be to feel his strong, bare
chest against the swells of her breasts ...

Shocked at where her thoughts had taken her,
Dawnmarie had to wonder if the trauma of yesterday
had caused her mind to snap, turning her into someone she did not know. She had allowed her mind to
wander to sensual thoughts of White Wolf before,
but never this brazenly.

Her thoughts were redirected back to White Wolf
as she heard him include her in his morning prayer
to the Great Spirit. She listened, moved to tears by
knowing just how much he loved her.

"Wenebojo, I give thanks for you having brought
Dawnmarie into my life," White Wolf said, sprin-
kling more tobacco into the fire. "She is all I have
ever wanted in a woman."

He hung his head, then gazed into the fire again.
"Wenebojo, she has suffered enough losses," he said,
his voice drawn. "Let my warriors bring her mother
back to her today. Let my woman's heart have a
measure of peace."

A soft sob behind him drew White Wolf's attention. He turned and gazed at Dawnmarie. Her face

was a vision, her tear-filled eyes making him even more determined to bring inner peace into her life once again.

"You are awake," he said, going to Dawnmarie, settling on his haunches beside her. "And you are crying. Cry, my woman, until your hurt has run from inside you like rivers flow through Chippewa country. Then you will feel free to enter into a new day with hope."

"It is hard to have hope when so much was taken from my world yesterday," Dawnmarie said, feeling weak in White Wolf's eyes as the tears continued to flow in torrents.

But she could not stop them. So much was bottled up inside her that she had to let it go. She must rid herself once and for all of these debilitating tears.

Burying her face in her hands, she cried until no more tears would come. Then when she felt the warmth of White Wolf's hand on her cheek she looked slowly up at him.

"A dress was brought for you to wear," he said softly. "I will go now so that you can dress. Then I will send my elderly aunt, Woman Dancing, to the lodge with food."

White Wolf smiled down at her as he pushed himself to his full height. "You need much nourishment," he said. "It will build your strength. When your body is stronger, your thoughts will be equally strong and direct. You will understand that fate has spared you for a purpose."

"What purpose is that?" she dared to ask.

"You need ask?"

"May I?"

"That purpose," he then said matter-of-factly, "is to be my wife."

She gazed at him with silent longing. Oh, how she desired him. How she wanted nothing to keep them apart. But there were other things that hastened to be done.

"I so badly want to be your wife," she said, forcing strength into her voice, though deep inside she felt weak and vulnerable. "But first I must go my*self* and search for my mother."

He smiled down at her. He admired her spirit. It seemed even more powerful than that of some of his very own warriors.

But there was a place and a time for such a determined mind. "Everything is being done that can be to find your mother," he said thickly. "It is not necessary for you to place your life in danger again. My warriors are capable of doing an adequate search for her."

He stared down at her for a moment longer, then turned on a moccasined heel and walked away from her, toward the entrance flap that led outside. "I leave you now," he said, giving her a glance over his shoulder. "Woman Dancing will arrive soon. I will follow shortly after to share the morning meal with you."

After he left, Dawnmarie felt the emptiness of his lodge without his presence. She gazed slowly around her, once again acquainting herself with those things that were his, and the way he lived. She had known only the ugly walls of the cabins at the various trading posts that her father had established during her lifetime.

This wigwam was not a *house,* with four walls and lovely furniture that she, as a small child, had dreamed of having one day. But it was pleasant, and, most importantly, it was *his.*

That in itself made it all that she needed.

Just being with him was all that mattered.

Guilt swam through her for having allowed herself to think too much of White Wolf and a future with him when she still had no idea what the fate of her mother was.

Yes, Dawnmarie's destiny was to be with White Wolf. But what was her mother's?

For the largest portion of her mother's life she had lived with one man and one daughter. How then, if she survived, could she live without either? If Dawnmarie were married, would her mother feel as though she had lost her?

Perhaps she could use the time to find her true people, the Kickapoo.

"Yes, that's the answer," Dawnmarie murmured as she stepped out of the robe and reached for the lovely buckskin dress that lay on the floor beside her. "She will be reunited with her true people. Surely White Wolf can help in this endeavor."

But first her mother must be found.

Just as Dawnmarie smoothed her hair over her shoulders and stepped into soft moccasins, a tiny, frail woman came into the lodge with a large tray of food. It was so heavy that to carry it weighed her shoulders down.

Dawnmarie rushed to the woman. "Let me help you," she said, relieving the woman of the burden. She placed the tray on the floor beside the fire, then turned to the woman who was still standing there, staring up at Dawnmarie from her short four-foot height.

"You must be Woman Dancing," Dawnmarie said, smiling down at her. She stretched out a hand of friendship. "I am Dawnmarie of the Kickapoo tribe of Indian."

"You are also part white," Woman Dancing said, twining her bony fingers around Dawnmarie's hand, holding it weakly. "Your eyes. They are the color of forest violets. They are beautiful."

Dawnmarie blushed. "Thank you," she said softly, slipping her hand away. "They are the color of my father's." Just the mention of her father made a renewed ache grab at Dawnmarie's heart. She turned and gazed into the fire.

A comforting, bony arm around her waist drew Dawnmarie's eyes back to the frail woman.

"White Wolf told me of your misfortune," Woman Dancing said, her voice full of sincere sympathy. Woman Dancing softly patted Dawnmarie's cheek. "He will make things better for you," she reassured. "You will see."

"I know that he will," Dawnmarie said, the smell of food wafting into her nose. Her stomach growled, embarrassing her. She giggled and placed a hand over her abdomen. "I did not realize just how hungry I was until you brought the food into the lodge."

"It is to eat," Woman Dancing said, gesturing down at the platter of food.

Dawnmarie gazed down at the abundance of food. She marveled at how much there was. She recognized stewed pumpkin and succotash, baked bread, and crisp little corn cakes, as well as berries pounded into little cakes.

Food had also been brought from the outdoor food pit that had been opened to retrieve seed corn, pecans, and hickory nuts stored from the autumn before.

She looked over at the pot of tea, and then at the

fresh blueberries. How good it was that food was so plentiful for the Chippewa. Their Great Spirit had blessed them twofold.

Soon, also, their blessings of wild rice would be celebrated. This year she would join the celebration. Hopefully by then she would have reason to enjoy it. It all depended on whether or not her mother was found.

Therein lay the *true* secret of her future happiness, whether or not she could accept everything White Wolf offered her with a happy heart or a burdened one.

"I mustn't," Dawnmarie finally said, feeling Woman Dancing's eyes on her, watching her as the tiny woman stepped away from her. "I will wait for White Wolf. It would be impolite to eat before he returns. I am in *his* lodge. His guest. I cannot be rude enough to eat without him."

"Violet Eyes, he would understand," Woman Dancing said, taking Dawnmarie's arm, leading her down on a mat beside the fire. "Now, *wee-si-nin*, eat, eat your fill."

Dawnmarie was torn with what to do. She was so hungry she felt as though she could eat everything on the platter. Yet she would not feel right eating without White Wolf.

She sighed with relief when he came into the wigwam, his eyes brilliantly dark in the light of the fire as he gazed down at her.

"Nephew, Violet Eyes waits for you," Woman Dancing said, smiling up at White Wolf. "You are here. *Now* she will eat."

"Aunt Woman Dancing, you brought a *wee-kon-dee-win*, feast, this morning," White Wolf said, gazing down at the platter.

He gathered Woman Dancing into his arms and gave her a warm hug, then stepped away from her and went and knelt on his haunches beside Dawnmarie.

"Violet Eyes," he said contemplatingly. He stroked his fingers through Dawnmarie's silken hair. "I believe I approve of the name my aunt places upon you today. Your eyes are mystical; to the Chippewa the color violet means someone of a high spiritual nature, someone who is direct, with a great knowingness."

White Wolf paused, then said, "Shall I call you my aunt's chosen name?" he asked thickly. "Or do you still prefer being called Dawnmarie?"

"Call me what makes you comfortable," Dawnmarie murmured.

"I will ease into it to make *you* more comfortable with the change," White Wolf said, looking quickly over his shoulder as he heard the shuffling of Woman Dancing's moccasined feet as she moved slowly toward the entrance flap.

"*Mee-gway-chee-wahn-dum*, thank you, Aunt Woman Dancing, for seeing to my needs this morning, as well as Dawnmarie's," he said, his voice filled with much compassion for his aunt.

"That is why your aunt is on this earth now that her husband walks the spirit path in the heavens," Woman Dancing said back to him, then left.

"I do love the name Violet Eyes. It seems more Indian in nature than Dawnmarie," Dawnmarie said as White Wolf settled down comfortably beside her on the mat. "My mother gave me a different name when I was born. An Indian name. But my father urged her to call me Dawnmarie. It was not only his mother's name, but it was easier for him to say than the Kickapoo name my mother gave me."

"*Ee-szhee-nee-kah-so-win*, names," White Wolf said, reaching over to get two small wooden platters from his store of eating utensils. He handed one to Dawnmarie and kept one himself. "*My* Chippewa name means many things—helper, messenger, tobacco runner, pipe carrier. It also means mentor, student."

"How beautiful," Dawnmarie said, her eyes eager as he piled her plate high with food, then gave her a wooden fork with which to eat.

She took a huge bite of stewed pumpkin, then succotash. Both were delicious.

"Your aunt," she then said, pausing before taking another bite. She watched White Wolf eat as though he was starved. "How did she come by her name? It is so beautiful. Does it hold a particular meaning for her?"

"It has particular meaning for everyone who has ever known her," White Wolf said, piling more crisp corn cakes onto his platter. He glanced over at Dawnmarie. "She was not always old and frail. When I was a child I so enjoyed looking at her and watching her dance."

He reached a hand to Dawnmarie's cheek and gently touched her. "Like you, she was a vision to behold," he said. "So delicate. So pretty. So vivacious."

"Although elderly, I can still see her loveliness," Dawnmarie murmured, relishing his hand on her cheek, leaning into it. "You mentioned enjoying watching her dance. Was she especially skilled at dancing?"

"Although names are generally given at birth,

there are exceptions," White Wolf said. "Woman Dancing's special name came from her ability to dance as a beautiful, young maiden. When she danced, the moon and stars shone in her eyes, and the world stood still."

"You are making me instantly jealous," Dawnmarie blurted out, then laughed awkwardly when White Wolf looked quickly over at her, his lips parted in surprise.

"White Wolf, I was only jesting," Dawnmarie quickly interjected. "I think it is wonderful for you to have such pleasantly warm memories of your aunt. Surely her own memories are what sustain her since she lives alone except for you. I hope that when I am as old, and if I am alone, I have something as beautiful and rewarding to sustain *me.*"

"We will grow old together," White Wolf said, his voice low and drawn. "I will never leave you to live alone on this earth. As for my uncle, his days were numbered, by a heart ailment. He was lucky to live as long as he did. I have no such weaknesses. My heart, my lungs, my legs and arms are all strong. Only a bullet or arrow could take them away from me . . . and *you,* my love."

"White Wolf," she said, looking slowly up at him. "Your caring touches my heart. You are so kind and so gentle."

"You have said more than once that I am gentle," he said. "*Ay-uh,* yes, in many ways that is so. Would you like for me to tell you why?"

"Yes, please do," Dawnmarie said, pushing her half-emptied wooden plate away from her. She drew her knees up and hugged them to her chest. "I thought a person was born to be either gentle or rough. Is there another way that somone acquires a gentle nature?"

"Ay-uh," White Wolf said, his eyes dancing. "You see, Dawnmarie, when I was a very young brave, I rubbed the wings of a butterfly over my heart and asked the butterfly to lend me its grace and gentleness. It listened and gave me what I asked. Since then I have followed the path of that butterfly, except ..."

He paused, and she saw a change in his eyes. When he looked away, she knew that he was no longer thinking of the butterfly. He was thinking of something that brought hate into a heart usually filled with love and caring.

"Except for what, White Wolf?" she asked softly. "Tell me."

He looked slowly at her, his eyes still troubled. "Sometimes I am forced to become a different man," he said thickly. "One who can defend my people and their rights to the land that some Sioux still claim as theirs. When this happens I cannot show a gentle side. I must appear fierce and challenging in front of my people."

"I too wish to be a Chippewa warrior," she said, swallowing hard as she remembered what Slow Running, the fiercest and least trusted Sioux of them all, had taken from her. "Given the chance, I would gladly send arrows into the hearts of those Sioux who follow Slow Running's lead."

She sighed and her shoulders slouched somewhat. "As it is, I am a Kickapoo maiden," she murmured. "Nothing more."

"A Kickapoo maiden who now has the strength and the power of my band of Chippewa behind you to help you in all of your endeavors," White Wolf said to reassure her.

"I appreciate that," Dawnmarie said. "But don't you see? That is not enough. I wish that I could make Chief Slow Running and his warriors pay for what he did to my life."

White Wolf set his plate aside and drew Dawnmarie into his arms. "My pretty woman, as a child, the first lesson I learned was patience," he said, cradling her close. "Be patient. In time you will get your revenge. I vow to you that vengeance shall be yours."

Dawnmarie clung to him. "I can't wait," she said, her voice breaking.

"Practice patience," White Wolf murmured. "Everything comes to those who have the patience to wait."

"I shall try," Dawnmarie murmured. "Oh, how I shall try."

Chapter Eighteen

Thy face, when seen, believe me, made every former fancy dim.

—*John Clare*

Chief Slow Running held his stomach as he rolled to one side of his bedroll in his lodge, then the other.

Star Flower knelt beside him and held a wooden vessel to his mouth as he once again retched into it.

When his stomach was drained of everything except a greenish, watery waste, Star Flower took the wooden vessel outside and dumped its contents far from the tepee.

She turned and stared at her brother's lodge, worried for him. She feared that he would not survive another full day, let alone another full night.

Her gaze went to the freshly sewn piece of buckskin that had been repaired where Dawnmarie had cut her way out of the tepee.

A bitterness filled Star Flower's heart, cursing not only Dawnmarie, but also the firewater that had made her brother so ill. The women of the tribe, the wives and sisters, had finally surmised after much deliberations that nothing *but* the white trader's firewater could be responsible for their men's discomfort.

Well, the trader was dead. But his daughter?

Hopefully she was lost in the forest, a victim of the fangs of many wolves. Star Flower had heard the long, haunting howls of wolves the entire night through. She had not wanted to believe they howled because they smelled upcoming deaths in the Sioux camp.

Star Flower wanted to believe they howled because they smelled and tasted the death of the halfbreed woman.

Hearing her brother coughing, and thinking that he was retching again, Star Flower broke into a run and went back to his side.

He was asleep now. He was coughing and talking in muddled phrases in his sleep.

"Breed, if you are alive, you will pay for the sins of your father," Star Flower hissed, her hand caressing her brother's brow.

Chapter Nineteen

Say thou dost love me, love me, love me—
Tell the silver iterance!
To love me also in silence, with thy soul.
               —Elizabeth Barrett Browning

The deep purple shadows of early evening fell over the Chippewa village. Dawnmarie sat beside the fire. There was still no word of her mother.

Dawnmarie was filled with despair, but she no longer felt alone. Although White Wolf was gone for the moment, attending to his chieftain duties, he and his sweet aunt had filled Dawnmarie's long day with much talk ... and more food than she wished to think about having devoured.

Strange how eating had taken the place of worrying. Up until now, eating was only secondary to everything else that she loved doing, such as her beading.

Oh, how she missed her beading. She cringed when she thought of everything that Slow Running had destroyed, including her precious loom.

She looked over her shoulder when she heard someone enter the wigwam behind her. Her eyes brightened and her heart leapt when she saw White Wolf walking toward her.

Then her gaze shifted. He was hiding something behind his back. She looked up at him and saw that his eyes were dancing mischievously. "What is it?" she asked, moving to her feet. "What have you got?"

"*Mah-bee-szhon,* come. Find out," White Wolf

said teasingly. "Come and see what I found in my canoe as I went there to remove the rest of my bride price pelts."

Realizing that he was trying to lighten her mood again by being sweet in that teasing way that she loved, she inched toward him.

"Come closer and you will see what it is," White Wolf said, smiling even more broadly as she walked toward him.

Dawnmarie gasped with surprise when he took a quick step and pressed her body into his.

"Kiss me, then I shall give you something special," he said huskily. "Isn't that a reasonable request?"

Dawnmarie drew a ragged breath. "Very," she whispered, gazing up at him.

Her senses reeled as his dark, stormy eyes claimed her, and then her lips. When he kissed her with a fierce, possessive heat, she gave herself to the rapture. At this moment in time she forgot everything but this man who fired her insides, who cradled her in his arms as though she were a precious rag doll.

Floods of emotions filled her, all exquisite.

And then he released her. "You pay well for your surprise," he said, his heart pounding, his knees weak with want of her. "You deserve having it now."

When he brought his hand from behind his back and she saw what he held, she sighed and reached a hand and took it. "My mother's friendship bag," she said, running her fingers over the shiny, beautifully colored beads. "I remember the last time my mother showed it to me. She said that whenever I found a special friend, the bag would be mine to give to her."

She gazed up at White Wolf. "I must have dropped it last night when I fell asleep in the canoe," she murmured. "Thank you, White Wolf. At least now I have this left of my life with my parents. I only wish Slow Running would have spared my loom and beads. They meant so much to me."

"You will have a loom and many beads again," White Wolf said, framing her face between his hands. He kissed her softly, then led her by her elbow down beside the fire. "I have something else to show you. It is time that I share it with you."

He sat down beside her. "Although you already know about the bundle that I wear at my waist, I think the time has come for me to share it with you again," he said, a knowing smile on his lips.

He gently took the friendship bag and laid it at her left side, then placed his love medicine bundle on her lap. "Open it," he said, his eyes searching hers. "See again what is inside my bundle."

She already knew from having sneaked a peek that one day, but she feigned innocence as she slowly opened the bundle.

"Empty its contents on your lap," he said thickly. "Then I will explain."

Dawnmarie shook the small buckskin bag and let its contents fall on her lap.

She could hear White Wolf's breath quicken as she picked up the small piece of her shawl in one hand and the small carved figure of a woman in her other.

She gave him a slow smile. "You charmed me into your life," she murmured. "That is the purpose of your love medicine bag."

He laughed softly. "I knew that you knew why I wore the bag," he said, placing a gentle hand to her cheek. "I saw your reaction the day that you gave it to me after I dropped it at your cabin. I was almost certain then that you knew. Are you not part Indian by birth? Did your mother not tell you of such charms and their meanings?''

"I was an astute student to my mother's teachings," Dawnmarie said, blushing.

Hopelessly in love, she felt like a bee that was drawn to honey as he reached for her.

The charms fell from her lap as she melted into White Wolf's embrace. A wild bliss overwhelmed her as he kissed her. She tingled all over with pleasure when he moved a hand and stroked a breast through the satiny fabric of the buckskin dress.

The feel of his hand caressing her breast made her dizzy. No man had ever taken such liberties with her body.

Now everything within her was awakened to these new wondrous feelings that robbed her senses of everything but this need she felt for White Wolf.

When she struggled to remain rational, to think on the trauma of past events, passion overtook her and protected her from the sadness brought on by such memories.

Oh, how wonderful it was that this passion, this *man,* was making her forget.

He took her by the hands and drew her to her feet. It seemed so natural when he began undressing her. Breathless, she tingled at the very touch of his hands as they brushed against her flesh.

She could feel his eyes on her breasts as he touched them. She was frantic with the need of him.

Her body turned to liquid as his gaze traveled away from her breasts and toward flesh revealed to him as he shoved her dress down past her thighs, soon revealing the secret place at the juncture of her thighs that seemed to have a heartbeat of its own. It throbbed so strangely; it seemed to be fueling the fires already burning deep within her.

And she had no shame over what she was allowing him to do. She had no regrets. It seemed so right. So very, very right.

The very air was filled with the promise of rapture, of paradise.

White Wolf's senses swam. Oh, how fiercely he wanted Dawnmarie. He had always known that her body would be wonderful to see and touch. But he could never hope for such perfection. Every curve. Every dip. Every secret place that his eyes touched was breathtaking. She was awesome, winsome in her beauty.

He bent to his knees before her and gently lifted one foot and then the other and slowly, almost meditatingly, removed her moccasins.

Then he turned his gaze slowly back up her body and drank in her nakedness. His heart raced as he reached up and cupped the weight of her silken breasts within the palms of his hands. He saw the passion leap in her eyes at the touch of his flesh against hers. He heard her quick intake of breath, and her face blushed as his thumbs circled the pink, tight nipples of her breasts.

Dawnmarie gave herself up to the rapture. She closed her eyes and threw her head back, trembling and weak as White Wolf's hands made a slow, soft descent along her body, searching and gentle. She was shocked by the raging hunger that filled her.

When his hands reached that part of her that throbbed and ached, his fingers caressing, she had to bite her lower lip to keep from crying out with ecstasy.

Consciously fueling her desire, White Wolf locked

his fingers on her hips and lowered his mouth to that part of her that had been created for loving. He found her hot and moist secret place. Her moans of pleasure reached clean inside him as he flicked his tongue for a moment, then caressed her.

Then, unable to stave off that which he needed himself to fulfill these raging hungers that swam through him, paining him, he moved to his feet and took one of her hands.

Dawnmarie's heart spiraled heavenward at the pleasure she had found with this man of her midnight dreams. She opened her eyes and gazed with wonder up at White Wolf. She felt as though the universe centered here in this lodge, as though nothing else existed, not even a sun, a moon, or stars outside this wigwam. Everything, all power, all passion, lay within these walls.

"Undress me," White Wolf said, leading her hand to the waist of his breechcloth.

Dawnmarie swallowed hard and smiled weakly up at him. She had never seen a man undressed before, not even her father. He had taken much care to keep himself clothed in her presence.

But soon she would know the mystery of a man, and not just *any* man, the man she *adored*. Dawnmarie both longed for and feared it. "Undress you?" she asked, trembling.

"*Touch* me," White Wolf said huskily. He lowered her hand and placed it over his tight bulge.

Sucking in a wild breath, he closed his eyes with ecstasy as her fingers closed over him through the flimsy fabric of his breechcloth.

Dawnmarie was stunned by what her fingers had discovered.

How large. How utterly fascinating!

Needing to have her, flesh against flesh, White Wolf wasted no more time with the preliminaries of leading her into how to make love. He eased her hand away.

He undressed quickly, his body revealing his total, undying desire for her.

"*Now* touch me," he said, his eyes filled with a hungry need.

Shakily, her eyes never leaving his, Dawnmarie reached out for him. She gasped at the heat she felt when she circled her fingers around him. She was stunned by how he was now even larger than before. *And* how this part of his anatomy *throbbed*. It seemed to have a heartbeat, a life all its own.

White Wolf covered her hand with his. He urged her into a slow up and down caress that brought a moan from the depths of his throat.

His legs stiffened and he reveled in the touch of her hand, in its movements.

Then wanting more than this, he eased her hand away again.

Placing his hands to her waist he slowly lowered her to the soft mats beside the fire. As she writhed and moaned with pleasure, he showered heated kisses over her taut-tipped breasts.

He then kissed his way down the full length of her body until once again he found her sweet, secret place. He pleasured her there for a moment, then rose over her and slowly parted her thighs with a knee.

"My love for you is greater than my need to breathe," he whispered huskily, then touched her lips wonderingly with his and kissed her.

Kneading her breasts, the nipples burning into his flesh, he entered her with one insistent thrust. He covered her cry of pain with his burning lips, his kisses now more heated, more eager.

Dawnmarie was shocked by the pain, a pain that soon melted into a wondrous pleasure. Sweet currents of warmth swept through her. And when his lips moved to her breasts again, rolling her nipples with his tongue, she twined her fingers through his hair and relished in this awakening, an awakening that caused a happiness to bubble from deeply within her very soul.

Enfolding her within his solid strength he ran kisses across the nape of her neck. He brushed her lips with soft kisses as he reverently breathed her name against them.

As White Wolf's mouth then seized hers in another kiss, this one more wild and demanding, she was shaken by a river of sensations. Her body was molded against his. She clung around his neck and rode with him as his rhythmic strokes within her hastened, filling her more deeply with his manly strength.

Suddenly a spinning sensation never before experienced by Dawnmarie rose up and flooded her whole body, filling her insides with a spreading, rapturous warmth. She moaned as she went over the edge into total ecstasy, his moans against her lips and the way his body tremored into hers proof that he had also found that peak of passion they had been working toward.

The tremors lessened, yet the pleasure still clung to Dawnmarie's insides. Not as intense, but wonderfully sweet and delicious.

Breathing hard, White Wolf lay his cheek against Dawnmarie's. He held her close a moment longer, then rolled away from her and lay on his side, gazing at her.

Still riding the waves of paradise, Dawnmarie turned on her side and faced him. She smiled at him, then traced his facial features with a finger.

"I never knew loving someone could be so wonderful," she murmured. "What I just experienced seems impossible, so unreal. I never knew that my body could become so alive, so ... so ... filled with feelings. It seems like pure magic how you awakened me to sensations I never knew before."

"As you have awakened me," White Wolf said, reaching for her, drawing her against his hard, muscled body. She trembled with pleasure when she felt that part of him that had just transported her to heaven and back rising in strength and length once again against her abdomen.

"Did I hurt you too much?" he asked, reaching a hand to her throbbing center, gently touching her there.

"Only for a moment," Dawnmarie said, gasping with pleasure when he thrust a finger inside her and moved it rhythmically within her. "I must confess that a slow ache is beginning again. But not the sort that hurts. It is an ache of wanting you, only wanting you."

He swept his arms around her and rolled her beneath him, his lips tremoring into hers. He placed his hands beneath her hips and lifted her to meet his entrance inside her again. He slipped his hands to the back of her legs and lifted them over his hips to give him easier access inside of her.

She sighed against his lips as he reached farther inside her with his large, throbbing shaft.

The pleasure was so wonderful, she caught her breath, not daring to breathe.

She never wanted it to end.

Chapter Twenty

My life and all seemed turned to clay.
—John Clare

The soft glow of the fire cast dancing shadows along the walls of the tepee. Star Flower knelt beside Slow Running, where he lay.

"My brother, now that you seem a trace better, should you not take broth into your body for nourishment?" Star Flower asked, holding a wooden bowl and spoon out toward Slow Running's pale lips. "The broth is warm and tasty. It will give you strength. It will enable you to leave your bed and reclaim what is yours."

She frowned down at him. "But I do not know why you would want that violet-eyed woman," she spat out venomously. "Is it her spirit that attracts you? Or is it something more that I, being a woman, cannot see?"

Slow Running ignored his sister's continued rantings and ravings about Dawnmarie. It was not her business why he did or did not want the half-breed as his wife. It was for him to know, and for him to accomplish. The next time Dawnmarie would not escape. He would tie her to a post inside his tepee until she accepted her destiny with him.

After many days and nights of being tied and helpless she would bend to his wishes.

His *every* wish, especially sexually.

Then she would have no choice but to repeat marriage vows with him.

"Send for my best, most trusted warrior, Yellow Tail," he said, his voice weak and drawn.

Star Flower's eyes widened.

"*Now*, sister," Slow Running said, trying to rise, only to fall back again on his blankets when he discovered that his knees were too weak to stand.

"My brother, now is not the time to involve yourself in tribal affairs," Star Flower said, again attempting to give him a spoonful of broth. "The elders are caring for everything. Just you rest. Take nourishment into your body. Then perhaps tomorrow I shall go for Yellow Tail."

Slow Running raised a hand and slapped the spoon away, splashing broth all over Star Flower's new, beautifully beaded dress. She gasped and stared down at the damage, then glared at her brother.

"I offer to feed you, care for you, and see to your health, and you repay me by doing this?" she shouted. She set the bowl of broth aside and rushed to her feet.

Glowering down at Slow Running, she placed her hands on her hips. "You are chief, but you are also my brother, and I do not have to bend to your wishes as though I am just some mere acquaintance to you," she ranted. "I shall not go for Yellow Tail. Get him yourself."

Gaining enough strength to reach out a hand for Star Flower, Slow Running placed a tight grip on one of her ankles and yanked.

Star Flower screamed as she lost her balance and fell backward, just barely missing the fire pit.

More stunned than enraged, she lay there for a moment trying to catch her breath. When she looked over at her brother, at the fire in his eyes and saw how tightly his jaw was set, fear crept into her heart. Growing up, if she ever crossed him, he spared her no mercy. He had beaten her into obedience then, and she knew he could do the same thing again.

Even now, when he looked too weak to stand, Star Flower knew that he would still manage to get his way.

Cowering, Star Flower moved to her feet. "I will go for Yellow Tail," she said, scurrying from the lodge.

"I have trained my sister well," Slow Running said to himself, staring icily into the fire.

Yellow Tail soon entered the tepee. He knelt on his haunches beside Slow Running. "What is it you wish of me?" he asked, his spine stiff, his voice filled with a strained caution.

"You are to search for the violet-eyed, half-breed woman," Slow Running said, looking stoically up at Yellow Tail. "Go alone. Warriors who travel in large numbers are easily spotted."

"I shall do this for my chief," Yellow Tail said, rising to his feet.

"While you search, be sure and check White Wolf's village," Slow Running flatly ordered. "It is known by all that he also wanted to offer a bride price for the woman. If she is with him, he will pay a price, but not to a dead father, to Slow Running."

"The price will be his life?" Yellow Tail said, his voice wary.

Slow Running nodded.

"Now go, Yellow Tail," he then said. "After you discover where she is staying, come back for more instructions."

Yellow Tail nodded and left the tepee.

Feeling smug and confident that the woman would soon be at his mercy again, Slow Running laughed heartily. "In *many* ways she will pay for her father's sins," he whispered huskily.

Chapter Twenty-one

My love draws near with airy tread,
And glances shy and sweet.
—Anonymous, nineteenth century

After Dawnmarie's morning bath in the river, she did not return to White Wolf's lodge right away. She had a lot to think about concerning her feelings for White Wolf, and how they had led her into lovemaking with him.

This morning, as she stood alone by the river, she felt no shame for having made love with White Wolf. Her main concern was that she had so easily forgotten the fate of her beloved mother. At a time such as this, the welfare of her mother should have come first.

Then again, how could Dawnmarie turn away from White Wolf after having shared such wild bliss with him? Her body had been awakened into the feelings of a woman.

Even now she trembled at the very thought of lying again with him, their bodies intertwined, his rhythmic strokes within her dizzying.

Swallowing hard, she shook her head in an effort to clear her thoughts. Then she flinched and her eyes flew upward as a shadow fell over her.

When she discovered White Wolf there she smiled softly up at him.

"You have shared the morning bath with the other women of my village?" he asked. He ran his fingers through his long, wet hair, proof that he had also taken an early morning dip in the river.

"Yes, I bathed," Dawnmarie murmured, feeling suddenly awkward in his presence.

Her eyes wavered as she looked away from him, knowing that if he drew her into his arms, her senses would leave her again.

With him so near, with her desires worn so close to her heart, her stomach felt strangely queasy.

"I, too, bathed," White Wolf said, sensing her uneasiness, and understanding why. Last night he had taken away her virginity. He had taught her that she was born to love and to be loved. "I went farther downriver. I bathed alone. I took time to swim . . . and to think."

Dawnmarie looked quickly over at him, a quiet alarm in her eyes. What if she had not pleased him enough last night? Maybe he no longer wanted her as she wanted him.

Had her inexperience turned him off?

There were many beautiful women who surely wished to be with him sexually. He had always had his choice of women but he still had not taken one as his wife.

Perhaps now he would cast Dawnmarie aside as useless and choose one of those other women? If so, she would not only feel foolish for having given herself so easily to him, she would feel betrayed.

"What were you thinking about?" she dared to ask, her insides tight as she awaited his answer.

"So many things," he said. He once again ran his

fingers through his hair, lifting it toward the sun's rays in an effort to dry it. "I am my people's leader. Like my uncle who was their chief before me, they depend on me. The winter is not that far in the distance, and one never knows if it will be a deadly or mild winter."

Dawnmarie relaxed when she realized that his worries were not of her, but instead his duties as chief.

"Today there will be a meeting between two chiefs," White Wolf said, tossing a rock into the river. He watched the minnows dart toward it, fooled into thinking someone had been generous enough to toss them food.

"Oh?" Dawnmarie said, her eyebrows forking. "You never mentioned that to me last night. Who is coming?"

"I only received word this morning that the Pota-watomis chief, Charging Deer, and his daughter, Swallow Song, will be here," White Wolf said, wondering why Dawnmarie looked so alarmed. "They will camp at the edge of our village. I will meet with Chief Charging Deer in council, and I am sure Swallow Song will enjoy chatting with the women." He smiled as though remembering something. "The women look forward to Swallow Song's visits. She is always smiling. She makes even the grouchiest women smile."

He paused, still studying Dawnmarie's reaction to what he was saying, wondering why she seemed so disturbed.

Then he spoke again. "Swallow Song and her father often visited the trading post. I have seen you talking together. Is she not a delightful person?"

"Yes, a delight," Dawnmarie murmured, jealousy suddenly flooding her senses.

Then she recalled her mother urging her to make a special friendship with Swallow Song and felt a keen melancholia rush through her. Her mother was a good judge of character. It should have been wonderful to have such a close friend as Swallow Song.

But even *then* Dawnmarie had found herself jealous of the beautiful Potawatomis maiden, and Swallow Song always paid way too much attention to White Wolf!

Noting the strange resentment Dawnmarie held toward Swallow Song, White Wolf changed the subject. Reaching a hand out, he caught the outer fringes of a wave as it swept onto the sandy beach. Bubbles clung to his fingers as the water receded and blended into the river.

"Hear the murmur of the waves?" he said thickly. "The river provides us with food to eat, water to drink, and water to bathe in. It has a *soul.*"

"I will never forget how frightened I was during the recent storm when my canoe was capsized," Dawnmarie murmured, gazing into the water, the reflection of the sun like sparkling diamonds across the surface. "It was as though I was attacked by an unseen force."

She looked quickly over at him. "A demon, perhaps?" she said, her voice guarded.

"Just like humans, the river listens to commands of the wind, sky, and rain," White Wolf said, sighing deeply. He rose to his full height and reached for her hand, helping her up beside him. "If someone is in the river when it receives these negative commands, it has no control over what happens to those who ride their waves."

Catching the sight of canoes coming into view around the bend in the river, Dawnmarie's heart skipped a beat. She knew they were Chippewa warriors. Not the Potawatomis chief and his daughter. She knew Sharp Nose, and he was in the lead canoe.

She also knew that Sharp Nose had led the search party for her mother.

Tears leapt to her eyes and a deep sadness engulfed her when she looked from canoe to canoe as they grew closer, not finding her mother in any of them.

"They did not find her," she blurted out, turning to clasp a hand onto White Wolf's bare arm. "White Wolf, they never found my mother."

Understanding her feelings, he drew her into his arms and caressed her back with a hand, his eyes following the movement of his warriors as they grounded their canoes a few feet up the beach, away from him.

Sharp Nose, looking bone-weary from his long search, came to White Wolf. He gazed down at Dawnmarie who looked at him with tear-filled eyes over White Wolf's shoulder as he held her close. White Wolf's feelings for this woman were more apparent than ever before.

"We searched wide and far and found no sign of your mother," Sharp Nose said, his voice drawn. "We surveyed many camps and villages. We questioned many white traders. We even stopped voyagers who traveled the avenue of the rivers and asked them. But no one knew her whereabouts."

Dawnmarie closed her eyes and clung determinedly to White Wolf. "She is gone," she whispered, fighting back the urge to shed any more tears.

She had to accept that she may never see her mother again.

She eased from White Wolf's arms and wiped her face clean of tears with her hands. "Thank you, Sharp Nose," she murmured. "Thank you for your efforts to rescue my mother. I shall always remember your kindness."

Sharp Nose nodded.

White Wolf gave his friend a fond hug before Sharp Nose walked away, then turned back to Dawnmarie.

"Those warriors who just returned will not attend the council with the Potawatomis chief," White Wolf said. "They need their rest. *Mah-bee-szhon,* come. Woman Dancing has taken food to my lodge. Let us eat. Soon Chief Charging Deer will arrive. You can sit at my side in council, or you can mingle with the women who will be discussing their beading and sewing. Perhaps you can lend them some of your knowledge of beading."

"Yes, I would like that," Dawnmarie said, falling into step beside him as they walked up the slight incline, into the outskirts of the village. "I would enjoy sitting with the women. Should they ask, I would be proud to share my knowledge of beading with them."

By staying with the women, she could also keep a closer watch on Swallow Song.

"It is my sincere regret that no good news was brought of your mother," White Wolf said, glancing down at Dawnmarie. He was proud of her for having accepted the news as one who was filled with much courage. Every day he saw reason to love her even more.

"I know that the chances of my mother being alive

get slimmer each day," Dawnmarie said, her voice breaking. She looked up at him, their eyes locking. "But I shall never give up on believing that she is alive. If I wish hard enough that it is so, just maybe we will discover that she *is*."

"*Ay-uh,* believing in the goodness of the Great Spirit makes me also feel that she is alive," White Wolf said, nodding. "I will send more warriors out to search for her. After the council today, I will choose those who have much strength and endurance, and whose pleasant personalities will enable them to mingle with the tribes that have not yet been questioned about your mother."

"But it seems as though Sharp Nose has already questioned everyone," Dawnmarie said.

"There are many villages that lay beyond the rivers and lakes that we normally travel," White Wolf reassured her. "If a group of voyagers found your mother and carried her far away, then she might have gotten farther than we originally thought."

"My mother would have asked anyone who found her to bring her to your village, because this is where she sent *me* for assistance," Dawnmarie said, not wishing to dash this hope that White Wolf was trying to raise in her heart.

"If she was unconscious when she was placed in a voyagers' water vessel, she would not have been able to tell them her wishes," White Wolf said, lifting the entrance flap of his lodge to allow her to enter.

Dawnmarie stopped and stared up at him. His logic was so pure and wonderful, she suddenly flung herself into his arms. "Thank you," she murmured. "Thank you for giving me reason to hope."

He swept his arm around her waist and led her inside his lodge where the tantalizing aroma of food wafted from a large kettle hanging over the embers of the fire.

White Wolf laughed good-naturedly. "We have just had food for thought," he said, reaching for two wooden bowls. "Now let us have food for our *stomachs*."

Giggling, Dawnmarie took one of the bowls. She smiled as she watched him ladle corn dumplings and boiled rabbit into her dish. His goodness and wisdom never ceased to amaze her. His knowledge exceeded his age of thirty winters.

"*Nah-mah-dah-bee-yen,* sit beside me," White Wolf said, patting the mat as he sat down. "Let us enjoy each other's company before the others arrive."

The thought of Swallow Song's arrival swept away Dawnmarie's feelings of security.

Chapter Twenty-two

She blushed a smile so sweetly kind,
Did all my fears remove.
—Robert Dodsley

Dawnmarie sat in the circle of women separate from the warriors' large outdoor fire. The shaman offered prayers to the spirits and drums echoed a steady rhythm in the dark shadows of night.

Dawnmarie loved watching White Wolf discuss matters with Chief Charging Deer. White Wolf spoke with a nobility that commanded the attention of everyone who listened to him.

She felt a deep pride knowing that a man of such power, charisma, and charm loved her so much.

"Dawnmarie, since you lost all of your beads during the Sioux raid, I would be happy to give you some of mine," Swallow Song said, interrupting Dawnmarie's thoughts.

Ever since she had arrived, Swallow Song had treated Dawnmarie like a long-lost friend.

But it was becoming more and more obvious to Dawnmarie that this behavior came naturally to Swallow Song. She could see why Swallow Song was so popular with everyone in the village.

She *did* smile all of the time. She *was* sweet and sincere.

"You wish to share your beads with me?" Dawnmarie asked, feeling a tinge of shame for resenting her, for being jealous of her.

But she had cause to. She would never forget White Wolf's praises of this lovely lady whose eyes gleamed with peace and happiness, and whose pretty face glowed with an inner radiance.

Dawnmarie could even understand why White Wolf might fall in love with Swallow Song.

Yet he could have taken a bride price to Swallow Song's father instead of Dawnmarie's. He could have taken her to his bed, instead of Dawnmarie.

Knowing this made some of Dawnmarie's confidence return. She tried to smile as Swallow Song lay a pouch of beads on Dawnmarie's lap.

"There are many beautiful beads inside my bag," Swallow Song said. Woman Dancing went on to comment on how kind and good Swallow Song was to be so generous to someone who had not been as fortunate as she.

"Thank you, Woman Dancing," Swallow Song said. "But always remember that it is easy to offer gifts of friendship to someone you like."

Swallow Song smiled over at Dawnmarie. "I have always wanted to be friends with you, Dawnmarie," she said softly. "Do you think that this friendship gift that I have just given to you might seal such a friendship? Or would you prefer I make you a friendship bag?"

Dawnmarie felt guilty over her misgivings about Swallow Song, but she still felt jealous when Swallow Song's attention moved slowly to White Wolf as she awaited Dawnmarie's response.

She grew cold inside when White Wolf seemed to return Swallow Song's attention he looked over his shoulder and smiled at her.

Frustrated, thinking that perhaps he was comparing her to Swallow Song, Dawnmarie rose quickly to her feet and let the bag of beads drop. Unable to speak, she ran to White Wolf's lodge and plopped down beside the fire.

Soft footsteps entered behind her. She turned with a start and swallowed hard when she found Swallow Song there, holding the friendship bag.

"I was sincere in my offering of friendship," Swallow Song said softly. "Please accept it."

Dawnmarie sighed heavily, then took the bag. "You must forgive me for behaving so rudely," she murmured. "But I am not myself since my father's death, and my mother's disappearance."

"I understand," Swallow Song said, her gaze shifting slowly to the blankets and furs that still lay across the mats, where the imprints of two bodies were still visible.

She looked quickly over at Dawnmarie again, her eyes filled with wonder.

But she would not ask the obvious. And even though Dawnmarie might have an edge over Swallow Song in gaining White Wolf's love, Swallow Song decided this very moment that she would risk this

new friendship, she would risk *everything*, to have
White Wolf for herself.

She placed an arm around Dawnmarie's waist.
"Come," she murmured. "Let us join the women
again. I shall even give you a needle and buckskin
that you can use to bead something pretty."

Dawnmarie cast her a suspicious glance, then
sighed and went back to the circle of women. She
sat down and gladly took the needle and buckskin
from Swallow Song. It was good to have something
with which to busy her fingers.

As she sewed beads onto the buckskin, her eyes
shifted to White Wolf more oft than not. She wished
the council would pass quickly so that Swallow Song
would leave and join her father at his campsite, away
from White Wolf.

Out of the corner of her eyes she suddenly spotted
someone else. Sharp Nose had just emerged from his
lodge after a long day of sleep. While he stood outside the circle, not daring to enter, she saw his eyes
lock on someone in particular.

She followed his gaze, and her heart leapt when
she realized that he was staring at Swallow Song. It
was obvious that he was most interested in the lovely
Potawatomis woman.

But when she turned to look at Sharp Nose again,
to study his eyes, he was gone.

She wondered if Swallow Song could return Sharp
Nose's love, or was she too intent on marrying a
powerful chief to give him a second thought?

Now deep in thought, she began to sew again but
pricked her finger as her thoughts strayed.

"Be careful, Dawnmarie, or you will get blood on
the garment you are beading," Swallow Song said,
her eyes twinkling devilishly at Dawnmarie.

Dawnmarie's insides tightened. Seeing the mischievous look in Swallow Song's eyes, and hearing the mockery in her voice, Dawnmarie glared at her.

She began to suspect that everything Swallow Song had given her, the gifts, the offer of friendship, had been done with an ulterior motive.

She could see that Swallow Song wanted only one thing, to have White Wolf even though she surely knew of his and Dawnmarie's love.

It was devious of Swallow Song to try to break the special bond between White Wolf and Dawnmarie, Dawnmarie thought bitterly. Although Swallow Song captured the hearts of many men with her false kindness, once her true nature surfaced, she would make a man's life miserable.

Aware of everyone's eyes on her, Dawnmarie forced a smile and returned to her sewing. But her insides quavered with an uneasiness she could not cast aside so easily. She wished that night would come quickly.

Then she would show White Wolf that he need never hunger for another woman.

Chapter Twenty-three

Eternity is here and now, I thought.
—Vita Sackville-West

White Wolf saw Dawnmarie flee to his lodge, Swallow Song following her. He was relieved to see them return to the circle of women, and that everything seemed to be all right between them again.

He returned his attention back to the business at hand. It was *nii-bin,* summer. The days were long, the wind was warm, and there was plenty to eat. It was a time for visiting with friends, holding feasts and dancing.

"And, White Wolf, what do you intend to do about the continued influx of white people on land that belongs to the red man?" Chief Charging Deer asked, resting his long-stemmed pipe on his knee, smoke spiraling from it.

Chief Charging Deer was a short and stocky man dressed in fringed buckskins, with hair that trailed down his back in one long braid. "The arrival of so many white people is overwhelming," he further stated. "Are you going to stay and tolerate the whites? Or are you going to move on to a place where whites are not so pronounced?"

"*Gah-ween-geh-goo,* nothing or no one will run me from this land of lakes and loveliness," White Wolf said without hesitation. "I will stay here forever, and I encourage you to do the same. There is enough land to share with the whites. Also the white people bring progress. My people have enjoyed more prosperity after learning the ways of the white traders."

"I have not been as fortunate," Chief Charging Deer mumbled. "I have been cheated too often. My trust is now as thin as dangerous ice which forms on winter rivers. For this reason, I am considering moving. I have heard of a place called Chicago. Or perhaps I will travel to Indiana."

"Are you leaving anytime soon?" White Wolf asked, resting his hands on his knees. "I will miss our councils."

Chief Charging Deer looked past White Wolf, at his daughter. "It depends on how quickly I can arrange my daughter's future," he said, giving White Wolf a sly gaze.

"*Gee-wee-ee-shee-chee-gay,* arrange?" White Wolf said, forking an eyebrow. "What sort of arrangement?"

"Not so much an arrangement," Chief Charging Deer said, clumsily clearing his throat, "as a marriage."

"Could she not find a mate elsewhere?" White Wolf prodded, curious about this chief's strange attitude toward his daughter who was as beautiful as a spring flower. "You talk as though you wish to give her away in marriage right here."

Chief Charging Deer shifted his weight. He crossed his legs and avoided White Wolf's steady, questioning stare. Instead, he busied himself by filling his pipe with the fresh tobacco that was a gift from White Wolf.

"I will remain in lake country one more winter before I make up my mind whether or not to go to Chicago or Indiana," he then quickly said.

"Life is like a circle sometimes," White Wolf said, wondering why Charging Deer would not answer his questions about his daughter. "Sometimes there is a hole in the circle, causing an imperfect balance between nature and man. One must adjust to the good or the bad. I wish you the best of everything, my friend."

Charging Deer puffed on his freshly filled pipe, then removed it from between his lips and passed it **around** the circle so that everyone could share the smoke of friendship.

"There are many forces and different directions that can help or interfere with the harmony of nature," Charging Deer said thickly. "I have dealt with many forces in my lifetime." He frowned over at White Wolf. "Ah, but if you only knew what I have been forced to endure."

"Do you wish to tell the council so that the burden

will be lifted from your heart?" White Wolf asked, taking the pipe and inhaling deeply from its stem.

"In time, things that have tormented me for so long will be behind me," Chief Charging Deer said throatily. "I see it coming closer, this release." He lowered his eyes. "It would have been easier if my wife had lived long enough to help me through my private woes. As it is, she has been dead now many winters. No woman has become special in my eyes since."

"Your daughter is there still to comfort you, to fill your old age with laughter," White Wolf said. "I would think you would not accept a bride price for her just yet."

Chief Charging Deer's shoulders tightened. He gave White Wolf a narrowed look.

Seeing this, and puzzled even more over this chief's strange behavior over his daughter, White Wolf changed the subject.

They continued to talk about troubles faced by other tribes and how they planned to make things better.

Chapter Twenty-four

Thy shape, thy size, could not deceive me;
Beauty seemed hid in every limb.
                                        —*John Clare*

Dawnmarie was glad when the council and the feasting were over. She waited for White Wolf beside the fire in his wigwam. No one had asked her to go with White Wolf when he accompanied Charging Deer and Swallow Song to their campsite.

She felt left out and nervous.

The time with White Wolf might be all the time that Swallow Song needed to lure him into her arms, she worried. What man would deny her? After all, she was so beautiful.

White Wolf came into the lodge while Dawnmarie was still deep in thought. He knelt down behind her and suddenly swept his arms around her. His hands cupped her breasts through her dress, drawing a surprised gasp from Dawnmarie.

She closed her eyes and sighed, realizing that White Wolf could not lie to her so easily about his love for her. He had hurried back to her. He shoved her dress down, the flesh of his hands warm and wonderful on her breasts as he caressed them, his thumbs circling her nipples, making them become tight with pleasure.

"The day was too *gee-nwah,* long," White Wolf whispered. He took her hands and drew her up before him. As he pushed her dress down the full length of her, he gazed heatedly at her ripe, full breasts, her suppleness.

"The night is here with its mystery, with its secrets," he said huskily.

"How I feel about you is no secret," Dawnmarie said, her voice trembling with building passion. "How I love you, my darling Chippewa chief. I want you. I ache all over with want of you."

He placed his fingers at her waist and drew her close, gasping with pleasure when her breasts ground into the bare flesh of his chest.

He sucked in a breath of building passion as she suddenly placed the palms of her hands on his chest and gently shoved him down in a sitting position on the mats, then swung her legs around him and sat on his lap.

Twining her arms around his neck she drew her lips to his and kissed him with abandon, her lips parting as his tongue probed for entrance.

She melted when his tongue danced against hers, his hands now traveling slowly over her body, stopping when he found her every secret place, caressing, teasing, arousing.

White Wolf felt the curl of heat growing in his lower body. His fingers pressed urgently into her flesh, then with a fierceness he held her close and at the same time rolled her over, away from him, then rose above her.

Her erect, rosy nipples tilted upward, he enfolded them once again within the heat of his fingers. Her hair was disarrayed around her smooth copper shoulders.

Her hips, curving voluptuously from her slender waist, framed the dark triangle of hair, beneath which lay the core of her desire. He nudged her thighs apart and with one thrust was inside her, reveling in the feel of her clasping, moist inner flesh against his throbbing member.

His hands slipped down her body and cupped the rounded flesh of her bottom, lifting her to meet his rhythmic thrusts.

She clung and rocked with him.

Her hips gyrated. She leaned her head back, lips parted, her moans matching his own groans of pleasure.

He kissed her long and deep. He moved slowly and powerfully.

He could feel the pulsing of the blood through his body, which made him feel alive with a raging fire.

Bright threads of excitement wove through Dawnmarie's heart as White Wolf's kisses became even more sensuous than before.

Hot, demanding, he crushed her so hard to him that she gasped.

He felt the urgency building. Their bodies strained together hungrily, fierce and fevered. His hands moved over her soft, creamy flesh. He darted his tongue moistly into her mouth. His lips lowered then and brushed the smooth, glassy skin of her breasts.

And then the slow, deep rumblings began deeply within him, like a volacno ready to erupt. He paused to get his breath.

Leaning a fraction away from her he smiled into her eyes. He reached a hand to her cheek.

She took the hand and placed one of his fingers into her mouth. Smiling seductively at him, she sucked on his finger.

His heart beating like thunderclaps within his chest, White Wolf eased himself from inside her. He moved to his knees and twined his fingers through her hair, and as he questioned with his eyes, her eyes looking wonderingly into his, he led himself to her sweet lips.

"What am I to do?" she asked, puzzled. She looked at his velvet tight hardness, just the very sight of it so near her lips causing her to feel strangely excited.

"Pleasure me," he said huskily. He did not tell her how. He showed her. He closed his eyes and groaned as she learned to do this as quickly as she had learned to find pleasure in his arms.

But when he feared that he might find release too quickly, he gently eased away from Dawnmarie. He swept her into his arms and burned kisses onto her lips and down onto her breasts.

And then he moved down and knelt over her and returned the same sort of pleasure that she had just given him. When she began to writhe and moan too much, he feared that she was too near the edge, also, then rose over her and thrust himself inside her again.

Dawnmarie clung to him, her eyes closed, her teeth clenched, the pleasure was so mind-boggling. When her spasms began, she threw her head back and emitted a guttural sigh, glad to feel him finding his own release, their timing as perfect as their love.

Afterward, they lay beside the fire, needing no words between them, finding everything right enough as they found a soft, quiet peace from just being together.

Chapter Twenty-five

I shall not have him at my feet,
And yet my feet are on the flowers.
            —Alice Meynell

"Father, tell me how I can have the heart of the man I love," Swallow Song said, gazing dreamily into the dark, star-speckled heaven, the campfire warm and soft beside her.

"You mean White Wolf?" Charging Deer asked guardedly.

Swallow Song turned to her father and took his hands in hers. "Yes, Father," she murmured. "Tell me how I can win him? I want him to be my husband."

"That is good," he said thickly. "Now listen well, my daughter, to your father's teachings. This man will be yours for the taking."

Chapter Twenty-six

She pressed me close, and with a sigh,
To melting joy's resigned.
                    —*Robert Dodsley*

The night air was still. Brother moon was only half-way across the sky as Chief Charging Deer talked quietly to his daughter. She sat wide-eyed beside him, listening.

"Swallow Song, the Chippewa warriors seek wives who are good workers," Chief Charging Deer said softly. "To them a woman's worth depends on her ability to work hard."

"Doesn't beauty attract them to a woman?" Swallow Song asked. She pictured Dawnmarie's exquisite loveliness and tried to fight off feelings of jealousy. She wanted to keep her mind clear so that she could pursue White Wolf with all of her energy.

"My daughter, did you not see how White Wolf's eyes lingered on you so often today?" Chief Charging Deer asked, reaching to take her hands. He held them on his lap. "And not only today. Many times at the trading posts his eyes took in your beauty."

"Yes, I have seen this," Swallow Song murmured. "But I have also seen his eyes linger on Dawnmarie. And *she* is the one staying in his lodge." She lowered her eyes, then raised them to her father again. "I do not wish to sound jealous, but White Wolf *is* giving Dawnmarie special attention."

"Only because he pities her," Charging Deer scoffed. "He is a man of heart, of deep feelings. He brought Dawnmarie to his village, and to his lodge, only because he pities her for having lost so much at the hand of Slow Running."

"I thought perhaps her lovely violet eyes may have cast a spell on him," Swallow Song said, sighing heavily.

"Nothing but your loveliness has cast a spell on this Chippewa chief," Charging Deer said, drawing her into his embrace.

He then held her away from him, his fingers gently resting on her shoulders. "But you must do more now than just look beautiful," he said thickly. "You must prove your worth as a wife to him. In time, he will send Dawnmarie away and bring you into his blankets as a wife. A wife is more important than a woman who merely needs pity."

"Then tell me what to do and I shall do it," Swallow Song said, moving to her knees.

"You must go tonight and cut the finest wood in the forest," Charging Deer said. "Then place this wood before White Wolf's lodge while he sleeps. This will show White Wolf your true worth and will bring his heart around to you."

"Is it really as simple as that?" Swallow Song marveled.

"As simple as that," he said, nodding. "*But* it is important that you choose the best trees from which to cut your offering of wood so that your father will be certain to be able to leave the Chippewa village without you."

"Do you wish to leave me so that I can find a husband, or because you wish to get rid of me?" Swallow Song asked, her lower lip drooping into a pout.

Charging Deer hesitated, his eyes turned from her, and then he slowly looked her way again. "I wish for my daughter to have the best of husbands," he said thickly. "Chief White Wolf will be that perfect husband. In order for you to become a perfect wife, I must leave you in his total care."

He placed a hand at the nape of her neck and drew her close to him. "Trust me," he said, warning in his voice.

"I do, Father," Swallow Song said, her insides tightening. "I know what must be done. I must go and select the finest wood. Then I must take a husband White Wolf."

He dropped his hand away, causing her to lurch backward from the suddenness.

"I grow weary of so many things in my life," he then said, heaving a quavering sigh. "Nothing is as I wished it to be. Nothing."

"I am sorry that I am a disappointment to you, Father," Swallow Song said, flinging herself into his arms. When he did not hug her for comfort, she shied away from him, cowering. "I shall not disappoint you much longer, Father. When I have a husband, your duties to me will be over."

He sighed, again, his face weary and drawn.

Overhead the northern lights suddenly flickered, like wind rustling the tent of the sky.

"Look heavenward, Father," Swallow Song said, pointing toward the lights that twinkled magically across the sky.

Charging Deer looked upward. "The great wide

sky has known many mysteries," he said softly. "The sky is filled with strange things unknown to man. So man has drawn his own conclusions. Stars are heavenly spirits which guide lost souls at night."

He pointed elsewhere. "As the Milky Way streams across the northern heavens, it becomes a white path to the unknown land of the spirits, a place of happy and endless hunting."

He gestured toward the moon. "The moon is like a person," he said softly. "The moon at one time was a man who, while on his way to fetch water, was taken up into the air. In a full moon one can always see a man with a pail."

"But what of the northern lights tonight, Father?" Swallow Song asked, still watching the play of lights in the sky. "Surely seeing them tonight is an omen, a good omen which tells me that White Wolf will be mine by tomorrow's dawning."

"You can take it as an omen if you wish, my daughter," Charging Deer said, wishing to have the same hope as she that she soon would be taken as a wife. "But there are more reasons for the northern lights than just to lead a man to my daughter's arms tonight. They are believed to be the torches held in the hands of the spirits, seeking the souls of those who have just died, to lead them over the abyss terminating the edge of the world. A narrow pathway leads across it to the land of brightness and plenty, where disease and pain are no more, and where food of all kinds is already in abundance. To this place none but the dead and the Raven can go. When the spirits wish to communicate they make a whistling noise and the earth people answer only in a whispering tone."

"I do not wish to lose my soul yet to the beautiful

lights," Swallow Song said, hugging herself as a chill swept over her flesh. "I wish to have a husband, perhaps many children."

"Children?" Charging Deer said, a warning suddenly flashing in his eyes. "Look only to have a husband. That will be a blessing enough for you, *and* your father."

Swallow Song lowered her eyes. "Yes, I know that you are right," she murmured, then looked pleadingly up at him again. "But perhaps, somehow, children will be possible?"

He placed a gentle hand to her cheek. "Do not wish for things that might lead to the death of you," he said thickly. "You know that it is best that you never have children."

"But White Wolf will feel deceived should I marry him, then refuse him children," Swallow Song said, her voice drawn and sorrowful.

"First get him to marry you," her father said flatly. "Then concern yourself with how he understands about other things, later."

"Other things?" Swallow Song said warily.

"You know what I mean. Do not make me say it out loud," he said, rising to his feet. "I never wish to speak of that which tears apart my very insides."

Swallow Song scrambled to her feet. She took a hatchet from her father's belongings. "I am sorry, Father, for my inability to be a perfect daughter for you," she said, then walked slowly away from him, her head hung.

He watched her for a moment, his heart aching, then went and fell into step with her. "I shall go with you and help you search for that perfect tree from which to cut the wood offering for White Wolf."

He grabbed her hand and drew her around to face

him. "I do not wish to hurt you," he said softly. "It's just that I cannot help thinking, you could have had so much in life, if not for . . ."

Again he could not find kind words for the physical flaw that plagued her birth.

"I understand, and I wish I could change things," Swallow Song said, tears streaming from her eyes. "Do you think I enjoy being . . . being . . ."

He placed a hand over her lips to keep her from saying anything else. "Say no more," he murmured. "I love you, daughter. No matter what, I love you."

Sobbing, she crept into his arms. She cherished his embrace, which she missed too often now.

"Now, now," he said, stroking her waist-length hair. "Cry no more. Let us go and get you that perfect husband."

She wiped the tears from her cheeks and nodded. "Yes, that perfect husband for a less than perfect wife," she said, then turned and walked away from her father. She hoped that she could capture White Wolf's heart soon, for she was growing weary of being with her father, a father who cared more for himself than helping her accept her shortcomings.

"We will place the *finest* wood on White Wolf's doorstep tonight," Charging Deer said, ignoring his daughter's reference to her being an imperfect woman.

Yes it was true, but not yet to everyone's naked eye. He had to wonder how White Wolf would react that first time he realized he married someone whose very soul seemed filled with demons!

Chapter Twenty-seven

I to cry out on pride
Who have won her favour!
—Tennyson

Still weak, his knees shaking, Slow Running stepped from his lodge and greeted Yellow Tail who had just beached his canoe.

"Have you come with welcome news?" Slow Running asked, clasping a hand on Yellow Tail's shoulder.

"You were right," Yellow Tail said, nodding anxiously. "She is in the Chippewa village, sharing White Wolf's lodge. Perhaps he has already taken her as his wife."

Slow Running's insides filled with rage. He knotted a hand into a tight fist at his left side. "If so, it won't be for long," he snarled. "You must keep an eye on her. Find a time when she is alone, then kidnap her and bring her to me. I will see that she becomes *my* woman, *my* wife."

"What if White Wolf comes after her?" Yellow Tail asked, frowning over at Slow Running.

"If you question my commands one more time, you will *die*," Slow Running hissed out as he leaned his face into Yellow Tail's. "Now go. Do as you are told. Bring her here. *Soon.*"

Yellow Tail nodded anxiously, then turned on a moccasined heel and ran to his canoe. His eyes flared with humiliation and hatred, hoping that this unwise decision of his chief's *would* bring White Wolf to this

camp. Yellow Tail would laugh as he watched Slow
Running's scalp sway from a scalp pole. Slow Running was bad for the Sioux nation. He always put
himself before his people. In time, he had to be
stopped. He *would* be stopped.

For now, though, Yellow Tail played along with
his chief's insane requests.

He shoved the canoe out into the river, then
climbed aboard. He did not hurry though. He would
take his time. He smiled, knowing how impatient
Slow Running became when he had to wait!

Chapter Twenty-eight

Your hands lie open in the long fresh grass—
The finger-points look through,
like rosy blooms.
                              —*Dante Gabriel Rossetti*

Having to relinquish White Wolf again to council
with Chief Charging Deer, Dawnmarie stepped out
of the lodge with him to say good-bye. She gasped
when he took a step outside the lodge and half stumbled over a pile of neatly stacked wood that sat
squarely in the way of their exit.

White Wolf regained his balance and stared down
at the wood for a moment. Then understanding the
meaning of the wood pile, he smiled knowingly and
turned his gaze to Dawnmarie. But before he could
say anything to her about this special sort of gift to
a warrior, she spoke ahead of him.

"Woman Dancing shouldn't have labored over
gathering such an amount of wood," she said, staring
down at it. "She is hardly strong enough."

She gazed toward Woman Dancing's lodge, then up at White Wolf. "Your aunt proves over and over again how much she loves you."

White Wolf was confused to learn that Dawnmarie was not the one who had placed the wood at his door. He knew that Woman Dancing had not done it, for he had not allowed her to gather wood for many moons now. He would always do the chore himself.

He turned and looked from lodge to lodge, wondering who was responsible for this offering of the heart. His heart skipped a beat as he figured it out. It must be the lovely Potawatomis maiden. Quite often he had seen her watching him. He had seen her flirting smile. The wood must be her way of declaring her love for him.

He also wondered if her father was behind any of this.

"White Wolf?" Dawnmarie asked, seeing his strange expression. She followed the path of his eyes, which stopped where the Potawatomis chief and his daughter made camp.

A coldness swept through her to see White Wolf's interest drawn to their camp. Visions of the previous night swept her thoughts. She shivered with ecstasy to recall her sensual moments with White Wolf when he professed his love for her. It did not seem possible that he could love her so dearly at night, then be thinking of another woman the next day.

"Why are you so suddenly quiet? Why are you looking toward Chief Charging Deer's camp?" Dawnmarie demanded.

White Wolf turned toward her. She knew many customs of the Chippewa, but it was obvious that she did not know the meaning of this offering of firewood.

And he would not tell her who he suspected brought it. He could tell Dawnmarie was jealous over Swallow Song's attentiveness toward him. He would not further feed such jealousy.

Placing his hands gently on her shoulders, he drew her close to him. "My thoughts are on the council this morning," he said thickly. "And what are you going to do to busy yourself while I am gone?"

She reveled in his closeness, the manly scent of him. "I shall pretend I am your wife today," she murmured. "I shall clean your lodge and prepare the meals."

She smiled up at him. "And then I shall enjoy my beading."

"Beading?" White Wolf said, questioning her with his eyes.

She paused, hating to mention Swallow Song to White Wolf.

"Swallow Song gave me some beads and a piece of buckskin upon which I have already started a lovely design," she said softly, watching his reaction to Swallow Song's name.

The mention of Swallow Song made White Wolf's insides tighten. If she had brought the offering of wood, that meant her father had expectations that White Wolf could not fulfill. He dreaded today's council.

"Swallow Song is a generous woman," he said, his voice drawn as he glanced down at the wood. He knew it must have taken many hours to gather it.

If he refused the offer, it would possibly sever his ties with the Potawatomis. But if he accepted, it would mean that he would lose the woman of his heart!

Dawnmarie observed White Wolf's uneasiness and not wanting to venture why, she fell to her knees and began gathering the firewood into her arms. "I shall place the wood away from the door of your lodge," she said softly.

Dawnmarie had told Woman Dancing yesterday that she wished to care for White Wolf's needs. Woman Dancing had then supplied her with much food to prepare and it seemed that Woman Dancing had even gathered firewood for Dawnmarie to use for the fire.

Dawnmarie was glad that she had asked Woman Dancing to remain in her lodge and take advantage of a full day of rest, or a full day of pleasurable beading. After a full night of gathering wood, Woman Dancing would need the day to rest from such hard labors.

"*Gee-mah-gi-on-ah-shig-wah,* I shall leave you now," White Wolf said, reaching a hand to Dawnmarie, stopping her chore of restacking the wood. He leaned down into her face, their breaths mingling. "Today you will miss this warrior chief?"

Dawnmarie nodded. She never wanted to lose him. Her eyes devoured his handsome face. "Today will seem forever," she murmured, almost floating into his arms as he took her hands and led her to her feet.

He cupped her chin in his hand and lifted her lips to his as he bent to kiss her.

He scarcely heard the drums that were now beating in the distance to announce that it was time for council to begin.

His insides a raging inferno, White Wolf did not want to leave Dawnmarie. But he knew that he had many important things to discuss with Charging Deer.

"I must go now," he said, relieved that she had not asked to accompany him this morning. He only hoped that Swallow Song would not accompany her father into council.

Yet he feared that she expected some sort of answer from him. Giving the wrong answer might place a wall of noncommunication between him and the Potawatomis chief.

Weak from the kiss and embrace, Dawnmarie looked up at White Wolf with wavering eyes. "Perhaps I should go with you today," she suddenly blurted. "I do not think I can part from you for even one second."

Alarmed, White Wolf took a step back from her. He knew he did not want Dawnmarie to be with him when he discussed Swallow Song with her father, for he knew the wood had not been innocently placed at his door. Swallow Song was the only one who could have done it!

"The day will be long again in council," he quickly blurted. "I do not believe you would enjoy yourself being there."

"I would enjoy being anywhere as long as you were there," Dawnmarie persisted, hoping he did not have a hidden reason for not wanting her to come along.

"I thought you said you were going to cook me something special for our evening meal," he said, trying not to sound desperate. "I would much rather sit there and think of the mysterious dishes that await me than worry about you being bored and uncomfortable in council."

"All right, then," Dawnmarie said, wanting to please him. "I shall prepare my surprise for you."

Seeing that the warriors were starting to gather around the large fire in the center of the village, and knowing that White Wolf's presence was needed, she stepped away from him.

"Go now," she murmured. "I shall be fine."

She watched him walk away with his proud, long-legged stride. She watched him sit down midst his warriors. Her heart sank further when she saw Chief Charging Deer arrive with his daughter.

When Shallow Song sat down beside her father in council, a keen, icy resentment flowed through Dawnmarie's veins. Now she wished that she had not given in so easily to White Wolf's suggestion that she stay away from the council. She had only given the Potawatomis maiden an open invitation to flirt with White Wolf!

Angry and frustrated, Dawnmarie stacked the rest of the wood away from the entranceway, then stormed inside and sat down beside the fire.

Suddenly she did not want to clean White Wolf's lodge, or cook. All she wanted was to go to council and sit at White Wolf's side.

She sat for a moment and glared into the fire, but after a few moments she pushed herself up from the floor and began her chores.

She moved begrudgingly through her work and wondered if White Wolf had purposely kept her away from council because he knew that Swallow Song would be there.

Chapter Twenty-nine

Take all that's mine beneath the moon,
So I with her but half a noon.
                                    —Wordsworth

The sun was just lowering in the sky when the council finished.

White Wolf walked Chief Charging Deer and Swallow Song toward their camp. It was their last night there now that the council was over.

"Did you not find a gift of wood at your door this morning?" Chief Charging Deer asked, giving White Wolf a steady stare as they walked toward the campsite.

White Wolf's heart lurched, as did his stomach, for he had dreaded the mention of firewood.

"*Ay-uh*, yes, I found much wood this morning," he said stiffly, feeling two sets of eyes on him now: Charging Deer's and Swallow Song's.

Swallow Song came around and stood at his other side. He now felt trapped between daughter and father, one on each side of him.

"That gift of wood is from my daughter," Charging Deer said, his eyes never leaving White Wolf. "Do you now wish to offer a bride price for her? If so, she is yours."

White Wolf was stunned by the obvious anxiousness of this Potawatomis chief to rid himself of such a lovely daughter.

Similarly, it was rare for a woman to almost throw herself at the feet of a warrior.

It made the situation very awkward for him. Even though he had never given Swallow Song cause to think that he had singled her out for a *wife*, he knew he had gazed at her with admiration.

She had simply read more into his admiring glances than he had intended.

Yet he must be careful. He wanted to maintain good relations with the Potawatomis.

"This is all happening too quickly," he said, looking from Swallow Song to her father. "I need time to think it over."

"It is normal to need time to adjust to the idea of having a wife," Charging Deer said, nodding. "But do not take much time. Otherwise I will take my daughter from your sight forever if a bride price is not promised by sunrise tomorrow."

"*Wah-bungh*, tomorrow then, Charging Deer," White Wolf said, then walked stiffly away.

How could this chief place such demands on him? It was as though Charging Deer's offer was also a threat.

White Wolf no longer cared if the ties between him and Charging Deer fell apart. He never allowed anyone to give him ultimatums!

Above all, he could not jeopardize his relationship with Dawnmarie.

Tonight he would prove his love to her in the only way he knew how. Tonight he would play the flute beneath the stars for Dawnmarie alone.

He only hoped that she would know the meaning of *this* special Indian custom.

Chapter Thirty

I guessed thy face without thee knowing,
Was beautiful as e'er was seen.
                              —*John Clare*

Warmed by the fire and snuggled between blankets, Dawnmarie smiled in her sleep. She was dreaming, reliving the ecstasy she had found once again in White Wolf's arms. After the second council with Chief Charging Deer, he had come home to her, and they had shared the meal she had prepared especially for him.

Afterward they had made love until they fell away from one another, satiated. They had come away from their lovemaking totally happy and at peace with their love for each other. Any doubts were swept away.

Dawnmarie turned over to her other side. Her dream took her into the magical world of lovemaking with White Wolf, his body hard and firm against hers, his lips demanding, his hands caressing.

But she was drawn suddenly awake by the sound of soft and sweet music wafting from the forest beyond. She moved up an elbow. The soft fire's glow revealed to her that White Wolf was not there.

She leaned her ear toward the sound of music again, now recognizing the instrument that was being played: a flute! She understood the meaning of the flute being played during the midnight hour of night. A Chippewa warrior in love would make a flute of cedar twigs or sumac stalks to play for his woman, to prove his undying love and to offer himself to her for a lifetime.

Again Dawnmarie looked at the empty blankets at her left side. She smiled and gently ran a hand over the impression of White Wolf's body, as though he were still there himself.

But he was gone. A feeling of joyous bliss claimed her very soul for she had no doubt that it was White Wolf who played the flute; who did this to stir her into again knowing his total commitment of love for her.

Deeply moved, Dawnmarie sat up and continued to listen. Feeling warm and wonderful inside, she sighed and held her head back, her eyes closed. Her desire for White Wolf made her giddy and weak all over.

Then remembrances of someone else slipped into her memory.

She lowered her eyes and held her face in her hands. "Mum, oh, where are you, Mum?" she whispered.

Still not knowing the fate of her mother made Dawnmarie's happiness over having such a wonderful man loving her waver somewhat.

If only the warriors could find her mother, everything would be perfect. Dawnmarie would be free to marry White Wolf.

Another person came to Dawnmarie's mind like a cold slap in the face: Swallow Song! What if she heard the flute? What if she thought it was being played for *her*? If she went to White Wolf beneath the moon and stars, looking exquisite, lovely, and seductive, would he be able to cast her aside and say that he was waiting for his true love?

Or would she beguile him into forgetting there was

another woman, one to whom he had professed his love, not only once, but many times?

Although Dawnmarie thought she had fought through jealousy over Swallow Song and won, she now realized that she could never take any chances where she was concerned.

Swallow Song was a determined lady who wanted White Wolf at any price.

Scrambling to her feet, Dawnmarie slipped a snow-white rabbit fur robe over her bare skin. She followed the sound of the flute, her heart singing in time with the sentimental music of the tiny wooden instrument.

She ran from the village into the forest. Stars flickered overhead like miniature lanterns and the moon's soft glow added to the effect of the music's lilting sounds. Brushing aside low-hanging tree limbs that lay in her path, Dawnmarie ran on and on.

Breathless, she finally saw White Wolf only a short distance away. He was sitting on a rock, the moonlight flooding over him, illuminating him as though he were a beacon in the night. He still did not see *her* but continued to play his flute, his eyes closed, his back resting against a rock behind him.

Dawnmarie stopped for a moment to get her breath and to marvel over White Wolf's handsomeness. As always, as if caught in his spell, she gazed in awe at his bronze, finely chiseled face and the expanse of his sleekly muscled chest and shoulders.

The more she watched him the more she was taken by the deep, sensual emotions he aroused within her.

The music stirred her insides into a deliciously sweet warmth.

Barefoot, she tiptoed onward then knelt beside the rock on which White Wolf sat and reached a hand to his bare knee. She laughed softly when he opened his eyes and found her there.

Glad that Dawnmarie had undertsood the bidding of his music, White Wolf gazed down at her. She was like a beautiful vision as she looked up at him, her violet eyes sheened by moonlight.

He slipped his flute into the waistband of his breechcloth and reached a hand to her face, his thumb lightly caressing her flushed cheek.

"You beckoned, my darling?" Dawnmarie murmured. "I came."

"How I do love you," he said huskily, the flawless features of her face vibrant and glowing. "You understood the meaning of why I played the flute. You followed the music of my heart. Don't you know that I would have sat here all night playing this sentimental music in order to soften the heart of the woman I love?"

"My love, you know that my heart is yours," Dawnmarie murmured. "I give my *all* to you."

She stood up before him and with trembling fingers slipped the robe from around her shoulders. As the robe fluttered to the ground, revealing Dawnmarie's full nudity to White Wolf, she heard his quick intake of breath and saw the surprise in his eyes as his gaze burned upon her bare skin.

White Wolf sat there for a moment longer, greedily absorbing the sight of her nudity as he slowly raked his eyes over her. He had seen it all before, but each time was more exciting than the last when he gazed at her slim and sinuous body, her liquid curves and perfect breasts.

Then his gaze swept down to that valley between her thighs, to that central muff of dark hair that beckoned.

Answering the call, he reached a hand out and cupped her there. When he thrust his middle finger into the depths of her tight cave of love, he felt a shimmer roll through her body and heard her gasp with pleasure.

The passion was so wonderful as he thrust his finger over and over again inside her that Dawnmarie's mind reeled with the pleasure.

Then when his free hand covered a breast, his thumb circling the soft pink crest of her nipple, the rapture was so overwhelming her knees almost buckled beneath her.

White Wolf stepped from the rock and swept Dawnmarie into his arms, then lay her down on the soft robe that had fallen at her feet.

Dawnmarie's heart throbbed erratically as she watched him remove his brief breechcloth and then his moccasins.

When he was finally standing nude over her, his readiness for her evident in the length and size of his manhood, she reached her arms out for him.

"Come to me," she whispered. "I need you. I've never needed you as much as now."

He knelt over her with his hard, taut body and parted her legs with a knee. He probed at the center of her desire, then with one shove delved into the rose-red, slippery heat of her body and began his eager thrusts.

The entrance inside Dawnmarie came so quickly, filling her so magnificently, it startled her. Moaning with pleasure, she arched toward him, the flesh of her thighs rippling in sinuous hollows. Their naked flesh seemed to fuse, their bodies sucking, flesh against flesh, in fiery pleasure.

Dawnmarie's lips were hot and sweet as White Wolf's mouth seized them in a torrid kiss. His hands took in the roundness of her breasts, stroking and kneading. His tongue brushed her lips lightly and he kissed her again.

His lean and sinewy buttocks moved, her fingers clasped on them, urging him deeper and faster.

Gripping her shoulders, his mouth brushed her cheeks and ears and lightly kissed her eyelids.

She moaned when his mouth moved over her nipple, his tongue flicking.

Dawnmarie whimpered tiny cries against White Wolf's lips as once again he kissed her. She was lost in a passion's reverie of need, unable to think beyond this wondrous moment with White Wolf. They surely were the only two people in the world . . .

Chapter Thirty-one

"Eternity is here and now," I thought.
—Vita Sackville-West

"My daughter, why are you dressing in your most beautiful doeskin dress with the sparkling beads?" Chief Charging Deer asked as he rose from his bed of blankets beside the outdoor fire.

"I did not mean to awaken you, Father," Swallow Song said. She dotted her cheeks with blood-root, then took a final stroke through her hair with her porcupine quill brush. "I must leave. I was awakened by someone playing a flute. It *has* to be White Wolf."

She fell to her knees beside her father and took his hands in hers and clasped them to her bosom. "Father, don't you see?" she asked, her voice breathless with excitement. "He had time to think about marriage and now he wants to marry me. He played the flute as warriors do to win the heart of their favored woman."

"I do not hear any music," Charging Deer said, moving to a sitting position.

"That is why I cannot waste any more time," Swallow Song said, rising quickly to her feet. "I fear I have already taken too much time as it is making myself look special for the man who beckons me with his flute. I must run now, Father, before he returns to his lodge."

"Swallow Song, wait ..." Charging Deer said, scrambling to his feet.

But his words fell on deaf ears. She was already out of sight, having run into the dark depths of the forest.

Charging Deer eased himself back down on the blankets. He stared into the fire. It must be White Wolf playing the flute for his daughter, since they had discussed Swallow Song only today.

He smiled, hoping that tomorrow he *would* be able to move on up the river in his canoe without the weight of his daughter. She had become a burden he no longer wanted. He only hoped that once she was married, her husband would not return her to him, saying she had oeen misrepresented to him!

He sighed, lit his pipe, settled down in his blankets, and waited to see if she stayed with her lover. One night with White Wolf would make her legally his.

If White Wolf tried to send her back to the Potawatomis camp later, he would risk the wrath of the Potawatomis!

Chapter Thirty-two

The mind, from pleasures less,
Withdraws into happiness.
        —Andrew Marvell

Heading in the direction of where she had heard the flute music, Swallow Song ran breathlessly onward. She wondered why White Wolf had stopped playing. Without the music to follow, it was difficult to find him.

Oh, why had she taken so long to make herself pretty? she despaired to herself. He had probably given up on her.

She smiled as another idea occurred to her. Perhaps she could meet him in the forest as he made his way back to his lodge.

Running blindly through the maze of trees and bushes, she searched and searched, but was disappointed when she found no signs of White Wolf anywhere.

Despair filled her, to think that she had lost this opportunity with him. She started to return to the village when suddenly she heard some sounds up ahead that sounded like soft whimpers.

Forking an eyebrow, she paused to listen better.

Her insides tightened and her heart sank when she recognized not only White Wolf's voice as he professed his undying love for Dawnmarie, but also Dawnmarie's when she returned the sentiment.

Closing her eyes, Swallow Song clenched her hands into tight fists at her sides. She tried to will herself not to go any farther.

She did not want to see White Wolf with that violet-eyed woman! Surely they had met in the forest to make love.

Tears splashed from her eyes when she realized that White Wolf had been playing the flute for Dawnmarie, not her!

She should have realized that White Wolf lodged Dawnmarie in his wigwam because he loved, not pitied her!

Swallow Song turned to run away, but stopped.

She could not help herself. She had to see what they were doing. She had to be certain!

She moved stealthily beneath the trees, then stopped, her eyes wide, her heart aching. What she saw made her senses reel with despair.

White Wolf and Dawnmarie were making maddening love.

As though in a spell, Swallow Song stood there and watched. She had never seen a man nude before, much less making love to a nude woman. The sight was mystical and somewhat beautiful.

Yet she wished this woman was herself!

Turning, she ran back toward the village, tears blinding her. She felt as though her heart were torn to shreds. She had never before felt so heartbroken and disappointed.

Now she felt as though she might never be free

from her father, a father who would never accept her shortcomings!

Wiping tears from her eyes, only to find more there, blinding her, Swallow Song continued to make her way back to the village, then suddenly was stopped as she collided into someone.

Stunned, wondering who else might have followed the lilting sound of a flute, she steadied herself and gazed through her tears up into the dark, piercing eyes of a Sioux warrior.

She knew him well.

It was Yellow Tail, one of Chief Slow Running's warriors.

Swallow Song started to scream but his hand came too quickly over her mouth. She squirmed and kicked and pulled at his arm as he locked it around her waist. She tried to yank his other hand from her mouth. But his strength was more than hers, and she finally went limp in his arms.

Even when Yellow Tail took her to his canoe and threw her into it she dared not scream. He quickly put a knife to her throat.

"Say nothing," Yellow Tail warned.

Knowing the dangers, and almost paralyzed with fear, Swallow Song nodded.

She lay perfectly still as he lay his knife aside long enough to gag her mouth, then tied her wrists and ankles.

Wild-eyed, she watched the land slip away as she moved farther and farther away from her father and the man who had betrayed her.

More helpless tears spilled from her eyes as she gazed with wonder at the strong, bare back of the Sioux who rhythmically drew his paddle through the water.

Why would he abduct her when he surely had any number of women at his disposal at the Sioux camp? she wondered. Was it because he had eyed her from afar and had hungered for her?

Was this at least a man who might end her father's misery by taking her from him?

Not wanting to be with anyone but White Wolf, Swallow Song closed her eyes and silently cursed her father. Then she cursed Dawnmarie and White Wolf, and finally her very miserable existence.

Chapter Thirty-three

Farewell to one now silenced quiet,
Sent out of hearing, out of sight.
                    —Alice Meynell

"Yellow Tail, you have seen Dawnmarie many times at the trading post, yet you brought the wrong woman to me?" Slow Running shouted as he glared from Swallow Song to Yellow Tail.

Star Flower smiled wickedly from the dark shadows of the tepee. She knew Yellow Tail better than her brother and knew that he had brought the wrong woman on purpose as a way of getting revenge for Slow Running's frequent berations.

Star Flower was glad that her brother would have to wait even longer for Dawnmarie. Perhaps, given enough time, he would forget his crazed desire for her and look elsewhere for a woman to warm his body at night.

"*Hecitu yelo,* that is true," Yellow Tail said, clasping his hands together behind him. "But it was dark, my chief."

Yellow Tail looked over at Swallow Song who stared back at him, her eyes wide and frightened over the gag in her mouth.

His gaze moved over her slowly. She was beautiful. Even though he had purposely brought the wrong woman, he knew Swallow Song was someone any man might want to take as his woman.

If Yellow Tail did not have a family of his own, he might even take the Potawatomis woman into his lodge tonight. He felt a sexual awakening, which he had not felt in years since he had long since tired of his wife.

"Is that your excuse?" Slow Running said, his weak legs trembling as he pushed himself up from his bed of blankets. "That it was too dark to see who you took as *winu*, captive?"

Slow Running moved shakily to the entrance flap, threw it aside, and looked heavenward.

He then went back and glared into Yellow Tail's eyes. "The moon is as bright as can be and you still say that you did not recognize this woman?" he grumbled, a hand fisted at his left side.

"Yes," Yellow Tail said, his voice tight and measured.

"Take her away!" Slow Running cried, flinging a hand into the air. "She is of no use to me."

"Should I take her back to White Wolf's village?" Yellow Tail asked, knowing that he was wrong to be enjoying his chief's frustrations.

"No!" Slow Running shouted. "Take her deep into the forest. Lose her there. Let her find her own way back to the Chippewa village. Best the wolves find her first, though. I need no trouble from her father, *or* White Wolf. At least not until I am stronger."

Slow Running went to Swallow Song and jerked

the gag down from her mouth. "Your father had council with Chief White Wolf," he said, glowering at her. "Tell me why."

Fear gripping her heart, Swallow Song scarcely breathed out her answer. "They have council often," she whispered. "They are friends."

"Why were you in the forest away from your father's campsite?" Slow Running demanded. "Yellow Tail says you were running through the forest when he found you. Why weren't you at your father's camp so late at night?"

Swallow Song lowered her eyes. "I cannot say," she murmured. "It is something I do not wish to talk about."

She looked up pleadingly at Slow Running. "Please do not turn me out into the night like an animal. Yellow Tail took me by mistake. Please allow him to return me safely to my father's camp."

Slow Running saw the fear etched across her face, but he felt nothing but loathing.

"Take her away, Yellow Tail," he said, his voice even and void of feeling.

"And what about Dawnmarie?" Yellow Tail said, slipping Swallow Song's gag back in place.

"It is too late for you to abduct her tonight," Slow Running said, sighing heavily. "Soon the heavens will be filled with sunrise. It will be a new day."

He glared up at Yellow Tail. "Take her away," he flatly ordered. "*Now*. We will discuss Dawnmarie another time."

Yellow Tail nodded, roughly grabbed Swallow Song by the arm, and yanked her outside the tepee. She sobbed and moved clumsily beside him, fearing the next hours and what might happen to her. Although daylight would soon enter this beautiful land of lakes, there was still enough darkness now to make wandering alone dangerous.

Yellow Tail held her arm tightly as he forced her to follow alongside him into the darker depths of the forest where the moon was all but hidden to the naked eye.

She silently prayed to her Great Spirit that this warrior would set her free from her bonds before releasing her into the wilds. If he left her there, without the use of her hands, she would eventually become food for the forest animals.

This stark fear made her feel as though she might retch. Her stomach churned and she could taste a bitterness in her mouth. She swallowed and swallowed to keep herself from vomiting.

And then suddenly Yellow Tail stopped and jerked her around to face him. She eyed him anxiously as he first removed her gag, then took a knife and cut the bonds at her wrists.

She emitted a low sob of relief when she felt the ropes fall away, totally releasing her to freedom.

Yellow Tail gave her a shove. "Go," he said thickly.

Swallow Song rubbed her raw wrists as she backed slowly away from him. Then she turned and ran as hard as she could. She wanted to get much space between herself and this warrior whose eyes told her that he desired her. He could rape her and no one would be there to stop him.

She did not want to lose her virginity to a stranger, to a man who saw her as a nobody. She had so often dreamed of White Wolf teaching her the mysteries of lovemaking.

Now that could never be. He had already chosen another woman.

Sobbing hard, tears blinding her, Swallow Song's knees weakened and buckled beneath her. She fell to the ground on her knees and held her face in her hands. She had lost everything. Even her abduction had not been as traumatic as seeing White Wolf make love to Dawnmarie.

Why hadn't she been more brazen while flirting with him those long weeks and months that she had first seen him? She could have made him love her. And now he was lost to her forever.

Another fear grabbed her. "Father," she whispered to herself, gulping hard, her eyes wild. "What will he say when he discovers that White Wolf is not going to offer his bride price for me after all? Father depended on White Wolf to release him of the burden of me. What now? How will my father react when he discovers that he will have to return to our village with me?"

She broke into tears again. Perhaps it would have been best if the Sioux chief had taken her instead of Dawnmarie. At least she would not have to return to her father.

"What is wrong with my appearance?" she cried to the heavens. "Am I so ugly to look at that two chiefs turn away from me in disgust?"

Shakily, feeling drained of emotion, she moved to her feet and began to half stagger forward. She was not sure which way to go in the forest. She was disoriented. Everything looked the same. If she could only find the river she could find her way back to the Chippewa village!

She made a sharp right turn and stumbled over broken tree limbs that lay in her path, crying out in pain when sharp briars pierced her tender flesh.

Finally, when the trees thinned and the foliage lessened overhead, she stared at the sky. She recalled her father saying that stars were heavenly spirits and guides to lost souls at night. She sought out the stars that would lead her back to the Chippewa village.

While searching the heavens for something recognizable, she paid no heed to what lay in her path. Suddenly she screamed with pain and fell to the ground. She grabbed for her ankle in severe pain.

Through her tears she saw the cause of her agony. She was caught in a trap used for wolves!

She stared at it. She was familiar with such traps since her father used to set them. A hooked stick was fastened to a tree with the hooked end five feet from the ground.

Now her ankle was caught on this hook just like a fish!

Writhing on the ground, she screamed and screamed. But no matter how much she wanted to remove the hook, she knew not to try. It was too deep into her flesh. Even touching the hook sent spirals of scorching pain through her body.

She clung to her leg above the wound, and finally, blessedly, passed out from the intensity of the pain.

The shine of the river was only a few feet away from where she had fallen.

Chapter Thirty-four

The mind, that ocean where each kind
Does straight its own resemblances find.
    —Andrew Marvell

Chief Charging Deer placed another log on his campfire and peered into the inky dark depths of the forest. He wondered what was going on. Had his daughter found White Wolf? Had he agreed to take her as his wife?

Charging Deer hoped White Wolf would be the answer to all his problems.

Just as he was thinking this, he saw a man and woman come out of the forest. They were arm in arm, walking so close together that it was like they were one person, instead of two.

The moon had slipped behind a cloud, so that Charging Deer could not see exactly who it was. But one thing was certain; this man and woman were greatly in love.

He took a step forward and smiled smugly when he finally recognized White Wolf's stance and noble presence.

But the woman at his right side, hidden by White Wolf's embrace, was not as easily identifiable.

"It *must* be Swallow Song," he concluded. He sighed deeply. "My daughter is with White Wolf, otherwise she would have returned to our camp. She must be with the man she loves."

Thinking that all was well, Charging Deer stretched out midst his blankets beside the fire and went to sleep.

Chapter Thirty-five

Who shall drive a mournful face
From the sad winds about my door?
                    —Alice Meynell

The rising sun mutely spread its color of orange through a heavy layer of fog over the river. Chief Charging Deer awakened and smiled when he saw that his daughter was still gone. This had to mean that White Wolf *had* taken her into his lodge as his wife.

Too anxious to eat his morning meal, or go to the river for his usual morning swim, the Potawatomis chief slipped a warm robe around his shoulders. He thrust his chest out proudly as he entered the Chippewa village.

He smiled courteously to those who were coming from their wigwams to grab armloads of wood for their fire pits. He patted a young brave's head as the brave ran up to him and smiled.

Charging Deer's daughter was now a part of this Chippewa village, of the Chippewa tribe. This made Charging Deer smile smugly.

His daughter's future was set in stone, unless ...

He would not let doubts ruin this special moment. Although his daughter had some serious problems that no one in the Chippewa village was aware of, surely White Wolf would not cast her aside. Her sweetness would touch any man's heart, especially White Wolf's. His reputation was that of a gentle and caring man. He would always go out of his way to be kind; and he was generous, almost to a *fault*. So then he would be kind and sympathetic to Swallow Song.

Charging Deer would not ask for any special celebration to mark the marriage of his daughter to the Chippewa chief. He would bless their union, then return to his village. After his daughter was born with her medical problems he vowed that he would never have another child for fear they might prove equally burdensome.

Stepping up to White Wolf's wigwam, Charging Deer leaned his ear close to the entrance flap. He smiled again. He could hear the voices of a man and a woman. They were talking so softly, he could not recognize his daughter's voice, but he knew for certain that she was there. He had seen White Wolf leave the forest with a woman at his side only moments after his daughter had gone to follow the magnetic music of his flute.

Charging Deer decided he could wait no longer to congratulate this Chippewa chief for having taken his daughter into his lodge.

"White Wolf?" he said, taking a step back from the entranceway so that White Wolf would not think that he had been eavesdropping. "May I speak with you for a moment? May I offer you my congratulations?"

White Wolf and Dawnmarie exchanged quick glances.

"What does he wish to congratulate me for?" White Wolf said, rising to slip on his breechcloth. "What have I done to deserve congratulations?"

"Did you come to terms yesterday over anything in particular in council?" Dawnmarie asked, drawing a blanket over her nudity.

"Far from it," White Wolf said, smoothing his long, lean fingers through his thick hair, to rid it of its tangles.

But he could not tell her exactly where the problem *lay* with Chief Charging Deer . . . that today he would have to tell this Potawatomis chief that he would not offer a bride price for his daughter.

White Wolf expected Charging Deer to come early in the morning demanding an answer from him. But to offer congratulations?

"What happened between you and Charging Deer yesterday?" Dawnmarie persisted, seeing how uneasy Charging Deer's presence made White Wolf.

White Wolf leaned down onto one knee before her and placed a hand to the nape of her neck. He drew her lips to his. "It is best that you do not concern yourself with things between two chiefs," he said thickly. He brushed a kiss across her lips, then rose to his full height. "I shall go now and find out the reason for Charging Deer's early visit and congratulations."

Dawnmarie watched him leave, then stretched out midst the blankets, yawning. She was bone-tired from the full night of lovemaking. She had learned more and more last night about things that pleased White Wolf. He had shown her ways to bring about more enduring pleasure. Even now her flesh tingled with aliveness.

"I could never have enough of you, my wonderful Chippewa chief," she murmured.

But now she wondered what was transpiring between White Wolf and Charging Deer.

Too tired to go to the entrance flap and listen, she curled up on her side and closed her eyes, smiling.

"Why do you offer congratulations to me this

morning?" White Wolf asked. He studied Charging Deer's expression, wondering what had happened to make him so unusually happy today. He even seemed *smug.*

"You pretend not to know?" Charging Deer asked clutching the robe more closely around him.

"*Gee-kan-dan,* know? Know what?" White Wolf said, arching an eyebrow.

"Shall I call to my daughter and ask her to confirm what has happened between you?" Charging Deer said, his lips quavering into a slow smile. "If so, step aside, White Wolf. Let me lift the entrance flap. Let me tell my daughter to step outside beside you. Let me see you together. That will be enough for me to know that I can return today to my village a happy father."

"Your ... *gee-dah-niss,* daughter ... ?" White Wolf asked, his voice drawn and wary.

"She is here," Charging Deer said, wondering what sort of game White Wolf was playing. "Step aside. I must speak to my daughter at once."

White Wolf's puzzlement was building. How could the chief think that his daughter was here? Why would he? And if he thought that Swallow Song was here, and she wasn't, where *was* she?

A slow panic rose within White Wolf. He half stumbled out of the way when Charging Deer gave him a shove and hurriedly pushed the entrance flap aside so that he could see inside the lodge.

Dawnmarie had heard the voices getting louder. She started to leave the blankets to see why, then drew one quickly up to her chin again when Charging Deer swung open the entrance flap and stared down at her, his face quickly paling of color.

"My daughter," he said after a short, stunned pause. "You ... are ... not my daughter."

He stared at Dawnmarie a moment longer, then dropped the entrance flap back into place and turned with glaring, angry eyes at White Wolf.

"Are you playing tricks on me and my daughter?" he shouted. "You played your flute of love for her last night. She came to you. I saw you take her from the forest. Where is she now? Why is she not in your lodge?"

"I never saw Swallow Song last night after I left your camp," White Wolf said blandly. "And I did not play my flute for *her*. It was for Dawnmarie. She was who you saw leave the forest with me. It was Dawnmarie who warmed my blankets last night. Not Swallow Song."

"You have betrayed our friendship!" Charging Deer shouted, drawing everyone from their lodges to stare.

Fully clothed, Dawnmarie stepped outside the lodge, just in time to see Charging Deer stamp away.

"What's wrong?" she asked, but was ignored as White Wolf went after Charging Deer.

"There is no betrayal here," White Wolf said, stepping in front of Charging Deer, stopping him. "There were no promises made to you about your daughter. My decision was reached between women. I chose Dawnmarie. She will soon be my *gee-wee-oo,* wife."

"You chose a half-breed over my daughter?" Charging Deer ranted. "You, a powerful leader, chose someone with white blood running through her veins for your wife? You will regret this, White Wolf."

"This is not the time for threats," White Wolf said,

glancing down at Dawnmarie as she rushed to his side. He looked at Charging Deer again. "Your daughter is not with me, so right now we should be concerned over where she is, and with whom. Save your anger at me for later."

Charging Deer's eyes wavered. He turned and stared at the river, then turned slowly toward White Wolf. "Where do you think she is?" he asked, his voice drawn. "Why didn't she return to me when she realized the flute's music was meant for another woman?"

Dawnmarie paled. She wondered if Swallow Song had seen her and White Wolf together in the forest? Had she fled from anger? From heartbreak? Had she fled, filled with humiliation?

White Wolf seemed to read Dawnmarie's thoughts. While he was in the arms of his woman, could Swallow Song have seen?

He looked at Charging Deer again. "We must send out a search party for your daughter," he said thickly. "I will send many warriors out in canoes. I will see to it that some go by foot into the forest too. We will find your daughter."

Charging Deer's jaw was tight. He refused to speak, but went back to his camp to sit beside the campfire.

Dawnmarie and White Wolf stared at him a moment longer, puzzled by his silence. First he was wrought with emotion over the disappearance of his daughter. Now he seemed almost uncaring.

"I know not how to understand that man," White Wolf said. But, as promised, he began his task of going from lodge to lodge, handing out orders to his warriors.

Dawnmarie boarded White Wolf's canoe with him.

She sat stiffly on the seat behind him as they wound their way down the long river, the veil of fog impeding their search as they tried to watch the shore for any signs of Swallow Song.

Sharp Nose ran desperately through the forest, his eyes ever searching for Swallow Song. There were no prints to help guide him. She was so tiny she would not leave prints beneath the umbrella of trees. If he was to find her, it would be by pure chance.

Now he regretted having not told Swallow Song of his feelings for her. But his pride had stood in the way. Seeing her constantly awestruck over White Wolf, he was afraid to approach her.

Now, however, he cursed his pride! He may never have the chance to tell Swallow Song that he could love her far better than any other man ... even White Wolf!

As the sun finally burned the fog away, Dawnmarie was able to see the shore much more clearly. She watched and hoped that she would see Swallow Song. If anything was to happen to her, war might break out between the Chippewa and Potawatomis. Charging Deer was angry enough before he realized that his daughter was missing. Now he might have further reason to get revenge on White Wolf.

Sharp Nose ran endlessly through the forest, his eyes moving steadily from side to side. On the left side of him he saw the shine of the river and then, to his surprise, he saw White Wolf's canoe come into sight around a bend in the river.

His heart lurched when he then saw Swallow Song lying on the ground either unconscious or asleep.

When he drew closer he felt his insides recoil. Swallow Song's ankle was caught in a wolf trap, and blood dripped steadily from the wound. She was pale white from the loss of blood, and definitely unconscious.

Sharp Nose ran to the river and shouted White Wolf's name, glad that his voice echoed down the river far enough for White Wolf to hear. White Wolf, hearing his voice, came toward him.

Sharp Nose bent to his knees beside Swallow Song. Gently, very carefully, he removed the hook trap from her ankle. Even though unconscious, she groaned from pain.

Sharp Nose lifted her into his arms and held her to his chest as he waited for White Wolf's arrival. He gazed down at Swallow Song, amazed by her beauty. Her lips were perfectly shaped, as was her tiny nose, and the contours of her face were gentle.

He had noticed how lovely she was before, but now, as she lay limply in his arms, close to his heart, he saw just how exquisite she truly was.

Now that White Wolf had taken Dawnmarie into his lodge to be his wife, Swallow Song must choose someone else. He hoped it would be him.

White Wolf beached his canoe and ran to Sharp Nose. He gasped as he reached a gentle hand to Swallow Song's pale face. "No," he said, his gaze taking in the wound at her ankle. "How could this have happened?"

He truly realized how. She must have seen him and Dawnmarie making love and fled blindly through the forest.

Looking at her, he could not help but feel responsible somehow for her situation.

He took Swallow Song from Sharp Nose's arms and carried her to his canoe.

Stunned not only by seeing Swallow Song in such a condition, but also seeing White Wolf's attentiveness to her, Dawnmarie followed White Wolf to the canoe. She climbed inside as Sharp Nose joined them, his eyes never leaving Swallow Song.

"You take us back to our village," White Wolf said, gazing up at Sharp Nose. "I will sit here with Swallow Song."

Sharp Nose gazed at White Wolf at length, yet did not question his sudden attentiveness to Swallow Song. He knew it was crucial they get Swallow Song back to their village to have her wound tended to, so he did not let jealousy stand in the way of her welfare.

He sat down and drew the paddle rhythmically through the water and headed for home.

Dawnmarie was torn about how to feel about White Wolf so gently cradling Swallow Song's head on his lap. Surely he felt responsible for her misfortune. But would White Wolf's guilt cause him to turn his back on the woman he professed to love?

Then Dawnmarie's own guilt set in. She felt selfish for thinking of herself when Swallow Song's life was in danger.

Yet how could she not fear losing the only man she ever loved, the only hope in her life that was so recently wrought with tragedy!

When they reached the village Swallow Song was taken to the council house, a haven for those who did not have a proper shelter in the Chippewa village.

Charging Deer was summoned.

Knowing various skills of medicating different sorts of wounds, Woman Dancing came and cleansed Swallow Song's ankle and applied a herbal poultice.

Then as everyone stood by, wondering and watching, a shaman came to perform a ceremony over Swallow Song's limp, pale body.

Wearing just a loincloth and a leather thong around his head, the shaman entered. His face was covered with bright paint. He placed tobacco on a rock just inside the entrance as an offering to the Great Spirit and told White Wolf and Swallow Song's father that he would cure Swallow Song through his power and the use of milkweed.

He held his medicine bag high, pointed it at her, and dropped a shell. He then began his chant, imploring the spirits to come in.

There was scarcely a sound as all eyes watched, and inner souls prayed to their own different Great Spirits for their own reasons.

Chapter Thirty six

I kiss'd her slender hand,
She took the kiss sedately.
—Tennyson

Everything was quiet in the council house when Swallow Song stirred slightly and awakened slowly.

White Wolf stroked Swallow Song's brow as the shaman made a quiet exit from the lodge. "It is good that you are awake," he said softly, glancing down at her ankle, which was wrapped in soft buckskin.

He looked into her eyes again. "The pain in your ankle will soon go away," he said thickly. "Our people's shaman, Mysterious Voice, has worked his magic on you."

Memories of the past events began to flood Swallow Song's mind. She closed her eyes and cringed as she remembered seeing Dawnmarie and White Wolf making love, of then running blindly through the forest, not caring what might become of her.

Next she remembered the Sioux's abduction and finally escaping only to fall to the ground in body-wracking pain, the wolf trap spearing her as though she were nothing more than a fish!

"The pain is still so bad you cannot speak?" White Wolf asked as Swallow Song turned her eyes away from him, tears splashing from them.

Sharp Nose edged closer. He wished he could soothingly talk her out of her pain, out of her obvious distress. He glanced over at Dawnmarie and could see the worry in her eyes. He knew she was worried that White Wolf's concern for Swallow Song might turn into something else.

Swallow Song sucked in a quavering breath of courage, then turned vicious eyes up at White Wolf. "Get away," she hissed. "Leave me be. I do not need you at my side."

She searched the faces of those who were there, for her father. When she did not see him, all hope left her. He was not there, and obviously cared nothing for her welfare. He too had betrayed her, and she did not know if she could ever forgive him.

White Wolf was not surprised by her attitude toward him. He knew he had caused her to flee into the forest where she had gotten lodged in a trap.

He was glad about one thing. At least the trap that had held her captive until Sharp Nose had found her was not Chippewa. The Chippewa did not believe in capturing innocent animals in such a way. Slow Running used such traps though.

White Wolf moved to his feet and stood back with Dawnmarie allowing Sharp Nose to kneel down beside Swallow Song.

"Will you allow me to sit with you?" Sharp Nose asked thickly, risking his pride by taking her hand. If she jerked it away, it would be hard for him to hide his rejection.

Swallow Song blinked her eyes up at him. She vaguely remembered something that had happened while she was supposedly unconscious. She recalled warm, strong arms lifting her from the ground after she had been released from the trap.

Sharp Nose had not noticed, but she had awakened long enough to see him in the moonlight as he had carried her toward the canoe that brought her back to the Chippewa village. He was her hero.

Not only had he found her, but he had rescued her from the trap!

"Listen well, Swallow Song," Sharp Nose said. "I shall sit by your side until you are well again. I shall feed you and bathe your brow with soft, cool cloths." He paused, then said, "That is, if you will allow me to do these things for you in your father's absence."

"My father," Swallow Song suddenly blurted. "Where . . . is . . . my father?"

"He has found a hillside on which to pray," Sharp Nose said softly. "He begs the Great Spirit for your recovery."

Relieved, and quickly forgiving her father, Swallow Song wept freely.

Dawnmarie could not help herself. Her heart went out to Swallow Song. Just watching her and thinking about what she must have gone through while lying injured in the forest made Dawnmarie want to reach out and help her in any way she could.

Dawnmarie decided she would not allow jealousy to interfere with these new feelings that she had about Swallow Song. She would even find a way to make things up to her, since she felt partly responsible for Swallow Song lying there pale and in pain.

Dawnmarie watched Sharp Nose with a curious interest. His feelings for Swallow Song were obvious, and it also seemed that Swallow Song echoed similar feelings for him. As he drew her into his powerful arms and held her while she cried, she twined her arms around his neck and clung to him.

Swallow Song suddenly pulled herself free of Sharp Nose's embrace. "The Sioux," she cried, staring up at Sharp Nose with wide, frightened eyes. "I was abducted by the Sioux."

"Sioux?" White Wolf said, his voice drawn. He knelt down beside Sharp Nose, his eyes imploring Swallow Song. "When? How?"

"I was running through the forest after . . . after . . ." Swallow Song said. "After I saw something that pained my heart deeply. A Sioux warrior was there. Yellow Tail. He . . . he . . . abducted me."

"Why would Yellow Tail do this?" White Wolf prodded. He had never had much of a problem with this Sioux who seemed to follow his chief's commands none too eagerly.

"Slow Running commanded him to," Swallow Song said, pausing before saying Dawnmarie's name. She looked up at Dawnmarie. Strange how looking at her now did not cause her insides to crawl with a festering hate. She knew Dawnmarie, like herself, had fallen victim to White Wolf's handsomeness.

"Slow Running commanded Yellow Tail to abduct you?" White Wolf prodded further.

Swallow Song looked over at him. "No," she said,

her voice breaking. "Yellow Tail mistakenly took me
for *Dawnmarie*. It was Dawnmarie who he wanted
to abduct, not me."

A chill of fear swam through Dawnmarie. If Slow
Running would go this far to have her as his wife,
there was no telling what he was capable of doing.
She listened and watched for White Wolf's reaction,
knowing that he was surely aware of the grave threat
to both their futures.

"Slow Running sent me away when he saw that
Yellow Tail had abducted the wrong woman. He
wanted me to die. He probably even purposely set
the trap in which my ankle became caught."

She stifled a sob behind her hand, then gasped out.
"I know that all Sioux are not evil," she said. "But
Slow Running is. He is an evil, dangerous man."

"But you are safe now," Sharp Nose said, wrap-
ping his arms around her. He cradled her against his
powerful chest. "I will never allow anything or anyone to harm you again."

Swallow Song snuggled against him, feeling more
protected than she had in her entire life. And she
felt suddenly *loved*.

She gazed up at Sharp Nose in wonder. Why
hadn't she seen the goodness in Sharp Nose earlier?
He was a man of genuine gentleness, the sort of man
she needed who could look past her shortcomings.

Charging Deer came into the lodge. He stood behind everyone and stared at his daughter. The Great
Spirit had listened. His daughter was conscious!

Not only was she conscious, it seemed that she had
found a man to love her. It was obvious how Sharp
Nose felt about her by the way he held her and
talked softly to her. It was obvious, also, that his

daughter was as taken by this man as she had been by White Wolf.

He smiled and sighed. Although it had happened in a roundabout way, his purpose for coming to this village was finally being realized. Perhaps now he could leave without his daughter. He only worried over whether Sharp Nose would continue to love his daughter once he became aware of her inner demons.

He moved past everyone and knelt down beside Swallow Song. "Daughter?" he said, reaching a hand out for her. "Your father is here at your side now. My prayers have been answered. You are awake. You are going to be all right."

Swallow Song turned slow eyes to her father. She gazed at him at length, then broke free from Sharp Nose's comforting embrace and into her father's. Charging Deer held her and ran his fingers through her waist-length hair.

White Wolf went to Dawnmarie. He held her gently. "You know what we must do now, don't you?" he grumbled.

"What?" she asked, searching his eyes for answers.

"It was you Slow Running sent for," he said, his voice drawn. "He is not going to give you up to me without a *fight*." He glared, his eyes glowing with fire. "Well, he will get a fight. I will gather together my warriors and make sure his threats become nothing more than dust in the wind!"

Sharp Nose came to White Wolf's side. "What are we to do about Slow Running?" he asked, having not heard White Wolf voice his decision to Dawnmarie.

White Wolf glanced down at Swallow Song. Her best cure would be if Sharp Nose kept Swallow

Song's heart from straying back in White Wolf's direction.

He turned his eyes to Sharp Nose again. "I will take many warriors to fight Slow Running," he said. "But you must stay and help Swallow Song recover. The bond that has formed between you is very unique."

"I understand," Sharp Nose said, glad to stay, but sorry to be left out of the fight. He also wanted to settle a score with the snakelike Sioux.

But he said, "I will take care of the Potawatomis maiden. But I must first wash my body in ashes with my brethren to prepare myself for warring against Slow Running. I cannot stay behind like a woman while the rest of my brothers fight like *men.*"

"Then, my friend, you shall fight," White Wolf said, placing a hand to Sharp Nose's shoulder. "It was selfish of me to ask you, my most valorous warrior, to stay behind." He gave Swallow Song's father a studious look. "I believe your woman will be all right until you return. For now I think father and daughter should spend some time together."

Sharp Nose stared down at Swallow Song and nodded.

Dawnmarie went with White Wolf from lodge to lodge as he gave the warring command. She helped White Wolf wash his body in cold ashes from the fire pit. But just as he started to draw war paint on his face, a commotion outside drew him from his lodge.

Dawnmarie went with him, her heart pounding with renewed hope of finally knowing something about her mother. The warriors who came from the beach were returning from their long excursion down the river.

She strained her neck, thinking she might see her mother at any moment.

But as the last of the warriors came into sight without her mother, Dawnmarie was filled with renewed despair. She realized that she might never see her mother again. They had searched so long without finding her.

But then she saw someone else coming up from the beach, a straggler, a *white* man. Dawnmarie watched him with bated breath as he came and stood before White Wolf.

"I am Peter Storm," the man said, extending a hand of friendship to White Wolf. He shook White Wolf's hand earnestly, his eyes traveling over to Dawnmarie, then back up at White Wolf whose tall height dwarfed his shorter one. "I'm a trader. I own a trading post many miles upriver. I'm new in these parts. It was just me and my wife, until ..." Again he focused his attention on Dawnmarie. "Until I found this young woman's mother in the forest."

Dawnmarie sucked in a wild breath of relief. "My mother?" she asked excitedly. "Where is she? Why didn't you find me sooner?"

"Your mother was dangerously ill for a while after I took her into our home," Peter said blandly. "She was out of her head with fever. She rambled rather than talked lucidly. I had no idea where she came from." He nodded over his shoulder at the warriors. "Then these warriors found me."

"Is she all right now?" Dawnmarie asked, grabbing the man's arm. "Tell me, is my mother all right?"

"She is fine," Peter said, patting Dawnmarie's

hand. "Weak, but fine. But she is too weak to travel just yet."

Dawnmarie turned anxious eyes up at White Wolf. "Please forget your warring today, White Wolf," she pleaded. "Please take me to my mother. I have waited so long to hear that she is all right. I don't want to have to wait longer to *see* her."

"Warring?" Peter said, his voice wary. He could see from the ash spread along White Wolf's body that the warriors were preparing to go to war with another faction of Indians. "I wasn't aware of warring in these parts," he said.

"We war only when necessary, in order to protect hunting grounds, the innocent, and ..." He gave Dawnmarie a quick glance, then looked at the trader again. "And *wives*."

He then turned to his warriors. "Those who were going with me into warring come with me now elsewhere," he shouted. He looked over at Sharp Nose. "If you wish to stay with the woman, stay."

Sharp Nose nodded.

White Wolf and his warriors went to the river and bathed the ash from their bodies, then boarded their canoes.

Dawnmarie sat in White Wolf's canoe, her heart pounding, her eyes heavenward with a soft thanks to her Great Spirit that her mother was still alive!

Star Flower sat beside Slow Running, tucking blankets and pelts around him as he shivered violently. "My brother, you are ill again," she said. "You have had a relapse. Now you are forced to focus on other things besides half-breed women!"

"She will be mine," he said between clenched teeth. "I cannot stay ill forever!"

Chapter Thirty-seven

Upon my heart thy sweetness lightened;
Life, love, that moment all were thine.
                                        —John Clare

Light as the wind, nimble as fish, the canoes swept up the river, a stiff breeze sending them surging through the light chop of water in the brilliant sunshine. Dawnmarie clung to the sides of the canoe, so eager to see her mother that she could hardly stand the waiting.

She busied her mind with other things. She focused her attention on White Wolf and how masterfully he drew his paddle through the water, his muscles cording with each movement.

Fluttering in the wind, his black hair hung long and loose down his perfect line of back. His skin was a smooth, copper sheen beneath the rays of the sun.

When he looked occasionally sideways, to watch the shore, she got the opportunity to see his handsome profile, one that drew her breath away and sent her heart into a hard thumping.

Averting her attention from him, since just looking at him made her insides feel mushy, she admired the canoe. The bark canoe of the Chippewa was the most beautiful and lightest model of all the water crafts. It was made with the rind of a birch tree and sewed together with roots of tamarack, which they called *wat-tap*. It rode above the water as tight as a cork, gracefully leaning and dodging about under the skillful hand of the Chippewa warriors.

A French-Canadian voyager's canoe went past, straining under a load of beaver pelts. Dawnmarie watched this canoe until it made a turn in the water and headed toward land, then her eyes fell on a cabin that sat high on a hill a short distance from the river.

Her heart skipped a beat when she saw a lot of activity at the cabin. Trappers were coming and going from its doors, and Indians camped by outdoor fires.

Dawnmarie realized this must be the trading post where her mother was staying. The lead canoe of the Chippewa procession headed toward the shore, confirming her suspicion that they had reached their destination.

The trader climbed out of the canoe as White Wolf beached his own.

Dawnmarie did not wait for White Wolf to climb from the canoe. She jumped out into ankle-deep water and ran past the trader, up a path, until she burst into the cabin, heaving for breath.

Several men were there along with a tall, stout woman behind the counter who was counting out pelts. When the woman saw Dawnmarie she stopped counting and went over to her.

"I'm Dawnmarie," Dawnmarie stammered out between deep breaths. "My mother. I have come to see my mother."

She looked overhead. The loft was dark. Surely her mother wasn't there. Her eyes looked past the woman at a door that led to a back room. In her father's trading post this room had been the storage room. But a soft flickering light wafting from the door suggested it was being used as a bedroom.

She didn't wait for the woman to lead her to the room. She ran to it, her knees almost buckling from relief when she found her mother there, propped up in the bed, her face drawn, but very much alive.

Dawnmarie hastened to the bed and sat on the edge and drew her mother into her arms. "Mum, oh, Mum," she murmured, careful not to squeeze too hard. In her mind's eye she relived the very instant her mother had been shot. The wound should be healing now, unless . . .

"Mum, you should be stronger than . . . this . . ." Dawnmarie said, easing from her mother's arms. "Unless your wound became infected. Is it, Mum? Is it infected?"

"You know how poorly I heal," Doe Eyes said, lifting a hand to Dawnmarie's face, slowly tracing her features. "My daughter. My beautiful daughter. You eluded the Sioux. How did you?"

"I did not actually elude them all that successfully," Dawnmarie said. "I was taken captive."

Dawnmarie heard her mother's quick intake of breath, then quickly explained how it had all happened.

"But I escaped," she quickly interjected. "A white wolf came mystically to me in the forest, and . . . and . . . then Chief White Wolf was suddenly there instead of the wolf. It is something you might dream, but not truly live."

"Then, while I have been in a deep, feverish sleep, you have been safely with White Wolf?" Doe Eyes asked, her insides warming to the thought of her daughter having found her way inside White Wolf's heart, possibly to stay there forever.

"Very," Dawnmarie said, smiling softly down at her mother. "And, Mum, there is more to tell you. I . . . I . . ."

She stopped when footsteps entered the room be-

hind her. She turned a beaming smile up at White
Wolf as he came into the room with the trader. He
came to her side, his hand warm on her shoulder as
he gazed down at her mother.

"And how are you faring, Doe Eyes?" White Wolf
asked, glad that she was alive, but saddened over her
looking so frail and gaunt.

"Now that I see that my daughter is alive and in
the best of company I shall survive," Doe Eyes said,
then her smile waned. "But I shall never forget what
Slow Running and his warriors have taken from us."

"Mum, I saw to Father's burial," Dawnmarie said,
her voice breaking. "He is at peace, Mum. He is in
the spirit world now. He has no more woes or fears
of this earth to face. That is long gone from him."

Doe Eyes looked up at Dawnmarie, then turned
her eyes away. "I shall miss him forever," she said,
sudden sobs wracking her body.

Dawnmarie gently drew her mother within her
arms. "It's going to be all right, Mum," she whispered. "White Wolf is righting all wrongs for us. Father can never return, but our dignity can be
restored. White Wolf has given our lives back to us
and I am ever grateful."

Doe Eyes clung to Dawnmarie for a moment
longer, then gazed up at White Wolf. "How can I
ever thank you," she murmured.

White Wolf sat down beside Dawnmarie. "It is *I*
who should be thanking you," he said huskily. "For
bringing such a daughter as Dawnmarie into this
world for me to take as my wife."

Doe Eyes looked from Dawnmarie to White Wolf,
then smiled her tears away. "You will marry soon?"
she asked softly.

"Soon," White Wolf said, slipping an arm around

Dawnmarie's waist. "Now that she knows that you are all right we can both move on with our lives."

"We will wait until you are able to travel to White Wolf's village to celebrate the marriage ceremony with us," Dawnmarie said, smoothing some locks of her mother's hair back from her brow. "It would not be right without you there to see your daughter become the wife of such a wonderful man."

Dawnmarie could see strange sorts of lights enter her mother's eyes. She did not seem as happy as she had moments ago. Something was still troubling her.

"I don't want you to wait for my arrival to marry White Wolf," her mother said somberly. "This world is an unsettled place." She gripped her daughter's arm. "Who can say who will even see another sunrise? Grasp life now as it is offered to you. I have lost so much in my lifetime: my people, my husband. Perhaps tomorrow *you*. Who can say?"

Dawnmarie could not argue this point. Not with the threat of Chief Slow Running always there, always serving as a reminder of how evil things can be.

Dawnmarie could tell there was still something else that bothered her mother to cause her to behave so strangely. It was as though something had snapped in her mind. One minute she was smiling and happy. The next she seemed remorseful, almost desperate.

"Mum, please do not worry about anything," Dawnmarie said, glad when her mother's grip on her arm lightened. She took her mother's hand and held it on her lap. "Just get well. That's all that matters now. Soon we will be together for all time. You will see."

The sound of footsteps behind her made Dawnmarie turn around and see her old friend, Father James, a Jesuit priest who everyone knew in these

parts, enter the room. He was a man who at one
time had been bent on "Christianizing and civilizing"
the red man, but who simply enjoyed their friendship
now as he ventured from village to village, camp to
camp, in an effort to keep peace among the various
tribes. Since the Jesuit priests always wore long,
flowing black robes, the Indians referred to them as
the "black robes."

"I see that you have company today, Doe Eyes,"
Father James said softly. He stepped up to the bed
and smiled down at Dawnmarie. "I am glad that you
are here. No one knew where to find you. I thought
perhaps you had not survived the attack which
caused your mother's injuries."

Dawnmarie rose to her feet and hugged Father
James. She had first become fond of him many years
ago when he came to her father's trading post. She
remembered his gentle voice and a face radiant
with kindness.

"I know you would have found me if you could,"
she murmured, enjoying the warmth of his embrace.
"But I am here now. That is all that matters."

She slipped away from him and stood beside
White Wolf. She took White Wolf's hand and
beamed up at him, then gazed over at Father James.
"Come soon to the Chippewa village," she murmured. "There is going to be a marriage ceremony
that I would like for you to see. I would love to
receive your blessing."

Father James smiled warmly as he placed a hand
on White Wolf's arm. "You are truly a brilliant
chief," he said thickly. "Never again will you find
such a young lady as this. You chose wisely, my son.
Very wisely."

"I am the lucky one," White Wolf said, nodding.

Then Father James went and knelt beside the bed on one knee. "Actually I did not come to join in your merriment of seeing your daughter again," he said softly. "I had no idea she was here. I came for another purpose. I have news, news of your true people, the Kickapoo. I sent many feelers out and discovered where your village is located, the village you were abducted from all those years ago."

Dawnmarie and her mother both gasped.

Father James took one of Doe Eyes's hands. "When you are well enough I will take you there," he said. "The Kickapoo encampment is two, maybe three days travel by canoe. Get well. Then I will take both you and your daughter to your true people."

Dawnmarie stifled a sob of happiness behind a hand. For so long her mother had hungered to see her people again, to be one among them as it was meant to be. Now she would get that chance. It was a miracle that it would happen now, when her mother's world had tumbled around her.

Dawnmarie, herself, was anxious to know her true people. But she had never been driven to know them. This was her mother's dream. Dawnmarie would be there mainly to see it happen.

Dawnmarie's life, *her* future, lay with White Wolf, not the Kickapoo, yet she would never forget her mother telling her that to enter the afterworld as Kickapoo, she must find and make peace with them while on this earth so that they could look past that part of her that was white.

For this reason, the journey was equally important to Dawnmarie as her mother. She was glad that her mother's dream was finally becoming a reality.

Chapter Thirty-eight

I never saw so sweet a face
As that I stood before.
                    —John Clare

The stars twinkled like miniature diamond brooches in the heavens. The air was warm and caressing as White Wolf lay another log on the campfire. Dawnmarie lay on rich, thick pelts while the river lapped lazily against the shore a short distance away. She kept her eyes on the trader's cabin. Inside, the lamplight was turned down low, meaning everyone had retired for the night.

Dawnmarie felt totally relaxed knowing that her mother was safely in that cabin, tucked in beneath warm blankets. Her mother's heart should be filled with joy over many things now. Her daughter was alive and would marry a wonderful Chippewa chief. And soon she would be reunited with her own people.

Yet Dawnmarie was haunted by that lost look in her mother's eyes. She wondered if it would ever be replaced by something even akin to peace. Had she suffered too much to be the same woman she once was?

"You seem lost in thought," White Wolf said as he stretched out beside Dawnmarie. He placed his hands to her waist and drew her next to him, the privacy of their campsite such that they could feel free to do as they wished. White Wolf had sent his other warriors back to the village. He and Dawnmarie stayed behind so that Dawnmarie could have one last day with her mother before returning.

"There is something about Mother that is not right," Dawnmarie said, stroking her fingers through White Wolf's wet hair. They had bathed only moments ago after having eaten a fill of the meal offered them in the cabin. She felt sparkling clean and smelled of fresh river water.

"She is still weak," White Wolf said softly. "She is still traumatized by past events. When she is fully recuperated you will then see your mother as you have always known her."

"I hope so," Dawnmarie said, her hands now moving along White Wolf's chest, loving the feel of his copper skin against the flesh of her fingers. She giggled when he sucked in a breath of pleasure as she caused his stomach to quaver with her soft, butterfly touches.

"You are starting something that I will want to finish," White Wolf said, turning on his side, facing her. He grabbed her hands away when she threatened to move them lower. "The stars are our only witness. Do you wish to wander farther with your hands? If so, I shall also want to touch you where you are soft and wet."

"Please do," Dawnmarie said, her heart throbbing with the anticipation of what was transpiring between them.

When he released her hand she shamelessly placed her fingers at the waist of his breechcloth and slowly lowered it, her gaze locked on that part of him that was aroused in his need of her.

She closed her eyes in ecstasy when his hands reached up inside the skirt of her dress and found the spot that ached for his touch. She trembled when he thrust a finger inside her, his thumb flicking the tightened nub where the center of her desire lay.

"It makes me mindless," she whispered, shuddering as his free hand reached down inside her dress and cupped a breast. She felt as though her whole body was throbbing as she became awakened anew to that wonderful bliss that White Wolf knew how to arouse inside her.

She lowered his breechcloth, then clasped her eager fingers around his tightness. She moved her fingers rhythmically on him as he lifted her dress and cupped that place between her legs that was already on fire from his caresses.

He eased her hand away from him, then positioned himself so that he could worship her body with his lips and tongue.

She writhed, her breath becoming erratic.

Her head rolled back and forth as her senses reeled from this frantic need that was spreading like wildfire through her.

And then he rolled away from her. He drew her dress over her head. When it was tossed aside he rolled her beneath him. In one thrust he was inside her, his hands on her breasts, his lips scorching hers with fevered kisses.

Dawnmarie felt the pleasure building. She was reaching that high plateau, where the most wondrous of feelings would be found.

White Wolf kneaded her breasts.

He licked the nipples into a tight peak.

His buttocks rose and fell, filling her to her innermost depths.

Then their bodies quaked. They rocked. They rolled and tangled, their sighs filling the night air as they came to that place in the heavens reserved only for lovers.

It was as if they flew on eagle's wings, then came back down to earth, their bodies stilled, their breathing ragged.

"I love you," echoed across the sky.

"I love you," the moon, the stars, and the river seemed to echo back.

Chapter Thirty-nine

Dreaming of beauty,
Ere I found thee!
          —John Clare

Several days had passed. Swallow Song gazed down at the wound at her ankle. She ran her fingers over the scar that was now healing. It was only slightly tender to the touch.

She was relieved that her body healed so quickly. She only wished that the ugly, hidden secrets of her body would heal as well and never embarrass her again.

She felt lucky that no one in this village knew yet of her affliction. Not many people from her own village knew. She did not mingle much, purposely keeping to herself so that no one would see her body shakes and how her eyes rolled back inside her head until her seizures finished.

For she suffered from horrible seizures. That was the secret she *and* her father guarded with their lives. So far during her stay at the Chippewa village, she had not been seized with her inner demons. They would not only have robbed her of her dignity, but also of the man she loved, Sharp Nose.

She awakened each morning in order to see him, to be with him, to feel his mighty arms around her. Never in her life had she felt such peace as when she was in his arms.

She frowned. When he witnessed her first seizure would he look away in disgust? Or would he continue to love her and want to protect her? She knew her father was weary of being her protector.

She could not blame her father for being frustrated. First he had a wife with the affliction, then a daughter.

She looked up as Sharp Nose came into the lodge, a colorful bouquet of wildflowers in his hand. She giggled and reached her hands out for the flowers, burying her nose in them, then clasping them to her bosom.

"Thank you," she murmured, beaming up at Sharp Nose as she laid the flowers on her lap. She felt lovely today wearing a dress that Dawnmarie had loaned her. It was beautifully beaded with intricate designs of the forest flowers.

Her hair smelled sweet after she washed it in water brimming with floating rose petals, which were a special treat from Dawnmarie.

These past several days she and Dawnmarie had formed a special friendship. She believed that Dawnmarie's attitude had changed toward her. Swallow Song no longer posed a threat since Sharp Nose was now her center of attention.

Swallow Song understood how Dawnmarie felt. At one time she had been as jealous as Dawnmarie.

Now they could laugh at their jealousies, and it felt good to have a special friend.

But Swallow Song also wondered what Dawnmarie would do once she found out about her ugly secret. Swallow Song did not want pity from Dawnmarie. She wanted understanding, something that would make the bond between them even stronger.

Swallow Song had always feared people's reaction to her affliction. She had saved herself the embarrassment by not becoming close friends with anyone.

Until now.

"Dawnmarie says that she is bringing you a special gift soon," Sharp Nose said, sitting down beside Swallow Song's thick, sumptuous bed of blankets.

He reached for one of the flowers he had given her. He smiled and slipped the flower into her hair above her left ear.

"A special gift?" Swallow Song said, her eyes brightening. "I wonder what it is. Her friendship is gift enough."

"It is good that you and Dawnmarie are becoming close," Sharp Nose said, placing his hands at her waist and lifting her onto his lap. He cradled her close, and she laid her cheek against his chest. "You see, White Wolf and I have been best friends since we were small children. In fact, we built our first canoe together and shared it for many years."

He placed his hand to her chin and lifted it so that their eyes met. "It would be good to share something more with White Wolf," he said thickly.

"What else would you like to share with him?" Swallow Song murmured.

"Marriage ceremonies," Sharp Nose said, searching her eyes for her reaction. "Yours and mine. His and Dawnmarie's."

"Are you asking me to be your wife?" Swallow Song asked, breathless at the thought of having finally found a man who would have her. Not only that, but she truly loved him, way more than she had ever loved any man.

"If I were to ask, what would your answer be?" Sharp Nose asked, his pulse racing as he took in her innocent loveliness, her utter beauty.

Swallow Song choked back a sob of joy. "I would say to you, Sharp Nose, that if I were well enough, I would bring a gift of wood and lay it at your doorstep to prove my worth as your wife."

Chief Charging Deer stood outside, listening. He leaned an ear closer, a slow smile lifting his lips.

Then a disturbing thought came to him that made his smile wane. He hoped that not too much time would elapse before the marriage ceremony. If Sharp Nose witnessed his daughter's seizures he might take back his offer of marriage.

Yes, he must hurry things along.

"Darling Swallow Song," Sharp Nose murmured, leaning to kiss her. Trembling, their lips met. He wove his fingers through her hair and held her close, his lips becoming more demanding, his kiss more passionately fevered.

Breathless, rapture filling her, Swallow Song twined her arms around his neck. She had never been kissed before and found the experience wonderful. She enjoyed her body's reactions. Her insides felt mushy, warm, and sweet. She never knew that a kiss could create such sensations throughout her body. Just being near Sharp Nose sent her head reeling.

But this!

The kiss!

And his kiss, the demand in his arms, the way his hands stroked her back, down to the curve of her buttocks, and then up again, the way he cupped her breasts through her buckskin dress, made her feel light-headed with passion, as though she might faint from the pleasure.

"I love you so," Sharp Nose whispered, brushing soft kisses along her lips. "I need you, Swallow Song. My body aches for you."

Unpracticed at such things, Swallow Song's face grew hot with a blush at the thought of him undressing in front of her, and her before him.

But she wanted the full experience of these new feelings.

She nodded anxiously, then grew ashen when she heard a noise outside the lodge and saw the shadow of someone standing there, the bright sunlight illuminating the shadow through the buckskin fabric of the council house.

"We are not alone," she whispered, wrenching herself from Sharp Nose's arms. "I must return to my bed. I think my father might be outside the lodge, listening."

Sharp Nose looked over his shoulder at the lingering shadow. His jaw tightened. Swallow Song's father was strange in his behavior toward her.

Sharp Nose had watched Charging Deer. His attitude was not so much one of concern, or of guarding a daughter who was being sought openly by a man. It was something else and Sharp Nose had not been able to figure out *what*.

He turned his attention back to Swallow Song. "Never forget how much I love you," he said thickly, gently placing her midst her blankets again. "I shall forever love you."

She smiled weakly up at him, hiding her shiver of doubt beneath the blankets. "I shall love you forever," she whispered back.

Sharp Nose gently placed a hand to her cheek, then gave her a feather's touch of a kiss. "So now I must go and speak with your father."

Swallow Song reached her arms quickly around his neck, to keep him with her a moment longer. "I shall not even breathe until you return to me," she said, consumed by love for him. He leaned over and placed another kiss on her lips, then rose and left the lodge.

She lifted her eyes heavenward. "Oh, Great Spirit, please do not take this away from me," she begged in a whisper. "Let my Chippewa warrior understand everything about me when he has to face it. I will kill myself if he cannot understand my demons, for Sharp Nose is my very last chance at salvation."

Sharp Nose and Chief Charging Deer gazed at one another for a moment, then Sharp Nose spoke. He folded his arms across his chest. He held his chin high. "When you return to your village, I will follow, with a generous bride price for your daughter," he said, watching a strange sort of light, an apparent relief leap into the Potawatomis chief's midnight dark eyes.

He was taken aback by Charging Deer's quick, abrupt reply.

"There is no need to wait until I return to my village," Charging Deer said tersely. "If you want my daughter, bring pelts *now*."

Sharp Nose quirked an eyebrow. He did not understand this chief's attitude and wondered why he was so anxious to give such a lovely daughter away.

This made Sharp Nose somewhat wary, wondering if there was something about Swallow Song that he should know.

Sharp Nose had lost his heart so hopelessly to Swallow Song, he chose not to bother himself with worries about the whys of things.

"If that is what you wish, then that is how it shall be," Sharp Nose said, nodding. "I am as anxious to have your daughter as it seems you are anxious to give her away."

When he saw the quick intake of Charging Deer's breath and the rage that marked his facial features, Sharp Nose changed the topic.

"I will go now for the pelts," Sharp Nose said, turning and walking away quickly.

Charging Deer watched Sharp Nose for a moment, then entered the lodge and sat down beside Swallow Song. "It is done," he said thickly. "Sharp Nose and I talked. He is paying a bride price. You will be married soon."

Brimming with excitement, Swallow Song leaned into her father's embrace as he reached for her. "Be happy for me for the right reasons, Father," she murmured. "Not for those I suspect you are feeling."

"Sharp Nose is a good man," Charging Deer said, patting her back. "He will be a good husband. Why should I not be happy for you?"

Suddenly Swallow Song's body stiffened. Her teeth clenched. Her eyes froze and her hands doubled into tight fists at her sides.

Charging Deer's insides tightened, and he closed his eyes as he held Swallow Song in his arms while her body lurched and tremored.

When her shakes were too violent for him to hold her, he laid her on the bed of blankets and watched her eyes roll backward as her whole body shook with violent spasms.

He looked away from her and closed his eyes as thin, white drool rolled from the corner of her mouth. Hanging his head in his hands, he waited until it was over and she was quiet again, her breathing shallow.

Charging Deer turned his eyes back to his daughter. Hers were wildly imploring him. Her face was pale, her lips purple.

"Father, why, oh, why?" she cried, lunging into his arms as he drew her up from the blankets.

"It is something no one understands," Charging Deer said softly, gently stroking her back through her dress. "It is something from your mother's family."

He gripped her shoulders and held her away from him, his face showing his weariness. "You will marry soon," he said thickly. "But bear me no grandsons. Give me no granddaughters. I would not wish this affliction on anyone else in our family."

"But what if Sharp Nose wants children?" she sobbed.

"Once he witnesses your demonic behavior, he will not wish to have children by you," he said, his voice drawn.

"I am not being fair to him by marrying him," Swallow Song cried. "Take me home, Father. Please take me home. I must forget him. I must."

"You will marry him," Charging Deer said, his voice flat and angry.

She nodded.

She looked quickly toward the entranceway when suddenly Dawnmarie appeared, all smiles, all sweetness. She was hiding something behind her back.

Dawnmarie came into the lodge, but her smile quickly faded when she saw how upset Swallow Song was. "What is wrong?" she said, settling down on the floor on the opposite side of the bed from Charging Deer. She still held the surprise for Swallow Song behind her. "Swallow Song, you've been crying."

"She cries from happiness," Charging Deer said quickly. "She is soon to be a wife."

Swallow Song felt around her mouth with her fingers to make sure there was nothing left there from her seizure. She smiled awkwardly over at Dawnmarie. "Yes, I will soon marry Sharp Nose," she said softly. "Right now he is gathering up pelts for a bride price for Father."

"How happy I am for you," Dawnmarie said. "And I can understand tears of happiness. Of late, I, too, have shed many."

Dawnmarie wondered why Swallow Song and her father exchanged strange, troubled glances. But anxious to give Swallow Song her special gift, so happy to have become friends with her instead of enemies, she cast aside her worries and pulled out the friendship bag for Swallow Song to see.

Swallow Song's eyes widened. "The bag. It is so beautiful," she murmured, staring in wonder at the beautiful glass "star chevron" beads, bright blue with red and white zigzag patterns, that covered the lovely bag.

Dawnmarie pressed the bag into her hands. "This is to seal the bond of friendship between us," she said, feeling so silly about her earlier feelings of jealousy of Swallow Song. The feelings she had for her as a friend, though, were much stronger than those she had felt when she saw her as nothing more than a contender for the love of White Wolf.

Charging Deer also recognized the importance of this gift. He knew the power that Dawnmarie now had over White Wolf, as women do when men first fall in love with them. By becoming friends with Dawnmarie, Swallow Song's power would also increase within the Chippewa community. Smiling smugly, he left the lodge without even being missed.

Swallow Song ran her fingers over the floral shape designs of the beadwork. "I have never seen anything as lovely as this," she murmured. She gazed quickly over at Dawnmarie. "Can you really part with this?"

"My mother was given this by a special friend many years ago," Dawnmarie said. "She gave it to me to give away when *I* found a special friend. Now I have found her. Please take the gift and know it is given to you from my heart."

Swallow Song's eyes pooled with tears again. Everything was almost too perfect now. She wondered how long it would be before her luck ran out and her body betrayed her again. She smiled weakly at Dawnmarie.

"Thank you," she murmured, choking back a sob. "I shall treasure it, as well as your friendship, always."

Dawnmarie saw something in Swallow Song's eyes that made her realize something was wrong. She reached over and gave Swallow Song a hug, feeling Swallow Song trembling, hesitant, and stiff.

She drew away and searched Swallow Song's eyes for answers. "Swallow Song, is anything wrong?" she asked guardedly.

Meekly, in a way which was less than convincing to Dawnmarie, Swallow Song shook her head slowly back and forth.

"I'm glad," Dawnmarie said, hugging her. "But remember, Swallow Song, we are best of friends now. There is no need ever to keep secrets from one another. I am here for you. Feel free to confide in me."

Swallow Song stared widely across Dawnmarie's shoulder as she clung to her, everything at this moment seeming to her to be frozen in time. She wished it could be that way. She dreaded these next days, weeks, and months.

She might lose everything she had gained.

Trying to keep thoughts of demons from surfacing, she closed her eyes tightly.

Chapter Forty

Pure-bosom'd,
And Heaven reflected in her face.
—*William Cowper*

As the sunset splashed orange across the horizon White Wolf sat in council with his warriors around the outdoor fire, Dawnmarie at his side. The night air was touched with coolness, a sign that winter would soon arrive.

Dawnmarie glanced toward the council house. She wondered how much longer Swallow Song would be sheltered there. Sharp Nose's absence at the council was noticeable. His usual place at White Wolf's side was vacant. Right now he was away on the hunt gathering together his bride price for Swallow Song.

Dawnmarie's thoughts went to Charging Deer. His urgency to rid himself of his daughter became more and more evident. But no one had asked him why.

There was no need humiliating Swallow Song any more than she already had been where her father was concerned.

"My warriors, Chief Slow Running has not been forgotten by this Chippewa chief," White Wolf announced as he gazed from warrior to warrior. "But there will be no attack at this time."

He glanced over at Dawnmarie, then looked toward his warriors again. "As you all know, my woman's mother survived the recent Sioux attack," he continued. "She is recuperating at a trading post up the river. When she is well, I will escort her farther upriver so that she can find her true people, the Kickapoo. I am asking for volunteers who will travel with the procession of canoes and for some who will stay behind and stand guard at our village to make sure our people are safe from attack. Slow Running tempts war in many ways. He might become impatient and bring warring to *us*."

Again he gazed over at Dawnmarie. "He has abducted my woman once, and tried a second time, but his warrior mistakenly took Swallow Song instead," he said thickly. He glowered at his warriors. "I am sure there will be a third attempt."

His warriors joined in by giving their loyal support to White Wolf in all of his endeavors.

"It is good that I have so many warriors to depend on," he replied, nodding.

He looked toward the river, then at the setting sun. "Tonight we must prepare ourselves for a possible sneak attack," he said. "Our scout has returned with news that Slow Running is no longer incapacitated. He is now standing on his feet, instead of lying in bed like a woman. Anything can be expected of him."

"What shall we do, my chief?"

White Wolf turned with a start when he heard Sharp Nose's voice.

White Wolf smiled broadly, rose to his feet, and clasped his hands on his friend's shoulders. "It is good to have you back," he said thickly. He glanced down at the river and saw the pile of pelts in Sharp Nose's canoe.

He smiled over at Sharp Nose. "So your bride price is ready," he said, his eyes dancing.

"Ay-uh," Sharp Nose said, proudly squaring his shoulders. His eyes wavered then when he saw Chief Charging Deer step from the council house, a blanket thrown over his left shoulder.

"It seems you have brought enough pelts to pay for *two* women," White Wolf said, chuckling.

When Sharp Nose made no reply, White Wolf followed his gaze and stiffened when he found Charging Deer moving toward them.

"I have brought enough," Sharp Nose said only loud enough for White Wolf to hear. "Even if I only had a few, Swallow Song's father would still accept. But I want to prove her worth by offering many."

He dropped his hands to his sides as Charging Deer stopped and stood before them.

"Down by the river you will find my canoe," Sharp Nose said, a hand gesturing toward the river. His eyes narrowed into Charging Deer's. "In my canoe you will find my bride price. If it is not enough, I shall gather together many more. I am quite skilled with the arrow. I am a skillful hunter. I can bring to you as many pelts as is needed to have your daughter as my bride."

Charging Deer did not bother to look at the canoe, or at what was being offered. "What you have

brought is adequate," he said tersely. "Now I will
go and transfer them to my canoe, then leave for
my village."

Dawnmarie was watching and listening, but this
last comment from Charging Deer drew her quickly
to her feet. Her eyes wary, she moved to White
Wolf's side. "Chief Charging Deer, why don't you
look at the bride price before you accept it?" she
asked, her voice drawn. "Why are you leaving this
quickly? Don't you want to stay and witness your
daughter's happiness in marriage?"

"Her happiness is mine whether or not I watch
her clasp hands of marriage with Sharp Nose,"
Charging Deer said in a monotone. "I have been
away from my people long enough. My daughter
does not need me anymore. My people do. They are
my world now, not my daughter."

Out of the corner of Dawnmarie's eyes she caught
movement at the door of the council house. Swallow
Song was standing in the doorway, looking forlorn.
She limped toward them.

Sharp Nose went to her and grabbed her up into
his arms. "You should not be putting weight on your
ankle just yet," he scolded.

Swallow Song looked adoringly at him, finding his
protectiveness so wonderful after hearing her father
relinquish his hold on her way too easily. "Thank
you," she murmured. "My wonderful Chippewa warrior. Thank you for caring so much."

Sharp Nose brushed a kiss across her lips, then
carried her over to her father. He still held her protectively in his arms, purposely proving to her father
that he would not let harm come to her. Not even
from a noncaring father.

"Father, are you leaving now?" Swallow Song asked, her eyes wavering into his.

"You know that I must," Charging Deer said. "My duty here is done. Sharp Nose's just begins."

She lowered her eyes. "I understand," she said, gulping back a sob that threatened to rise in her throat.

Charging Deer ran his hand across the gentle lines of her face, then turned and walked away.

Dawnmarie was stunned. She watched Charging Deer until he had placed all of the pelts in his canoe. When he did not even turn to give his daughter a last farewell look, nod, or wave, she went to Swallow Song and tried to comfort her.

"You will soon be a beautiful bride," Dawnmarie said, taking Swallow Song's hand. "Isn't it wonderful, Swallow Song? We will be married at almost the same time. Perhaps we might even become heavy with child at the same time."

Dawnmarie's smile faded when she saw a quiet panic leap into Swallow Song's eyes.

"What did I say that alarmed you?" Dawnmarie asked.

Swallow Song forced a smile. "Nothing alarmed me," she said, twining an arm around Sharp Nose's neck. "I am ever so happy, Dawnmarie."

"*Ay-uh,* there will be two marriages soon," Sharp Nose said, his eyes eager as he looked over at White Wolf. "Perhaps we all could share a marriage ceremony?"

His gaze turned to Dawnmarie. "Dawnmarie? Would you want to share ceremonies?"

He turned anxious eyes back to White Wolf. "Perhaps we could even have the ceremony tomorrow?"

White Wolf's eyes filled with a sudden excitement

at the suggestion. They gleamed as he gazed questioningly down at Dawnmarie. "Do *you* want to share ceremonies?" he asked. "I have delayed warring. But I see no reason to delay marriage between you and me. We have waited long enough to seal our bond of love."

"Yes, oh, yes," Dawnmarie said, flinging herself into his arms. "I would love to become your wife tomorrow."

White Wolf kissed her, then remembered his waiting warriors when he heard some of them chuckle at his open demonstration of love for Dawnmarie.

Remembering what the council was being held for, White Wolf broke free of Dawnmarie and went to sit back down midst the circle.

"We were discussing a possible Sioux attack," White Wolf said. "We must take preparations even tonight to guard against such an attack. Guarding the village is not enough. Slow Running is like a snake who sneaks slyly and noiselessly about. We will make sure that he cannot approach us by river. We will stretch nets with bells along the most shallow part of the riverbank where canoes are usually more easily beached. It will not be detected by the Sioux until they are tangled in the nets. The bells will alert us that we have caught our prey."

Everyone agreed, and the council disbanded to go stretch the nets wide and far.

Night came.

The towering pines and beautiful white birch trees were dappled with moonlight. Dawnmarie strolled hand in hand with White Wolf along the riverbank, checking the nets one last time, while Sharp Nose and Swallow Song sat beside the lodge fire in Sharp Nose's wigwam.

"It is good to be in your lodge," Swallow Song said, snuggling in Sharp Nose's arms. "The council house was spacious but unfriendly."

"Many councils of warring were discussed there and still lay in the council house shadows like ghosts," Sharp Nose said, cupping her chin in his hand, turning her face up to his.

He kissed her softly, then eased her down onto the mats. As she lay there, so beautiful, so petite, he roamed his eyes over her, at her flawless features, at her soft glimmer of hair.

Careful not to touch her injured ankle, he inched one of his hands up her leg, inside her dress.

When he splayed his fingers over her mound of hair at the juncture of her thighs, he heard her quick intake of breath. "I need you," he said huskily. "Tonight, Swallow Song. Not tomorrow after the ceremony."

Swallow Song's insides grew tight with alarm. She loved him dearly, yet she feared the trauma of making love for the first time might throw her body into one of her spells. She must be sure he was her husband before chancing that. Perhaps then he might not turn her away.

"I am afraid," she murmured against his lips, her face warming with a blush as he stroked her secret place. "You are the first man for me."

"Then tonight I shall only touch and caress you," he said throatily.

He reached for her hand and placed it over the bulge that lay hard and anxious beneath his breechcloth. "Touch *me*," he whispered. "Acquaint yourself with the size and length of me before I place it inside you tomorrow."

Swallowing hard, Swallow Song's fingers spread

out over him, her heart pounding at the very feel of him. "It is so big," she whispered.

"That assures you more pleasure," he whispered, kissing her eyelids closed. "You shall see what I mean tomorrow, my sweet."

She savored the moment *now*.

Chapter Forty-one

She walks among the loveliness she made
Between the apple-blossom and the water.
                    —*Vita Sackville-West*

"Let's sit by the river for a while," Dawnmarie said, swinging around to face White Wolf. "It is such a lovely night."

He took her hand and led her down on the soft sand.

Watching the waves urgently seeking the shore, she snuggled next to him.

"It is so peaceful and serene here," Dawnmarie said, sighing with happiness.

"In this great north country the woods and water are one with their god," White Wolf said, watching the fireflies lighting their lamps over the water. "We are in nature's cathedral. She is all around us. You just have to attune yourself to her wonders. The spirits lift you and you are at peace."

He drew her closer to his side. "Cry to the sky," he said, gesturing with a hand heavenward. "You will be answered. Take the time to listen. You will hear the voice eternal—our wild rice, our cranberries, our forest animals."

"This is so beautiful," Dawnmarie said, gazing in wonder up at him. "Your words hold such magic in them."

"It is because I believe that everything has a soul," he said, smiling down at her. "Trees, birds, our lakes, the river itself. I learned long ago to achieve harmony with nature. The elders always stressed the importance of maintaining balance in one's life, and looking to nature as a model. If you lose balance, bad things happen."

Dawnmarie's thoughts went to Swallow Song's father. "Were my father alive he would not have been as anxious to part with me as Swallow Song's father so cold-heartedly left her," she blurted out, finally saying what she had been feeling all evening.

She gazed up at White Wolf. "You are a powerful chief," she said. "Is it because Charging Deer is a chief and is burdened with the worry of his people that he left so quickly?"

"Who is to say," White Wolf murmured. "I do know that the Potawatomis have been duped often by treaties. Charging Deer is an unsettled person because of this. You heard how he feels that he must move onward, to settle his people elsewhere. Perhaps he thought it best to get his daughter settled in with a husband before he left for unknown parts. Who is to say if he and his people will arrive safely while on their journey. While Swallow Song is here, among my people, her chances of survival are much better than if she went with her father."

"I hope that *is* his reason," Dawnmarie said, snuggling closer. "But no matter what, his behavior, his quick exit from her life, hurt Swallow Song as if he pierced her heart with an arrow."

White Wolf placed a hand to Dawnmarie's chin

and tilted her face so that he could gaze into her eyes. "My woman, the woman who will soon be my wife, please do not concern yourself over Swallow Song's welfare any longer," he said softly. "She is now under the care of my best friend. He will love her hurt away. Let us center our thoughts on our happiness, yours and mine. My Violet Eyes, I've never been so happy."

"It's been so long since you called me Violet Eyes," Dawnmarie said softly.

"Do you mind?"

"Not at all."

"I prefer it to the name that your father gave you, which is a white name," he said thickly.

"Won't it confuse people if my name changes now, at my age, and after they have known me so long as Dawnmarie?"

"You are new in my village," he said, her hair spilling over her shoulders, tumbling beneath her as she stretched out on the soft, warm sand.

Eager to taste of her passion-moist lips, White Wolf looked down at her, greedily absorbing the sight of her. He smoothed fallen locks of her hair from her eyes. "The name Violet Eyes will come naturally to them."

"But my mother ... ?"

"She will call you what she will call you," White Wolf said, lowering his mouth to her lips. He spoke softly and gently against them. "It does not matter. Right now all that matters is that you are here. You are in my arms. And tomorrow our lives will become like one heartbeat, one soul, one being."

His mouth seized hers in a fevered kiss, his hands eagerly disrobing her.

She lifted her hips to help him, and when she felt

the sting of the wind on her flesh, she slipped her mouth free and reached for his breechcloth, quickly slipping it over his hips and away from him.

"Warm me, darling," she murmured, her voice foreign to her in its huskiness. "Feed my flesh. Feed my desires."

He ran his hands over her body, taking in the roundness, stroking. He bent over her and placed his hard, taut body against hers, with one thrust entering her where she offered him paradise.

She clung around his shoulders. Her tongue parted his lips and flicked inside his mouth.

His response was a moan of pleasure when she thrust her pelvis toward him, allowing him to move more deeply within her.

She touched him all over, hungrily, desperately. She clutched his buttocks with her fingers. Inside she throbbed in a frenzied rhythm, her heart pounding, the warmth of pleasure flooding through her body.

A loon sent its mysterious warble across the water. Nearby frogs and crickets serenaded their mates. Dawnmarie's groans of ecstasy challenged the other night sounds as White Wolf's hands swept down and cupped her breasts, his lips following, his tongue flicking across her nipples.

Dawnmarie drew in her breath sharply and gave a little cry when his lips fastened on a pliant, pink nub, sucking it hard.

His mouth was hot and demanding as he once again kissed her, darting his tongue moistly into her mouth. She was vaguely aware of herself making soft, whimpering sounds as he pressed endlessly deeper inside her, seemingly touching the very core of her being with his rapid, wondrous thrusts.

White Wolf felt the energy building. Drawing

closer to that ultimate of release, he gave himself over to that feeling of agony and bliss.

He clung to Dawnmarie's slim, sensuous body. He came to her, thrusting, ever thrusting, each sending a message to her heart.

Knowing that he could not hold back any longer, he stiffened for a moment, buried his lips along the delicate, vulnerable line of her throat, then gave one last, deep thrust inside her.

When it came to him, that rapture, that moment of wild bliss, he held her tightly. He groaned against her neck, his body quavering into hers.

Dawnmarie was mindless with pleasure and gave herself up to the rapture, the feelings inside her blazing, searing.

She shuddered.

She clung to him.

Afterward White Wolf rolled away from her and lay on his back on the sand beside her.

Her body turned to liquid when his eyes touched her, and he smiled.

"Everything in my life is so perfect now," Dawnmarie whispered, scooting over to mold herself against his body. "My mother is alive. You and I are going to be married. Surely nothing else will happen to spoil our happiness."

Slow Running's knees wobbled as he slowly paced before the outdoor council fire at his village. "Do not waste time bringing the woman to me," he flatly ordered his warriors who sat in council, their faces black with ash, war paint drawn on them. "Watch the village closely. When you see White Wolf alone, capture him. Bring him to me. That will, in turn, lure the woman here. And if the Chippewa warriors accompany her, we shall kill them all. It is time they know who is master of this lake country!"

Yellow Tail glowered, then went along with the others to their canoes. He had received word by one of his closest friends that if he crossed his chief just one more time he would be staked in the center of the village and tormented until dead.

He would much rather follow Slow Running's twisted orders than die. So he shoved his canoe out into the water, then leapt aboard. He followed the others down the long avenue of the river, the canoes sliding noiselessly along, except for the low hissing sound of the paddles as they plunged rhythmically through the water. Soon they would arrive at the Chippewa village.

Chapter Forty-two

My beloved spake, and said unto me,
Rise up, my love, my fair one, and come away.
                        —The Song of Songs, 2:10

It had been a long day of excitement, celebration, feasting, and laughter. The dancing still continued, several drums beating their steady rhythm for the dancers, rattles shaking out their own rhythmic beat.

The woman dancers with hundreds of metal cones sewn to their dresses made a soft chorus of clattering in passing in and from the dancing circle. The men dancers wore beaded outfits.

Some men proudly displayed their beautiful head-dresses of eagle feathers that waved as they danced. Eagle feathers represented honesty and courage. The right to wear them was earned by deeds of valor and served to honor the person who had performed them. It was said that one could not speak a lie in the presence of an eagle feather.

Dawnmarie held White Wolf's hand as they sat before a huge outdoor fire with Sharp Nose and Swallow Song, the licking orange flames of the fire just strong enough now to cast shadows into the softly falling darkness of night.

Dawnmarie turned beaming eyes up at White Wolf. They were now officially man and wife. She cast Swallow Song a glance, happy for her. She had never seen her as radiant and as beautiful as now, on her wedding day. Her dress matched Dawnmarie's, thanks to Woman Dancing who had assigned several women to make them in time for the quickly planned ceremony.

The two women's white buckskin dresses were long and flowing, topped off by a white manta, snow-white moccasins, and a headdress of feathers and snake skins.

Their faces were painted with the color of corn, their lips ruby with the color of the bloodroot. They wore their hair long and flowing down their backs with beautiful pastel shawls that dripped from their shoulders to ward off the chill of the early evening air.

Dawnmarie once again looked over at White Wolf. Today, he and Sharp Nose wore a full outfit of buckskin, the sleeves and leggings fringed and heavily beaded.

White Wolf's hair hung in a single, long braid down his back. A beautifully beaded headband held his hair back from his brow, a lone feather hanging from a coil of his hair at the back. His face was a handsome copper sheen beneath the glow of the fire, and Dawnmarie's insides melted and trembled to know that White Wolf was her husband, someone who had surely been sought by many beautiful maidens.

But out of them all, he had chosen her!

Still it seemed surreal, like a wonderful dream that she would soon awaken from.

But when he squeezed her hand, it reminded her that this was real, that this was life as it should be. She sighed and smiled at him adoringly.

Finally the ceremony ended and congratulations were completed. The outdoor fire was now only glowing embers as White Wolf swept Dawnmarie into his arms and carried her toward his lodge. She looked over his shoulder and got a last, fast glimpse of Swallow Song as Sharp Nose carried her into his lodge.

"They are so happy," Dawnmarie said, laying her cheek against White Wolf's powerful chest. "I am so happy for them."

"I am happy for *us*," White Wolf said, brushing aside the entrance flap as he entered his lodge. "If I could have made it happen, I would have married you many winters ago."

Dawnmarie giggled. "I would have then been too young to be your wife," she said as he placed her to her feet beside the fire pit. "I doubt you would have wanted me then. My body was slow developing into a woman. My breasts were just tiny things for so long. I did not start my monthly flow until only two winters ago."

"I have loved you forever, even when you were but just a seed in your mother's womb," White Wolf said, framing her face between his hands. "Even before then it was written in the heavens that you and I would become man and wife. It is my belief that things are planned at the beginning of time. It is charted in the heavens who will be born and who they will take as their mate."

Dawnmarie hugged herself as she gazed up at White Wolf. "If that is true, then it has already been determined how many children you and I will bring into our lives," she said. "Even how many *grand*children."

"*Ay-uh,* that is so, Violet Eyes," he said throatily. "And it also known how many times we will make love tonight." His eyes danced into hers. "Do you want to venture a guess?"

"Many times," Dawnmarie said, mesmerized by his chiseled features as though she were looking at him for that first time. "The full night is ours, isn't it? I do not want to sleep at all. I just want to make love."

She reached her hand to his headband and slipped it away from his head. She tossed it aside, then placed her fingers to the fringed hem of his shirt and slowly pushed it up across his muscled chest and wide shoulders, then over his head.

After dropping the shirt to the floor, she splayed her hands across his chest and ran her lips over his flesh, and then her tongue. When she nipped at his nipples, first one and then the other, she watched his eyes close in ecstasy, his groans filling the empty shadowed corners of the lodge.

Her heart pounding, already warm and wet where the center of her own passion lay, Dawnmarie placed her hands at the waistband of his leggings. She became breathless with anticipation as she shoved them slowly downward. She gasped at the sight of him as his arousal sprang into full view, all velvety tight, a pearl bead of moisture at the very tip.

As his leggings dropped to the floor, Dawnmarie brazenly swept her fingers around his taut manhood, eliciting another groan from deep within her husband. She moved one hand on him, her other hand reaching around to stroke his muscled buttocks.

Remembering another way that brought him much pleasure, she flicked her tongue over where her hand had just been.

His hands framing her face, drawing her up away from where he throbbed so mercilessly, made her realize that he was too near that pinnacle of pleasure. He unselfishly wanted to delay it until later, after they had shared much more mutal touching and caressing.

"While I stoke the lodge fire, my eyes will be on you as you undress," White Wolf said. "Watching you, seeing your body, will stoke the fires inside me."

Dawnmarie's fingers trembled as she disrobed herself. As he placed wood into the glowing embers, her eyes were on him, and how when he stirred the muscles moved down the length of his body.

After he placed the last log on the fire he reached out for her and led her down onto a thick pallet of furs. "My wonderful Violet Eyes," he whispered, his hands moving over her liquid curves, then to that central muff of hair that lay at the apex of her long, smooth thighs. "Tonight will be forever. Let it be our guideline throughout the rest of our marriage. Let there never be distrust or reason for arguing between us. Our marriage will be that which will live on into eternity, when we will then walk hand in hand on the road of the hereafter."

"I once witnessed a white man's wedding ceremony," she murmured, sucking in a breath of pleasure as he caressed her center of desire. "In the ceremony the woman vowed to love, honor, and obey her husband. I understood why she would say she loved the man she married. But to obey? I was not sure I could ever commit myself to obeying any man. But now? With you? Whatever you wish will be my desire. My life is yours."

"I will never order you around like you are my child or my pet," White Wolf said thickly. "We will share in our decisions for our family." He straddled her with his knees. "Let us begin a family now, my woman. Tonight."

Dawnmarie smiled shyly up at him with a secret that she wanted to wait until later to share with him. She wanted to be certain why she was missing her monthly flow since having made love with him.

Was she with child? she wondered. Or was her body confused by the new lovemaking sensations she was experiencing? Her whole body was so alive now, so responsive to every little touch, to every little caress.

She hoped with all of her heart that the cause of her lapse of menses was because she *was* with child. She would cherish every moment of her pregnancy, because the child was also White Wolf's.

"Yes, let us make a child," she said, her hands exploring his long, lithe, and well-aroused body. She ran her fingers over the sinews of his shoulders, then over his flat belly, down to where his proof of love for her lay long and thick against her abdomen. She placed her hand around his hardness, opened her legs to him, then led him inside her.

He filled her so magnificently she closed her eyes with rapture. She lifted her hips and met his eager thrusts, his hands on her breasts, his thumbs caressing her taut nipples.

His mouth came to hers with an explosive kiss. He swept his hands down the full length of her body, then clasped his fingers beneath her buttocks, lifting her closer, allowing him to penetrate much more deeply.

His mouth moved down from his lips, kissing his way to her breasts. She moaned and twined her fingers through his hair when his lips moved over her nipple, his tongue flicking.

She swung her legs around his hips as he plunged into her pulsing cleft more quickly. Her frenzied desire peaked. She swirled in a storm of passion that shook her innermost senses. The very air was charged with their fire, their energy, their wild bliss.

White Wolf's insides tightened, the warmth spreading. Again he moved his lips to her breasts, his tongue titillating her nipples, swirling, flicking, licking.

Gasping spasmodically, Dawnmarie tossed her head from side to side, her hair thrashing like a whip around her face.

Their bodies moved together, rocked and swayed, in a wild, dizzying rhythm.

She moaned when he gripped her shoulders and made one last deep plunge inside her, their climax coming so suddenly their gasping breaths of pleasure were like sudden lightning flashes midst their minds.

When their pleasure subsided, White Wolf rolled away from Dawnmarie, then lifted her atop him. Her breasts crushing his chest made his senses reel. He closed his eyes as her teeth nipped at his lips, his chin, and then his neck.

He rolled her to his side, his mouth brushing her

cheeks and ears. Lightly, tenderly, he kissed her eyelids.

Then their eyes flew widely open when White Wolf heard his name being spoken frantically just outside the entrance flap.

"White Wolf, come, I need you," Sharp Nose pleaded. "It is my wife. Something is terribly wrong with my wife. I do not know what to do to help her. It is . . . as . . . though a demon has her in its grip!'"

White Wolf and Dawnmarie exchanged quick, troubled glances. Then they scrambled to their feet and quickly dressed. When they stepped outside the lodge, Sharp Nose was gone.

White Wolf grabbed Dawnmarie's hand. They rushed to Sharp Nose's lodge and hurried inside. What they saw made them gasp and take a shaky step backward.

Sharp Nose tried to gather Swallow Song into his arms but she was thrashing her arms and legs too much. And her head. It was thrown back and thumping hard against the mats, her eyes rolled almost completely from sight in their sockets.

"Swallow Song," Dawnmarie cried, rushing to the other side of the mat, opposite where Sharp Nose sat, obviously struck numb by what he was witnessing, and so obviously very helpless.

"How long has she been doing this?" Dawnmarie asked, finally achieving being able to grab one of Swallow Song's hands. She held it with all of her might, her eyes never leaving her friend's face that was distorted almost into someone she could hardly recognize.

And the fact that Swallow Song was nude did not even penetrate Dawnmarie's consciousness. Her concern, her *fears,* overpowered anything else that would most normally embarrass her.

"We were making love ..." Sharp Nose stammered. "We had just achieved a satisfying climax. I was holding her. Kissing her. She stiffened in my arms. Then her body jerked backward. She went into some sort of trance, her body jerking and ... and ..."

His words broke off when Swallow Song suddenly lay quiet, her breathing labored. When her eyes focused, and she was able to realize things around her, she died a slow death inside to know that what she had dreaded happening, had happened.

Ashamed and humiliated, she turned her eyes away and began softly crying. "Now you all know the worst about me," she sobbed. "I had hoped that you would never need know. I was foolish to stay here."

She turned wild eyes to Sharp Nose. "I was foolish to marry you," she cried. "Oh, how you must hate me. Do you see me as a deceitful, lying, crazed woman?"

She eased her hand from Dawnmarie's and reached her trembling fingers to Sharp Nose's face. She gently touched it. "I love you so, but I will leave now," she said, her voice breaking. "I will return to my father. I can see by your silence and by the fear in your eyes that you no longer wish to have me as your wife."

White Wolf knelt down beside Sharp Nose. He placed a comforting arm around his shoulders.

Dawnmarie gazed at Sharp Nose, fearing what his next words might be. *She* felt no pity for Swallow Song. She felt a true sadness.

But could Sharp Nose be loath to think of this

woman whose body betrayed her as his wife any longer?

She scarcely breathed as she waited for his answer.

While waiting, Dawnmarie gently placed a robe around Swallow Song's frail shoulders.

Chapter Forty-three

In one another's being mingle—
Why not I with thine?
                         —Shelley

Still stunned over Swallow Song's seizure, and her subsequent feelings of hopelessness, Sharp Nose gazed in wonder at her. Now he understood why her father had handed her over to him so easily. To rid himself of a daughter who was not like all other daughters.

This embittered Sharp Nose even more against her father. He was a callous, thoughtless man. How could he love his daughter less because of something that she could not help?

Sharp Nose loved her no less. He would make sure she was pampered. He would never allow her to feel ashamed over that which she had no control.

"Swallow Song," he said, his voice drawn. He went to her and drew her up into his arms and held her close. "My sweet Swallow Song."

As she clung to him, sobbing hard, he caressed her back. "Do not cry and do not be ashamed," he whispered. "I love you. Can you not see that? Do you not know that nothing can make me love you less?"

"How can you?" she cried, pressing her cheek against his chest, her tears wetting his flesh. "Did you not see? My body betrayed me *and* you. I am not pretty anymore in your eyes. How can you ever think me pretty again after you saw how I turned into something so ugly? What you feel for me is ... is ... *pity.*"

Dawnmarie moved to White Wolf. She leaned against him as he swept an arm around her waist. She placed a hand to her mouth to stifle a sob of anguish for Swallow Song behind it.

"Swallow Song, you are even more beautiful to me," Sharp Nose said, clutching his fingers to her shoulders to lean her away from him, so that their eyes could meet and hold. "I could never pity you. My love for you will sustain us both through your moments of terror."

"Then ... then ... you will not send me back to my father?" she asked, her eyes wide and imploring. "I can stay? I can still be your wife?"

"I would never let you go away from me for any reason," Sharp Nose said, drawing her back into his embrace. He smiled at White Wolf and Dawnmarie over Swallow Song's shoulder. "And you not only have your husband to love you. So do White Wolf and Dawnmarie."

Shyly, Swallow Song turned her gaze slowly over to them. When she saw no loathing or pity in their eyes, she broke from Sharp Nose's embrace and ran to them. She hugged Dawnmarie, and then White Wolf. Then gave them a soft smile. "Thank you," she murmured. "I love you both for caring so much."

They hugged her again, then left the lodge so that Swallow Song and Sharp Nose could be alone.

"It is as though a demon lives inside Swallow Song," White Wolf said, pushing aside the entrance flap of his lodge, entering after Dawnmarie. "But I am confident that Sharp Nose will find the means to chase the demons away. His love for her is strong."

Feeling blessed for what she and White Wolf had, Dawnmarie turned and flung herself into his arms. She did not say it aloud, but she feared the future for Swallow Song and Sharp Nose ... and their children.

They undressed and returned to their bed of blankets. Dawnmarie welcomed White Wolf's arm around her as he drew her against his muscled body. Sleep did not come so easily though, since she was plagued by troubled thoughts.

Then she finally felt herself floating into a soft sleep, smiling when she felt White Wolf's hand cup a breast and softly knead it. It was a wonderful way to go to sleep. Yes, she felt so very, very blessed.

Chapter Forty-four

My heart has left its dwelling place and can return no more.
—John Clare

White Wolf stirred in his sleep. He turned to his side, the slow, lapping flames of the fire along the logs casting a golden glow on his face. In his sleep he drew a blanket up closer beneath his chin, then awakened with a start when he heard something outside, something down by the river.

He leaned up on an elbow and listened more closely. His senses alert, he grew rigid at the sound of bells tinkling and jangling.

"The net," he whispered to himself. "Something has disturbed the net of bells. Or . . . someone . . ."

He gazed quickly over at Dawnmarie. She had not been disturbed by the bells. She still slept soundly, ah, so beautifully.

Careful not to awaken her, he slipped from beneath the warm blankets. Trying not to make a sound, he hurried into his breechcloth and moccasins, then moved stealthily to the back of his lodge. From his store of weapons he chose a knife that he sheathed quickly at his waist.

Then he grabbed his rifle that he kept loaded for such an emergency.

Again he moved stealthily through his wigwam. When he stepped out into the darkness, he gazed from lodge to lodge. No one stirred. That had to mean that he was the only one to have heard the bells.

After quick thought he decided not to awaken anyone else. Even his guards. Had everyone not had a tiring day? He felt confident that he could handle anything alone. If there were intruders near his village he felt that he might have a better chance at stopping them if there were less in number to surprise those who had arrived in this dark midnight hour of night.

This decision made, he ran into the dark depths of the forest, then slowly, cautiously, made his way toward the river. He stared ahead when he saw the shine of the river beneath the moonlight, his eyebrows quirking when he saw no signs of canoes.

As he got closer he smiled to himself when he realized just what *had* tangled itself in the net. He could see the shine of a deer's panic-filled eyes in the darkness, and then he made out its shape as it struggled to get free of the net, tangling itself even more severely into it.

As White Wolf reached the deer, he accessed the situation. He lay his rifle on the sandy beach. "You came to the river for a drink and instead found a net," he whispered to the deer, taking his knife, slicing into the net to set the animal loose.

Just as the deer leapt free and ran into the forest something else drew White Wolf's attention. So intent on freeing the deer he had not noticed it before. He sniffed the air. That smell. How could he have not noticed before? The smell of Sioux tobacco.

That had to mean that . . .

He started to turn, to retrieve his rifle.

But he was not quick enough. He was grabbed around the throat and wrestled to the ground.

The last thing he saw before the butt of a rifle cracked him across the brow was Yellow Tail leering down at him, his eyes like dark gleaming coals in the night.

"Two nights we waited for you to come alone to the river," Yellow Tail grumbled as two other warriors stepped up to his side. "Grab him. Let us hurry now to our canoes. Bind his ankles and wrists. Place him in my canoe. I want to be the one to take credit for bringing the Chippewa chief to Slow Running."

Yellow Tail sneered as he gazed at the netting that was now in disarray because of the deer. The prior evening Yellow Tail's canoe had tangled in it.

But the Chippewa had been too busy celebrating and feasting to notice the jangle of the bells. Yellow Tail had freed his canoe and had instructed his warriors to beach their canoes farther up the river away from the village. Cleverly he had repaired the net so that no one would notice.

Fiercely, his muscles cording, he took his knife and shredded the net into tiny pieces, then ran off into the cover of the darkness of the forest. He made his way to his canoe, then gave it a shove from the shore.

Climbing aboard, he felt his smugness leaving him. He knew what the wrath of the Chippewa might be when they found their chief gone.

But whatever happened as a result would not lay on *his* conscience. It was his chief who had ordered this capture. He could not help but think that in so doing, Slow Running might have signed a death warrant for his band of Sioux.

His shoulders slumped as he drew his paddle through the water, he did not feel the heat of eyes on his back.

White Wolf awakened with a throbbing brow. Trickles of blood flowed into his eyes. He wrestled with his bonds, only succeeding at making his flesh raw where the leather bit into his wrists and ankles.

He glared up at Yellow Tail's bare back. Did the small Sioux not realize that soon many Chippewa warriors would follow, decked out in their war paint? He did not understand the logic of what the Sioux had done tonight.

Then he realized that Dawnmarie had to be the motivated the Sioux chief.

Slow Running had devised a scheme to somehow assure that Violet Eyes would be his and only White Wolf's death would make that possible.

"Sioux, you will be the one to die," White Wolf said, knowing that Yellow Tail heard him by the way his back stiffened, and his breath came in sharply.

Chapter Forty-five

When love has come to you,
So genuinely real and wonderful,
Fight, if must, to keep it!
              —Kathryn Edwards

Disturbed by a dream, Dawnmarie woke with a start. She reached out for White Wolf in the dark for comfort, then lurched and sprang to a sitting position when she found him gone. The fire had burned down to glowing ashes, emitting only a scarce amount of light for her to see that her husband was nowhere in the lodge.

She rushed to her feet and pulled a dress over her head and slipped into moccasins. Not allowing herself to be alarmed, wanting to believe that White

Wolf had not slept well himself and had gone outside to get a breath of air, she went from the lodge and stiffened when she saw no signs of him anywhere.

Her heart thumping, many thoughts rushed through her mind, none pleasant. She hurried back inside the lodge and went to White Wolf's store of weapons. Indeed, his favorite rifle was gone. Her gaze shifted. His favorite knife was also gone, as well as its sheath.

"He would not leave in the middle of the night to go hunting, especially without telling me first," she said, puzzled over his absence, her mind swirling with wonder. "Unless he has gone to hunt the *Sioux.*"

She rushed from the lodge again and looked toward the river. Nothing seemed out of place.

"The net!" she gasped, running now toward the river.

When she reached the sandy beach and looked a short distance upriver, where the net had been cleverly placed across its narrow channel, she was gripped with a crushing coldness.

"It's not there," she whispered harshly against a hand.

Half stumbling she ran hard up the beach, then stopped when she found the shredded net. She fell to her knees and gathered bits and pieces of it into her hands, her eyes studying the footsteps in the sand as the moonlight swept over them.

There were deer hooves.

There were several footprints.

And then she died a slow death inside when she realized the place in the sand where there had been an obvious struggle.

Something else then caught her eye. She dropped the pieces of net and placed a trembling finger to the small pool of blood on the sand. She touched it gingerly and placed her finger before her eyes, knowing that, yes, it was blood.

"Oh, please don't let it be White Wolf's!" she cried.

As she inhaled a quavering breath of despair she noticed something else. The strong stench of Sioux tobacco. They had been there. They had obviously struggled with someone on the beach.

And that someone had to be White Wolf. Everyone else in the village seemed to be asleep. Tired from the long day of celebration and feasting, even guards had carelessly gone into their lodges to sleep.

"No!" she cried, scrambling quickly to her feet. She stretched her hands overhead and cried to the heavens. "Great Spirit, hear my plea. Let nothing happen to my husband!"

She broke into a mad run down the beach, cursing the sand. It was not easy to walk through, much less run, but speed was of the essence. She had to get to Sharp Nose. She had to alert him and all of the Chippewa warriors that their chief was in mortal danger.

The blood! she despaired to herself. Where had it come from? How badly was he injured?

She was breathless. Her knees were weak when she reached Sharp Nose's lodge. She didn't even stop to voice her entrance first. She hurried inside and fell to her knees beside Sharp Nose.

"Wake up!" she cried. "Oh, Sharp Nose, something has happened to White Wolf! I believe the Sioux have abducted him!"

His eyes wild, his heart racing with fear for his best friend, Sharp Nose bolted to his feet. He pulled on his breechcloth and stepped into moccasins.

Swallow Song pulled a robe around her shoulders

and went to Dawnmarie. She gave her a warm hug, then stepped out of the way as Dawnmarie left with Sharp Nose to awaken the rest of the warriors.

In a short time many had been assigned to go on the warpath with Sharp Nose, while others had been instructed to stay behind and guard their village. Woman Dancing was summoned to sit with Swallow Song.

Chanting, the warriors covered their bodies in ashes and painted their faces.

Their hands filled with various weapons, they ran toward the river.

Dawnmarie followed, a pistol that she had taken from White Wolf's store of weapons in her right hand.

When Sharp Nose realized that Dawnmarie was beside him, he stopped and gripped her shoulders with tight fingers. "You cannot go," he said, frowning down at her. "Warring is not for women."

"My husband's life is in danger," she cried. She stubbornly lifted her chin. "I cannot . . . I *will* not . . . stand by and wait to see what has happened to him. I will go with you. Please do not try and stop me."

Sharp Nose gazed down at her. He saw her insistence and need to see that White Wolf was all right. He nodded. "You can go, but once there, do as you are told," he said flatly. "I will do what I can to protect you, but only if you are willing to follow my lead."

"I will do anything to go with you," Dawnmarie said, nodding her head anxiously.

They ran toward the beach, then stopped suddenly when two Sioux warriors stepped out of the cover of the forest, white cloths tied to their lifted rifles.

Sharp Nose shoved Dawnmarie behind him. He glowered at the warriors. "Where is White Wolf?" he asked thickly.

"He has been taken to Slow Running," one of the warriors said. "We have come to deliver a message."

"And that is ... ?" Sharp Nose asked, looking guardedly from one to the other.

"Let us take this woman to my chief, then in return, White Wolf will be set free," the other warrior said. "Or we will have total warring between two factions of Indians."

"You chose warring the moment you stole our chief," Sharp Nose said, protecting Dawnmarie with his body as arrows whizzed through the air and lodged into the chests of the two Sioux.

Dawnmarie peeked around Sharp Nose and at how quickly death had come to these two warriors. She felt faint to know that it could come as quickly to her husband.

Chapter Forty-six

I think true love is never blind,
But rather brings an added light.
—Phoebe Cary

Drums beat out a low and monotonous sound. The moon was high in the sky, the air cool and crisp. Stripped of his clothes, White Wolf struggled with the thongs at his wrists and ankles that were tied to stakes buried in the ground.

His legs wide apart, his arms above his head, the bare ground cold against his back as he lay there,

White Wolf glared at the Sioux men and women who bent over him, tormenting him with their hands, pinching him, poking him, prodding.

He flinched but willed himself not to cry out with pain when one of the Sioux warriors slowly drew the blade of a hatchet across his hairless chest, leaving a trail of blood droplets in its wake.

But the true pain was in his brow. It pounded mercilessly. He could even feel dried blood stretching against the flesh of his forehead.

He felt lucky, though, that the blow to his head had not rendered him senseless, perhaps unable ever to lead his people again.

He was *not* senseless. He was only for the moment helpless because of his bonds.

But soon he would be free and he would make these Sioux pay for the degradation of the moment. His warriors, as soon as they found him gone, would come for him. It made no sense to him whatsoever that Slow Running could think that he could achieve anything from capturing him, except by bringing death to his people.

White Wolf knew that he and Slow Running were very different in that sense. White Wolf tried to keep warring from his people while Slow Running did not hesitate to bring it to his. His goals were always selfish ones. Whatever he might gain, if only momentary success against his enemy, he would do, no matter the cost.

White Wolf's eyes narrowed angrily when Chief Slow Running came from his lodge a short distance from where White Wolf was held captive. Seeing that Slow Running was still not entirely well from having consumed the tainted brandy was the only thing that made White Wolf smile.

If Dawnmarie's father had known what Slow Running's true intentions were, he would have poisoned the brandy with something even more lethal.

Gaunt, frail and trembling, and leaning heavily on a tall staff, Slow Running snickered as he stopped close beside White Wolf. "You do not look superior to the Sioux *now*," he said, laughing throatily.

He nudged White Wolf's private parts with the blunt end of his staff. "You look less than a *man*," he said, chuckling. He leaned against the staff again. "Soon Dawnmarie will see this herself. When she arrives at my camp she will be disgusted by the sight of you lying there so helpless and degraded. She will turn her back on you. She will walk proudly into my lodge and become my *wife*."

"I always knew that you were a demented man, but I did not know you were so *ignorant*," White Wolf said, straining again at the bonds that held him hostage.

"You speak foolishly while at my mercy," Slow Running warned, scowling down at White Wolf.

"I speak the truth," White Wolf said stiffly. "If that looks foolish in your eyes, so be it."

"Believe what you wish to believe and blind yourself to the truth," Slow Running said. "You are my captive. Soon there will be an exchange. Your warriors will bring Dawnmarie to me. In turn, you will be set free. If the exchange is not done peacefully, then you will die instantly."

"You prove your ignorance again," White Wolf said, smiling smugly up at Slow Running. "You will bring death to your *people,* not me. My warriors are clever, and they will never do anything to jeopardize their chief's, or his woman's, safety. Soon you will see just how clever they are."

"The only thing I see is that my warriors should have stormed your village and taken it by force instead of trying to reason with you peacefully," Slow Running said, turning to walk away. He looked over his shoulder. "It is not too late to agree to my terms. If Dawnmarie does not come to me soon, my warriors will go for her. Many of your people, perhaps *all* of them, will die!"

"Any way you choose to involve my people in warring you will end up the loser," White Wolf shouted after Slow Running. "You who shame the very name Sioux, for those who have tried to reach a measure of peace with the Chippewa, will die. If not by the hand of the Chippewa, by the hand of your very own Sioux who are loath to even speak your name!"

Slow Running turned and glared at White Wolf. "You still dare to speak while you are captive?" he hissed out. "Say any more, Chippewa, and your tongue will be cut out, and that long and flowing hair will be removed from your scalp."

Slow Running paused and leaned into his staff. "It won't be long before Dawnmarie is brought to me," he said, smiling slowly. "My messengers have probably already arrived at your village."

White Wolf was not at all alarmed by this. He smiled knowingly up at Slow Running. The Sioux chief would soon realize exactly how wrong he was to mess with the destiny of the Chippewa and their women. Slow Running's own destiny, even his life, was soon to be short-lived.

Slow Running went to his tepee and moaned as he settled down beside his lodge fire. Star Flower came to him with a bowl of soup. He knocked it out of her hands and glowered up at her. "I do not need sisterly pamperings any longer," he grumbled. "Soon I will have a *real* woman to make my meals and warm my bed."

"Big brother, soon you may not have a bed, or a lodge, with no woman to be at your beck and call," Star Flower said, inching away from him toward the entrance flap. "I have watched you these past sunrises. You are not thinking clearly. What you did tonight, abducting White Wolf, was very foolish. The Chippewa outnumber the Sioux in this lake country two to one. And what Sioux, besides those who foolishly follow your command, would come to your aid?"

A deep sob surfaced from the depths of her throat as she stopped before leaving. "My brother, in my dreams I see many dead, many *graves,*" she cried. "I have seen *yours,* my brother."

She placed a fist to her lips and bit into the flesh.

"Do you not you hear me? I have seen *many* graves, and all because of your stubborn pride and your need for a woman."

When he did not venture to respond, her eyes filled with frustration. "You cannot want this woman so much for your pleasure," she said, her voice breaking. "It is only because she is White Wolf's woman that you want her. It is a challenge between two chiefs that makes you do such reckless, mindless things. If you claim her and make her your wife, you can laugh at White Wolf. You can torment him. Is losing everything else worth proving such foolish things to White Wolf?"

Still he did not answer her.

He stared ahead past her, as though she were not there.

Shaken from her building frustrations, Star Flower

turned and ran from the lodge. She went and stood over White Wolf, her eyes wavering into his, and then ran to her lodge and threw herself onto her pallet of furs, sobbing.

Slow Running pushed himself up from the floor of his tepee and left his lodge again. He waved to several warriors to come to him.

"Pale Cloud and Red Squirrel should have returned by now," he said, staring past his warriors to White Wolf. He shivered inwardly as White Wolf's eyes bore into his like two hot coals.

He swallowed hard and looked quickly away. "Shining Moon, Wind Whistling, take warriors in your canoes. Go and see what has happened to them."

Wind Whistling took two shaky steps toward Slow Running. "Like you, my chief, I am still weak from my recent illness," he dared to say. "I do not feel able to defend myself should we run into a Chippewa warring party."

Shining Moon agreed with Wind Whistling. "Many of us are doing too poorly to defend ourselves," he said. "The timing is not good, my chief, for what you have set out to do. We will surely fail. Many will surely die."

Slow Running reached a hand out and gripped his fingers painfully into Shining Moon's shoulder. "You whine too much," he said, his voice filled with threat. "You go, or die at the hand of your chief."

Slow Running dropped his hand down to his side and gazed from warrior to warrior. "Take as many warriors as will fill two canoes. Go downriver to check on the two men who were sent to bargain with White Wolf's warriors," he said, his voice raised in pitch. "Go. *Now*. And do not return unless they, or you, have the woman!"

Midst bowed heads and low grumblings the warriors went to their canoes and boarded them and rode away in the soft waves of night.

Slow Running clamped his lips tightly together and glared over at White Wolf. When he found White Wolf still staring at him he became unnerved.

Frowning, he went back inside his lodge and sat beside the fire. He peered into the dancing flames, shaking his head to clear his thoughts when in those flames he saw beckoning hands, as though the mistress of death were tempting him.

Chapter Forty-seven

Silent and chaste, she steals along,
Far from the world's gay, busy throng.
—*William Cowper*

Afraid that it was taking too long to get to the Sioux camp, Dawnmarie strained her neck to see around Sharp Nose. She peered into the moonlit darkness, seeing nothing but water, which seemed like a dark bottomless pit beneath the veil of night.

She looked toward the shore. Some of the dead trees resembled old men, twisted and gnarled with age.

She shivered when, in the distance, she heard the mournful howl of a wolf.

Then she closed her eyes and remembered the night that she had dreamed of the white wolf, and when she had awakened, had seen one loping away into the forest, and White Wolf soon there, taking its place.

"My darling husband, please be all right," she whispered, then quickly opened her eyes when she heard Sharp Nose's quick intake of breath.

She stiffened when he dropped his paddle to the floor of the canoe and raised his rifle and aimed it.

Dawnmarie scooted over on the seat so that she could get a better view.

Her insides splashed cold when she caught sight of two Sioux canoes coming around the bend in the river a short distance away.

"Get down!" Sharp Nose shouted at Dawnmarie over his shoulder. "Lie flat in the canoe. Those approaching are from Slow Running's camp!"

"No!" Dawnmarie cried, lifting her pistol. "I won't let them interfere in our going to rescue White Wolf. I will fight for my husband. We must get to White Wolf."

Sharp Nose had no time to argue. The Sioux canoes were bearing down upon them. Arrows flew from their bows, and rifle fire whistled past.

The canoes were almost nose to nose as the battle continued. Through a barrage of arrows, several Chippewa dove into the river and swam underwater toward the Sioux canoe.

Dawnmarie aimed and fired her pistol, groaning when she realized that her aim was off and she had hit no one.

She screamed when one of the Chippewa warriors behind her in the same canoe slumped over, blood pouring from a chest wound.

She froze inside when she looked back at the other canoe and saw casualties there also.

Then she resumed firing, proud when at last one

of her bullets found its target. She watched the Sioux drop his firearm, clasp at his chest, then topple over the edge of the canoe into the water.

Suddenly both Sioux canoes tipped, spilling all of the warriors into the water. Dawnmarie felt like shouting with glee when the Chippewa warriors who had forced the canoes over came to the surface. They went on with their business of fighting the Sioux. She could tell that the Sioux seemed weaker than normal. They did not seem to have the will to fight back.

Then she smiled. Those exact warriors were the ones most affected by her father's tainted brandy. It was obvious that they were still suffering its side effects. They would lose the battle because of it.

She had to look away when hatchets took off the heads of the disabled Sioux. She could hardly stand to hear the cries of pain, or see the smearing of the blood in the water.

And then everything was quiet. Dawnmarie slowly turned her eyes around. The Chippewa who had survived swam back to their canoes, while dead Sioux warriors floated strangely in the water for a moment, then slowly sank.

Immediate attention was given to those warriors whose wounds were bad, but not fatal. After their wounds were bound and the warriors were stretched out on the floors of the canoes, the Chippewa canoes forged ahead up the river.

"You did well," Sharp Nose said to Dawnmarie over his shoulder as he did not miss one stroke with his paddle. "White Wolf will be proud to know that his wife has the ability to fight as valiantly as a man."

Dawnmarie smiled weakly, glad that Sharp Nose could not see the trembling of her fingers, or feel the pounding of her heart.

She placed a hand to her abdomen, praying to the Great Spirit that if she was with child, nothing she did today while attempting to save White Wolf's life would make their child come prematurely. Surely there could be nothing more fulfilling in life than to have a baby with the man she loved, except perhaps that look that White Wolf might have on his face at the first sight of his child.

In truth, she knew the chances of losing both tonight, the father *and* the tiny seed that he may have planted deeply wihin her womb.

She grew somber with worry.

Chapter Forty-eight

If ever two were one, then surely we.
  —Anne Bradstreet

The Chippewa beached their canoes far enough from the Sioux encampment not to be noticed. Dawnmarie clasped her fingers tightly to the pistol as she left the canoe and ran to the cover of the woods with the others.

They moved stealthily through the forest, the stillness broken by the hoarse gobble of wild turkeys.

Dawnmarie knew that the wild creatures roamed these woods without fear.

She shivered, for she was not a wild creature, and she was certainly not fearless. Every cell in her body seemed to tingle with an anxious concern over what she was about to do. She was not that skilled with firearms, yet she knew that, when faced with danger, anyone could use one.

And, she reminded herself, she had already proven her ability to fire a gun accurately enough. She had shot one of the Sioux just prior to the capsizing of his canoe.

When the glow of the outdoor fires of the Sioux encampment showed golden and wavering through a break in the trees a short distance away, Sharp Nose held out an arm and stopped Dawnmarie.

He nodded to several of the warriors. They nodded back, then moved on through the darkness.

"Where are they going?" Dawnmarie whispered, her eyes wide as she tried to keep focused on them.

"They will render the guards helpless and then we can sneak into the village and release White Wolf without taking any more casualties," Sharp Nose whispered back.

"Any more casualties?" Dawnmarie gasped. "Does that mean that the warriors will kill the guards?"

"*Ay-uh*, that is the only way; it is either kill or *be* killed ourselves," Sharp Nose whispered, turning to gaze down at her with affection. He placed a gentle hand to her cheek. "You should not have come. We may be pushed into a full-fledged battle. If you get killed, White Wolf ..."

"*He* is our only concern now," Dawnmarie said, interrupting him.

A sudden rash of gunfire drew their eyes around. Dawnmarie's heart skipped a beat when she realized that the guards had been alerted to intruders in the night.

Had the Chippewa warriors been shot? she wondered.

Or the Sioux?

Sharp Nose gave a sudden war cry that rang through the air.

Dawnmarie felt dizzy with fear when she realized what that cry meant. That they would not be entering the encampment quietly. They were atttacking.

Sudden doubt swept through her like wildfire.

But she had hardly time to think about it or even consider backing out on her decision to join the Chippewa. She had to follow or be left behind in the dark.

Her knees trembling, the pit of her stomach weak, she broke into a mad run with the warriors. She tried to stay close to Sharp Nose, but his long strides were no match for her smaller ones.

When she reached the encampment and caught sight of White Wolf spread-eagled on the ground, all fears, all doubts, were gone. All that she could think about was setting him free.

Everything was frenzied in the Sioux camp.

Women screamed, and children cried. Arrows flew through the air like flames.

A scream froze in Dawnmarie's throat when a Sioux warrior stopped and stood over White Wolf, his arrow drawn back on his bow, ready to shoot.

Sharp Nose then stepped into view. He brought a knife down into the Sioux's back. The arrow slipped from the bow and fell to the ground. The Sioux struggled to reach back to remove the knife from his back, then gave up and crumpled to the ground beside White Wolf. The warrior's body lurched, and then he lay quiet, his eyes locked in a death stare.

Dawnmarie ran to White Wolf just as Sharp Nose kicked the dead Sioux away. Her eyes locked with White Wolf's. "My darling," she cried. She started to move to her knees, to help free him, but Sharp

Nose was already there cutting the leather bonds at his wrists, and then at his ankles.

Dawnmarie stood guard. She held her pistol ready for firing as she looked guardedly in one direction, then another. Her insides recoiled as she saw the death and destruction that already lay on the ground around her, and yet the fighting continued.

She could not help but feel sad for the children who stood at the far edge of the encampment clinging to their mothers.

Nor could she help but feel sad for those Sioux warriors who had been forced into cruel acts by their chief. As they lay sprawled across the ground now in pools of their life's blood, resentment boiled inside her against Slow Running.

"Slow Running!" she suddenly gasped, her eyes moving to his lodge. "Where is *he*?"

A Chippewa warrior came from Slow Running's lodge. He sounded off a series of war whoops as he held several scalps in the air, then set fire to them while another warrior tossed a torch inside Slow Running's tepee.

"Can he truly be dead?" Dawnmarie whispered to herself as she watched the tepee become engulfed in flames. Yet she cringed at the sight of the scalps still burning on the ground where the warrior had thrown them.

"Violet Eyes, you should not have come," White Wolf said, suddenly pulling her around to face him as he stood tall and nude before her.

Dawnmarie gazed up at him, so thankful that he had survived. Her heart ached when she saw the large purplish lump on his brow, the blood caked on it and in his hair, and then the smaller wounds along the flesh of his chest.

"My darling," she said, flinging herself into his arms.

Sharp Nose kept watch, then gave White Wolf a look over his shoulder. "It is done," he said solemnly as the firing ceased all around them. "We have finally beaten this band of Sioux."

"And what of Slow Running?" White Wolf asked as one of his warriors brought him a robe made of white rabbit, slipping it over his shoulders to hide his nudity beneath it.

Another warrior came to him. "He eluded us," he said thickly. "Slow Running and a few of his warriors escaped. They fled to the river and got away in their canoes before we could stop them."

"But I saw you burning scalps as you left Slow Running's lodge," Dawnmarie blurted out.

"Those were Chippewa and white man scalps that Slow Running had collected through the years of his reign as chief," the warrior said, his teeth clenched in anger as he spoke.

"Lord," Dawnmarie said, trembling through and through at the thought. She felt lucky now, at least, that her father had not been scalped.

Then she gazed up at White Wolf, her eyes wavering. "Now what of those Sioux who are still alive?" she asked as Sharp Nose went and checked on the injured Chippewa. Dead or alive, those that had been downed by the Sioux were lifted and taken to the remaining Sioux canoes that lined the riverbank.

"They are now our captives," White Wolf said. "Men, women, and children, alike, will be taken to my village. We will, in time, give them over to another band of Sioux, if they will have them."

"If they will not?" Dawnmarie was afraid to ask.

"They will conform to our rules and live as Chippewa, or go away to wander alone or die," White Wolf said blandly. "Either way, it will be way better than living under the rule of Slow Running."

"Since Slow Running has escaped we still have him to worry about," Dawnmarie said as she watched the captives rounded up and marched, single file, toward the river.

"Destiny did not lead us to killing him at this time," White Wolf said, taking Dawnmarie's elbow, leading her around the strewn bodies. "But soon he will meet his end. Without his warriors, there is only so much havoc he can reek. He had best flee altogether. But being as ignorant as he is, he will come back for more. Then he will get his just punishment."

"I'm so glad he spared your life," Dawnmarie said, gazing up at him, never wanting to let him out of her sight again.

"You should not have come here with my warriors," he scolded again.

Knowing that she might have this to hear for some time to come, Dawnmarie smiled up at him. "I know," she murmured. "But I came anyhow. No one could have stopped me. I had to help free you. Please understand."

"I understand, yet still you should not have come," he mumbled tightly.

Dawnmarie nodded and smiled again, then her smile was wiped away as Star Flower stepped suddenly in the way, stopping White Wolf and Dawnmarie.

Dawnmarie cringed and had a strong urge to retch when Star Flower spat in her face. A shiver coursed across her flesh as she wiped her face clean of the sticky mucus.

She glared at Star Flower as Sharp Nose jerked the Sioux maiden away and forced her to the beach.

Star Flower was still staring at Dawnmarie as she stumbled into a canoe with the rest of the prisoners.

Untouched by Star Flower's steady stare, Dawnmarie started to move onward with White Wolf, then stopped and gaped openly at a Sioux warrior who lay dead on his back a short distance from the beach, an arrow lodged in his chest.

White Wolf also stopped and stared. "Yellow Tail," he said, surprise registering in his eyes when he noticed that it was not a Chippewa arrow that had downed him. It was Sioux!

"Slow Running must have killed him," White Wolf said thickly. "Yellow Tail must have said one last wrong thing to his chief at the wrong time."

"How horrible," Dawnmarie breathed out. "To have your own chief take your life is perhaps the worst way to die."

"He did not die without honor," White Wolf grumbled. "Slow Running dishonored himself by killing one of his own warriors."

Several warriors had retrieved the Chippewa canoes from hiding and brought them through the water to beach them alongside those occupied by Sioux captives.

White Wolf walked Dawnmarie down to the beach, then lifted her into a canoe.

She pulled a soft pelt around her shoulders as White Wolf positioned himself on the seat before her. He let the robe fall away from his shoulders, to rest around his waist, a paddle already lifted and sending the canoe out into deeper water.

"I shall doctor your wounds when we return home," Dawnmarie said, trying not to think about his embarrassing ordeal of being staked to the ground at the mercy of his enemy, unclothed. "I shall make everything all right for you, darling. You will see."

"It is for the man to make things right for the woman," he said, giving her a half frown over his shoulder. "I *will* remove the danger of Slow Running. He will slip up. He will make a wrong move. Then he will *nee-boo,* die."

Dawnmarie watched the land for movement as the canoe gently rode the waves. The moon played tricks on her eyes. Sometimes the shadows seemed to be dancing.

The limbs of the trees creaked and groaned as the wind blew against them and then there was the mournful howl of a wolf. She peered intensely at a rise of land at the side of the river. She gasped and stared at the white wolf as it stood with its eyes lifted to the moon, crying to it as though it might, in part, be human.

"Do you see?" Dawnmarie cried, pointing to the wolf as White Wolf looked at her over her shoulder. "I bet it's the same white wolf that came to me the night I was thrown from the canoe."

"It smells death tonight," White Wolf said thickly, turning his eyes toward the wolf. He admired the sleekness of the wolf's pelt. It was as white as all snows in winter. And it made him proud that it was his namesake.

"The wolf is so beautiful," she sighed.

"My mother told me that when I was born, the white wolf came to the very edge of our village," White Wolf said to her over his shoulder. "Twice I saw the wolf, on the day of my birth, and when I sought my vision at puberty. My name White Wolf came from *both* occasions."

"And so you still see it from time to time," Dawnmarie said, marveling over this.

"It is my spirit guardian," White Wolf said, nodding. "It will be with me always."

"I'm sorry you suffered losses tonight," Dawnmarie murmured. "Those who died, died valiantly rescuing you."

"They need not have died," White Wolf said tightly. "Warring has been left behind us. It does not pleasure this chief's heart to go into warring with the Sioux. It is sad my warriors were forced into it."

"How many Sioux warriors do you think escaped with Slow Running?"

"Not enough to fight off the wrath of the Chippewa, that is certain," White Wolf said, his gaze going to the shore. "They are there even now watching us. They will not wait long before showing their faces again. Slow Running is driven by many demons. They will multiply within him the longer he lives."

Demons, Dawnmarie thought to herself. She recalled how Swallow Song's body had betrayed her, clouding her sweetness. But it had nothing to do with demons, as Dawnmarie had first thought. There had to be something medically wrong, for when Swallow Song was not midst a seizure, no one could be any purer of heart and mind than her.

Dawnmarie looked over her shoulder at Sharp Nose as he commanded the canoe behind White Wolf's. For a while, during his warring time, he had probably been able to forget a wife whose body behaved strangely.

But now, he would soon have to face it again.

Chapter Forty-nine

His tears must not disturb my heart,
But who shall change the years and part
The world from every thought of pain?
                        —*Alice Meynell*

The sight of the outdoor fire at White Wolf's village spraying a brilliant color of orange against the dark heavens made Dawnmarie sigh with relief.

After the canoes were beached, the captives were taken to the center of the village and given blankets beside the outdoor fire for sleeping. Guards were posted all around them, their rifles reflecting the fire in their barrels.

The dead were seen to; their burials were set for the break of dawn.

Dawnmarie and White Wolf were finally able to go to their lodge. Woman Dancing was there, bent over the fire, tending it when they entered. She looked quickly up at them, relief flooding her eyes.

"You are safe," she cried. "You have come home to me." She embraced White Wolf and then Dawnmarie.

"Many died," White Wolf said thickly. "It is a sad night for the Chippewa."

Woman Dancing turned to White Wolf. "It is sad, yet *you* are still alive to lead your people," she murmured. "Had you died, so much faith and hope would have been lost to us all."

She placed a gentle hand on White Wolf's cheek, smiled softly up at him, then turned and shuffled toward the entranceway. "I must go now and see to those who are not as fortunate as I," she said, yet stopping again to stare at White Wolf.

Then she looked over at Dawnmarie. "I leave him in your care, Violet Eyes," she murmured. "See to his wounds with gentleness."

"I will," Dawnmarie said, smiling. Then she grew serious again, stopping Woman Dancing just before she lifted the entrance flap to leave. "Woman Dancing, you looked after Swallow Song in Sharp Nose's absence. How is she?"

"She is very worried about Sharp Nose's welfare, but other than that, she came through the night without problems," Woman Dancing said. "I held and rocked her. She is so much like a child. She behaves as though she has never had enough loving."

"Yes, I have also noticed that," Dawnmarie said softly.

Woman Dancing left.

Dawnmarie turned to White Wolf. As he gazed down at her with his midnight dark eyes, she slipped the rabbit robe from around his shoulders. "I shall make you feel much better," she said, tossing the robe aside. "Point me to your herbs. I shall prepare some medicine for your wounds."

"You know the art of herbal medicating?"

"You forget that in many ways I am more Indian than white."

"You are now Chippewa," he said, taking her to the back of the wigwam. He took several leather pouches from his store of herbs and gave them to her.

"I am Chippewa by marriage," Dawnmarie said, preparing the medicine. "But I shall never forget the

Kickapoo side of my heritage." She paused, her eyes wavering into his. "Does that anger you? Do you mind that I feel strongly about my Kickapoo heritage? It is so important that I never forsake it. My afterlife depends on it."

"Your afterlife is already taken care of," White Wolf said, stretching out on a pelt beside the fire. He closed his eyes and raised his arms above his head as her soothing fingers rubbed the herbal concoction over his flesh. "Don't you remember my belief that one's destiny is charted even before they become a seed in their mother's womb?"

"Yes, I remember," Dawnmarie murmured. "But I shall also never forget my mother's teachings about such things."

"Listen to the teachings then of both your mother and husband and you have nothing to fear of death," White Wolf said, smiling.

He wove his fingers through her hair, then placed his hands at her shoulders and urged her up next to him. "I have missed the taste of your lips, my Violet Eyes."

"Then kiss me," she whispered, leaning up so that their mouths could come together. She melted inside. She forgot the ugliness of only a short while ago when she was at the Sioux camp.

Several loud, uncontrollable screams drew them apart and to their feet.

"Swallow Song?" Dawnmarie blurted out as White Wolf quickly drew on a breechclout. "Is she having another seizure?"

They ran outside, then stopped when they saw who was making the commotion. Star Flower. She was being held between two warriors as she tried desperately to escape.

"Let me go!" she screamed. "I must find my brother! Let me go!"

White Wolf and Dawnmarie went to her. White Wolf nodded to his warriors to release their hold on her. Then he stepped closer to her. "Sioux woman, if you do not want to be tied and gagged like a true captive, then I urge you to be quiet and lay down with the rest of your people and sleep," he warned. "You have pushed my patience a last time. I did not strike you when you spat on my wife's face. But I will do worse if you continue making a disturbance that keeps my people from their rest."

"She is your wife?" Star Flower asked, looking disbelievingly at Dawnmarie. "My brother ruined all of our people's lives for a woman who was already a man's wife?"

"White Wolf is very much my husband," Dawnmarie bragged as she possessively placed an arm around White Wolf's waist.

Her eyes cast downward, her shoulders slumped, Star Flower stretched out on a blanket between two other women. "This was all for nothing," she whispered, tears splashing from her eyes. "I told him. I told my brother he was wrong. He did not listen. Now all is lost."

White Wolf and Dawnmarie stared down at Star Flower as she talked like a mindless person to herself, then went back to their lodge.

"I am bone-weary," Dawnmarie said sullenly.

"Then let us sleep," White Wolf said, guiding her to the bed of blankets. "You have medicated my wounds enough. Now let us medicate our souls.

Sleep is good for the soul. It is good, because for a while so much ugliness can be forgotten."

Dawnmarie snuggled next to White Wolf.

They clung together as they fell into a deep sleep.

Chapter Fifty

Sing little birds above our heads,
Bloom, flowers beneath her feet.
—Anonymous, nineteenth century

Swallow Song gazed down at Sharp Nose. Asleep, his head was resting on her lap. She ran her fingers gently across his brow. "My husband," she whispered. "I have never seen you so exhausted. Sleep. Sleep, my love."

In the quiet of the night, as the flames in the fire pit drew dancing shadows on the curved walls of the wigwam, Swallow Song became sullen. She closed her eyes as she recalled having a seizure in the presence of her husband. All through her lovemaking, even to the end, when she had found utter paradise within the arms of her husband, she had thought that perhaps she would be saved the humiliation of the seizure.

But fate would not allow it. How embarrassed she was when she recovered.

She had wanted to die!

"Swallow Song," Sharp Nose whispered in his sleep. "My sweet, sweet Swallow Song."

She smiled through her tears down at him. He loved her anyhow. And because he could forgive her body's weakness, she felt as though she might burst from the intenseness of her feelings for him.

"I shall always, forever, love you," she whispered back to him, although knowing he could not hear. But that was not necessary.

He knew. Even in his sleep he knew.

Doubts then filled her when she allowed her thoughts to stray to the possibility of having children. Her father had warned her against it.

But loving a man as much as she loved Sharp Nose, how could she not want to have children by him?

"We shall, my darling Chippewa," she whispered. "We shall have children."

Chapter Fifty-one

The red rose is a falcon,
And the white rose is a dove.
—John Boyle O'Reilly

Slow running stopped to get his breath. He leaned against an outcropping of rock, his warriors tumbling from weakness to the ground.

They had beached their canoes and now searched for a safe place to make camp.

Except for the nuisance of a white wolf prowling about, they felt they had found a perfect hideaway where rocks formed a half cave in the side of a hill.

"Rest, my warriors. Then tomorrow we must move onward," Slow Running said, stretching out on a blanket that one of his warriors spread for him. "But not too far. We must always stay close enough to

White Wolf's village. At our first opportunity we shall get vengeance. We shall release those who were taken captive. My sister is among them. She cannot be allowed to mate with a Chippewa!"

Chapter Fifty-two

Compare with me, ye women, if you can,
I prize thy love more than those mines of gold.
                                        —Anne Bradstreet

Dawn had banished the curling shadows of night. Smoke from the smoke holes made a gray blanket that spiraled high into the sky.

Dawnmarie was so warm and cozy midst her blankets that she had no desire to get up and begin her morning chores. She stretched and tossed to her left side before opening her eyes.

She smiled to herself when she saw White Wolf tending to the fire, sparks rising from the timbers as he lay another log across those that were already sizzling and taking flame.

Her eyes never leaving the expanse of White Wolf's sleekly muscled back, her hands reaching out to touch him, Dawnmarie quietly crept from her blankets.

Her heart raced as her hands grew closer, her insides mushy warm with need of him. Several days had passed now and the war wounds placed on his chest and brow by the Sioux were healed. The warriors who died during the attack on the Sioux village had been buried. Those who had lived grew stronger each day.

The captives were restless, the children crying most of the day, the women wailing.

Plans were made to meet and have council with a neighboring Sioux with whom White Wolf had won an alliance of peace. White Wolf was going to take the captives there. It was his deepest desire to leave them so that he could return home with a clear mind to do his chieftain duties for his *own* people.

But this was now. Except for those who tended the early fires in their own lodges, to ward off the chill of the September morning, it was the time of day when hardly anyone stirred.

It was the perfect time of day to draw warmth and love from one's husband.

Splaying her fingers against White Wolf's back, Dawnmarie laughed softly when she felt the sensuous rippling of his flesh at her very touch.

"My husband, you have tended to the fire enough," she said, now pressing her breasts against his back. She wrapped her arms around him.

"Come back to bed with me, White Wolf," Dawnmarie pleaded, sending featherings of kisses along his back.

He turned toward her and led her down onto the blankets, sucking in a wild breath of pleasure when one of her hands crept around his manhood and moved on him.

She felt him growing in length within her fingers. She ran her thumb over the tight tip of his manhood, smoothing the pearly liquid she found there into his flesh.

White Wolf's pulse raced. He closed his eyes and for a moment longer enjoyed how she was pleasuring him.

Then he reached for her hand and moved it away.

He traced her facial features with a finger. "This early in the morning, the fire casts its glow on your face. You are the most beautiful of women," he said huskily. "You are the most beautiful woman in the world."

His hands moved lower. She closed her eyes and threw her head back with ecstasy when he cupped her breasts, his thumbs circling and teasing her nipples into tight, pink crests.

When his mouth covered a breast, his tongue flicking its nipple, Dawnmarie sighed and twined her fingers through his hair to draw his face even closer. Her whole body seemed to have turned into heartbeats, throbbing sensually, aching with the wild bliss of the moment.

White Wolf's hands went to Dawnmarie's waist. Gently he shoved her down onto the bed of blankets. He knelt over her, his tongue and hands pleasuring her exquisite, satiny flesh.

His mouth browsed over her, and being loved so unhurriedly, so wondrously, Dawnmarie's insides melted away, her senses soaring.

When his lips found that place between her slim, copper thighs, where her passion was centered, and he kissed her there, she felt giddy the pleasure was so overwhelming.

Dawnmarie's hands clung to his sinewed shoulders, her head swimming with the wonder of the moment as his tongue moved on her, making her writhe and whimper tiny cries of ecstasy.

White Wolf's eyes were hollow pits of burning passion as he rose over Dawnmarie and nudged her legs apart with a knee. He twined his fingers through hers and held her hands over her head as he plunged into her pulsing cleft.

White Wolf watched Dawnmarie's expression and the hidden flames behind her eyes as her body lurched with each thrust, her eyes hazed with passion, her cheeks flushed.

And then he kissed her, his hands at her breasts, kneading, his body moving into her in a wild, dizzying rhythm.

His tongue parted her lips.

Their tongues touched, danced, and sucked.

Sweeping his arms around her, he drew her even more closely to the contours of his body. Holding her in a torrid embrace, his mouth was hot and sweet as he showered her face and neck with kisses.

"My love," Dawnmarie whispered, her voice quivering emotionally in her excitement.

Delicious shivers of desire rushed up and down her flesh. She thrilled inside when she reached around to get instant, brief touches of his manhood as he withdrew from within her, and then thrust inside her again with his powerful, manly strength.

He filled her, she gloried to herself. Oh, how magnificently he filled her. She was swirling in a storm of passion that shook her innermost senses.

White Wolf could feel the storm building within him. His mouth seared into hers with intensity, every nerve in his body tensing. His eager mouth drank from hers, tasting her sweetness. He anchored her fiercely as the blood spun through his veins, the silver flames of desire leaping higher within him.

Pausing to get his breath, and readying himself for that final plunge inside her that would fill her with his seed, White Wolf's eyes swept over her face, a drugged passion seizing him when he saw the hunger in her eyes, the beckoning.

Then he kissed her again, a kiss that stole her

breath. He made a maddening, deep thrust inside her, the silent explosion of their needs finally reached, accompanied by their sighs and groans of ecstasy.

White Wolf lay his cheek against Dawnmarie's. He caressed her center of desire as he rolled away from her. He could feel her tremor with wild bliss as he endearingly stroked her where she was still tender and hot from their lovemaking.

Moaning from pleasure as her breasts pressed into his chest, he reached for her and drew her against him. His hands moved between them and cupped her breasts. He leaned down and sucked a nipple between his teeth.

"We might never leave the lodge today if you continue with what you are doing," Dawnmarie whispered. She giggled. "My darling Chippewa chief, let us save some for tonight."

"My Violet Eyes, are you saying you do not have enough loving to last from morning 'til night?" he asked, chuckling against her lips when she brushed his mouth with soft kisses.

"I shall always have enough loving whenever, *wherever,* you desire it," Dawnmarie said, reaching down to touch that part of him that only moments ago sent her to paradise and back. She felt him tremor as she began stroking him. "And if you wish more loving this morning instead of breakfast, I am more than willing."

Voices outside as his people began emerging from their lodges for their morning chores drew White Wolf's attention. He regrettably reached for Dawnmarie's hand and slid it away from his throbbing hardness.

"We had best fill our other hunger so that this

chief can be strong enough to see to his chiefly duties," he said, smiling into her eyes. "I must go into council this morning with my warriors and elders."

He gave her another brief kiss, then rose to his feet. He slipped his fringed shirt over his head first, then stepped into his leggings.

"We have much to discuss," he said thickly. "There will be a meeting, hopefully tomorrow, with Chief Buffalo Cloud. This meeting with the Sioux chief is necessary. It is important to strengthen our relationship since my people have lost so much recently at the hand of another Sioux. *This* Sioux chief will reaffirm my people's belief that not all Sioux are bad."

Dawnmarie rose from her bed. She reached for her beautifully beaded dress and slipped it over her head. "When you go for council with Buffalo Cloud, may I go with you?" she asked as she ran her hands down the front of the dress to smooth out the wrinkles. "Otherwise I will worry every minute that you are gone. No one has any idea where Chief Slow Running is or when he might decide to reek more havoc on our lives."

"*Ay-uh,* you can accompany me there," he said softly. "I would like for you to witness that there are peaceful ways of settling things with a band of Sioux. It will be good for you to witness this."

"Your people have warred often with the Sioux," Dawnmarie said. She smiled at Woman Dancing as she entered the lodge and hung a pot of breakfast foods over the fire, then left as quickly without a word, yet leaving White Wolf and Dawnmarie warmed through and through with her pleasant smile.

"I always thought that you hated the Sioux," Dawnmarie said. "*All* Sioux."

"Too many times, *ay-uh,* the Chippewa have warred with the Sioux," White Wolf said blandly. "And warring was needed then. Too often the Sioux, even Buffalo Cloud, were guilty of such things as being too greedy. Most of those warring, greedy Sioux have been chased from this land of lakes. Buffalo Cloud and I came to terms. There is peace between us now. Slow Running was the only one who still remained a thorn in the sides of not only the Chippewa, but the Sioux and white people alike."

"Slow Running seems invincible," Dawnmarie sighed. "He is like a cat who has nine lives."

"No man is invincible," White Wolf grumbled, slipping his moccasins on. He handed Dawnmarie a hairbrush made from the quills of a porcupine. As she had these past mornings, she brushed his hair until it glistened.

He in turn then brushed hers.

She sighed with happiness as he ever so gently braided her hair into two long braids down her back. He stood tall and straight as she placed his beaded headband around his head, then tied a lone feather into a loop of hair at the back of his head.

Dawnmarie stepped around to stand before him. She placed a hand to his cheek. "My wonderful Chippewa chief, I love you so," she murmured.

He took her hand down, kissed its palm, then yanked her against his hard body. "My Violet Eyes, you stir my very soul with your sweetness," he said huskily.

He lowered his mouth to her lips and kissed her, then smiled down at her. "Perhaps it is not best to take you with me to the Sioux village to meet in council after all," he said, his eyes dancing into hers.

"Why *not?*" she asked, her chin high.

"When you are near, it is hard not to kiss or touch you," he said. "My thoughts will be channeled from the discussion at hand to *you.*"

Dawnmarie's lips parted, then his laughter proved that he had only been jesting about not taking her. But she didn't mind. She loved this lighthearted side of him. She took his hand and led him beside the fire with her.

"I think we should eat," she said, her eyes twinkling. She reached for two wooden bowls and spoons. After ladling food into both their bowls, she sat back and ate hungrily.

"Have you heard the tale about how the squirrel got his stripes?" White Wolf asked, between bites of the hearty breakfast of scrambled fried rabbit and eggs.

"I don't believe so," Dawnmarie said. "My mother told me many stories, but not that one. Please tell me." She scooped another large bite of food into her mouth.

He finished his meal. Feeling comfortably full and warm inside, he shoved his bowl aside. He moved to his haunches and laid more wood on the fire.

"The ground squirrel got his stripes because he said that a good man was his arch enemy," he said, smiling over at her. "Man and other animals scratched the ground squirrel's back in anger. From thereon he had the stripe. It is a brand of sorts."

Dawnmarie laughed softly. She shoved her empty bowl aside and went and climbed onto his lap. She twined an arm around his neck. "Tell me more," she murmured. "These moments with you are so special. I shall never forget them."

"It is good to teach you, as I will also teach our children," White Wolf said, smoothing a fallen lock of her hair back from her brow. "I will tell our sons and our daughters about the deer and the skunk."

"What about them?" Dawnmarie asked, her thoughts straying to his mention of children. She thrilled inside to be even more sure now that she was with child. She had just not been sure enough until these past few days, sure enough at least to share this marvelous secret with White Wolf.

She had confided in Swallow Song.

Swallow Song had, in turn, shared her own secret with Dawnmarie, that she, too, thought she might be with child.

Dawnmarie had wanted to be happy for Swallow Song and Sharp Nose. But she could not help but worry that the seizures might be passed on to the child.

"The antler of a young deer is considered a valuable charm," White Wolf said, drawing Dawnmarie's thoughts back to him. "The skunk, with its odor, is considered important in keeping diseases away from people."

"Is that myth or truth?" Dawnmarie asked, eyes wide.

"It is hard to tell myth from truth most times," White Wolf said, chuckling. Then he saw the seriousness in her eyes and in the way she gazed at him. "Why do you ask?"

"It would be wonderful if we could find a way to charm away the terrible disease that plagues Swallow Song," Dawnmarie blurted, then flung herself into his arms and held him tight. "Hold me, darling. We have so much to be thankful for."

White Wolf realized the truth in her words. He gently caressed her back, hearing the laughter of Swallow Song as she walked outside with Sharp Nose, perhaps on their way to the river for their morning swim and bath.

He wished he *did* know of a way to make the world perfect for his friends.

As it was, he had never felt as helpless. This was something way beyond his power as chief to find answers for.

Chapter Fifty-three

*We loved with a love that
was more than love.*
        —Edgar Allan Poe

The very next day the council fire burned high and bright in the gray noonday light. Clouds hung low in the sky as those in council at the Sioux village sat in a wide circle around the fire. Dawnmarie sat proudly beside White Wolf, Sharp Nose also there on his other side.

Dawnmarie felt the absence of Swallow Song who was not with her husband. It saddened her to know that Swallow Song had been plagued by another seizure late last night. Woman Dancing was with her now, giving her the special caring only she knew how to give.

Dawnmarie looked past the council circle, at the Sioux captives who were huddled together. Their heads were ashamedly hung as they listened to White Wolf offer them to Chief Buffalo Cloud, a young Sioux who perhaps matched White Wolf's age of thirty winters.

Her attention returned to the council. She watched
White Wolf pass a "talking stick" to Buffalo Cloud.
While on their way to Buffalo Cloud's village White
Wolf had explained the meaning of the "talking
sticks" to her. The sticks were passed from one person to the next, allowing each person, in turn, to
speak their point of view, and only the person holding the stick was allowed to talk.

Everyone's point of view was considered sacred
and was recognized to be so and was never
interrupted.

The "answering feather" was also held by the person who was speaking, unless the speaker asked a
question of another council member. The "answering
feather" was then passed to the person being
queried.

White Wolf had explained that the "talking stick"
brought specific medicine to the council, the symbol
for seeing clearly while others may represent peace,
truth, strength, gentleness, and wisdom.

The colors of the stick had meaning. Gray stood
for friendship and knowledge. Black stood for
harmony.

The feathers and hide on the sticks were important, also. Each creature they had been taken
from had its own medicine and contributed to the
medicine of the "talking stick." The rabbit fur handle
represented the ability to listen. The horse hair, dyed
green, red, and blue, brought perseverance and
added a connection with the earth and to the spirits
of the wind. Deer antlers imparted gentleness.
Leather brought about abundance.

White Wolf had told her that through listening we
are taught life has millions of options and answers
to any predicament. When even a whisper is spoken

across the wind, someone's point of view is being sent for a listener to learn from.

"And so you say you took these captives from Chief Slow Running's encampment?" Buffalo Cloud asked, his legs crossed at his ankles, his hands resting on his knees.

"*Ay-uh,* that is so," White Wolf said guardedly, his jaw tightening.

Buffalo Cloud gave the captives a wavering look. His gaze stopped on one captive in particular and lingered. She was the only one who was defying the Chippewa warrior who stood at her side, holding her immobile by a wrist.

Buffalo Cloud saw much fire in this young woman's eyes as she kept trying to wrench her wrist free. He knew her. He had always admired her wild spirit. He had always silently admired her beauty. He had been interested in her the first time he saw her many moons ago.

But because of who her brother was, more enemy than friend to Buffalo Cloud, he had not pursued her as a love interest.

But now?

Even though Slow Running was still alive he was no longer in control of his people's lives, especially his sister's. This gave Buffalo Cloud free rein to approach Star Flower.

He would tame her. He would make her his wife.

Buffalo Cloud looked at White Wolf again. "And what was your reason for the attack on Slow Running's camp?" he asked, not visibly disturbed by the fact that the Chippewa had attacked another band of Sioux.

"I, myself, did not lead this attack against Slow Running," White Wolf said, his jaw tightening. "I was his captive. My warriors came to my rescue. In doing so, they were forced into a fight which left many dead and injured, both Sioux and Chippewa."

White Wolf gestured with a wave of a hand toward the women and children and the few warriors who stood with their heads bowed as they were being discussed. "The Sioux captives were treated well at my village," he said thickly. "But it is not a normal thing for my band of Chippewa to take, much less keep, captives."

He dropped his hand and folded his arms across his chest as he locked eyes with Buffalo Cloud. "I offer you the captives," he said, watching how Buffalo Cloud's eyes roamed more than once to Star Flower. "Will you take them into your camp, to be one with your people?"

Buffalo Cloud kneaded his chin, his thoughts once again on Slow Running. "Their chief is still alive, is he not?" he then asked.

"*Bee-mah-dee-zee*, alive, but without power to lead," White Wolf said, slowly smiling. "And let me say this, Buffalo Cloud. Slow Running's interests do not lie with his people as much as with *neen*, self. I do not believe he will attempt taking them back. He is, as I see it, glad to be free of his responsibility of them."

White Wolf gave Dawnmarie a wavering glance, then frowned over at Buffalo Cloud. "If anyone must keep guards at the fringes of their villages, it is the Chippewa," he said, his voice drawn. "As long as Slow Running is alive he is a threat to my wife and to my people as a whole." He firmed his jaw and lifted his chin. "He will not be a threat for long. This chief will see that his end comes soon."

"I understand the wrong Slow Running has done

many people," Buffalo Cloud said, sighing. "The world will be a better place without him. Warring makes one's soul weary. I watched my father and my grandfather before him and what warring against the Chippewa did to them. They both died way before their time. Although some see us as enemies, White Wolf, because we are from the opposite tribes who fought one another for hunting and trapping grounds, it is good that we have found a measure of peace between us."

"I feel the same," White Wolf said, almost humbly. "Fighting only takes away fathers and husbands who are necessary providers for our families."

"Come," Buffalo Cloud said, motioning with a hand. "Sit closer beside me. Let us first be entertained by 'friendship drums,' let us share the moccasin game, and then a smoke. It is good that we have a peaceful way of settling disputes between us."

Buffalo Cloud rose and motioned with a hand toward one of his warriors. When the warrior came and stood before him, Buffalo Cloud clasped his hands on his shoulders. "Take the captives and see that they are fed," he said, his glance shifting smoothly to Star Flower. "Except for one, that is. Bring Star Flower to me. She will join the council. She will feast as we feast."

Dawnmarie rose beside White Wolf and walked with him toward Buffalo Cloud. She watched with much interest as Star Flower was taken to the Sioux chief. It amazed her how Star Flower became quickly humble in the Sioux chief's towering presence.

Dawnmarie looked over at Buffalo Cloud, never having noticed just how handsome he was. Now she understood why Star Flower seemed in awe of him.

He had singled her out, more than likely, for his woman.

"Do you want me to sit with you?" Star Flower asked, her voice lilting as she gazed up at Buffalo Cloud.

"I have watched you from afar often," Buffalo Cloud said, running a hand down the full length of her coal-black hair. "What I saw pleased my eyes. To have you this near pleases my *heart*. Will you feast with me? Will you go with me to my lodge tonight? I have searched long for a perfect woman who will fill my lodge with sunshine."

"Am I that woman?" Star Flower asked, searching his eyes for answers.

"I believe so," Buffalo Cloud said, chuckling. He placed a gentle hand to her elbow and led her down on a blanket beside him. He nodded a welcome as White Wolf and Dawnmarie sat on his other side as people made room for them.

Dawnmarie and Star Flower exchanged heated glances. Then their attention was drawn to the sound of drums suddenly being played midst the circle.

Dawnmarie knew the meaning of these particular drums. She had listened to them being discussed while Indians traded at her father's trading post. They were called "friendship drums."

These drums stressed alliances between groups of peoples and peace and friendship. One of these drums would be given to White Wolf at the end of the council.

As everyone politely listened to the performance of the drums, Dawnmarie admirably gazed at them. They were very large, over two feet in diameter and a foot in thickness. They were made from iron tubs with a large circular hole cut in the bottom of the tub and thick moose skin drum heads fastened on each end.

Inside the drum, a little bell was strung across the top just under the head. When the head was struck, the bell jingled, adding another sound. The drums hung from four curved sticks, much like shepherd's crooks turned outward.

The drums were decorated with a skirt of red velvet covering the outside. Narrow blue trim and a band of otter fur went around the drums at the rim. Below the fur, a wide band of beadwork encircled the rims with four pocket-shaped beaded tabs suspended from it.

Feathers, ribbon streamers, and silver discs were also used for decoration. An important mark of the "friendship drums" was a broad yellow stripe painted down the middle of the upper head. Above the stripe, the head was painted blue. Below, it was painted red. These colors were symbolic of dark and light, cold and warm seasons.

A young brave brought a pipe to Buffalo Cloud. Dawnmarie admired the pipe. It was made of wood with a long, flat stem, hung with feathers and decorated with paint, beadwork, and quillwork.

Today the Sioux chief did not use the usual brand of tobacco used by most Sioux. He graciously used the tobacco that White Wolf had given to him as a gift. This tobacco was made from the inner bark of the red dogwood, sometimes referred to as the "red willow." The outside bark of a twig was removed with the thumbnail and the remaining layer of bark, when carefully shaven off, served as *kinnikinnick,* tobacco.

Another young Sioux brave brought a burning twig and set it to the tobacco. After only inhaling once, the pipe was lit. The brave placed the twig into the outdoor fire, then joined the other young braves who were readying to perform as dancers.

Buffalo Cloud handed the pipe to White Wolf who took several puffs. The smoke from the tobacco carried the word of peace shared between two bands of Indians to the Great Spirit.

He then sent the pipe around the circle until all of the Sioux and Chippewa braves had partaken in a smoke, the women only momentarily touching the pipe as they passed it on down the line to the next warrior.

A young brave came and got the pipe from Buffalo Cloud as it came back to him. Almost meditatingly, the pipe was laid before Buffalo Cloud, the stem pointing his way as he nodded toward the dancers, giving them a silent command to begin.

As the many grandfather pines in the nearby forest sang and swayed in the wind, deerskin moccasins moved to the heartbeat of the drums. It was known to everyone that each child made their own costumes with help from their family. From the moment they could walk the children were taught songs and dances and encouraged to participate at an early age.

These young dancers wore various outfits made by their own ingenuity and hands. Some wore beaded eagle headbands with a single feather. The leather strips that hung from the headband were tipped with eagle plumes.

Some of their braids were decorated with conch shells and beaded rosettes. Some wore breastplates made from bones, beads, fur, and sinew while others wore porcupine broaches, beaded wristbands, and ribbon shirts.

Each wore his costume proudly as they whirled

and stamped and bounced in time with the drum's beats.

The crowd watching broke into a low chanting, some moving into singing, others quietly nodding their heads and clapping.

Dawnmarie felt herself drawn into the moment. She slowly swayed her shoulders back and forth, her insides bubbling from happiness. At this moment everything seemed magically wonderful, except for two things she could not shake from her mind: Swallow Song and Sharp Nose's shared trauma.

Also Slow Running was out there somewhere, surely making plans to interfere in the lives of White Wolf's people again.

Other than that, Dawnmarie felt as though things were finally becoming right in her world. Soon she would be with her mother again. They would travel to the Kickapoo village where they would both be acquainted with their true heritage.

She smiled as she turned her gaze to White Wolf. He was the most precious of her blessings. He, and . . .

She paused and slipped one of her hands over her abdomen. He and their baby who was growing inside her womb.

The dancing came to a halt. Dawnmarie watched two young Sioux braves lay four moccasins and four smooth bones, one of which was marked with two crosses carved on opposite sides, before White Wolf and Buffalo Cloud. The moccasins consisted of four oval-shaped pieces of blue serge about the size of a man's hand, lined with brown cloth, and hand-sewn about the edges. The serge was the upper side.

They were going to play the moccasin game, which was like shoe gambling. On her way to the village White Wolf had told Dawnmarie they would be play-

ing this game, and that he and Buffalo Cloud had
played it since their very first council.

He had explained to her that if two bands of warriors faced each other and the outcome of warring
could only mean the death of many, they chose a
different way of settling the dispute.

Although there was no more warring between
White Wolf and Buffalo Cloud, it was a routine thing
now to continue playing the moccasin game when
they met in council. It was a simple challenge, a time
of camaraderie.

Other items were laid before the two chiefs: a
switch of the hazelnut bush, used in designating the
moccasin under which the marked bone was hidden;
twenty knitting needlelike sticks of wood used in
paying the penalty for wrong choices; and ten small
slabs of cedar wood, pointed at one end so that they
could easily be planted in the ground.

The small slabs were counted and each represented twenty of the small knitting needlelike sticks,
their total making up the final score and showing the
winning side.

Since he was Buffalo Cloud's guest, White Wolf
was the first to hide the bones. He performed many
amusing gestures with his arms and hands, following
the rhythm of the drums and the songs. The drumbeats, songs, and gestures were intended to confuse
the opposing person whose turn it was to find the
marked bone.

When White Wolf had the bones all hidden, he
clapped his hands.

Buffalo Cloud whipped the ground slightly with
his stick, then finally slapped the moccasin under the
one he suspected was hiding the marked bone. Be-

fore doing so, however, he could uncover two of the moccasins, if he so wished.

His choice was undeniably indicated by the decided manner in which he slapped the moccasin. A wrong choice was penalized by passing a knitting needlelike stick to the opposite side. A bundle of twenty sticks was used to keep score, and a stick was given for each correct guess.

The game continued until it was obvious that White Wolf was the winner. None of the Sioux seemed bothered or surprised by their chief losing. Never had he won against White Wolf.

Buffalo Cloud moved to his feet, and White Wolf rose beside him, smiling.

"You are the winner again," Buffalo Cloud said, good-naturedly reaching a hand out for White Wolf. "But I still won't give up. We will play again when we meet in council."

"We both are winners in the moccasin game," White Wolf said, clasping Buffalo Cloud's hand. "Because we play a nonwarlike game, our people live, not die."

"That is so," Buffalo Cloud said, smiling at Dawnmarie as she rose to White Wolf's side. "Your husband is clever in many ways, Dawnmarie."

"Violet Eyes," White Wolf was quick to correct. "She is now called Violet Eyes."

"And so she should be," Buffalo Cloud said, openly admiring Dawnmarie's eyes. He looked suddenly to his left side when he felt a soft hand on his arm.

He smiled down at Star Flower and slipped a possessive arm around her waist, then turned his gaze back to White Wolf. "Today I have won something more important than a mere moccasin game," he said, squaring his shoulders. "This woman whom I have held within my heart for many moons. You have brought her to me. This special gift outshines all others that I have ever gotten in my lifetime."

Shivers ran up and down Dawnmarie's spine when Star Flower gave her a smug smile. This smugness filled Dawnmarie with a warning. She knew that men could be persuaded to listen to women they loved. Women could work mischief with their minds. Could Star Flower, hating White Wolf and Dawnmarie so much, cause Buffalo Cloud's heart to harden toward the Chippewa again?

Dawnmarie was glad when food was brought on trays and placed on the ground near the outdoor fire. She sat down with White Wolf and ate, but only halfheartedly.

She could not get her suspicions of Star Flower off her mind.

Chapter Fifty-four

The angels, not half so happy in Heaven,
Went envying her and me.
                    —*Edgar Allan Poe*

The council was over. It had been a good one, hearts warmed with renewed friendships. Dusk was falling as the canoes moved smoothly down the river. Everything was serene, the world touched by a glorious sunset.

Dawnmarie clutched a robe around her shoulders as she sat in the canoe behind White Wolf. Her thoughts ran through the day's activities, and she smiled when she recalled how nobly her husband presented himself in council. Who wouldn't be pulled into liking him?

She grabbed the sides of the canoe, her robe tumbling from her shoulders, when White Wolf suddenly steered his canoe away from a huge pile of debris floating in the middle of the river.

Frowning, Dawnmarie caught her balance as she eyed the debris. Something occurred to her, but she did not have time to warn White Wolf that this tangle of limbs seemed too man-made to have come together on its own.

Before she could speak, arrows shot past her and gunfire broke out along the shore.

"Ambush!" White Wolf shouted, his arms moving like streaks of lightning as he guided his canoe past the ambush point.

He and his warriors were forced to beach their canoes as more debris came into sight. The narrow passage on the one side of the rubble of limbs and freshly cut trees was not large enough for the canoes to pass through.

"Hear me well, my woman," White Wolf shouted at Dawnmarie as he grabbed his rifle from the canoe. "You must hide yourself midst the bushes behind those trees over there!"

He took her by the hand and ran with her into hiding. He kissed her brow, gave her a lingering stare, then left again.

Her heart pounding, her throat dry, Dawnmarie watched White Wolf, Sharp Nose, and the other warriors move stealthily through the forest toward the spot of the ambush.

Afraid of what might happen to her husband in the next few minutes, Dawnmarie wished that she had a firearm. She felt way too helpless and vulnerable without one.

She clasped and unclasped her hands nervously when she heard the renewed outburst of gunfire and then the war cries. All of the combined sounds tore at Dawnmarie's heart. She covered her ears with her hands and lifted her eyes heavenward.

"Please keep him alive," she begged her Great Spirit. "He is all that is good on this earth. Don't take him to the spirit world. Give him more time to spread peace and friendship among the neighboring tribes and among the white people. Most importantly, do not take him from *me*."

Unable to stand not being with White Wolf, Dawnmarie ran from her hiding place. She followed the sounds of the warring, knowing Slow Running was responsible for the attack.

"Let him die, instead," Dawnmarie whispered, again looking heavenward. "He is all that is *evil* on this earth. Take him! If someone must die, let it be Slow Running!"

Breathless and unable to see well now that the sun had dropped fully out of sight along the horizon, Dawnmarie stopped running.

She peered intensely through a break in the trees a short distance away and gasped when she discovered just how close she was to the site of the battle. She also realized that no more weapons were being fired.

Everything was quiet.

Her eyes frantically searched those who were still standing, and those kneeling over the wounded or dead in the clearing.

Her heartbeats faltered when she saw White Wolf kneeling beside someone on the ground.

Oh, yes, she was so wondrously happy that White Wolf had come through this ambush alive.

But, oh, Lord, she did not want to look at the person who had fallen, obviously severely injured as blood poured from a wound in his chest.

"No," she sobbed, shaking her head. "Please not Sharp Nose. Please ... not ... Sharp Nose."

Emotions swelled inside her as she ran and knelt down beside White Wolf. Tears splashed from her eyes as she reached for one of Sharp Nose's hands while he lay there gasping for breath.

He turned his dark, pain-hazed eyes to Dawnmarie. "Be Swallow Song's friend forever," he managed to say. "She needs you." He looked up at White Wolf. "Please watch out for her. She ... needs ... much loving and understanding."

"*You* will be there for her," White Wolf said thickly, pressing a strip of buckskin against the wound, trying to stop the blood flow.

White Wolf turned desperate, anxious eyes up to those warriors who had lived through the ambush. "Go and remove the debris from the water!" he shouted. "Make room for the passing of our canoes! With speed, my warriors, make room for the passage of our canoes!"

His eyes wavered as he looked around him, and at those of his warriors who had not lived through the ordeal, or who were wounded.

Dawnmarie followed his gaze. She felt sick inside to know that only moments ago these warriors had been happy, their hearts filled with peace after the council.

How quickly that had changed.

"We owe this all to one evil man," White Wolf said, his gaze stopping farther than where his warriors lay. A slow smile quavered across his lips. "But he is now dead, never to alter history for my people again!"

Dawnmarie's eyes widened and her heart stood still for a moment when she followed his gaze and discovered who he was looking at. "Slow Running!" she gasped. She looked quickly over at White Wolf. "Is he dead? Truly dead?"

"So are the Sioux who sent death and injury to my warriors today," White Wolf said. "They have paid with their lives."

He turned his gaze down at Sharp Nose again and placed a gentle hand to his brow. "My friend, we were as *neekaunssidag,* brothers. You are my best friend in the world. What could I have done to have avoided this?" he said, his voice breaking. "Where did I go wrong?"

Sharp Nose reached a weak, trembling hand to take White Wolf's hand in his. "Never blame yourself," he said, blood spewing from his mouth as he stopped to cough. "Did we not enter all skirmishes and decisions together that had to do with Slow Running? There was nothing else that could have been done. He was evil, through and through. I die willingly if it means that he is gone from this earth."

White Wolf slipped his hand free. He swept his arms beneath Sharp Nose and lifted him slowly from the ground. He nodded to Dawnmarie. "Hold the strip of buckskin over his wound as I carry him to my canoe," he said softly. He looked over his shoulder as the others were lifted from the ground, some lifeless, others groaning with pain.

Dawnmarie nodded and walked slowly beside White Wolf as he carried Sharp Nose from the battle scene. Her heart ached as she heard the rattle sounds in the depths of his throat, his eyes closed now to the pain.

She understood what those rattles meant. She had heard them once before when a trapper had died from a gunshot wound after a small skirmish with Slow Running's Sioux. He was brought to her father's trading post. There was nothing anyone could do for him. He died only a matter of hours after having arrived there.

Death rattles, she thought with dread. Knowing that Sharp Nose was truly dying, she cried anew. When she thought of Swallow Song and how she would soon be widowed, it tore her with sadness.

Her eyes wavered as she gazed at Sharp Nose again. Such a gentle, caring man did not deserve to die.

And she felt guilty and selfish at this moment. When she had prayed to her Great Spirit, she prayed only for her husband and herself. Why hadn't she thought to include Sharp Nose in her prayer? Could that have helped?

They finally reached the canoes. White Wolf gently placed Sharp Nose on the soft pelts at the bottom of his vessel. Dawnmarie scrambled into the canoe and sat beside Sharp Nose. She lay his head on her lap, her hand devotedly keeping his wound covered with the cloth. Even so, the blood bubbled around it, soaking into his buckskin shirt like a sponge.

The waterway was cleared enough now for the canoes to pass through with the injured and dead. The downhearted drove their canoes past the debris, the canoes moving like missiles through the water.

The moon was bright overhead.

Suddenly from across the way came the mournful

song of a *mong*, lune, echoing ... echoing ... echoing.

It seemed to match the mournful beat of White Wolf's and Dawnmarie's hearts.

Chapter Fifty-five

My friend of friends, whom I shall miss,
He is not banished, though for this—
Nor he, nor sadness, nor delight.
                                   —Alice Meynell

In the sky great eagles dipped their beaks to the earth, their wings producing powerful whirring winds. Near the shore on the far side of the river, flocks of ducks swam, dove, and quacked loudly, their din and clatter carrying across the water.

Silence fell in a deadly gloom throughout the Chippewa village as White Wolf's people watched the arrival of their warriors' canoes. Chants and mournful cries filled the air as they ran toward the river, the sight of their fallen loved ones lying on the floors of the canoes filling them with grief and despair.

Swallow Song half stumbled along with the others, her eyes misting over with tears when she realized that Sharp Nose was not among those sitting in their canoes. A warrior she did not recognize manned her husband's canoe.

But where was her husband? Her eyes moved frantically from canoe to canoe, stopping suddenly on White Wolf's as he beached his on the sandy shore. Dawnmarie was tending to a wounded warrior in White Wolf's canoe.

A frenzied dread soared through Swallow Song as Dawnmarie looked up at her with such pity in her eyes.

"Tell me it is not my husband!" Swallow Song cried, reaching her hands out toward White Wolf as he came to her and grabbed her into his arms.

White Wolf held her away from him, steady as he peered down at her. "We were ambushed," he said, his voice drawn, his eyes wavering into hers. "Swallow Song, your husband lies in my canoe, a mortal wound in his chest. His time on this earth is short. You stay here. I will bring him to you. You must say your final words to him in haste."

Swallow Song's shoulders began to sway as her eyes closed in an almost faint.

White Wolf drew her fully into his arms. "Swallow Song," he whispered into her ear. "This is not the time to be weak. Your husband needs you. Will yourself to be strong enough to last through your last good-byes."

Her head spinning, her heart throbbing, Swallow Song listened, yet did not want to hear what was being said to her. How could she have found paradise on earth only to have it taken from her? How could she go on without Sharp Nose? He was her savior, the very reason for her to breathe!

White Wolf gripped Swallow Song's shoulders. He held her away from him. "Swallow Song, you must listen to what I say," he said, his voice firm. "Be strong. Do you hear me? Be . . . strong."

Swallow Song wiped tears from her eyes with the back of her hand. She nodded and gazed up at White Wolf. "Please bring my husband to me," she said, stifling sobs at the base of her throat. "I . . . will . . . try my hardest . . . to . . . be strong."

White Wolf stared at her questioningly for a moment longer, then turned and went back to his canoe. He first lifted Dawnmarie from the vessel and placed her on her feet on the silken sand. Then he eased Sharp Nose into his arms and carried him slowly toward Swallow Song.

Swallow Song's knees almost buckled when she saw the severity of her husband's wound, and the blood that had clotted on his clothes.

Dawnmarie went quickly to Swallow Song and braced her midst her arms and led her to the ground as White Wolf lay Sharp Nose on thick, cushiony tufts of grass. The blood no longer flowed from his wound. His eyes were closed, his color a pasty, gray pallor.

"My husband, my husband," Swallow Song wailed, taking one of his hands, kissing its palm.

She winced when she heard the death rattles. From this she knew that she was losing her Sharp Nose. She knew that these last moments with him were critical.

"Please look at me, Sharp Nose," she pleaded. "Please let me know that you are aware that I am here."

His fingers stirred against her hand, then slowly entwined around it.

She sucked in a breath of relief and forced a smile when he opened his eyes and looked up at her.

"*Neen mee-kah-way-diz-ee-ee gee-wee-oo,* my beautiful wife," Sharp Nose managed in a whisper. He coughed. Blood curled from the corners of his lips. He clasped harder to his wife's hand when he saw tears fill her eyes. "I will always love you, my little one. Remember, we have vowed our love one for another for eternity. Never forget. Remember that."

"Yes," she murmured. "For eternity."

"This husband of yours is not on this earth for long now, but I will watch and look over you from the spirit world in the heavens," Sharp Nose said, each word a labored one.

"Please do not die," Swallow Song sobbed, a desperation rising inside her as she felt the last minutes of his life slipping away. "Sharp Nose, I am with child. I promise to give you a boy child if you promise not to die. I will also promise that our son will not have seizures."

"A *ah-bee-no-gee,* child," Sharp Nose said, tears filling his eyes as he released her hand and placed it on her abdomen. "A *gee-wee-gance,* boy child. I could have taught him so many things." He looked up at White Wolf. He gestured with a trembling hand for him to come closer to him.

Dawnmarie knelt with White Wolf on Sharp Nose's other side. Sharp Nose placed a hand on White Wolf's shoulder. "My friend, you are the brother I never had," he said thickly. "My memories go with me to the spirit world. I shall cherish them. They will keep me warm. Look after my wife. Please teach my child as I would."

Sharp Nose glanced up at Dawnmarie. "Beautiful woman," he said, reaching his hand over to her face, to gently touch it. "Keep my friend White Wolf happy. Help my wife through the coming days, weeks, and months."

Dawnmarie nodded. She blinked tears from her eyes as Sharp Nose once again looked up at White Wolf.

"My friend," he said, his voice quickly failing him.

'A year from this day, the day that I die, when it is again *dag-waagi*, fall of the west, go to my favorite praying place. Bring my wife and child and your wife. Once there, do not talk. Do not move. Just wait and I will meet you there."

Sharp Nose paused and sucked in a desperate, shallow breath, then spoke again. This time his voice was scarcely discernible. "White Wolf, I will come only once to my favorite praying place," he said. "Next year, on this same day I died. Come. Wait and I will meet you there. You will know it is me. I wish to see you all one last time. That then will be our final farewell."

"We will be there," White Wolf said, his heart skipping a beat as Sharp Nose stopped breathing, his eyes locked in a death stare on White Wolf's face.

With trembling fingers, White Wolf reached and lowered Sharp Nose's lashes over his eyes. "He . . . is . . . gone," he said, fighting back the urge to cry to the heavens, to ask *why?*

But his thoughts were taken elsewhere when Swallow Song fainted. He was grateful that she had lasted as long as she had.

White Wolf gave instructions for Sharp Nose to be taken to his lodge. White Wolf then carried Swallow Song to his own lodge.

Dawnmarie sat down on the floor beside the fire pit, Swallow Song's head resting in her lap. Numb from having lost such a special friend, Dawnmarie slowly stroked Swallow Song's brow, feeling only half there; the other half of her seemed to be elsewhere, in a world of nonbelief.

"Do not despair so much over Sharp Nose's passing," White Wolf said throatily as he knelt down beside Dawnmarie. "Think of the brighter side of his death and you can accept it much easier. Don't you realize that the storm of Sharp Nose's life is over? He is now at peace. It is not momentary peace that can be disrupted by those who have evil in their hearts. His is an everlasting peace. He is even now walking the road to the hereafter. Can you not see that smile on his face? I can see it. I can feel it. That is what shall sustain me during the burial rites of my friend. Let it also sustain you, my Violet Eyes."

"It just isn't fair," Dawnmarie said, gazing down at Swallow Song, wondering about her future.

Then she froze inside when Swallow Song awakened only long enough to go into one of her seizures.

Dawnmarie held Swallow Song in her arms, then had to release her and lay her on the floor when this seizure became so violent, it seemed to last an eternity.

And then it was over. Swallow Song went quickly into a deep sleep instead of waking up to the realization of what she had just gone through as her body once more betrayed her.

Woman Dancing came into the lodge. "I shall sit with Swallow Song," she offered softly. "Go, my little ones. Sit by the river. Be away from your sorrows for a while. Tomorrow they will return twofold when we bury so many of our beloved warriors."

Sighing heavily, White Wolf nodded. He reached a hand out for Dawnmarie. She rose to his side. They stopped only long enough to slip into thick rabbit robes. Then they left the lodge and walked down to the river and sat down on the sand.

"It is the worst of days," White Wolf grumbled. "I hope to never relive it."

"You won't have to," Dawnmarie murmured. "Slow Running is dead."

"There are more Slow Runnings in this world," White Wolf said, glowering over at her. "I only hope they are far, far away from this land of lakes."

Dawnmarie recalled Star Flower's mocking look. If she was able to sway Buffalo Cloud's opinion, he might become the same sort of man as Slow Running.

She cast the thought aside. It was too troubling.

"And Swallow Song is with *child*," White Wolf suddenly blurted out. "Swallow Song carries Sharp Nose's child? What of *its* future? He will be without a father's guidance."

"You are here for the child," Dawnmarie said, taking his hand, hugging it to her bosom as she turned on her knees to face him. "And, my darling, while you are teaching that child the ways of his Chippewa father, perhaps you could also teach *ours*."

White Wolf's lips parted in a soft gasp. "Are you saying that a child is growing inside you?" he asked, his eyes suddenly wide and bright as he stared down at her in wonder.

"*Ay-uh*," she said, giggling softly.

White Wolf drew her into his arms and held her tightly. "Much of my world was taken away today," he said, his face burrowed into the sweet fragrance of her hair. "To know that we will soon have a child makes the sorrow not as heavy inside my heart."

"Nor mine," Dawnmarie whispered, clinging.

Chapter Fifty-six

White his shroud as the mountain snow,
Lorded with sweet flowers;
Which bewept to the grave did go,
With true-love showers.
—Shakespeare

The sky was as dark as black marble. No moon shone, and no stars flickered their miniature lanterns in the heavens. Since the warriors had been brought home to be laid to rest among their ancestors, the drumming in White Wolf's village had not stopped.

The sound of the steady *tum-tum* of the drums could be heard across the lake and river.

It seeped through the walls of the wigwams.

"*Aaaayee, eeeeyae,*" came the constant chanting, accompanying the drums that would continue even long after the burials of the fallen loved ones.

White Wolf's face was black with ash, the color of mourning. He had started his duties to his fallen friend before the sun rose so that before sunset of this same day Sharp Nose would be properly buried in the burial grounds of the Lac du Flambeau Indians, tucked away on a hill overlooking Flambeau Lake.

Tending to his duties to his friend, while Dawnmarie and Woman Dancing looked after Swallow Song, White Wolf worked with much emotion by the faint light of the fire in Sharp Nose's lodge. He braided his friend's hair and slowly and meditatingly washed his body.

Before rigor mortis had set in, White Wolf had flexed Sharp Nose's body into the position needed for burial, with his knees pulled toward his chest, his arms extended straight down on each side of him.

It was the custom of the Chippewa to bury their dead in this way. It seemed only befitting that people should leave this earth in the same position in which they had come into it, the position they were in while in their mother's womb.

This made dressing Sharp Nose more difficult, but with much care and affection White Wolf placed Sharp Nose in his best clothing adorned with his favorite beadwork and moccasins.

This done, White Wolf went to Sharp Nose's store of personal belongings. Tears shining in the corners of his eyes, he went through Sharp Nose's possessions and chose the personal articles that his friend had favored most: his rifle, his pouch of tobacco and pipe, and the tiny bow that his father had made for him when he had been only old enough to shoot arrows into crickets instead of larger animals.

White Wolf handled the tiny bow delicately, studying the intricate designs that had been carved into it. Sharp Nose had cherished this bow after the death of his father many moons ago.

These things in place, White Wolf had one last thing to do. He purposely left one lock of hair free of Sharp Nose's braids at the back of his head.

Slipping his knife from the sheath at his waist, White Wolf slowly cut off the lock of hair. He slipped his knife back inside its sheath, then reached for a tiny piece of birch bark.

With care he wrapped the hair with the birch bark. This was for Swallow Song's "spirit bundle." He would give it to her and she would bring the spirit bundle to the fire ceremonies on the three nights of Sharp Nose's soul's journey to the hereafter.

She would then keep the "spirit bundle" with her forever. At meal times she would place food before it, and at night she would place it in her bed beside her.

After laying the "spirit bundle" aside, White Wolf wrapped Sharp Nose and his possessions in sheets of birchbark, held in position by tied cords of basswood fiber.

This done, he notified everyone that he was ready to proceed with the burial rites. But first he knelt down beside the bundle in which his friend lay so quietly. He lowered his head humbly. It was the custom that immediately preceding the removal of a body from their lodge, relatives spoke to it.

Sharp Nose took the time now to speak with his friend in private. This was something between them. No one else. Swallow Song would have her moments soon. This was White Wolf and Sharp Nose's moments, when friends shared company one last time before burial.

"Sharp Nose, as your spirit soars overhead, awaiting burial so that you can then be free to walk that wondrous road to the hereafter, listen to what I have to say and hold it dear and close to your heart," White Wolf said softly, tears splashing from his eyes.

"No one could have fit into my heart and life as a best friend but you," he murmured. "No one will ever replace you. Our bond will stay intact and will continue when I join you in the spirit world."

White Wolf cleared his throat. "I will carry my memories of our times together always. They will sustain me when I feel sad over not having you at my side on the hunt. When I fish by torchlight in Flambeau Lake, it will not be the same without you there laughing over whose fish is the largest."

He stopped and frustratingly wove his fingers through his hair, then continued. "I bid you good-bye, my friend, but I look forward to the day you promised you would return to the fall season of next year. As I perform my chiefly duties, day by day, I will think of that day, when we will meet for the last time."

He sighed heavily. "Good-bye for now, my friend," he said, his voice breaking. "I hope that your travel on the road to the hereafter is, as I had always thought it might be, filled with wondrous peace, a place where you will finally be able to embrace those loved ones who have gone before you."

White Wolf flicked tears from his eyes and swallowed hard. "Please tell my mother, father, and uncle that I think of them daily," he said thickly. "Tell them that I shall love them forever. Tell them that I have chosen the most perfect wife and that I will soon be a father."

Satisfied that he had spoken his heart, White Wolf rose slowly to his feet. He stopped long enough to stare at length down at the wrapped body. He would return soon to remove the body from the wigwam.

But for now he must go for Swallow Song and take her back to her husband.

He did not do this eagerly, for he knew what her reaction would be to seeing her beloved husband wrapped in birchbark.

It was the final act of life, to be wrapped in birchbark and placed in the burial grounds among others who have already died.

Dawnmarie and Woman Dancing rose to their feet

when White Wolf entered the lodge. They stood together while White Wolf knelt down beside Swallow Song and gave her Sharp Nose's "spirit bundle."

Dawnmarie stifled a sob behind a hand when Swallow Song took the bundle and grasped it to her bosom, her eyes wide and mournful as she spoke a soft thank you to White Wolf.

White Wolf reached a hand out for Swallow Song. "It is time for you to have a moment with your husband before we take him to his burial place," he said thickly.

Swallow Song pushed herself slowly up from the floor. White Wolf grabbed for her when her knees buckled beneath her. Dawnmarie rushed to Swallow Song's other side.

Together she and White Wolf took her from the lodge, Woman Dancing following, her voice a monotone of low chanting sounds.

When they reached Sharp Nose's lodge, several warriors were removing the west wall. This made Swallow Song groan with remorse, knowing that her husband would soon be carried through that vacant wall because the "land of the dead" was located in the west.

Dawnmarie stepped away from Swallow Song and White Wolf as they entered the lodge. Through the hole in the wall she watched Swallow Song, glad that Swallow Song had full composure of herself now, instead of being so overwrought with grief she could not spend these last moments with Sharp Nose.

After Swallow Song returned to Dawnmarie's side, Dawnmarie clung to her around the waist and held her steady as Sharp Nose's body was finally taken from the house through the hole in the wall. A warrior helped White Wolf carry Sharp Nose away from the village.

Dawnmarie and Swallow Song followed. The Chippewa people sang and shook their rattles close behind them on their way to the burial ground, their way of asking the Great Spirit to take Sharp Nose home to the land of promise in the heavens.

Just as the sun was rising in the sky, with its glorious pink light, they reached the burial grounds where a shallow grave had been dug, the bottom of the grave lined with bulrush mats.

Dawnmarie clung to Swallow Song as they stood back from the grave and watched Sharp Nose being placed there in a sitting position, facing north.

Several women came forth and placed dried meat, berries, bread, wild rice, and a frying pan in the grave with Sharp Nose, foods to sustain him on his long journey to the hereafter.

Before covering the grave with earth, White Wolf spoke from the heart again over his fallen warrior. He knelt down, his hands touching the birchbark-covered body. "We leave you with much sorrow," he said. "Be not far from us in the heavens, Sharp Nose. Let us hear your laughter in the cry of the eagle. Let us share your tears in the rain. Let us feel your warmth in the sunshine. Let us hear your words in the whispering winds. We leave you now, but we will never be truly apart."

He stood tall and square-shouldered as others danced around the grave three times, giving the spirit a start on its way to the hereafter.

Then everyone stood away from the grave, softly chanting, as two warriors pushed the black soil into the grave.

Once that was done, a warrior brought a wooden

plank and placed it over the mound of dirt. White Wolf held onto Swallow Song as she walked across this plank of wood, signifying thereby that she was letting her dead partner go, but that she was not yet ready to go herself.

Dawnmarie then held Swallow Song's hand as birchbark, poles, brushes, and rush mats were spread over the grave; those were then weighted down with poles and rocks.

A grave marker made from a small piece of wood with the representation of Sharp Nose's *do-dam* carved into it was placed at the foot of the grave.

Since Sharp Nose's best friend, White Wolf, had killed a minimum of four warriors collectively, it was White Wolf's duty to place a "brave stick" on the grave. He had whittled the stick in four places, the shavings projected upward into red stripes that represented blood.

This stick protected Sharp Nose's soul and meant that the dead warriors killed by White Wolf would help Sharp Nose's soul on his spirit journey. They also acted as his soul's mates.

After this, White Wolf lit a torch and stuck it in the ground at the head of the grave. Several women brought food and placed it on the ground close to the fire; the spirit of the fire would be used by the deceased in the preparation of the food while the soul was on its journey. Swallow Song would keep the fire burning for three successive days and nights, the amount of time required for her husband to reach the hereafter.

There was a moment of silence. Then everyone but Swallow Song turned and walked slowly back toward the village. The air was filled with the mourn-

ful chanting, the drums in the distance still rhythmically throbbed their beats.

Dawnmarie stopped and turned to go back to
Swallow Song, but White Wolf discouraged her by
taking her hand, forcing her to walk on beside him
toward the village.

Dawnmarie leaned closer to White Wolf so no one
would hear what she was going to say. "But what if
Swallow Song should need me?" she whispered as
she watched Swallow Song place a bouquet of wildflowers on her husband's grave. "White Wolf, I don't
think she should be alone."

"She is not alone," White Wolf said thickly, gazing
at Swallow Song over his shoulder. "Do you not
know that even though Sharp Nose's spirit has already begun his long journey to the spirit world, he
is, in part, still with his wife? She is feeling his comfort now."

They walked onward, then stopped when they saw
the arrival of a canoe. Dawnmarie's pulse began to
race when she recognized who was being carried to
dry land from the canoe.

"Mum," Dawnmarie whispered, somewhat ashamed
for the excitement she felt at seeing her mother after
having just buried a beloved friend.

But she had been without her mother for so long.
It had seemed like an eternity.

She broke away from White Wolf and ran toward
the river. Not wanting to interfere with the mourning
of White Wolf's people, she did not shout her mother's name.

Yet every fiber of her being was happy that her
mother had finally been able to travel. Her mother
had fought for her life. She was most definitely not
one of Slow Running's casualties!

Peter Storm was just placing Dawnmarie's mother on the ground when Dawnmarie reached her. Sobbing, Dawnmarie flung herself into her mother's arms.

"Mum, I've missed you so," she whispered.

"Life has been empty without you and . . . and . . ." Doe Eyes said, stopping before she mentioned her late husband's name.

Doe Eyes eased from Dawnmarie's arms. She gazed somewhat blankly at her daughter, then her eyes widened with fright when White Wolf came to Dawnmarie's side. "Your body is covered with ash," she said warily. "You are dressed for burial rites. Whose?"

"My friend, Sharp Nose, was just buried," White Wolf said thickly. "Many other warriors were also buried today. They were slain in an ambush. Slow Running was responsible."

Doe Eyes gasped.

"But Slow Running and his warriors are now dead," White Wolf quickly interjected when he saw the fear that Slow Running's very name caused her. "You, my people, and my wife no longer need to fear them."

"Wife?" Doe Eyes said, shifting her gaze to Dawnmarie.

It seemed to Dawnmarie that her mother lacked excitement over the news. She seemed way too sullen, not like her usual self. There was no emotion when she embraced Dawnmarie upon seeing her, and there was nothing much in her eyes except a strange sort of hollowness.

"Yes, Mum, we are married," she finally said. "White Wolf fills my life with such joy, Mum."

"That is good," Doe Eyes mumbled, still lacking enthusiasm.

White Wolf also noticed the change in Doe Eyes. He swept a comforting arm around Dawnmarie's waist.

"I am anxious to be reunited with my true people," Doe Eyes said, her voice drawn. "Will you go with me to Father James's mission, White Wolf? We will let him show us where my people's encampment is?"

White Wolf's gaze shifted to Dawnmarie, their eyes momentarily locking. Then he turned to Doe Eyes again. "After my mourning period for my friend is over, *ay-uh*, yes, I will take you there," he said thickly.

Doe Eyes said nothing more. Not even a thank-you. She began walking away, her eyes downcast.

Dawnmarie stared at her. She started to reach a hand out to her, to tell her about the child that she was carrying. But she chose not to. Even that might not penetrate her mother's reasoning nor bring out warm feelings that were no longer there.

All that seemed to matter to her mother was finding her true people. She seemed centered only on the Kickapoo, as though they were her very reason for breathing!

Her mother's change in personality made a quick anger rush through Dawnmarie. Slow Running was responsible for this change. He had killed her *spirit*. He had killed her very soul!

His death did not come soon enough, she thought wearily to herself.

Chapter Fifty-seven

*Our love was stronger by far than
the love of those who were older than we.*
—Edgar Allan Poe

Because of the need for the Chippewa to get on with
their lives, only a week had been taken to mourn for
their fallen brethren. It was time to prepare for the
wild rice harvest. Rice was one of their most important staple products that would feed them
through the long and blustery months of winter.

Many families had already gone upriver a short
distance where the rice fields grew midst the water
and marshes. The wigwam pole frames were on the
shores of the rice fields, left there from last year's
harvest.

The wigwams were now covered by temporary
mats and birchbark rolls. There the people camped
together, each harvesting their own part of the
marsh.

Dawnmarie and White Wolf would not join the
harvest until they returned from finding Dawnmarie's true people.

Dawnmarie looked over at White Wolf as he
sheathed his knife at his waist. She gazed at the extra
amount of beadwork on his fringed shirt, and smiled.
While waiting out the mourning period, she had lov-
ingly sewn the beads on his shirt.

She shifted her gaze to his headband that she had
also beaded.

White Wolf knelt down and gathered up several

blankets that he had rolled tightly and tied with leather thongs. As he took them toward the entranceway, to place in his canoe at the river, Dawnmarie's gaze followed him.

"Do you really think it is all right for you to leave now?" she blurted out, pausing from her chore of packing foodstuffs into a buckskin bag for the long journey down the river.

Her mother was already outside, awaiting the moment when she could board the canoe. Dawnmarie could hear her chatting with Woman Dancing. There was an anxiousness in her mother's voice that Dawnmarie feared. It seemed an unnatural anxiety.

Dawnmarie was faced with the reality that day by day her mother was no longer the same person. Not since the Sioux attack and the death of her husband.

Dawnmarie truly worried about her mother's reaction if she was not able to find her true people after all. Could she bear another big disappointment in life?

White Wolf turned to Dawnmarie. He saw the shadows in her eyes that meant that she was worrying again. And he knew her worries were for her mother. He had seen how her mother sat, smileless and somber. He had seen this happen before with women whose husbands had died. Some did not make it through their sorrow.

Like Dawnmarie, he saw the importance of finding the Kickapoo camp. It seemed to be Doe Eyes's idea of salvation. He wondered why she was not content to have a daughter, and soon a grandchild? There was something haunting about Doe Eyes's determination to reach her people. He doubted he would ever understand.

White Wolf explained that it was all right to leave.

"It is a while before the actual harvesting of the wild rice," he said. "The rice is now in the 'milk' stage where each family ties some of the stalks in bunches, to mark their harvest area and to protect the rice from the impending poor weather."

"We will be home then for the harvest," Dawn-marie said, going over to him. The blankets in his arms in the way, she leaned over them and brushed his lips with a kiss. "I will enjoy harvesting rice with my husband."

Then her eyes widened and she took a step away from him. "If we are not there, how will we be able to have our own area for ricing?" she asked. "All of the spaces in the rice fields in the river will be taken by someone else by the time we return."

"Violet Eyes, did you not miss me during the night last night?" White Wolf said, chuckling.

"I do believe I vaguely remember turning over and finding you gone," she said softly. "But I was so sleepy, I went back to sleep and thought nothing more of your absence."

"I was at the river tying off our own stalks," White Wolf said, his eyes dancing into hers. "It will wait now for our return. Also, Woman Dancing and Swallow Song will be responsible for our rice while we are gone."

"But Swallow Song is with child and Woman Dancing is not all that young any longer," Dawn-marie said, concerned for both her two friends. "They surely cannot man a canoe."

"Violet Eyes, they will not do any actual harvesting. Until our return they will take our place in our wigwam that I prepared for us all beside the river," White Wolf further explained. "When we return they will join in the fun of the harvest with us. They will continue sharing our lodge by the river. While you and I do the actual harvesting, *they* will gather chokecherries and early cranberries that need to be picked, dried, and stored. Then we will store away all the food, which will then sustain us through the long winter."

"It will be my first winter with you, my husband," Dawnmarie said. "I am anxious for the first snowfall. Can we make a sled and go sledding?"

"Never forget that you are with child and must take care not to place our child in danger," he said, his voice drawn. Then he smiled down at her again. "But we can walk hand in hand through the snow and marvel at nature's white dressing."

"Yes, hand in hand," Dawnmarie said, thrilled at the very thought of going through the rest of her life, and all nature's seasons, with her husband.

"I must go now and see that everyone is ready for the journey to the Kickapoo camp," White Wolf said.

Suddenly he dropped the blankets and grabbed Dawnmarie's wrists. He yanked her against his hard body and bent down so that their breaths were mingling. "My woman," he said huskily. "I shall miss our lovemaking while we are with the others on the journey."

He covered her mouth with a frenzied kiss, his hands now on her breasts, kneading them through her buckskin dress.

When he stepped away from her, his eyes were filled with a soft amusement. "When I cup your breasts with my hands now, I feel much more heaviness, much more breast," he said "Our child will have much warm milk to make him strong and healthy. He will have his mother to thank for that."

"As though you had nothing to do with my pregnancy?" Dawnmarie teased back. She snuggled into his arms again, crushing her breasts against his chest. "I love you so, White Wolf."

"Dawnmarie? White Wolf?" Doe Eyes called from outside the wigwam. "Everyone is waiting in their canoes. We are the only ones not yet ready for travel. Please hurry."

"One day soon we can begin the true course of the rest of our lives," White Wolf said, bending to pick up the blankets. "But for now we must set your mother's future right."

He looked over his shoulder at Dawnmarie's two traveling bags. "Are you ready?" he asked. "Is there enough food do you think for the full travel?"

"Woman Dancing has done herself proud again, caring for us as though we were her own children. She must have cooked for days to give us such wonderful food for our journey," Dawnmarie said, laughing softly as she turned and picked up both buckskin bags. She turned toward White Wolf. "Yes, m'lord, I am ready as I shall ever be."

They left the lodge together and boarded the canoe. As they traveled down the river, Dawnmarie sighed as she absorbed the wonders of nature into her heart. Heralding the arrival of autumn, the leaves of the sumac, sweet gum, and dogwood flared red in the woodlands, turning the shores into gauntlets of flame.

Dawnmarie breathed in the air of this sun-ripened morning and let God's paintbrush heal her spirit. Just a quick blown kiss, summer was now only a memory.

Finally, after many hours of steady travel, they reached Father James's mission, which consisted of only a bark chapel and cabin.

Father James was soon ready in White Wolf's canoe, sitting himself beside Dawnmarie's mother at the back.

As the canoe made its way down the river again, Father James's black robe fluttered in the breeze. His soft voice filled the air with a sound almost as beautiful as music as he spoke comfortingly to Dawnmarie's mother.

Dawnmarie gazed at Father James at length, viewing him as a man of hope, a man who would perhaps bring her mother out of her strangely induced private hell.

If he could not do it, no one could.

Chapter Fifty-eight

Though I shall walk with him no more,
A low voice sounds upon the shore.
                          —*Alice Meynell*

After traveling for two days and stopping each night to make camp in the damp, foggy air, the long procession of canoes finally reached the spot where Father James told them to stop.

"I see nothing," Doe Eyes cried, paling. "White Wolf, go onward. This cannot be the right place. I see no lodges. I . . . I . . . see no people."

"I know it was here," Father James exclaimed. His soft blue eyes wavered as he clung to the sides of the canoe. He found himself staring across land that was barren except for some scattered debris. "I met with the Kickapoo. They listened to my words of God."

Holding his paddle across his lap, the canoe rocking freely in the river, White Wolf turned to Father James. "How many moons ago was it that you were here?" he asked thickly. "Was it recently?"

"Not long ago, but I cannot say how many weeks it has been," Father James said, kneading his brow. "Perhaps it was *months*. My disappointment in finding them gone keeps me from thinking clearly."

"He is wrong," Doe Eyes cried, scrambling to the front of the canoe, clasping a hand to White Wolf's arm. "Travel onward. You will see that he is wrong. My people must be upriver somewhere *else*. If Father James cannot think clearly now as to when he saw them, how can you trust his judgment when he says he met with them *here*?"

White Wolf took Doe Eyes's hand and removed it from his arm. He gently held it. "Look across the land, Doe Eyes," he said, his voice drawn. "Do you not see the signs of people having lived here? Look on yonder hill. There is a burial ground. Someone lived here. It had to be the Kickapoo. Father James could not be wrong about such a thing as that."

"Beach the canoe," Doe Eyes pleaded, her voice filled with emotion. "I must wander along the ground that housed my people. I must pray over the graves. My very own cousins, aunts, and uncles may be among the dead. Perhaps even my mother and father." Tears splashed from her eyes. "I wished for more, to embrace and love my people. Now only scraps of my people are left for my viewing."

"Mum, please sit down," Dawnmarie urged as she reached a hand out for her mother.

White Wolf gazed over at Dawnmarie, then as

Doe Eyes sat down beside her, he turned his canoe toward shore, the other canoes following his lead.

Once on land, Dawnmarie stood back and watched her mother walking listlessly about, stopping to pick up a household item whenever she would find one. She seemed to be in a trance as she turned an object from side to side, then laid it down to go to another. It was as though touching these various objects were a means of touching her people.

"Come with me, daughter," Doe Eyes said as she held a hand out for Dawnmarie. "Come to the burial ground of your ancestors."

Stiffly Dawnmarie went to her mother and took her hand. She looked over her shoulder at White Wolf who nodded at her to go on, that he would wait for them.

One by one they went to the wooden markers. Upon them were engraved names that Doe Eyes sometimes recognized.

Tears spilling from her eyes, Dawnmarie watched as her mother fell to the ground upon one grave, covering it with her body.

"Mother," Doe Eyes said in her Kickapoo language. "My beloved mother."

Now knowing that this was her grandmother's grave, Dawnmarie went and knelt on both knees beside it. "Mum, please get up," she said, her voice breaking as she reached out for her. "Please do not lie there like that. Seeing you like that breaks my heart."

Doe Eyes moved slowly to her knees, then went and knelt down beside Dawnmarie. "Send a prayer to your grandmother in the sky," she said, lifting her eyes heavenward.

Dawnmarie did as she was asked, then a sick sort

of feeling swept through her. And not from emotion. She felt as though she were coming down with something, perhaps from having slept out in the open these past two nights. Her throat felt tight and hot. Her pulse was racing.

"Mum, I don't feel so well," she finally blurted, dizzy as she moved to her feet. "I ... must ... go and sit down."

Doe Eyes seemed not to hear. She continued to sit beside the grave, her chants filling the air.

Dawnmarie went to White Wolf. She reached a shaky hand toward him. "Husband, something inside me is not right," she said, breathing hard. "I feel suddenly ill." She coughed several times, then leaned into his embrace as he started to walk her to the canoe.

Doe Eyes came then to Father James. "Where do you think my people have gone?" she asked blandly.

His response made Dawnmarie and White Wolf stop and stare at him.

"I must confess to you all that I have recently heard that the Kickapoo *may* have traveled on to Mexico," he said, his eyes wavering from one to the other. "It appears that my informant was right."

"You heard this yet you brought us here anyway?" White Wolf said, his voice rising in pitch along with his anger. He glanced down at Dawnmarie whose face was flushed, possibly with fever, then glared at Father James. "Black Robe, I do not understand your reasoning."

Father James gestured toward Doe Eyes. "I had hoped, for the sake of this woman, that what I heard was wrong," he said softly. "Chances were, it was. As it is, it seems we have traveled these past two days for naught. I hope you will accept my apology."

No one had a chance to say anything. Doe Eyes crumpled to the ground in a dead faint. Dawnmarie rushed to her mother and knelt over her. "Mum," she cried.

When she got no response, she gazed quickly up at White Wolf. "I am so afraid for my mother," she said, her voice breaking. "Did you not see the hopelessness in her eyes after knowing where her people may have fled to? She knows that Mexico is too far away for her to travel there. White Wolf, my mother's hopes are totally shattered. I fear that has taken her reason for living away."

White Wolf knelt down and swept Doe Eyes into his arms. "I fear more for *you* than for your mother," he said, his voice drawn. "She has only fainted. *You* look feverish. We are far from our home. If you are sick for two days and nights without the medical assistance you can find among my people, I fear not only for you, but also our child."

Weak, her vision blurred from the sudden fever, Dawnmarie placed her hand across her abdomen, her fears for her child matching White Wolf's.

Chapter Fifty-nine

The moon never beams without
bringing me dreams.
                        —Edgar Allan Poe

The journey back to his village had been a grueling one for White Wolf. He had resented having to stop at night for everyone to rest, for if he had been alone he would have traveled onward without stopping, in order to get his wife home so that she could be cared for more properly.

Mysterious Voice, White Wolf's shaman, could perform his magic on Dawnmarie.

As it was, White Wolf had held back his rage when Father James had prayed his white man's prayers over her. He was responsible for this lost journey in the first place.

But finally Dawnmarie lay midst her plush bed of blankets beside White Wolf's lodge fire. White Wolf sat beside her and held her hand as she coughed incessantly.

He gazed over at Doe Eyes. She was sitting in the deepest shadows of his lodge, lost in her own world. She sat for hours now, staring lifelessly straight ahead, seemingly unaware that her daughter was so violently ill. It was as though Doe Eyes were in a distant world, void of mind.

White Wolf turned his gaze back to Dawnmarie. Her face was crimson with fever and her eyes were sunken. Her dark eyelashes lay like soft veils across her cheeks as she slept.

"My *gee-wee-oo*, wife," White Wolf whispered as he wrung out a cloth in a basin, then gently lay it across her forehead. "Open your eyes. Let me wonder again over their violet color."

But she only broke into a great fit of coughing. When it subsided, her whole body seemed to shudder with relief.

White Wolf gazed at her mother again. The last thing that Doe Eyes had said to White Wolf before she had gone into what seemed a self-induced trance was that she felt responsible for Dawnmarie's illness. If her daughter died, the guilt would lie on her shoulders. It was Doe Eyes who insisted that they travel down the river to look for her people. The nights had been too cold to sleep without proper lodging, and now Dawnmarie was ill from having slept out-of-doors.

A shuffling of feet behind him made White Wolf rise to his feet. He stepped aside and made room for Mysterious Voice as he arrived with his symbolic medicine bag and bear paws.

The shaman was dressed in a long, flowing robe, his gray hair reaching the floor behind him as he stood over Dawnmarie. While exercising his power, he beat a special *cige-gwan,* drum, with two small drumsticks, and sang his special songs.

Knowing that Dawnmarie was in good hands, White Wolf felt free to leave to go to the forest to search for a skunk. He had his own remedies. After boiling the skunk, he would have cough syrup for his woman, as well as salve for her chest, to help relieve not only the cough, but also her congestion.

Moving quietly to the back of his wigwam, White Wolf grabbed his bow and arrow, then left the lodge and ran into the forest.

After he had gone a short distance, voices drew his attention elsewhere.

He stopped and paused. He gazed with a longing toward the river where his people had begun harvesting rice. And none too soon. There were many signs of an approaching winter storm.

The wooly worm's coat was thick and black as midnight. White Wolf followed its sign while readying himself for winter. Black meant a long, cold winter.

He wished that the worms' coats were white instead of black this year. He had too many problems to deal with already. He did not need the rivers and lakes frozen so hard no one could cut through to the water. He did not need snows so deep no one could walk through them.

He was filled with all sorts of dreads, yet he enjoyed watching his people work. Despite the work, they found pleasure in what they were doing. Since the wild rice grew in water, a team of two harvesters worked together in a canoe. One person stood in the back of the canoe pushing it through the watery field with a long pole, without using paddles that can bruise the plants.

The other person sat in the prow with two ricing sticks. He used one stick to bend the tall plants over the canoe, the other to tap the grain heads so that some of the ripe kernels would rain down into the canoe and others would fall back into the water as seeds for next year's harvest.

His gaze moved through the throng of people in canoes. When he found Swallow Song and Woman Dancing in his canoe, harvesting the rice that White Wolf would normally harvest, he smiled. They had

promised him that he and his wife would not go without rice just because he could not harvest his own.

They laughed and talked even now as they moved
through the rice, their canoe heavy-laden with what
they had already harvested.

At first White Wolf had concerned himself over
Woman Dancing's age and Swallow Song's condition.
But watching them gave proof that he had nothing
to worry about. They saw what they did as enjoy-
ment, not hard labor.

Sighing heavily, White Wolf ran farther into the
forest. When he reached a meadow that stretched
away from the forest, he stopped and waited, watching the hollow logs that lay strewn at the edge of the
forest. Skunks were like children. He had seen them
play in and out of the logs, as though they might be
playing hide-and-seek.

His gaze searched through the thick grass and
weeds. He also had to find some wintergreen plants
for which to flavor the cough syrup. The more pleasant the taste and smell, the more he could get down
his wife's throat.

A stirring in the bushes made him stiffen. He readied his bow and arrow. When a skunk waddled into
view, then pattered on inside the hollow log, White
Wolf crept to the log.

As quick as lightning flashes across the sky during
a raging storm, White Wolf sent the arrow into the
side of the skunk. He was too quick for the skunk
to spray its defensive odor.

Reaching in to grab the small animal, White Wolf
winced with pain when he realized the animal had
enough life left in him to bite him.

He withdrew his hand and studied the wound. The
teeth had only grazed the flesh. No blood was drawn.

He was grateful for that. It would not do for him to come down with a fever from an animal bite. His wife needed his full attention. He must make her well.

And he could not keep the child she carried in her womb from his mind. What if her illness caused her to lose their child? It would be like losing a part of himself to death.

The skunk now dead, White Wolf grabbed it, then searched and found wintergreen. He rushed back home. The shaman was gone. Dawnmarie lay much too quiet. Her mother had not moved. She still sat there staring into space, seemingly uncaring or unfeeling.

A short while later White Wolf sat beside Dawnmarie's bed with the broth made from the boiled skunk. He lifted her head with one hand while tipping the bowl of medicine to her lips with his other.

It was a struggle to get the broth down her throat. While she was asleep there was a threat of choking her. Slowly he allowed the liquid to trickle down her throat. He persisted until he felt she had had enough.

He placed her head back down on the blankets. Then he lowered a blanket enough so that her chest was fully exposed to him.

Taking the boiled fat of the skunk onto the tips of his fingers, he slowly rubbed this over Dawnmarie's chest. Her voice, speaking so low he scarcely heard her, made him look quickly up at her eyes.

Everything within him became mellow when he saw that she was awake. It seemed an eternity since she had been awake and lucid enough to speak his name. And now she was even smiling.

"Violet Eyes," he said, grabbing her hands. He chuckled when they slipped away and he realized why. The fat from the boiled skunk. His hands were as greased as her chest.

He reached for the cloth that he had placed on her forehead. He wiped his fingers clean, then swept Dawnmarie into his arms.

He trembled inwardly when her breasts pressed against his chest, their very heat reaching through the buckskin fabric of his fringed shirt.

"You are going to be well," he said, caressing her back. "My sweet wife, I have prayed often to the Great Spirit. And Mysterious Voice visited you each day with his magic."

"How ... long ... have I been this ill?" Dawnmarie asked, perspiring now as the fever began lowering.

"Many nights and days," White Wolf said, softly gripping her shoulders with his hands. He held her away from him so that their eyes could meet. "I was so afraid that you would not survive the fever."

Dawnmarie coughed into a hand, the pain in her lungs frightening. "But the fever is now leaving me," she murmured.

"The cough has been as threatening as the temperature," White Wolf grumbled, gazing at the shine of the grease on her breasts. "But even that seems better."

Dawnmarie sniffed. Her gaze followed his and saw the grease on her chest. "I smell horrid," she said, touching the grease, lifting her fingers to her nose. She sniffed again. "What is it?"

"It was obtained from a skunk," White Wolf said, then laughed and drew her into his arms again when she showed surprise in her eyes.

Dawnmarie looked over White Wolf's shoulder.

Despair filled her when she saw her mother sitting in the shadows, unresponsive.

"How long has Mother been like that?" she asked, easing from White Wolf's embrace. She placed a robe around her shoulders and started to get up to go to her mother, but White Wolf stopped her.

"You are not strong enough to leave your bed," he said flatly. "Stay. Give yourself time to fully recover before you start worrying about someone else."

"But my mother ... ?" Dawnmarie said, sighing heavily when she realized that White Wolf was right ... that she *was* too weak to leave her bed.

White Wolf turned and stared at Doe Eyes. "She has been this way since our return from the search for your people," he said softly. "When she eats, I have to feed her. Even then she sometimes puts her tongue in the way so that we cannot get food into her mouth. She wishes to die, Dawnmarie. In a sense, she is already dead."

Dawnmarie stifled a gasp behind her hand. She stared wistfully at her mother. "Mum," she said, a sob lodging in the depths of her throat.

Then something else, some*one,* came to her mind. She looked wildly up at White Wolf as she placed a hand on her abdomen. "Our child?" she asked, her eyes searching White Wolf's to seek true response from him.

"There is still life in your body besides your own," White Wolf said, himself placing a hand over Dawnmarie's. "Our child is still nestled sweetly within your womb. But I did fear so for our child. When you coughed so fitfully, it seemed your whole body was being torn apart. That was what I feared most for our child."

Dawnmarie coughed, her face growing red from the effort. She wheezed and lay slowly down on the blankets.

White Wolf covered her to her chin with a blanket, then lay down beside her. "You will cough some more, but not as much or as strongly," he reassured. "My woman, you are going to soon be able to go and see the rice that Swallow Song and Woman Dancing harvested for our long winter months."

Dawnmarie turned to White Wolf. She traced his face with a finger. "They did this for us?" she murmured. "But what of *their* health? Are they truly able to labor so hard without it harming them?"

"While in the canoe, the wild rice falling at their feet as they harvest it, they are happy *and* safe," White Wolf reassured. "I would not allow them to be there if I felt they shouldn't be."

"Has Swallow Song had any more seizures while I have been too ill to know what is happening around me?"

"Not one."

"And her and Sharp Nose's child?"

"The child is healthy. Their child and ours will become best friends, as it is meant to be, since their fathers were devoted to one another."

"What if we have a son, and Swallow Song has a daughter?"

White Wolf paused, cocked an eyebrow, then chuckled. "We will have to see what destiny does about that," he said, snuggling closer to Dawnmarie.

Dawnmarie looked past him again at her mother. "What are we to do about Mother?" she asked softly.

"Her fate is also a matter of charted destinies," White Wolf said thickly.

"Suddenly I am so tired again," Dawnmarie said, her eyes slowly closing.

"Then sleep, my pretty one," White Wolf said, gently stroking her brow. "Just sleep."

After she was asleep, White Wolf went outside and looked toward the heavens. "Great Spirit, thank you for bringing my woman back to me. But I must implore you to let there be no more complications in my people's lives," he cried. "Have we not had enough sadness and heartache? And please bring my woman quickly to her feet. She has always been a woman of such energy. Allow her to be the same person again."

He then returned to his lodge to watch Dawnmarie. He now felt peaceful with himself.

In his mind's eye he recalled Dawnmarie's radiant face when she laughed. He could feel her lips against his, warm and vibrant. It would be the same again, *soon*.

He shifted his gaze to Doe Eyes. A sadness overcame him to see her so empty-eyed. He saw no hope for her. Her mind was separated from her body.

Going to Doe Eyes, White Wolf placed gentle hands to her shoulders and lowered her to her blankets. "Doe Eyes, close your eyes and join your daughter in the dream world in the heavens," he whispered. He placed his fingers to her lashes and gently closed her eyes for her. "Find solace in sleep, Doe Eyes."

He was relieved when she heaved a sigh and slept. He covered her with a blanket, then resumed his vigil beside the fire, his eyes focused on his woman, his *gee-wee-oo*, wife.

Chapter Sixty

And so, all the night-tide, I lie
down by the side of my darling—
my darling—my life—
      —Edgar Allan Poe

Many months later, even though she was big with child, Dawnmarie went with White Wolf in his canoe to watch him spear fish by the light of flaming torches in Flambeau Lake. The practice of fishing at night was what gave the name of "Lake of the Torches" to the beautiful, serene lake that sat close to their village.

The warm night air enveloped the earth and the moon lit up the countryside with its pure, white radiance before it began its slow slide below the horizon. The torches were fastened to the prow of all of the canoes that sat calmly in Flambeau Lake, the warriors in them actively filling their canoes with their night's catch.

Dawnmarie watched with much interest as White Wolf made his torch. He gathered resin that he collected at a gash that he had slashed in the trunk of a Norway pine tree several days previously. He heated the resin, saturated birchbark with it, and while they were still hot, wound them around the end of a stick. He told her that sometimes he split one end of a green sapling into splinters and filled the space between the splinters with spruce pitch.

The fish in the lake—some of which were musky, walleye, bass, whitefish, trout, and panfish—were enticed by the torchlight to the surface of the water. White Wolf told her that the lake trout fed on smaller fish, such as herring, and grew slowly to lunkers of twenty to forty pounds.

A shawl around her shoulders to ward off the evening chill, Dawnmarie sat at the back of the canoe. White Wolf stood a few feet from her, spearing fish with a spear tipped with a stone point.

As he brought in the fish one by one on his spear, he killed them with a club made from a knot of a tree. The knot formed the club and an attached portion of the tree was the handle.

He had told her earlier that a warrior could spear more than twenty pounds of fish in less than an hour. She gazed down at the huge basket of fish that he had already caught. The harvest was good for him and the other warriors.

Dawnmarie looked from canoe to canoe. Almost methodically the warriors caught fish with their various equipment. Some used a leister while others used harpoons. But for the most part they used the same sort of spear that White Wolf was using.

A sudden pain in Dawnmarie's abdomen made her flinch. She slipped a hand over the large ball of her stomach as a worse pain followed.

Then the pain was gone, so quickly it seemed not to have happened at all.

"Look and see what I have just caught on my spear," White Wolf said, chuckling. He looked over at Dawnmarie and held the spear out for her to see.

Repulsed at the very sight of the ugly fish, Dawnmarie placed a hand to her mouth. It was flat-headed and potbellied, and dripped with slime. As White Wolf brought it back closer to himself and removed it from the spear, the ugly fish wrapped its slimy tail around his forearm. It was hard to believe it came out of this beautiful lake.

"What kind of fish is that?" Dawnmarie asked, visibly shuddering. "My father fished often, but he never brought home anything as ghastly as that." She laughed softly. "My mother wouldn't have cooked it in *her* fry pan."

"Your father should have brought it home," White Wolf said. He uncoiled the fish's tail, then killed it with his club and placed it with his other fish. "Although ugly, the strip of meat along the back is delicious."

His eyes twinkled as he leaned down closer to Dawnmarie. "Violet Eyes," he said, his lips quavering into a smile. "Eating the eelpout meat is a bit akin to kissing an ugly person in bright light."

She giggled, then her eyes grew wide as a wrenching, sharp pain shot through her abdomen.

White Wolf saw her instant agony. He noticed how she now clutched her abdomen. "The child?" he said thickly. "It is coming?"

Dawnmarie sighed with relief when the pain subsided. "*Ay-uh*, I am sure that what I have just felt is the start of labor," she said, gasping when another pain came so quickly, this one much harder than the last.

White Wolf's heart pounded. For a man who was never flustered, suddenly he seemed too disoriented to know what to do.

"The paddle," Dawnmarie said, wheezing as she clasped hard to her abdomen. "Darling, the paddle. Pick it up. Row me to shore. Take me to the birthing hut. Quickly. I doubt we have much time to spare."

Finally getting his bearings, and knowing that he needed to be levelheaded at such a time as this,

White Wolf fell to his knees and searched for the paddle. Finally he found it. It had slipped beneath the basket of fish.

Dawnmarie perspired heavily as the pains racked her body unceasingly. "Hurry, White Wolf," she cried. "Please ... hurry."

White Wolf wasted no more time in getting her to shore. After beaching the canoe he lifted her into his arms and carried her toward the birthing hut that he had built away from his village.

The birthing hut, he worried to himself. He must get her to the birthing hut that he had built for Dawnmarie *and* Swallow Song, since their children were due at almost the exact time.

A loon sang its mystical tune from somewhere across the river. An owl hooted.

A white wolf came at the edge of the clearing and stopped and stared, its eyes gleaming into the night.

"The white wolf," Dawnmarie said, having seen it. "It has come to witness the birth of our child."

"I would have been disappointed had it not come," White Wolf said. His heart thumped wildly at having seen the wolf himself, feeling the renewal of bonding between himself and the creature of the night. It seemed only natural that it would be there to share White Wolf's excitement.

A torch burned softly outside the small birthing hut. As White Wolf approached the entranceway, his eyebrows forked. "Violet Eyes, do you hear voices?" he asked. "Do you think that ..."

He didn't get the chance to finish his question. Woman Dancing came from the hut and reached for more firewood that sat beside the entranceway. He gazed up at the smoke hole. *Ay-uh,* smoke was spiraling from it, which mean that a fire was burning inside the hut. Had Woman Dancing known it was Dawnmarie's time?

Or was it because . . .

"Swallow Song is in hard labor," Woman Dancing said as she met White Wolf's approach, her arms now burdened with wood.

She gazed down at Dawnmarie. She smiled. "We will now have two babies born this same night," she murmured. "It is a good thing for best friends to have children born at the same hour. It gives a special bond to the children."

Dawnmarie clenched her teeth and closed her eyes. "I feel pressure between my legs!" she cried as another pain shot through her. "The baby. I . . . believe . . . it is coming now!"

White Wolf rushed her on into the hut where a fire burned softly in the center of the lodge. He placed her on a mat covered with hay beside Swallow Song.

Dawnmarie looked over at Swallow Song. Her hair was soaked with perspiration. Her face was flushed red. Yet she managed a smile and reached a hand out for Dawnmarie. Dawnmarie took her hand and squeezed it when another pain shot through her abdomen.

"Drink this," Woman Dancing said as she placed a small wooden cup to Dawnmarie's lips. "The herbal medication will ease your pain somewhat."

Dawnmarie did not have to be asked twice. She could hardly get a breath of relief before another pain was there, torturing her.

White Wolf undressed Dawnmarie while Woman Dancing removed Swallow Song's clothes.

After giving Dawnmarie a kiss of reassurance, White Wolf left the hut and gave the two women over to Woman Dancing's skilled care. The number of children that Woman Dancing had brought into the world numbered close to a hundred.

Yet she had no children of her own. That had not been too great a disappointment to her chieftain husband, for while he was alive, he had centered his fatherly attention on White Wolf after White Wolf had been orphaned way too young.

"Now, both of you, kneel on your knees," Woman Dancing kindly instructed. "Do you see the ropes that I have tied to stakes in the ground? Grab them. Pull them as the pains come to you."

Dawnmarie groaned and held her stomach with one hand as she turned on her side, then managed to get to her knees. Panting, her hair now soaked with perspiration, she laid her face on the soft hay facing Swallow Song. They smiled at one another, then softly cried as another pain came to them.

Dawnmarie closed her eyes when the pain subsided. "Mum," she cried softly to herself. "I need you, Mum."

But she knew that she hungered for her mother's presence in vain. Even if her mother had been told that her daughter had gone into labor, Dawnmarie knew that she would not understand. Her mind was gone, as though something or someone had gone inside and wiped all her memory away.

Dawnmarie wheezed as another pain enveloped her. She pulled on the ropes until they cut into the flesh of her fingers.

Then, again, she had a moment of peace.

"Woman Dancing, do you need someone else to assist you?" she asked, fearing the next round of pains. Each was worse than the last. She knew that

the child would be coming soon. "Isn't this too much
for just one woman?"

Dawnmarie turned her eyes in the direction of the
entranceway. "White Wolf," she pleaded. "Please
tell White Wolf to come back inside. I . . . need . . .
him. I would think he would want to be here. He
has told me often that it is from the man that the
child comes as well as the woman."

"Woman Dancing is enough woman, and White
Wolf need not be here," Woman Dancing said, wiping perspiration from Dawnmarie's brow with a soft
cloth, and then did the same for Swallow Song. "The
man's part in bringing the child into this world is
over. Now it is the woman's private moment. Husbands only get in the way."

Swallow Song groaned and stiffened, then cried
out when the pains were there again. She looked
wildly over at Woman Dancing. "I feel it!" she cried.
"Surely you can see the head!"

Woman Dancing knelt between Swallow Song's
legs. She reached her arms out just as the child
slipped from the birthing canal.

Dawnmarie cried and clutched to the ropes. "It is
also my time!" she cried. "I feel it. The child, it . . ."

She almost blacked out as the final pain went
through her like white lightning.

And then it was over.

She blinked her eyes, and when she heard the
sound of two babies crying, not one, she became
choked with a happy sob.

"Swallow Song, you have a son," Woman Dancing
said, working with Swallow Song's child, cutting the
cord.

She laid the child down on the hay, then cut the

other child's cord. "Dawnmarie, you have a daughter," she murmured.

She smiled from Dawnmarie to Swallow Song as she waited for them each to expel their placenta, the afterbirth.

"A son and a daughter," Woman Dancing murmured. "Perhaps destiny has worked a miracle today. The bonding I spoke of earlier? Perhaps it might even be stronger than I earlier imagined. Perhaps we have here a son and daughter who will become man and wife. There is enough difference in their background. One who is not only of Chippewa heritage, but also Kickapoo, and one who is also part Potawatomis. As sure as I am standing here, the destinies of these two children are intertwined, as were their births. It is as though they are twins, except they came from two separate wombs."

The placentas finally expelled, Dawnmarie and Swallow Song turned over and stretched out on their backs.

"A daughter," Dawnmarie sighed. She reached a hand out toward Woman Dancing. "Please let me hold my child. Please call for White Wolf."

"First I must give both children a herbal bath," Woman Dancing said, placing Dawnmarie's daughter in a birchbark receptacle in which herbal water had been prepared earlier. "This bath promotes a strong constitution."

She quickly bathed the child, then laid her in Dawnmarie's arms. "Nurse her now, my sweet one," she said softly. "Nursing must be done immediately after birth."

Dawnmarie looked in wonder at her daughter, at her tiny fingers, toes, and nose. She placed the child's lips to her nipple and felt a warmth flow through her

never known before by her as her child began suckling nourishment from her breast.

After Swallow Song was nursing her own child,
and blankets were covering both new mothers,
Woman Dancing sighed with relief, glad for Swallow
Song that she could nurse her child. She had wondered if Swallow Song's condition would permit her
to nurse her son. If not, he would have sucked porridge from a small hole punched in the bladder of
an animal. The porridge would have been made by
boiling wild rice in fish or meat broth.

Feeling that all was well, and as it should be,
Dancing Woman left the lodge and went to White
Wolf.

When he turned anxious eyes down at her, she
placed a gentle hand on his arm. "Your wife and
daughter are eager to see you," she said. "Both
mothers and both children are doing well."

"A daughter?" White Wolf said, beaming. "And
you say both children and both mothers? Swallow
Song also had her child?"

"A son was born to Swallow Song," Woman Dancing said, nodding.

His pulse racing with excitement, he gave Woman
Dancing a hug, then rushed inside the dimly lit hut.
His eyes misted with tears as he knelt down beside
Dawnmarie, his trembling hand reaching to touch the
tiny child suckling at her breast.

"A daughter," he said, his voice thick with emotion. He stroked his daughter's arm, the flesh as soft
as a rose petal against his fingertips. He smiled at
Dawnmarie, then leaned over and gave her a quavering kiss.

Dawnmarie felt as though she might be in heaven
she was so happy. When White Wolf drew away from

her, she blinked tears of joy from her eyes. "Our firstborn is not a son, but, oh, my darling, our daughter so resembles you," she murmured. "White Wolf, I cannot explain to you how I feel at this moment. I am so content and at peace with myself, it is as though I am soaring with the eagles in the heavens. Is it the same for you?"

"I *am* that eagle," White Wolf said, laughing softly.

Then his gaze shifted to Swallow Song as she lay feeding her son. Suddenly the bliss of the moment wavered into a melancholia. It was at this moment that he realized just how much he missed Sharp Nose. He held back a sob of despair that his friend was not there to witness the birth of his son.

And his heart went out to Swallow Song. Although she was in a world of wonder and exhilaration over having given birth to a son, he knew that deep inside her heart she was crying out for the father, wishing he were there.

He turned his gaze back to Dawnmarie. He leaned low, so that what he said would not reach Swallow Song's ears. "Can you share your husband for a moment or two with a woman whose husband is not here to glory with her over their child?" he whispered.

Dawnmarie smiled softly up at him. "White Wolf, surely you know you need not ask," she whispered back. "I love Swallow Song as though she were my sister. Please go to her. Let us all share one another on this more than perfect day."

Swallow Song's child was finished nursing.

Woman Dancing left the lodge to place the placenta of both women in the crotch of a tree, then returned and placed a diaper made from the down of cattail on Swallow Song's child after having powdered him with the ashes of cedar bark to prevent chafing.

The child's first clothes were rabbit skins in which he was now wrapped on a cradleboard. The child was propped up beside Swallow Song, where she could constantly view him.

White Wolf knelt beside Swallow Song. Dawnmarie watched, sad for Swallow Song that her husband was not there to fill these precious moments with his special love.

Something came suddenly to Dawnmarie. Swallow Song had given birth without going into a seizure! In fact, it was hard for Dawnmarie to recall Swallow Song's last seizure.

That was something to marvel at, to be happy for. Her best friend had not only had a beautiful child, but one who also seemed free of demons!

"Your son is as handsome as his father was," White Wolf said, gazing at the child, again feeling something tugging at his heart, knowing that Sharp Nose would never see his son.

White Wolf vowed to himself that this son would know all things that fathers taught their young braves: the hunt, the spearing of fish by torchlight in the lake, and the ways of a warrior.

All of these things this son would learn from White Wolf, his substitute father.

"Sharp Nose is here," Swallow Song said, stifling a sob behind a hand. "Do you not feel his presence, White Wolf? He sees his son. He knows him. He will even smile down from the heavens when he realizes that his son will bear his name."

"Tomorrow we will have the naming feast," White Wolf said softly. "The namer will name your son

Sharp Nose. Your son will carry your late husband's name proudly through his long years of life."

"And what will you name your daughter?" Swallow Song asked, gazing from White Wolf to Dawnmarie.

White Wolf moved to Dawnmarie's side. His daughter had just finished feeding.

Woman Dancing placed her on a cradleboard.

White Wolf had not only made a cedar cradleboard for his wife, but also Swallow Song. Made not only to carry the child, but also to develop the child's posture, the cradleboards were each two feet long, a foot wide, and one inch thick.

At one end was a foot brace, and at the other end, a hickory hoop. The hoop was to protect the head in case the cradleboard tipped. Moss cushioned the board.

The umbilical cord was saved. It would be sewn into a little buckskin bag and hung on the cradleboard. Maple sugar, wrapped in a little cloth, would be hung, as well as other items to amuse the child along with other items of significance.

"And what name shall we give our daughter?" White Wolf asked, taking Dawnmarie's hand.

A commotion outside the hut made her forget the question. She watched White Wolf leave the lodge, then listened and tried to make out what was being said. But the voices were too low, seeming to be deliberately so.

When White Wolf came back into the hut, his face was drawn and sullen, his eyes wary as he knelt down beside Dawnmarie.

"What is it?" she asked, feeling a coldness creep into her heart, pushing away the warmth of happiness that she had felt only moments ago. She leaned up on an elbow. Clasping the blanket to her bosom, she implored him with pleading eyes. "It's my mother, isn't it? Something has happened to my mother!"

White Wolf placed his hands at her shoulders. He slowly drew her into his embrace. While holding her tightly he told her that her mother's body had been found deep in the woods.

And knowing that she would see her mother while preparing her for burial, he had to tell her how she had been found.

"Your mother cut her hair off and burned it," he said, almost choking on the words. He felt her wince, then sob.

"My mother so often worried aloud to me about being afraid that some medicine men, one who does evil for vengeance, might turn himself into a bird, pick up her hair, and then work it over to make a nest. This . . . is . . . why she burned it."

"I do not understand the logic," White Wolf said blandly.

"There is none," Dawnmarie said, her voice breaking. "It was only my mother's fears of being punished for not having found her true people that plagued her way before she finally escaped into a world of silence."

And by telling this story to White Wolf that she had heard so often, she realized just then that her mother had been battling mental problems of one kind or another even way back when Dawnmarie was a child.

"Your mother has finally made peace with herself," White Wolf said. "She will soon be in the spirit world with your father."

"But she never ever found her true people again before she died," Dawnmarie cried. "Will I even?"

"Perhaps in time, you or our child might be with your Kickapoo people again. As for your mother, *she* will soon be with them in the *spirit* world. Then she will truly be at peace with herself. Remember *that* when you are filled with remorse and despair over your mother's death. Sometimes, my Violet Eyes, it is best for someone to enter the spirit world instead of staying on this earth where there are so many trials and tribulations and sadness to face. I, myself, do not dread the spirit world. I know that it is a place of pure happines. It is *paradise*."

"Hold me," Dawnmarie cried. "*My* paradise is on this earth, with you and our child."

Their daughter started crying, drawing Dawnmarie from her world of torment. White Wolf lifted the cradleboard and took his daughter from it. "She is most beautiful," he said. He held her in the crook of one of his arms and slowly rocked her back and forth.

"Baby mine, daughter mine, give me a smile, give me a sigh," he sang in Chippewa. "Baby mine, daughter mine, I give you my everything."

Dawnmarie smiled, the love she felt for White Wolf and her daughter overpowering all other emotions that plagued her. They were her life, her universe. They were all she truly needed to make her whole again.

"She wishes to sing *you* a lullaby," White Wolf said, easing his daughter into Dawnmarie's arms. "Hear her sweet cooing sounds? She is singing to you, Violet Eyes."

"And ah, how beautifully she sings," Dawnmarie said, warming through and through when her daughter's tiny fingers circled one of hers, clinging.

Dawnmarie watched Woman Dancing place Swallow Song's son in his mother's arms. It was wonderful to see Swallow Song so at peace with herself, lost again in her own little world as she held her son close to her heart.

Her thoughts went to her mother. She gazed up at White Wolf. "You asked me a while ago what we would name our daughter?" she said softly. "Can we name her Doe Eyes, after my mother?"

White Wolf nodded, then drew Dawnmarie up into his arms, their child snuggled between them. "Our daughter's name will be Doe Eyes," he whispered. "That is how it should be."

"Thank you," Dawnmarie whispered back. "Oh, thank you."

Chapter Sixty-one

I love you for laying firm hold on the possibilities of the good in me.

—Anonymous

The sun was just rising. The birds were awakening and filling the air with their joyous music. Squirrels scampered around, their tails bushy, their eyes eager.

Dawnmarie sat beside Swallow Song in the large council house, ten drums playing in cadence, the naming feast soon to begin.

Dawnmarie gazed down at her child as she lay in her arms, a tiny rabbit skin thrown loosely around her. It was hard for her to hold back her deep emotions. Before daybreak Dawnmarie's mother had been buried. And because of her responsibility and duty to her newborn child, Dawnmarie could not allow herself to go into deep mourning for her mother. She did not want to disturb the peace of her child. She did not want to cause her milk flow to cease because of her inner turmoil.

Dawnmarie had to look forward into the future, not dwell on the past. And she knew that her mother would understand. Her mother would only want what was best for her daughter, and her precious granddaughter.

Dawnmarie could not help but feel pain in her heart over her mother having not seen her grandchild. Just possibly if she had held her granddaughter at least *once,* it might have brought her back to the world of knowing, of loving, of caring.

Swallowing back a lump in her throat, Dawnmarie gazed over at Swallow Song. Her eyes were filled with a soft inner peace, yet an anxiousness. Dawnmarie knew that Swallow Song had to be filled with all sorts of emotions. Soon she would name her child after her late husband. That had much meaning for this Potawatomis woman whose husband had left this earth way before his time.

White Wolf came and sat down beside Dawnmarie. She eased their daughter into his arms.

"She still sleeps?" White Wolf asked softly, peering down at the veil of lashes that lay over his daughter's tiny, copper cheeks. "Even with the drums playing? Even with the people crowding into the council house?"

He brushed a soft kiss across his daughter's brow. "She is a happy child," he murmured. "That is good."

"And why shouldn't she be?" Dawnmarie asked softly. "Look whose arms are holding her. Even now, as tiny as she is, she realizes handsome over ugly."

She gazed at her husband's handsomeness this morning. He had just taken a dip in the river. His hair hung wet and sleek down his back, his beaded headband holding it in place. His sculpted face was clean of hair stubble after having plucked the whiskers even way before his bath.

His buckskins were new and heavily beaded. He was the epitome of man, so wonderful to look at he would forever quicken her breath when she was in his presence.

White Wolf watched his people file into the council house. They each passed three bowls that were placed on the floor. These were the offerings of tobacco as payment to the "namer" for naming the children today.

Proud to be chief of such fine people, White Wolf continued watching as they settled down in a wide circle around the large central fire. He nodded to one and then another as they looked his way and smiled. He gazed at the children, so proud of the young braves and maidens that he thought he would burst from it. In them lay the future of his people.

As babies, the parents had guarded these children carefully, to make sure they did not allow them, as infants, to touch the fingers of one hand with those of the other. It was their belief that should they touch the fingers of one with those of the other they were counting the days the child still had to live.

He singled out first one child, and then another. They were the most intelligent of them all. They had talked early in life, a sign of intelligence to the Chippewa. Their parents had been wise to feed them the raw brains of a small bird. It was a well-known fact that this would cause the development of early speech in the Chippewa children.

He had already instructed Dawnmarie of these Chippewa secrets.

Their children would be wise. Their sons would be great leaders.

The drumbeats of the ten drums in attendance continued, but the assembled crowd grew quiet as the "namer" came into the council house.

Dawnmarie gazed up at him. She had been told that the "namer," the one who approved of or gave the newborn children their names, was a person grown old in continuous good health.

Spotted Ear, the "namer" for this band of Chippewa, was a round, elderly man. He waddled past those who would witness his "naming" this morning, followed then by a feast of feasts. He wore a long and flowing buckskin robe, sparse of design. His hair was worn in one long braid down his back. His round, fleshy face was flushed; his midnight-black eyes were brilliantly bright.

White Wolf placed his daughter in Dawnmarie's arms, then rose and welcomed Spotted Ear with a warm embrace.

"It is good that you are the one who will legally name my daughter," White Wolf said. "It is only fitting that you are the 'namer' today, since it was you who named me."

"I have seen in a dream that I will also name a son for you," Spotted Ear said, placing a gentle hand on White Wolf's shoulder. "A name has come to mind for your son. But perhaps it is best not to give a name to an unborn son before I name your daughter, true?"

"I would be interested to know the name chosen by you now, if you do not see it as a taboo to say it," White Wolf said softly. "I do not see how it could place a shadow over the naming of my daughter today."

"If that is what you wish, then that is how it should be," Spotted Ear said, smiling. "I would name your son Proud Heart. Do you not think that name is fitting for the son of a chief as noble as you?"

Spotted Ear placed a gentle hand on White Wolf's shoulder. "My chief, you carry much pride in your heart," he said thickly. "I can see it. Your son will be named for the pride his father carries in his heart."

Touched by what Spotted Ear was saying, White Wolf was rendered speechless.

But it was not necessary for him to search for the right words to respond. Spotted Ear seemed to realize his awkwardness. He moved past him and sat down on thick mats before Dawnmarie and Swallow Song.

The naming would soon take place.

White Wolf sat back down beside Dawnmarie, his back straight, his shoulders squared.

All was silent.

Even the drums had stilled their throbbing beats.

Spotted Ear reached his arms out toward Dawnmarie.

Dawnmarie removed the blanket from around her daughter, then handed her to Spotted Ear.

Tears misting her eyes, she watched him hold her daughter up above his head, for all to see.

He then placed her on his lap and spoke in his Chippewa tongue as he named her, the name Doe Eyes sounding wonderful and perfect as it passed across his thick lips. This act, the "namer" giving the child her name, placed the child under the protection of the namer's guardian spirit.

After Doe Eyes was in Dawnmarie's arms again

and snuggled in her blanket, Dawnmarie watched, moved deeply inside, as Swallow Song's son was given his name.

Then everything changed from merriment to dread. As Spotted Ear held Swallow Song's son up for all to see, she was seized by a violent seizure. Her head thudded against the floor as she was thrown backward, her body trembling with spasms.

White Wolf took Doe Eyes into his arms so that Dawnmarie could help Swallow Song. She had learned to cover Swallow Song's body with her own, to keep her body from thrashing about.

There was a muted, strained silence in the council house when Dawnmarie stretched out over Swallow Song, the force of her body thankfully holding Swallow Song in place.

Gripping Swallow Song's hands strongly above her head, tears splashed from Dawnmarie's eyes to know how embarrassed Swallow Song would be once she recovered and saw that the eyes of the people were no longer on her beloved child, but herself.

Although it seemed to last an eternity, this seizure was brief. Dawnmarie moved to her knees beside Swallow Song. She drew her into her arms as she became aware of things and people around her. Dawnmarie held her as she sobbed.

"It's going to be all right," she whispered to Swallow Song. "Please don't cry. And don't be embarrassed. Everyone—*all* of White Wolf's people love you."

Swallow Song soon regained her composure. Her face flushed, her chin held proudly high, she resumed her place beside Dawnmarie.

Everything proceeded as though nothing had hap-

pened. Sharp Nose was given back to the care of
his mother.

Spotted Ear then took two necklaces from a deep
pocket at the side of his robe. The head of an eagle
carved into a piece of cedar hung from the end of
each necklace. "I give these gifts to both children as
a keepsake to be hung now on their cradleboard,
then to be worn around their necks when they are
old enough to understand their meaning. These
keepsakes from their 'namer' must be kept by the
children for the rest of their lives. They have been
given the same keepsake because they are of a special bond."

Dawnmarie took the necklace and softly thanked
the "namer." White Wolf brought her Doe Eyes's
cradleboard. She placed her daughter on it and secured her in her security of tied blankets, then
attached the necklace to the hoop where other trin-
kets hung for the child's pleasure.

Woman Dancing brought Swallow Song's child's
cradleboard to her. She placed her child, then the
necklace on it.

"More and more our children's lives are linked,"
Swallow Song said, smiling at Dawnmarie, then
White Wolf. "I am anxious to see how their futures
are intertwined, as well."

"They will be the very best of friends, I am sure,"
White Wolf said, nodding.

"Perhaps more than that," Swallow Song whispered to herself, hoping for her son's security in that
he would marry a Chippewa woman.

She shuddered visibly when she thought of something else. That he might too live day by day in fear
of becoming a victim of seizures. If he was a victim
of such seizures, Swallow Song was not sure if she

could stand by and watch his life ruined by them. He was next in line to be chief of his Potawatomis people. Everyone knew that a chief must be strong in all ways, physical *and* mental.

If he, in fact, became plagued with seizures, she might take the same road as Dawnmarie's mother. She could take her own life and finally be at peace with herself.

Though perhaps cowardly of her, she would leave her son to find his own way of salvation.

The ceremony now over, much food was passed around in the council house, piled high on wooden platters. Everyone dined on fish, venison, squirrel, beaver, muskrat, succotash, rice pudding, and wild rice. They were entertained by dancers. Children ran and played. An occasional dog would sneak into the council house and grab a piece of meat and run away with it.

Later, when everyone had returned to their chores, Dawnmarie was glad to find refuge in her lodge. It had been a tiring day. It had begun way too early for someone who had only recently given birth. As her child fed from a breast, her head bobbed.

Then she quickly awakened when she felt warm lips on her cheek. She smiled into White Wolf's eyes as he leaned down over her.

"My love," she murmured, reaching a hand to trace the outline of his lips. "I hunger for you more than you can know. I wish we did not have to wait."

"Sometimes waiting is best," White Wolf said, settling down beside her. "Did you not know that waiting oft times enhances the pleasure?"

He reached for the necklace on the cradleboard. "I wonder what the future *truly* holds for our daughter and Swallow Song's son?" he said thickly.

Chapter Sixty-two

To you, to you, to you
The dues of love and honour is.
  —Nicholas Breton

It was *dag-waagi*, the fall of the west again. It was autumn, when the cold set in and the drumming rains dulled the bright leaves. The dewy fresh air drifted in from the lake into White Wolf's village, where his people's wood fires were burning.

The wild rice that had just recently been harvested was drying. A contented feeling of well-being filled the village. The first grain of the season had been offered for a blessing from the Great Spirit.

White Wolf's people were enjoying the gift of grain. The aroma from the cooking pots wafted through the morning air. Boiled in with venison or with ducks or rice hens, it was nourishing and delicious.

The time had also come to follow Sharp Nose's bidding when he had offered his last farewell to White Wolf. It was the one-year anniversary of Sharp Nose's death.

Anticipating this morning, and how Sharp Nose might come to him in the forest, White Wolf had not slept the entire night. He had lain midst his blankets recalling his many ventures with his dearly departed friend: the shared hunt, the foot races, the camaraderie while warring with the Sioux.

White Wolf closed his eyes and envisioned himself with Sharp Nose again, reliving all of these things that had given them cause to grow close as brothers might feel for one another.

Then he opened his eyes to the new risen dawn. He slipped into his fringed buckskins, glad when Dawnmarie seemed to sense his urgency and dressed quickly with him.

Wrapped snugly in their fur robes, White Wolf, Dawnmarie, their daughter, and Swallow Song and her son now walked midst the flaring red autumn leaves of the forest toward the place where Sharp Nose had promised to be with them one last, final time.

Dawnmarie was in awe that White Wolf believed that somehow he might come in contact with his best friend again, yet she followed along beside him, anyhow. She had never met a man as intelligent as White Wolf. There was nothing he could not do.

And his belief in the hereafter was strong. He was a believer in many things spiritual. Perhaps . . . even . . . reincarnation? Dawnmarie wondered to herself.

As far as she was concerned, that, and only that, could be the way Sharp Nose could appear on this earth since his spirit was now a part of the heavens.

As they walked White Wolf saw strands of deer "velvet" hanging in strips from saplings. He noticed a number of hefty shortleaf pines that had been pummeled into the ground near the same spot.

His astute eyes then found a large deer scrape on a tree, scrupulously clean, yet rank with the undeniable scent of buck musk.

A devout, skilled hunter, such a sight made White Wolf's heart skip a beat. Any other time he would have carried his bow and arrow. He would be on the hunt. His arrow would soon find its target and he would carry home much deer meat for his family.

But this was not a hunt. He was there for a purpose much holier than that.

Then his eyes widened and he held his arm out to
stop Dawnmarie's and Swallow Song's farther approach. He just realized where he was. Through a
break in the trees a short distance away there was a
tall outcropping of rock that overlooked a slight incline of land. Autumn flowers covered the hillside in
a myriad of colors, a delectable mixture of aromas,
both sweet and spicy as they spread their fragrance
through the air.

Sharp Nose had pointed this place out many times
while they were on the hunt. Sharp Nose had said
that he had come there often to pray. He had told
White Wolf that always, while there, he had felt the
presence of many spirits. He had told White Wolf
that he might have found the very entrance to the
spirit world!

"We are almost there," White Wolf said quietly.
"Come. Walk softly. Scarcely breathe."

They moved stealthily onward. Dawnmarie soon
realized that everything had become quiet. There
was a silence in the forest never known to her before.

It was then that she had a splash of fear. This
seemed eerie. Perhaps, even, *wrong.*

She started to tell White Wolf that she wanted to
return to their lodge, but stopped when a large buck
came into view, sniffing noisily as it neared the hillside of spotted flowers. Nervously it stopped to nip
a sassafras bough and chewed quickly.

White Wolf nodded a silent command to Dawnmarie and Swallow Song not to go any farther. They
were only a few yards from the hillside and the
large deer.

The hackles on the deer's neck rose, his ears flick-

ered, and his nostrils flared and tested the wind as
he looked for those whose presence he smelled.

When he found the humans, he did not leap with
fear into the brush. He moved from the outer fringes
of the trees and stopped at the foot of the hillside,
his eyes bright, his eyes warm and friendly.

Being the skilled hunter that he was, White Wolf
could not help but marvel over this magnificent deer.
He gazed at him as though measuring him for a kill.
His rack of horns was wider than the breadth of a
large man's shoulders. They were horns of great
honor and sleekness of spirit.

Main beams sprouted like small oaks from his
skull, gnarled and knobby where hair met base. Its
brow tines glinted like daggers in the sunlight.

Suddenly White Wolf's thoughts of the hunt were
replaced with awe as the deer crept closer, leaves
crunching underfoot as he made his way toward
them.

White Wolf watched the deer pause for a moment,
the animal's nostrils flaring as once again he tested
the wind. The magnificent buck turned his head to
his other side and tested again.

As though sensing no danger from the humans,
the deer's nose dropped to the ground. Several fat
acorns caught his attention and he greedily gobbled
them down.

Then the deer's ears flickered. His nose sniffed.
His eyes rose when he realized he was still being
watched. In his eyes there was no fear. There was
warmth and peace.

"Remove the children from their cradleboards,"
White Wolf whispered, standing motionless. "Slowly.
Do not frighten the deer."

"Why must we remove our children from their cradleboards?" Dawnmarie whispered back, yet already doing as he asked, for he never did anything without a purpose.

"Do you not realize in whose presence we stand?" White Wolf whispered back, his eyes locked with the deer's.

"I see only a deer," Swallow Song whispered, taking her son from the cradleboard. The child snuggled warmly in his tiny rabbit wrap, Swallow Song held him in her arms.

"You are in the presence of a deer, but yet also your husband," White Wolf said, his insides quavering with excitement as the deer took slow steps forward. "Hold your son low enough now for the deer to see and marvel at."

Dawnmarie's pulse raced as she held Doe Eyes in her arms, slowly rocking her back and forth as she watched the deer move closer. How could this be? she marveled to herself. Yet she felt it with every fiber of her being that she was somehow in the presence of Sharp Nose.

She sucked in a wild, awestruck breath when the deer came and stood before Swallow Song, its eyes imploring her.

Then what happened next was so incredible, Dawnmarie's knees grew weak with the marvel of it. The deer nuzzled the child in Swallow Song's arms as though it were a way to show his approval, his love.

Swallow Song almost went faint with the uniqueness of what was happening. "Sharp Nose?" she cried, reaching a hand out to touch the deer's shiny, black nose. "You have returned, as promised. Oh, how can I tell you how much you are missed?"

He nuzzled her hand, remained there for a moment, then moved to stand before White Wolf.

White Wolf placed an arm around Dawnmarie's waist and drew her and his child close. "My friend," White Wolf said, his voice breaking.

The deer gave White Wolf a more playful nudge, then turned and ran slowly away.

Choked with emotion, they all watched the deer until he came to thicker fringes of forest, where the sun barely shone through the thick foliage overhead. Before entering, the deer stopped and looked back.

He turned away one last time and hesitated with ears cupped, then leapt over a hedge and was gone.

"*Miigwetch-ga-waa-ba-min,* we will be seeing you again, my friend, when we walk together as friends in the hereafter," White Wolf shouted, his voice echoing into the dark fringes of the forest.

Although the deer could no longer be seen, he stopped when he reached the bottom of a small ravine. He turned his head again. The only noise he heard was the yapping of a she-fox and her pups close by.

Seemingly satisfied, the buck leapt high, then low, as it moved through the forest, until it became only a shadow in the wind.

Chapter Sixty-three

He is not banished, for the showers.
Yet wake this green warm earth of ours.
—Alice Meynell

"And so, Swallow Song, are you content enough with your last farewell to your husband?" White Wolf asked as they walked back toward their village.

"It is something that I shall carry with me forever in my heart," Swallow Song said, still in awe of what had happened only moments ago. "I wish my son could remember, How blessed he would feel that his father came back to earth to be with him, if only for a moment."

"I feel that he will somehow remember," White Wolf said, nodding. He glanced over at Dawnmarie. "Violet Eyes, you have been so quiet since having witnessed Sharp Nose's return. What is it? What troubles you?"

"Nothing troubles me," Dawnmarie said, smiling over at him. "I just cannot get over the miracle we only moments ago were a part of. It is something that is so wonderful, it is hard to find words to describe how I feel about it."

"Just enjoy your memories of it," White Wolf said thickly. "That is enough."

Dawnmarie cast Swallow Song a wavering look. "Your leaving today, Swallow Song, to return to your father and your Potawatomis people, casts much sadness on the experience," she murmured. "Would you please change your mind? You have been happy among the Chippewa. Why must you live elsewhere?"

"It is important that I raise my son to become a great Potawatomis chief," Swallow Song said softly. "He *will* be the chief of my people after my father. It will be good to show my father that there *is* a grandson worthy of chieftainship from his daughter who he cast aside as useless."

Swallow Song met Dawnmarie's steady gaze, understanding the worry in their depths. "And do not worry about how I will be received by my father," she murmured. "Although he warned me against having children, I know that having his grandson to hold and marvel over will erase from his mind how he feels when ... when ... I suffer my seizures." She swallowed hard. "Perhaps they will come less frequently as I grow older."

"I will pray to the Great Spirit they will," Dawnmarie murmured. When Doe Eyes began fussing on her cradleboard, Dawnmarie's thoughts leapt to another concern. "Our children. They were meant to be together. Now that will be impossible. You know that your father has been talking about relocating to another land far from this land of lakes. If he does, not only will we miss you, my sweet friend, but also the children will be deprived of ever knowing one another."

"My father has spoken and threatened to relocate often," Swallow Song said, laughing softly. "I do not take his words seriously any longer when he speaks of moving to this place called Chicago, or to the great expanse of land called Indiana. His roots are in Wisconsin. He will stay there until he is part *of* the land, when he becomes but a small seed planted in the earth on the day of his burial."

"You must promise to visit often so that our children can romp and play together," White Wolf interjected. "It will not be the same as when I was friends with Sharp Nose as a child, enjoying the games of boys. But their bonds will strengthen into adulthood into perhaps something stronger."

"It is my hope that they will be attached by their heartstrings," Swallow Song said, nodding. "This is why I see the importance of raising my son as a Potawatomis chief, instead of a Chippewa warrior. I want to make sure that our children can legally marry, if they wish to. If they were raised together, as one tribe, one band of Indian, they would not be able to seal their hearts with marriage vows. It would be forbidden."

White Wolf laughed throatily. "Here we are speaking of marriage and the children are not even yet weaned of their mother's milk," he said, his gaze locked now on the canoe in the river as they approached the outer fringes of the Chippewa village. In the canoe were all of Swallow Song's belongings. Even the cradle that he had made for her child, a bed of fresh, dried moss lining the bottom.

"I wish you would change your mind," Dawnmarie persisted, herself eyeing the canoe, where two warriors waited to transport Swallow Song down the river to her father's encampment.

"For our children I will sacrifice anything," Swallow Song said, moving toward the canoe, her footsteps slowing as she reached the sandy beach. She turned to Dawnmarie. "Even a friendship like yours that is nourished from day to day with our speical bond. It is for our children that we both must sacrifice seeing each other each day, taking from one another those special feelings that make us smile."

"*Ay-uh,* I know," Dawnmarie said.

White Wolf removed the cradleboard from Swallow Song's back for her. He held it in the crook of his left arm as he peered down at the tiny copper face, the dark eyes gazing intensely back at him. He kissed the child's brow. "I shall always miss you," he said thickly.

He felt cheated that he would not be the one to teach this child all ways of young braves who would move into the status of warriors proud and strong. But he understood why this was being denied him, and stepped forward with a noble grace as he lay the cradleboard in Swallow Song's arms.

"Let me hold him one last time," Dawnmarie murmured, tears streaming from her eyes as Swallow Song gave her the cradleboard. Dawnmarie gazed down at the tiny face, then softly kissed the nose that was as sharp and pointed as his father's.

"You will see us soon and often," Swallow Song promised. She giggled. "You might tire of us we will visit so often."

"*Gah-ween-wee-kah,* never," White Wolf and Dawnmarie chorused together, laughing and exchanging smiles at their unique timing.

Dawnmarie lay the cradleboard back in Swallow Song's arms. Kissing Swallow Song on the cheek, she hugged her.

Stepping back, making room for White Wolf as he came to Swallow Song to help her into the canoe, Dawnmarie forced herself not to burst into a frenzy of crying. She *would* see Swallow Song often, for *she* would make the journey up the river herself, if Swallow Song did not come often enough.

She would worry about Swallow Song's peace of mind while living with her father. If he shamed her for her weakness, he would take the spirit from her that had grown inside her while among the Chippewa people.

Had he not avoided coming to the village to see her and her son?

He had come only once.

A warrior shoved the canoe out into the river, then boarded it. White Wolf and Dawnmarie waved at Swallow Song.

"May the Great Spirit see you safely home!" White Wolf shouted.

"Not only the Great Spirit, but also my husband's spirit!" she shouted back. "I feel him here with me! Did he not promise that he would look after me even in death from the spirit world?"

White Wolf nodded. Dawnmarie felt a part of herself slipping away as the canoe went farther and farther from view.

Willing herself not to behave childishly any longer about losing a daily friendship with Swallow Song, she smiled bravely up at White Wolf as he swept an arm around her waist and led her away from the river.

"Swallow Song and her son will be all right," White Wolf reassured, understanding his wife's worries even though she no longer voiced them aloud.

Doe Eyes began to wail. This gave Dawnmarie a reprieve from her worries of Swallow Song. She had a daughter who was very verbally reminding her that it was past feeding time.

Then Dawnmarie thought of something else. Was Doe Eyes hungry? Or did she somehow miss Sharp Nose? For the past three months they had been a part of each other's lives. Could her daughter sense that this had been suddenly taken away from her?

Dawnmarie glanced up at White Wolf, but did not voice her wonder aloud. There was no need in allowing him to know that it was this hard to break her ties with Swallow Song and her son. It might make him feel less important in her life.

And she would never allow him to think that. He and their daughter were her everything.

"Darling, after our daughter is fed I would like to show you again just how much I love you," she murmured. "I want to show you just how glad I am to still have you, to hold, to love, to adore."

Anticipating the moments promised him, White Wolf gave Dawnmarie a most wicked smile, his eyes dancing into hers.

Chapter Sixty-four

The winds of heaven mix forever,
With a sweet emotion.
—Shelley

As the harvest moon cast its orange pallor over White Wolf's village, he reached his hands out for Dawnmarie, beckoning her to come midst his blankets with him. Doe Eyes was comfortably filled with her mother's sweet milk. She now lay in her cradle on fresh, dried moss. A doll made of buckskin stuffed with moss lay beside her.

Nude, her pulse racing with the anticipation of their secret, treasured moments together, Dawnmarie took White Wolf's hands and moved down beside him.

The wind blew cold and brisk outside, but the firelight from the burning, sweet-smelling logs in the fire pit gilded everything within with its golden, mellow light.

White Wolf urged Dawnmarie to her knees. "Let me look at you," he said huskily. He cupped her breasts in the palms of his hands. "Let my eyes fill with pleasure from seeing you, as though it was that first time I saw you unclothed."

"Am I still as pleasing to your eyes?" Dawnmarie asked, knowing herself that her breasts were way larger, and that her waist had not narrowed down to its earlier size.

"*Ay-uh.* To my eyes, to my hands . . ." he said, pausing to bend and flick his tongue over one of her nipples. "And to my tongue."

Dawnmarie wove her fingers through his hair and brought his mouth closer. "It is such a different feeling when your lips cover my nipples," she whispered, her heart pounding as he kissed first one nipple, then the other. "Oh, what rapture swims through me. Our child's lips bring a gentle peace within me. *Yours* cause such rushes of pleasure."

He leaned away from her and led her down on the bed of blankets beside the fire, then knelt over her. His night-black hair spilled over his shoulders as he kissed her, his tongue searching through her lips, flicking.

As he moved fully over her with his body, molding perfectly to the curved hollow of her hips, his eyes became charged with deep emotion.

Her hands strolled over him. She could never get enough of touching him, of marveling anew over his muscles. She closed her eyes as their kiss deepened.

Her hand searched and found his pulsing hardness. She ran her fingers slowly along the sides, teasingly up and down, then she fully cupped him and moved her fingers on him. She could sense his pleasure by the way his breathing quickened, soft moans repeatedly surfacing from somewhere deeply inside him.

Then he reached for her hand. He moved it away and held it down at her side.

She melted inside when she felt the satin-hard length of him probing for entrance where her very soul seemed centered. When he plunged inside her, she sighed against his lips and lifted her legs around his hips.

She rocked with him.

She swayed.

She felt herself climbing to the sky, an eagle soaring, the sun's rays warm on her wings, the wind soft on her face.

White Wolf pressed endlessly deeper inside her. He could feel the pleasure growing. He had almost reached that bursting point. His breathing was ragged, overwhelmed with this surge of ecstasy that was welling up within him.

Then like a rush of wind in a spring storm, the pleasure erupted into something he no longer had control over. It was spreading, spinning. He gripped her shoulders. His burning hot kiss had become frenzied ... eager ... hard.

Dawnmarie whimpered tiny cries of pleasure against his lips as he thrust inside her with a wild, dizzying rhythm. She clung to him around the neck as she entered that realm of passion she hungered for.

She sank in a chasm of desire, smiling as she felt White Wolf find his own release. He held her tight as his body quavered into hers. He whispered her name against her cheek as he made the final plunge inside her.

Afterward, he did not roll immediately away from her. He straddled her. As he gazed down at her through his passion-heavy eyes, his hands sought the erect rosy nipples of her breasts.

Her lustrously long hair was disarrayed around her smooth, copper shoulders. A bead of perspiration lay beneath her nose and across her brow.

"One of these nights we will make a son," White Wolf then said, smiling down at her. He crawled to her side and stretched out beside her. "We will make a son who I will show how to throw a tomahawk so that it will split a twig at twenty paces. A son who I can teach well to watch out for snakes and spiders and white berries and mushrooms. When our son kills his first game we will give a 'feast of first game' for him."

"A son who can brother our daughter," Dawnmarie said, smiling as she turned to her side to face him. "You already miss baby Sharp Nose, don't you?"

"It is my right to miss him as I might miss a son," White Wolf said thickly.

He sat up and drew a robe around his shoulders, then went to the back of the lodge and brought something to Dawnmarie that was wrapped carefully in a thin sheet of buckskin.

"No more talk of sons," he said. "*Anyone's* sons. Let us talk of gifts to my *wife.*"

"Gifts?" Dawnmarie asked, eyes wide as she sat up and slipped into a soft rabbit robe. "What have you got there for me, sweet husband? And why? Have I done something that pleases you so much you felt the need to thank me with a gift?"

"Do I need a reason to give my beautiful wife a gift?" White Wolf said, handing it to her.

Eager fingers threw back the corners of the buckskin. Dawnmarie's eyes widened and she gasped when she saw the most perfect gift of all! A brand-new cedar bead loom!

"Oh, my," she sighed, her fingers tracing the loom from top to bottom. She gazed up at White Wolf as she held the loom to her bosom. "Darling, oh, darling, you remembered my having told you about the loom my father made for me that got destroyed in the Sioux raid. You, yourself, have made me another. I . . . don't . . . know what to say, except thank you, my darling. I am so happy."

He leaned back and brought a bag into view, then scooted it across the mats of the floor toward her. "This, too, I give to you," he said, smiling at her continued gasps of surprise. "I traded many furs for this second gift I give you tonight."

Dawnmarie laid her loom aside. Her fingers trembled as she opened the bag. She laughed, cried, then giggled as she gazed down into the bag, seeing so many various types of beads to use while sewing garments for the people she loved. She would make Woman Dancing something very special soon for all that she had done for her!

Reaching inside, she ran her fingers through the beads, the glass beads cold against her flesh.

Then she lay this aside and climbed on White Wolf's lap, straddling him as she placed her legs on each side of him. She twined her arms around his neck and drew his lips close to hers.

"I feel as though I have neglected you," she murmured, her lower lip curved downward in a pout. "I have no gifts for you tonight."

"How can you say that?" White Wolf said, reaching his hands inside her robe, finding her breasts. He kneaded them, his thumb circling the nipples. "Violet Eyes, you are gift enough for *any* man. But you are mine." He brushed a kiss across her lips. "*All* mine."

She flung herself into his arms, her robe falling away from her shoulders.

He shoved his own robe aside, sighing with wild bliss when she pressed her breasts into the flesh of his chest.

"May I ask for another gift tonight?" Dawnmarie whispered against his lips.

"*Ay-uh,* ask for anything and it is yours," White Wolf whispered back.

"Make love to me again?" Dawnmarie whispered, then received his response as quickly as he could push himself up and into her.

"Thank you, darling," Dawnmarie whispered again, then kissed him with a fiery passion. She felt as though he was lifting her to the stars with each shove inside her. She enjoyed the euphoria of the moment.

She smiled to herself and silently gave thanks that she had such ... a ... generous husband!

At the outer fringes of White Wolf's Chippewa village, a deer's eyes suddenly appeared like two shining lights in the night. Behind him there was a faraway scream of an owl, and then a long, quavering wolf's howl.

The deer turned its head. Its ear flickered as though in recognition, as though in *knowing*.

Then following the sound of the wolf, it turned and leapt eagerly into the darkness.

When it reached the spot where the wolf stood all white and sleek, the deer showed no fear. It moved closer to the wolf, gave it a friendly nudge in the side with its nose.

As friends might do midst the shadows of night, they ran off together, not knowing at this moment in time the meaning of the words "natural enemy."

Author's Note

Wild Bliss is the first book of a three-book series connected by the Indian tribes that will appear from time to time in all three books. This first book in the series will place emphasis on the Lac du Flambeau band of Chippewa; the second, *Wild Thunder,* the Potawatomis; the third, *Wild Whispers,* the Kickapoo.

Lac du Flambeau (Lake of Torches), in northern Wisconsin, at the head of the Wisconsin River, has been a permanent settlement of the Chippewa Indian Nation since about 1745, when Chief Sharpened Stone led his band to this lake. Nearby lakes furnished a fine setting for Indian life, with wild rice in season and plentiful fish that were taken at night by the light of flaming torches, hence the name "Flambeau."

Dear Reader:

I hope that you have enjoyed reading *Wild Bliss.* My next Topaz book, *Wild Thunder,* is the sequel to *Wild Bliss,* and will be in the bookstores six months from the release of *Wild Bliss.* This latest Indian book in my "Wild" series that I am writing exclusively for Dutton Signet offers much passion, excitement, and adventure. I hope you will buy it and enjoy it!

To receive my quarterly newsletter and fan club information, please send a legal-size, self-addressed stamped envelope to me at:

R#3 Box 60
Mattoon, IL 61938

Warmly

Cassie Edwards

FROM THE LEADING LADY OF INDIAN RO-
MANCE, EXPERIENCE THE MOST POWER-
FUL LOVE STORIES THAT BRIDGE THE
BOUNDARIES BETWEEN CULTURES. CAS-
SIE EDWARDS WILL BRING TEARS TO
YOUR EYES AND JOY TO YOUR HEART
WITH THE BEAUTY OF HER ROMANCES
FROM TOPAZ.

Wild Splendor

A hothouse flower in the parched, rugged desert of the Arizona Territory, beautiful and headstrong Leonida Branson wasn't about to let her youth dry up in a duty-bound marriage to the pompous General Porter. And when she first saw Sage, the fierce Navaho chieftain her fiancé had sworn to crush, she knew that the comforts of civilization were no match for the adventurous passion the copper-skinned brave awakened in her.

Darkly handsome, Sage's flashing black eyes smoldered with forbidden heat each time he caught sight of Leonida's porcelain beauty. But nothing had ever prepared this hardened warrior for the feelings that suddenly raged within him . . . and for his intense desire to sweep this exquisite woman into his powerful embrace, to teach her the ancient ways of his people . . . and the timeless ways of love.

Wild Desire

With her magnificent copper hair and lovely gray eyes, Stephanie Helton contrasted starkly with the famous "white Indian," Runner, adopted by the Navaho as a child and now destined to be their leader. Tall, lithe, and darkly sensual, Runner immediately recognized Stephanie as the fire that set his blood blazing . . . and as his sworn enemy.

Her father's railroad had pushed deep into the Arizona Territory, breaking the promises made to the Navaho, bringing grief and betrayal to the native people. But the hard, urgent force drawing Stephanie and Runner together defied reason and triumphed over old hatreds. Even as he drank deeply of her forbidden kisses and surrendered to the savage desire of their love, Runner felt his soul riven by conflict—he could not both lead his people and join his destiny to this woman's. And Stephanie knew her heart might break when he made his choice.

Wild Embrace

Exquisite, flame-haired Elizabeth Easton had thought Seattle a raw, rough frontier harbor after her elegant upbringing in San Francisco. But she discovered what the real wilderness was when the noble Indian brave, Strong Heart, forced her to go with him in a flight back to his Suquamish people. There, deep in the breathtaking forests of the great Pacific Northwest, Strong Heart was free from intolerant injustice. There Elizabeth was free of the smothering control of her ambitious businessman father. There both of them were free of all the pride and prejudice that kept them apart in the white world . . . as this superbly handsome, strong, and sensitive man became her guide on passion's path to unfettered joy . . . and she stood beside him to defy all that sought to end a love that would not be denied. . . .

Wild Abandon

The tragedy of the Civil War had forced Lauralee Johnston into an orphanage, and years passed before she found her beloved father and heeded his dying wish: that she place her trust in the handsome Cherokee brave, Joe Dancing Cloud. The sheltered Lauralee was wary of unfamiliar Cherokee customs and of Dancing Cloud's powerful, exotic presence, but he gradually gentled her with quiet strength ... teaching her about the kind of passion they had in common ... lighting the fires of love as he claimed her for his bride. But the bond forged between this bronzed, proud man and the shy, beautiful woman was rattled by the prejudice and hate that swirled around them ... as a red-haired Yankee villain from the wartorn past threatened to tear their union asunder. Yet this venomous enemy was no match for the fierce power of two lovers defending their one glowing dream, their destiny....